An unflinching indictment of luk[...]
call to fiery living. In Mike's sto[...]
stable ground between hot and co[...]

2015

AUTHOR OF *T*[...]

With an eerie and thrilling premise, *The Resurrection* is a riveting story that touches on the raw nerve of every person of faith—that unasked question of whether it is, ultimately, all possible, truly believable...all true. Whether the great miracle of faith still exists in a world populated by deceit. A brooding and suspenseful debut that will give you goose bumps and make you think long after you've turned the last page.

—TOSCA LEE
AUTHOR OF *DEMON: A MEMOIR*

In *The Resurrection*, Duran's prose is both lyrical and captivating, his storytelling entertaining yet thought-provoking. It was easy to forget this is his debut novel. I can't wait to see what he has in store for us next.

—MIKE DELLOSSO
AUTHOR OF *SCREAM* AND *DARLINGTON WOODS*

Like the ominous events creeping into the lives of these colorful characters, *The Resurrection* sneaks up on its readers, alternately charming and challenging assumptions until the very end. Though this is Duran's first novel, it speaks volumes about what lies ahead for this exciting new voice in Christian fiction.

—SIBELLA GIORELLO
CHRISTY AWARD–WINNING AUTHOR OF
THE RALEIGH HARMON MYSTERIES

Mike Duran's chilling debut depicts a raging battle of faith as mysterious powers of darkness war over the inhabitants of a small coastal village. With echoes of Frank Peretti's spiritual warfare and Athol Dickson's lyrical prose, *The Resurrection* is a tale that is one part ghost story, one part supernatural thriller, and one part spiritual awakening.

Duran leads the reader on a metaphysical journey where dangerous forces are unexpectedly unleashed when a boy is raised from the dead.

—MERRIE DESTEFANO
AUTHOR OF *AFTERLIFE: THE RESURRECTION CHRONICLES*

Mike Duran masterfully blends fear, evil, hope, and redemption to paint a memorable portrait of how even the least of the servants of the Light can overcome the prevailing darkness around them. *The Resurrection* is a debut novel that promises many more are sure to follow.

—TIM GEORGE
FICTIONADDICT.COM

THE Resurrection

THE Resurrection

MIKE DURAN

REALMS
A STRANG COMPANY

Most STRANG COMMUNICATIONS BOOK GROUP products are available at special quantity discounts for bulk purchase for sales promotions, premiums, fund-raising, and educational needs. For details, write Strang Communications Book Group, 600 Rinehart Road, Lake Mary, Florida 32746, or telephone (407) 333-0600.

THE RESURRECTION by Mike Duran
Published by Realms
A Strang Company
600 Rinehart Road
Lake Mary, Florida 32746
www.strangbookgroup.com

Cover design by Gearbox Studio
Design Director: Bill Johnson

Visit the author's website at www.mikeduran.com.

Library of Congress Cataloging-in-Publication Data
Duran, Mike.
  The resurrection / Mike Duran. -- 1st ed.
      p. cm.
  ISBN 978-1-61638-204-9
  1. Resurrection--Fiction. I. Title.
  PS3604.U723R47 2011
  813'.6--dc22

                                        2010041844

E-book ISBN: 978-1-61638-415-9

First Edition

11 12 13 14 15 — 9 8 7 6 5 4 3 2 1
Printed in the United States of America

To my father, who died trying

Acknowledgments

"THE JOURNEY OF A THOUSAND MILES," SAID THE SAGE, "begins with the first step." Like many authors, my journey to publication has felt like a thousand miles. It's hard to even say when that journey began. Perhaps it was as a kid reading Ray Bradbury, Weird Tales, and Marvel Comics. At the weekend matinees enamored with Sinbad, the Wolfman, or Bonnie and Clyde. Or at church hearing tales about a paradise lost and another to come. Somewhere along the way I fell in love with stories and the words that comprise them. Whatever that "first step," there are many who inspired me to begin this journey and to keep trudging forward.

My mom, who bought me my first book on the craft of writing and encouraged me to never stop growing. My wife, Lisa, who has endured my immaturity, idiosyncrasies, pessimism, and oddball hours. And shared the best times of my life. There is no one else I'd rather be with than you. My kids, their spouses, and children: Jacob, Melody, Theo, and Cadence; Chris and Krystal; Jon, Trish, and Arayla; and Alayna. You all make me proud and very happy.

Pastor Dave Jacobs, who saw something in me and did not break this bruised reed. My first congregation, Oasis Christian Fellowship of Fontana, who followed me...even into the wilderness. Veronica Fletcher, who prays for me, and Karen Woodall, who has encouraged me throughout this process.

The Penwrights, my first writing group. In particular, Gina Holmes, Ane Mulligan, and Jessica Dotta. Without your wisdom and encouragement, this book would not have been possible. To Rebecca Miller, Merrie Destefano, and Rachel Marks—the Borders Gang. You guys saved my writing life.

Janet Grant, for "finding" me, and Rachelle Gardner, who, I'm convinced, does not realize what she's gotten herself into.

Thank you both for your professionalism and sound advice. Alton Gansky for his editorial prowess on this project. Debbie Marrie and all the good folks at Strang Communications who took interest in this story and let me tell it. I am forever indebted!

The FUSD Paint Department, especially Rick Stanfield, Joe Sacco, and Danny Gutierrez. Your banter, crude humor, and encouragement have kept me down to earth.

And to my readers, thank you for taking this journey with me. Here's to a long and scenic one.

Chapter 1

No sooner had he removed the chunk of jet-black obsidian from atop his sermon notes than Reverend Ian Clark realized he had a visitor.

A ripple of electricity swept through the room, and the atmosphere tingled in its wake. It was a precursor to the manifestation, further evidence that his shrinking imagination—his world without wonder—had been invaded. The hair along Clark's forearms bristled, and his body grew tense. He knew what was coming. The stench of burning flesh fouled the air, forcing his throat into a knot. He stood rigid by the filing cabinet.

Mr. Cellophane had arrived.

Clark swallowed hard, his mind churning in indecision. Should he look at the spirit? Sometimes if he ignored it, the thing would go away, seeping back into the netherworld from where it came. But he didn't have time to waste. The girls would be here any minute, so he had to hurry. He gritted his teeth and turned toward the far end of the bookshelves, glowering.

The specter rose in the corner—its usual spot—and watched him with sallow eyes. An opaque, gauzy sheath seemed to cloak the presence. Pale organs throbbed beneath its translucent skin. It appeared to be a young man, or the remnants of one, caught between worlds. A demon or ghost, he speculated, maybe a transient from a parallel plane. How it had come to haunt the church, Clark could not say. Nor did he really care.

He'd been forced to call it something, what with the frequency of its visits and his interminable need to bleach existence of its mystery. *Beings aren't anonymous*, he often reasoned. *Amoebas, yes.* As far as Clark could tell, Mr. Cellophane was more than an amoeba or an ectoplasmic phenomenon. His repeated attempts to evict the entity had proven futile—no doubt an extension of his spiritual impotence. But Clark was history; soon the ministry would be nothing more than a bad dream. As far as he was concerned, the swirling bag of bones could rot over there.

The apparition rose to the ceiling and hovered, undulating; its head tilted forward, a brooding presence in the corner of the church office. Elastic arms braided with sinews dangled at its side as it stared dispassionately at the minister.

That look—that pleading, defenseless gaze—always unnerved Clark.

He wiped the moisture from his eyes and, with a type of resolute indifference, snatched his notes from the cabinet. He scowled at the glassy wraith—a childish, demoralized pout—and turned away. As he went to the coat rack and removed his black leather jacket, he sensed the sad, empty eyes following him. He flung the jacket over his shoulder and marched toward the exit.

"Leave me alone," he muttered.

He marched out of his office and slammed the door. Clark stormed past Vinyette's desk, dragging cords of the fetid vapors with him. Opening the front door, he peered into a dense spring fog. Intermittent droplets pattered the welcome mat, and something rustled in the camphor branches. Other than that, the parking lot was silent.

A groan of relief left him. At least he didn't have to deal with Ruby and her fanatical entourage. Clark locked the door, rolled his notes into a tight baton, and plunged into the misty veil.

A chill clung to the church office, as usual. Ruby Case shivered and yanked the sleeves of her sweat jacket over her wrists. *Why was it always so cold in this building?*

Once again it was just the three of them, but Ruby didn't mind. She had given up trying to generate enthusiasm in Canyon Springs Community Church. In a way she preferred the anonymity of her little prayer group. Vinyette, on the other hand, used it as motivation. "Goliath went down with one stone," she'd say. "So's the three of us should do some damage." Vinyette was not one to aim low. For Ruby, it was more about doing right than getting payback. The fact that her two best friends shared the burden every Sunday morning before church made the commitment a lot easier.

She slipped her eyes open and peeked at them. The girls sat as they always did—Vinyette propped forward with her elbows on her thighs, rocking back and forth, the tattoo on her bicep in full display, and Marje at attention, hands folded on her lap like a prim schoolgirl, eyes squeezed into a fine line of lashes. Vinyette had the lead—her natural position. Ruby smiled and shut her eyes again. She needed to concentrate and stop letting her mind wander.

As she settled in, something brushed past and sent goose bumps skittering up her spine. She thrust her eyes open, fully expecting to see someone standing near. There was no one. *Weird.*

Suddenly her insides somersaulted.

Ruby leaned back, forcing a metallic groan from the folding chair. She picked at her jeans, waiting, hoping for the wave of nausea to go away. Instead a flush of warmth cascaded over her, and the room turned fuzzy.

She unzipped her jacket and shook the collar of her shirt to let some air in. What was going on? Ruby blinked hard, trying to regain her mental equilibrium. She wasn't one to not be in control, and this, well, this wouldn't do. Her scalp tingled, as if invisible fingers caressed her hair. Maybe this was premature menopause. Like fifteen years premature. She frowned at the thought and kept flapping her collar.

That's when an image sprung into her mind, sharp and inescapable, and snatched her breath away.

Ruby slowly rose with one hand over her mouth, gawking at the vibrant impression that sketched itself in her mind's eye. She fumbled behind her for the chair, trying to steady herself, trying to comprehend what she was seeing, what she was feeling.

"Speak to him, Lord," Vinyette prayed in her slight Southern drawl, unaware of Ruby teetering in the circle. "Would you please get that man's attention?" Marje nodded in agreement, her gold hoops swinging in confirmation.

Ruby swayed, fighting to retain control of her senses. "The boys, Vin," she mumbled with a lightheaded lilt. "Can you…"

Vinyette snapped her eyes open and stopped rocking. She shouted something and leaped forward, grappling for Ruby, but she wasn't fast enough. Ruby collapsed. Her head struck the chair and sent it clattering. Then her body thudded to the carpet and she gasped.

Formless figures and indistinct sounds whirled around her, but the image remained. She lay spellbound, captivated by the bizarre vision.

It was stark in its simplicity: an immense gray tree with barren, arthritic limbs tilted on a high hill. Behind it stretched an unending curtain of crimson sky.

She commanded her body to move, but it could not. Even her heart seemed to freeze at the sight of the unfolding revelation.

The tree towered over her, its skeletal limbs like a vast umbrella speckled with blackbirds. She lay mesmerized, not at all fearful, just captivated by the terrible dream. As she studied it, her thoughts went to a single leaf blooming on a craggy bough, bright and green like newly sprung grass. It seemed incongruent, so out of place on the pale dead branch, like a glorious banner unfurling in some bomb-blasted war zone.

Ruby's bad leg lay crumpled underneath her. Someone wrestled it free and hovered overhead, shouting gibberish. Just behind her right ear a hot, sharp pinging began and tugged her back to reality. The vision dimmed, ebbed back into the recess of her psyche, the fuzz cleared, and she recognized her friend.

"Breathe, Ruby!" Vinyette's forearm quivered, and the tattoo-green barbed wire shown under her receding shirtsleeve. If Reverend Clark were here, he'd make her cover the darned thing. "Call them. Hurry!" Vinyette ordered someone. "Breathe!"

"No," Ruby gasped, struggling to sit up. "No."

"Stay down." Vinyette placed her trembling hand flat against Ruby's tummy with the perfect amount of pressure.

"I can't find the phone." Marje stumbled past them in her heels, sending a stapler tumbling off Vinyette's desk followed by fluttering papers.

"Then use your cell, Marje. C'mon!"

"No." Ruby groaned, pushed aside Vinyette's hand and sat up, still loopy. "I'm all right."

"All right, my butt!" Vinyette glared at her. "You fainted. Nearly cracked your head open."

Ruby touched the knot behind her ear and grimaced. The image of the tree finally faded. The coffee pot gurgled and the aroma hit her, as did a faint whiff of smoke. She wiped moisture from her eyes, drew a deep breath, and the church office came alive again. The lime green, low-back leather chair, excavated by Vinyette from some vintage thrift store, assured Ruby she was back on Earth.

"Here! Found it!" Marje held the cordless up. "Should I call?"

Vinyette stood and fidgeted with her turquoise rings, one after the other, biting her lip.

"No, Marje, I'll be OK." Ruby patted the back of her head to ensure her ponytail was intact. Marje stood ogling, and Vinyette knelt next to Ruby. They watched as she sat and brushed carpet fibers off her jeans. *Great!* She was now officially something she hated most—the center of attention.

Ruby drew her legs up and struggled to her feet.

"Careful." Vinyette had her by the elbow.

Marje rushed over, picked up the chair, and steadied it behind Ruby.

"Here," Vinyette said, "sit down. I'll get you some water."

She stomped across the room in her cowboy boots, plucked a paper cup from the water dispenser, and filled it. As she did, Ruby squinted and scanned the office to make sure the fuzziness was gone.

Vinyette returned and extended the cup, her long auburn hair gracing her lean frame. "What happened? Good Lord, Ruby. You scared the wits outta us."

Ruby savored the cool water, which gave her time to consider her options. She'd had intuitions before, subtle discernments about people or events. Her husband, Jack, called it her *baloney detector*. Sometimes harebrained words would pop into her mind, real off-the-wall like. Of course, she refused to consider herself psychic or profess some otherworldly calibration, but no amount of dismissal had stifled the gift.

Still, she'd never experienced anything like this.

She finished the water, brought the cup down, and squinted. "Is something burning? That smell. I can barely..."

Vinyette and Marje looked at each other and started sniffing the air like a couple of hound dogs. After a moment, Vinyette shrugged. "I don't think so." Then she pointed to the cup. "Do you want some more?"

"Please." Ruby coveted the chance to stall.

Spinning on the toe of her boot, Vinyette clomped to the cooler again and refilled the cup.

Ruby surveyed her nails for damage as she pondered her next step. She'd heard about things like this before. Trances and ecstatic visions, however, were the stuff of religious wackos. The fanatics up in Northfork were always touting premonitions and foreign tongues. Once they announced that God had turned some members' fillings into gold. The ensuing media curiosity was short-lived when the church refused to have the miracle verified. Of course, this only buttressed Jack's cynical sentiments. He wondered aloud about hillbillies actually having enough teeth to turn to gold and why God should bother with starvation in sub-Saharan Africa when some yokel needed precious metals gracing his diseased gums. That was Jack. As much as she believed in miracles and hated validating her husband's warped sense of humor, Ruby was hard-pressed to concede *that* kind of miracle. Besides, if Reverend Clark learned that a parishioner of his church had had some wild vision, he would have a field day dissecting it—that is, after the board's inquisition. She clucked her tongue as she spotted a chip in the polish on her right index finger.

Vinyette returned, and Ruby took the water and sipped it. Should she tell them? The thought made her stomach somersault again. *Why not?* Vinyette and Marje knew how to keep a secret. They had proven that. However, something this big always leaked out. The last thing Ruby Case wanted to do was start a scene. Besides, she needed a better handle on this before she went yakking.

"You said something about the boys?" Marje peered at Ruby. "Right before you—"

"That's right!" Ruby nodded enthusiastically. "That's right. They've been sick. Sean brought something home from preschool, and I must've got it." She smiled sheepishly.

"Yeah, but you passed out." Vinyette sounded skeptical. "That's it. I'm getting my truck and driving you home. You can have Jack take you to the doctor." She snatched her keys from the desk, jangled them, and arched her eyebrows in her usual mother-knows-best expression.

Ruby scrunched her lips. "Mmm, well..."

"Don't you dare."

The haunting dreamscape lingered—she could feel it. The invisible fingers were nearby, waiting to draw Ruby back.

Gulping the last of the water, she crumpled the paper cup in her fist. "I just...I probably caught something, Vin. I'm feeling better now." She studied the chip in her soft ivory polish and said unconvincingly, "Really."

Chapter 2

RUBY WENT TO HER USUAL SPOT: THIRD ROW, RIGHT SIDE, center aisle. She removed her sweat jacket and placed it in the corner of the pew, along with her purse and Bible. The Sunday service was about to begin. Mrs. Collison waved from the other side of the room, and Mr. Barkham, all six-foot-five of him, stood in the center aisle greeting people with his typical bland, businesslike demeanor. Several rows behind her the Raynee family scooted into their seats, one after the other. Jilly, the youngest, had taken a liking to her, and Ruby satisfied the girl's hungry gaze with a wink.

Small factions were scattered throughout the spacious sanctuary, making the place seem bigger than it was. Vinyette always said the spaces in the pews showed the distance between the people. If that was the case, the members of Canyon Springs were worlds apart.

She gingerly tapped the swollen lump behind her ear. The hot pinging persisted, and since she had no aspirin in her purse, she tried to ignore it. If she closed her eyes long enough, she knew the bizarre image would be there burning a hole into the back of her lids. The vision that had overwhelmed her that morning probably had some natural explanation. Maybe it *was* a bug, or a hot flash, or perhaps the stress had finally caught up to her.

Then again, maybe someone was trying to get her attention.

But a premonition of a dead tree?

Ruby shook her head. She was such a wet blanket. Jack always said she was a perpetual pessimist. As much as she hated to admit it, standing there, trying to downplay the visionary experience only confirmed her husband's conviction.

Ruby slipped into the pew and, as she sat, hissed. Her rear end smarted from the fall. *Great!* Now she had a dinged-up head and a bruised bottom to go along with her hallucination. What else could go wrong?

Reverend Clark climbed the steps to the platform and welcomed everyone. Vinyette hurried into a pew on the other side. Did that woman ever stop? The reverend led them in prayer, returned to his seat, and the congregation sang several hymns, led by Willis Richter. The stout, bald-shaven, ex-military chaplain brought tremendous energy, but his sweeping gestures and booming voice often upstaged the timid congregation. The last time Jack came, he rolled his eyes and called it *The Willis Richter Show*, which was unusually kind by Jack Case's standards.

Molly Ersvitz accompanied on piano and, after three hymns, made several announcements, including a reminder about the upcoming Easter pageant. Then Reverend Clark ascended to the pulpit. "Thank you, Miss Molly." He spoke above scattered applause. "I'll be continuing my series from the Gospel of Matthew. Please turn to chapter thirteen."

The fluttering of pages stirred throughout the cavernous room.

In his late twenties, Ian Clark was an odd match for the aging, listless congregation. His braided choker, with its ivory beads and rustic diamond-shaped pendant, peeked from beneath his collar. Affectionately labeled "Surfer Dude" by the youth group, the man had an affinity for peculiar jewelry—an observation that rarely went unnoticed when the critics raged. With his wire-rimmed glasses, youthful gait, and intellectual energy, he exuded collegiate airs. Still a year after Reverend Lawrence's abrupt resignation, Clark had yet to endear himself to the congregation.

Ruby reached for her Bible and adjusted it on her lap, but she did not open it. The ping in her noggin had become a warm throb, a reminder of this morning's strange occurrence. She sat wincing, drifting in thought, fearful that the fantastical vision would blast into her brain again and render her senseless.

Reverend Clark launched into his sermon, but try as she might, Ruby could not engage. The room seemed infused with a new, unfathomable energy—as if the premonition had rattled something loose inside her, sensitized her to a dimension just beyond the range of normal. Behind Reverend Clark, the five black, high-back argyle chairs for the church elders looked on like silent custodians of a long-forgotten history. Light from the wrought iron chandeliers sparkled in Clark's glasses, and the tall, stained glass windows created kaleidoscopic pools throughout the room. He gripped the top of the pulpit, one hand on each side, but his words seemed nonsensical, void of truth or passion. As much as she'd trained herself to resist the thought, Ruby could not shake the impression that Reverend Ian Clark was a complete phony.

Stop it! Stop thinking like that!

She opened her Bible and fiddled with its pages. She had to get out of there, go home and read, eat—something.

Clark rambled on, citing definitions and anecdotes, but unable to pierce the malaise that was Canyon Springs. Mule Walla, a local alfalfa farmer, sat hunched forward, head lolling on his chest in slumber, while the Lafortune children fidgeted under their mother's apathetic gaze. Miss Molly fanned herself with a bulletin while her current boyfriend glanced at his watch and bit back a yawn. Finally, Reverend Clark, seemingly oblivious to the disconnect, concluded his sermon. Willis Richter came forward and sang another hymn, evoking snickers from the Lafortune clan. Then the reverend made an innocuous appeal to "live large" and "stay true." The service ended.

Ruby sat dumfounded as the congregation rose and the sanctuary filled with the sound of voices and movement, oblivious to her dismay. After a moment she shrugged, got up, put her sweat jacket on, and looked for the quickest way of escape.

She slipped her Bible under her arm and picked up her purse. Turning into the aisle, she bounced off a heavyset man blocking her path.

"Whoa!" He chuckled and reached out to steady her.

"Oh, Oscar. Pardon me."

"No, pardon me." Thin, black hair greased over a balding scalp accentuated his oval face. A round, jovial man, he spread his plump arms and stomped his foot on the carpet. "What? Jack stayed home again?"

"Jack stayed home again," Ruby said in a sing-song voice. She'd gotten tired of answering questions about her husband and knew it was starting to show.

"He'll be back." Hayes creased his lips and nodded. "You can count on that."

Dark circles encased his once jolly eyes and a hint of stubble shaded his squat neck. He leaned toward her, bringing with him the smell of cheap cologne, and spoke with a tired wheeze. "Ruby, Luz has gotten worse. She doesn't have much time."

"Oscar, I am so sorry. Is there anything I can do to help? Do you need some errands run? Or some cleaning? Anything."

He reached across and touched her forearm with his fingertips. "You have the gift, Ruby. They say, ya know, God listens to you."

"Please, Oscar—"

"I believe it! I do. I... Will you come see her? Will you pray for my Luz? Ask God for..." His gaze faltered. "For..." He removed his hand and stepped away, his lips trembling.

"Oh, of course, Oscar." She reached over and squeezed his hand. "This week, OK?"

"Would you?"

"I promise."

"Next year will be our thirtieth...if she makes it that far."

"Oh, don't say that. You never know what's up God's sleeve." She shifted her Bible and purse to the other side and wrapped her arm around his massive shoulders, patting him as if he were a huge child. "We can only pray and hope for the best."

He thanked her, told her to bring the boys by the pharmacy for floats, and lumbered down the aisle past the Raynees, who stood waiting for Ruby. Jilly waved a sheet of paper and rocked side to side while her mother smiled and attempted to restrain the five-year-old.

As much as Ruby wanted to get out of there, the glimmer in Jilly's hazel eyes brought pause. They said the little girl was mildly autistic, but apart from her spacey gaze and a few minor tics, Ruby couldn't tell. In fact, Jilly had an uncanny psychic radar—an intuitive sense about people and events—that made her way above normal. She wore jean overalls and a yellow plaid flannel shirt, with her blonde hair pulled back in a nubby ponytail. Grasping the sheet of paper at her waist, she bounced on her toes and spastically wiggled her tongue across her lips. Mrs. Raynee patted the girl's shoulder, shook her head at Ruby, and smiled apologetically.

"Oh, she's got something she just has to show you."

Ruby smiled and winked. "How could I say no to my all-time favorite little person?"

"Thanks, Ruby," Mrs. Raynee said.

Ruby bent down and got level with Jilly's eyes. "Ya know, I keep all your things in a very special place. Whatcha got for me now, angel?"

"Mmm, hmm. It's special, Ruby Rainbow."

Jilly had christened Ruby with the nickname one day. *Behind the clouds*, the little girl noted, *there's colors*. And she saw both in Ruby, although lately there'd been way more clouds than colors.

Jilly stopped bobbing on her toes and proudly handed Ruby a folded sheet of drawing paper. "I saw it this morning." Suddenly she turned and looked away, as if disinterested.

Ruby glanced at Mrs. Raynee, who shrugged. Straightening up, Ruby unfolded the drawing paper.

Her breath caught and her eyes froze in disbelief. She steadied herself on the nearby pew, staring at the picture in her trembling hand.

It was a tree—a gray tree, inscribed in crayon, with branches rambling across the page. And on one side, a bright green leaf.

"It's the tree on the mountain," Jilly said, looking nowhere. Then she spread her arms, twirled, and lifted her voice with glee. "Everything's ready to go."

Chapter 3

STALKING INTO HIS OFFICE, IAN CLARK FLUNG HIS BIBLE ON the desk, sending loose papers scattering. What a terrible performance this morning. The congregation probably didn't believe a word he said. And why should they? He didn't believe it himself. He unbuttoned the cuffs of his shirt and glanced at the far end of the bookshelves. It was vacant.

Mr. Cellophane picked his own times.

Clark first encountered the spirit almost a year ago, shortly after arriving on the West Coast and taking the Canyon Springs job. At first he tried evicting the devil. He marched around the room shouting Bible verses like a demented exorcist in a low-budget horror movie, but the specter wouldn't budge. Why should it? Clark had as much spine as a jellyfish. His brief study of demonology didn't help either. *All hauntings have explanations*, the experts said. *Fear. Revenge. Hatred.* Some called it *entity attachment*. But after a year, he still had no clue what this entity was and why it was attached. Had someone died there? Or worse, had someone been murdered in the old church? Whatever the reason, no one else had apparently encountered the spirit. Cellophane was Clark's little secret, something he learned to live with.

Just like the rest of his ghosts.

He rolled up his shirtsleeves and stared at the massive photo in the gilded frame suspended behind his desk like an obnoxious billboard. The aerial shot of Canyon Springs Community was a constant reminder of his fall from grace. He shook his head and retrieved his laptop briefcase from the side of the desk. Then he made a beeline for the door. As he rushed from his office, he spotted a note on the floor. *Not again.* He picked up the light green paper and unfolded it.

Praying for you, Reverend. It was signed, *Vin, Ruby, and Marje.*

He winced. Their devotion was unnerving; their faithfulness put him to shame. He didn't deserve their support. If they knew the truth about him, they'd cease and desist.

Clark refolded the note and stared at it. The ticking of the wall clock jabbed at the stillness. He sighed, crumpled the paper into a tight ball, and tossed it toward the wastebasket. It banked off the filing cabinet, rolled on the rim, and fell to the bottom of the bin next to last week's note. Then he snatched his briefcase and marched out.

Ruby hurried through the foyer as fast as her limp would allow, sights set on the rustic wooden doors. Between the foreboding vision and little Jilly's crayon rendition, Ruby was practically numb. She needed some time to dig out from under this avalanche, wrap her mind around the possibilities. At least get this day behind her.

Vinyette poked her head out of the storage room. "Hey, you all right?"

"Oh, I didn't see you." Ruby carefully folded Jilly's picture and slipped it in her purse. "Yeah. Been a rough morning. Think I need to relax, take it easy the rest of the day."

"So you're not going this afternoon?" Vinyette ducked back into the tiny room with a stack of leftover bulletins and emerged dusting her hands off.

Ruby stared at the vaulted plaster ceiling and the wrought iron chandeliers. "Going?" Then she pressed the heel of her hand to her head. "The funeral! I almost forgot."

"You sure you're all right?" Vinyette's forehead creased with suspicion.

"I'll call you later. Thanks again for everything, Vin."

"You take care of yourself, ya hear me, Ruby?"

"I hear you."

She padded across the red floral carpet and pushed the door open. The smell of hyacinths clung to the dissipating fog, and she stood with her hand on the door, savoring the fragrance. She descended the broad, semicircular stairs—*hitch, step, hitch, step*—and followed the path across the church property. The flagstone trail passed a large, oblong planter made of river rock. Inside it, the church sign tilted forward slightly, one leg rotted by age and water damage. As far as bad legs went, Ruby was the expert. Still, the old wooden sign was an embarrassment. She followed the path through a small grove of olive trees and several sprawling avocadoes and headed home.

Fog lingered in the canyon behind the church like a lazy gray swamp, lapping at the brushy edges. Unseen beneath the mist, the creek whispered its joyful cadence, but like most of the streams in Stonetree Valley, Canyon Springs had withered to a trickle.

Ruby clenched the sweat jacket around her shoulders, and the fronts of her thighs tightened as the road began its descent. *Hitch, step. Hitch, step.* "Congenital dysplasia of the hip" was the medical term. To the uninformed, it was just a limp, but Ruby called it her gimp from God.

Swatches of warmth passed over her. Ocean air rose up the canyon, and the salty oxygen stung her nostrils. The walk to and from church had become a necessary ritual, a quiet time. The road formed a broad U-turn, looping around the canyon, connected in the middle by a narrow, two-lane bridge made of railroad ties and old steel trusses. By the time she reached the bridge, Jack was usually at the forefront of her thoughts. Sometimes the entire walk was devoted to praying about her cynical husband. Today, even he took a backseat to the vision.

Why, on a day this rich, green, and beautiful—during prayer, no less—did she get a premonition of a dried-up old tree?

Ruby stopped in her tracks. She spun around and gazed up the valley. Through the clearing the hills rose in waves, speckled with spring flowers between dark gorges and granite crags. At its peak a small, shadowy form notched the eastern skyline overlooking the city.

They called it the Sailor's Oak.

According to local lore, at one time it was the biggest, grandest oak in the area, a sprawling cloud of greens and browns rising on the cliff like an unearthly sentinel. It could be seen for miles, as far away as the sea, where mariners used it for navigation. Now it stood blighted and withered, a spectral figure haunting the heights of the quiet town.

That's where the stories diverged.

Ruby squinted and studied the distant silhouette. What could an old cursed tree possibly have to do with her? She touched the knot behind her ear, shrugged, and turned back to the sidewalk.

The road descended until it met the bridge. Her footsteps echoed in the gulch beneath the bridge. As she chugged up the street, Ruby looked back across the canyon. Eucalyptus trees lined the rim, long, slender branches still dripping dew. From here she could see the backside of the church and the parsonage cloistered near a thick grove. Voices rose in conversation, and she turned to see the Besbecks on their front porch, sipping tea. She waved and started up her driveway.

Sandy, the big gray tabby, sprawled near the porch and watched Ruby's arrival with disinterest. Somehow the cat avoided the marauding coyotes that roamed the canyon. The boys stood at the door, still in their nightclothes. The smell of frying bacon drifted from within.

"Brian keeps poking me." Sean pointed an accusatory finger at his big brother.

"Then just stay away from him, Sean." She drew her nails along Sean's back as she entered and shot a stern glance at Brian, who slouched on the sofa, clicking away at the video controller.

Jack stood at the stove with the hood fan rumbling, bacon sizzling in the cast iron skillet. "Want something? Eggs? Bacon?"

"It's almost lunch."

"Well, we gotta late start."

Ruby pressed her stomach, cringing at the memory of the mysterious nausea. "Nah. Maybe some toast."

She set her Bible on the Formica table, along with her purse. Then she retrieved Jilly's picture, went to the refrigerator, and stuck it up with a magnet. Ruby paused for a moment, staring at the decrepit crayon tree and the shiny leaf. Then she shook her head, walked back across the linoleum, and sat at the kitchen table. Sean thumped into the kitchen with his pajama jumpsuit unzipped down to his navel and draped his head and arms across her lap. She felt his forehead to make sure his fever was gone, then ruffled his wild, blond curls.

Jack wore his usual jean and T-shirt combo, sandy hair still plastered down from the shower. "So, how's everyone?" he asked, without looking at her, a plate of bacon at his elbow.

"Well, it depends on who you mean by *everyone.*"

He turned around, scowling. "Vineyette. Marje. Ian *Einstein.* I dunno."

"Jack." Ruby frowned. "They're fine. They still ask about you."

"Yeah, well, I'm around if they're *that* concerned." He turned back to the stove. "What time are you leaving tonight?"

"The service is at five. Are you sure you don't want to come?"

"You're the one that works with her. I didn't even know the kid, Rube."

"No." Ruby looked down at Sean's turbulent locks. "But you *do* know Marcella."

"I'm not going." Jack went to the refrigerator, glanced at the new picture, and plucked some eggs from the flat. "I hate funerals. I'm not going to another one…unless it's my own."

"Oh, stop it."

Brian shuffled into the kitchen doorway and stood cracking his knuckles, a bad habit he'd acquired from his father. He wrinkled his nose at his little brother, then turned to Jack. "Is it almost done?"

"In a minute. Go on."

Sean rolled over on Ruby's lap and looked at Brian, who moped out of the kitchen. A moment later Sean burst up and rushed after him, slipping across the linoleum in his pajama treads. She folded her hands on the table.

"What do you know about the Stonetree curse?"

Jack glanced at her with one eyebrow raised. "Why're you worried about that?"

"Well, I'm not."

"Then don't bring it up."

Ruby shifted in her seat. "No, really. What do you know about it?"

He removed the last of the bacon, clicked off the fan, and wiped his hands on a wadded towel. "Well, I know it's a buncha crap."

She folded her arms and rolled her eyes at him.

"Somebody was murdered up there." He tossed the towel, and it plopped on the table in front of her. "The tree died, they abandoned the old graveyard, and now it's haunted, or somethin'. And if you're not good," he crept toward her with his fingers curled into talons, "I'm gonna take you up there and drop you off 'til morning." He pounced on her, and she pushed him off, trying not to laugh.

He stood, wringing his still greasy fingers. "The only ones who go up there now are college kids on dares and people who don't believe that nonsense."

She stared forward, without response.

"Why?" Jack tilted his head and squinted at her with his green eyes. "You wanna take a little ride?"

"Yeah," she snapped. "Come to the funeral with me."

He backed up with his hands raised. "Sorry, lady, you're on your own tonight."

Clark hit the mossy flagstone walkway in full stride, briefcase swinging wildly at his side.

He lost traction and flailed in the air, arching himself backward until he regained his footing. He slowed his pace and glanced side to side. The stress was starting to show. He needed to get as far away from this place as possible, and after tonight, he'd be one step closer.

The brief walk from the office to the parsonage usually calmed his nerves. He followed the verdant path as it wound its way to an ivy grotto, shaded by a massive jacaranda. In the center the foliage opened, creating a dappled pool of sunlight. He stopped before a thin, elegant sundial. It rose from the earth like an arm, and on its oxidized fingers, a platter. Upon the face of the sundial danced carved images of fairies, lithe and supple. Engraved around its perimeter, a poem:

With ev'ry hour 'n passing day
You've less of me for work or play.
'Til in the twilight hour, you'll find
The one who holds the hands of time.

Two ornate stone benches faced the sundial, ivy eating its way up their sides, casting green tendrils skyward. On many occasions Clark sat on the benches contemplating the cryptic poem, mulling over the wreckage of his life. But today he frowned and kept walking.

The path slanted across the church property through a small grove of avocado trees to the parsonage on the northwest corner. Flagstone faded into redwood bark, and he crunched along, releasing its crisp scent. Through the stands of eucalyptus, on the far side of the canyon, he often saw Ruby Case trudging home after church. Her thin blonde ponytail would sway with every stride. Even from here her limp was unmistakable.

He looked away, biting back the tide of guilt. She'd been through a lot—more than he could imagine—and still she clung tenaciously to her faith. Some would probably call it naiveté, even obstinacy. In a world where science pushed the boundaries of human knowledge, where progressive philosophers ran circles around religious conservatives, how could one continue to believe in a two-thousand-year-old creed? Ruby Case was evidence enough that those people existed. She'd limped through life, soft-spoken and gracious, always holding out hope. And here he was throwing in the towel. *Clark, you're a worm!*

Approaching the parsonage, he shifted his briefcase to the other side and removed his keys. Why didn't Cellophane ever come here? One of these days Clark expected to open the door and have the monster swoop on him. The groundskeeper would find his body in the morning, drag him off, and they'd have a new minister by nightfall.

That wouldn't be all that bad.

He let himself in, slid his briefcase on the wall table, and placed his keys on the black leather bag. Then he went straight for his desk and removed his address book from the top drawer. He fingered through it until he located Professor Benjamin Keen's phone number. He removed his cell phone, added the number to his contacts, and saved it. Tonight he'd make it official. His days as a minister were over.

The sealed, unsigned envelope peeped from the folds of the desktop dictionary. In it his resignation letter waited. He slipped it out, blew the dust off, and laid it on the cherrywood surface. Highlighting Keen's number in his phone, Clark prepared to hit Send.

But the plaque over the desk caught his eye, as usual.

Stacie, his little sister, had made it in her high school woodworking class. She gave it to him the day he left for seminary, a going-away present. More than that, it was a benediction, a proclamation of good tidings to him. Yet now after his failed marriage, a fruitless ministry, and a second circling the drain, he felt shamed by it.

Clark snapped the phone shut and laid it on the desk. Then he removed the plaque from the wall.

He studied the crude handiwork—uneven cuts and loping beveled edges—but it was the message that haunted him. *Follow Your Dreams.* It was Stacie's favorite saying. Her fair, pale hands once carved the letters, and he traced his fingers through the rough-hewn words, as if trying to extract her memory from the shellacked surface. *Dreams? What dreams?*

He nibbled on the inside of his lip.

"Sorry, sis," he finally muttered.

Then he marched through the house, opened the back door, and tossed the plaque into the dimpled metal trash can. It rattled to the bottom. He hung his head for a moment, then brushed off his hands and returned to his desk.

At least he could exorcize one demon.

Chapter 4

GOLDMAN'S MORTUARY WAS JUST OFF RIVERMEER HEADING inland, a seven-minute drive on most days. Yet between the tourists and weekenders shuttling to and from the coast, it took Ruby fifteen minutes of exhaust-tangled, stop-and-go frustration.

Seeing the tiny lot was full, she parked her white RAV4 on a side street lined with budding myrtle trees. She was relieved to be out of traffic. A moment later she pulled down the visor and flicked open the mirror, removed her sunglasses, and inspected, from top to bottom, her hairclip, lavender eye shadow, clear lip gloss, and thin silver necklace. She'd given up trying to compensate for her handicap a long time ago. Besides, no amount of cosmetic detailing could beautify her fatal flaw. Snapping the visor back into place, she breathed a heavy sigh.

Her rear end was sore from the morning's fall, and she caught herself touching the tender area. As far as she could tell, the vision and its crayon likeness meant nothing. Just an oddball coincidence—life was full of them. Anyway, if there really was something behind the freakish daydream, she'd figure it out. She always did. Regardless, she'd already exerted far too much energy pondering interpretations. The funeral only added to her fatigue. As much as Ruby hated to admit it, her heart wasn't in it, and she felt guilty because of it.

She stepped out of the mini-SUV and squinted as the sun angled toward the western horizon. Over the sloping street, past the quaint shops and residential neighborhoods nestled into the green foothills, she could see a ribbon of shimmering Pacific: Stonetree Cove. Ruby closed the door, the alarm chirped, and she walked toward the funeral home.

Walking itself was a statement for Ruby. Growing up with a hobble earned her embarrassed glances and special treatment—flip sides of the coin of sympathy. She didn't need it. More than that, she loathed it. She'd come to believe that walking was a declaration of independence.

And Ruby was an expert on independence.

Her black leather loafers scuffed across the sidewalk. She turned the corner and walked past a neighborhood market and a barbershop before coming to the chapel. Two men in black suits stood stiffly at the open double doors. A young man with a pubescent black mustache handed her a pamphlet with a photocopied picture of Armando Amaya on the front. She thanked him and proceeded into the mortuary.

The familiar trace of formaldehyde struck her and she grimaced. The low yellow-tinged acoustic ceiling made the room appear cramped, constricting, and awakened pangs of claustrophobia. Plush curtains muffled the day's leftover light and candles flickered up front, casting a pulsating orange halo around the boy in the coffin.

Ruby stood there so her eyes could adjust then scanned the room. As expected, she did not recognize many people. Of course, Marcella was there, and some of her other coworkers from Livery's. One of the elders from Canyon Springs, Doyle Thomas, sat near the back. Other than that, she was on her own, just like Jack said.

Her eyes watered. She'd excavated her gray pantsuit for the service. It was the only one she owned and far too businesslike for her tastes. Maybe that's why she christened it her *funeral suit* and banished it to the farthest reaches of the closet. The last time she wore it, they buried Jack's mom. The smell of dust and mothballs coming off the fabric threatened to unleash her sinuses.

She undid the bottom button and slid into the wooden pew—three rows back, near the center aisle, next to a middle-aged woman wearing a poorly camouflaged wig and a short dress with black nylons. They exchanged smiles and Ruby glanced through the pamphlet. The woman picked at the hem of her dress with her long nails.

"What've they found out?"

"Excuse me?" Ruby replied.

"About the boy." The woman glanced behind them and leaned closer. "You know, the cause of death?"

Ruby eased back from the woman. *Who is this lady?* Scanning the pamphlet again, she said, "Respiratory failure. But they're not really sure."

The woman nodded. "They think it's that fever."

Ruby squinted. "Fever?"

"The one that wiped out half the city almost a hundred years ago."

"Um, I don't know anything about that." This woman was turning rude. They were here to pay last respects, not second-guess the cause of death. Ruby crossed her legs, brushed a wrinkle out of her pants, and angled the other direction.

"Well..." The woman returned to fidgeting with her hemline. "They better hope that's not it. Good kid. What a shame."

Flower arrangements surrounded the coffin, and two candle stands, twelve candles in each, stood on each end. Mondo wore a tuxedo, which seemed extravagant for the humble, uneducated boy and his simple family. Marcella and her three daughters sat ensconced in a dense circle of mourners, sniffling, holding hands, and dabbing their swollen eyes.

The chapel filled, and the track music faded. A priest emerged from a backroom, and the candles danced with his passing. A short, Hispanic man with gray hair and a thin mustache, he took the pulpit and addressed the crowd in a thick accent. The group rose as he commenced a lengthy prayer, reciting Scripture in Spanish and English. Upon mention of the boy's name, sniffles and sobs let loose in the room. He concluded and the crowd was seated.

The priest made the sign of the cross, took up an ornate black book, and repeated a succession of Latin phrases—*Beata Virgo Maria* and *Deo gratias* and *lachryma Christi*, words Ruby could only guess the meaning of. A cue was given, and the congregants said the Lord's Prayer, then the priest walked in front of the body, flicking holy water. He lit a censer of incense and carried it around the coffin, creating a thin layer of wispy blue haze that spread through the chapel. The pungent aroma merged with the mothballs and the odor of the flowers and turned Ruby's stomach. She hated the smell of funerals.

She sighed, and the woman next to her rummaged through a sequined purse. Across the room a child chattered, and someone shushed her. Ruby hung her head. Would something even be said about Mondo? Something endearing, personal? She had come to pay her respects and instead got trapped in a pointless, mechanistic ritual. Ruby closed her eyes and drifted in thought.

The service meandered. Scriptures referencing eternal life and heaven were cited, until the priest finally read a doxology and a prayer for the dead. Then the body was blessed, and the ceremony mercifully ended.

The track music resumed and people shuffled to their feet. "Is it over?" the young voice queried from across the room, eliciting nervous whispers and reprimands from those nearby. Someone sobbed in the front, and a line formed to view the body and extend a final farewell.

Ruby glanced at Marcella. More than anything she wanted to hug her and thank her for raising such a fine boy. Funerals were not the place to offer answers. Anyway, she didn't have one. God decided to take the boy, just as He decided to take Jack's mom and cripple Ruby's leg. She'd been through the tears and angry debates, but Daddy's saying stood the test of time: *God can't be explained, but He can be trusted.* Here, at Goldman's Mortuary, amid candles, incense, and formaldehyde, Ruby still believed that.

The line grew. Heavy sobs sounded near Marcella, followed by a flurry of embraces and loud consolation. Ruby's head throbbed. She took her purse and walked to the end of the line. *What a day.* When she got home, she would make some tea, phone Vin, and go to bed early.

The line crept forward. A middle-aged man in a cheap polyester suit placed something in the casket, made the sign of the cross, and walked away. The line moved. A teenage boy, looking uncomfortable, glanced at the corpse, tapped his fist on the edge of the coffin, and rushed off. The line moved. A woman with bleached hair and large sunglasses leaned across the body and sobbed, rocking the casket, until a man nearby drew her away. The line moved. A short, hunchbacked woman with a black veil shuffled forward. The old woman stood on her toes, kissed her fingertips, and touched the lips of the dead boy. She muttered something in Spanish and stepped away. The line moved, and Ruby stepped up to the casket.

A dull, pasty sheen clung to Mondo's flesh. He lay yellow and waxy, chest sunken, jaw frozen in mocking neutrality. Black droplets—tear stains—sprinkled his lapel.

She placed her hand on the boy's forearm without reservation and closed her eyes. What more could be said? *Thank You for the Amayas and sweet, simple Armando. Have mercy on them, O God.* Ruby sighed—a slow, concentrated breath that carried both frustration and resolve—removed her hand, and turned to leave.

Someone shrieked—a shrill yowl that ripped through the subdued atmosphere like a terrorist blast.

Ruby jolted to a stop and turned.

The room exploded with commotion. People were standing in shocked disbelief. Others stumbled from the pews, grappling sleeves and shoulders, clambering their way into the aisles. The chapel doors burst open, and frantic shadowy figures careened out of the building, sending uneven shafts of light into the room. On the carpet a young girl knelt with her hands over her head, protecting herself against the onrush. A wail erupted from the other side as a woman collapsed. Near the casket another commotion ensued, and Ruby turned as someone tumbled backward, taking several stands of flowers with him. An elderly woman in the front row stared forward, her face ashen, a trembling hand over her mouth.

And they all looked at Ruby.

She staggered back, struck the coffin, and gasped. Maybe she'd ignited herself on a candle or cut herself or something worse. She patted her hands along her torso, frantically inspecting her clothing for fire or blood, but the pantsuit looked as bland as ever.

Someone shouted the Lord's Prayer, and several others joined the refrain. Marcella stood limp, pale, her eyes wide and jaw gaping. A crowd huddled at the back, clinging to each other, eyes fixed forward. They were no longer looking at her, but at something else.

The hair on her neck bristled.

Ruby turned to see Armando Amaya sitting straight up in his coffin.

Chapter 5

A HORN SOUNDED AS CLARK WEDGED HIS BLACK JEEP INTO traffic. Rivermeer was a parking lot on the weekends. Now with the weather warming, it would only worsen. He glanced in the rearview mirror. The fog had given way to sunshine, turning the Pacific into a shimmering blue basin. Tourists lined the sidewalk cafés and art galleries, and the aroma of coffee and pastries roused his taste buds.

This was small-town Americana at its best: produce stands, delicatessens, even a pharmacy with an old-fashioned soda fountain. But the influx of artists and avant-garde occultists had slowly transformed the quaint downtown complex into an offbeat enclave, a watering hole for surfers, poets, and neo-pagans. College kids descended with their swagger, filling the pubs and unsettling the atmosphere, returning each weekend for a repeat performance. These eclectic forces had combined to make Stonetree something of a dark novelty.

But the spiritual climate of the city no longer concerned Reverend Ian Clark.

He passed into the residential district, driving inland. To his right, the ridgeline rose and meandered eastward. He followed it with his eyes, glancing from road to hilltop until he spotted the Sailor's Oak perched on the precipice.

Even Windayven, the upscale East Coast city where he last served, had its peculiar history and quirky landmarks. Stonetree was no different. However, the petrified oak and the folklore surrounding it did little more than bolster his intolerance for superstition and confirm his convictions about human nature. The world was far too big a place to believe any one religion, and people who did so were myopic, self-deceived. At least that was his going theory.

Professor Keen's ranch lay just outside the valley, a forty-five-minute trip. As Clark settled in, he checked the clock in the dash. *Five fifty-seven.* Traffic permitting, he'd be there well before dark. He glanced in his rearview mirror and did a double take.

A police car barreled toward him with its lights on, scattering leaves like a miniature cyclone. He tapped his brakes, unsure whether to stop in the middle of the street or get out of the way. Maybe he'd drifted across the center line, made an illegal turn, or had a burned-out taillight. Either way, the last thing he needed was a ticket. He pulled to the curb near the lumberyard. The police car swerved, sped past him, and dipped over the hill.

He sat for a few seconds, heart thumping.

When were the cops ever in a hurry around here? Maybe they'd caught a vagrant shoplifting or the college kids were getting rowdy at the Green Man pub again. But on a Sunday evening? Besides, they were headed the wrong direction.

Clark turned into traffic, and the Jeep crested the hill, where he met a chain of idling cars. He slowed and craned to see the source of the commotion. A block ahead, the police car stopped, lights spinning, in the middle of the street. Alongside it sat an ambulance and a hearse. People in dark attire huddled together and milled about in front of the mortuary, and someone engaged the police officer in animated discussion.

Goldman's Mortuary. What could be the problem? Maybe someone passed out during a funeral or had a heart attack. One time a distraught spouse pulled a gun on Reverend Moss and shot up the place. Luckily no one got hurt.

Despite his religious equivocations, Clark had given himself to serve. Until he pulled the plug on the whole thing, that's exactly what he needed to do. He might be a coward, but he wasn't heartless. At least not yet.

He veered out of traffic and parked behind a charcoal van with a dove decal and a religious bumper sticker. He got out and brushed his hands down his polo shirt in an attempt to press out any wrinkles. Then he pocketed his keys, walked around the Jeep, and followed the sidewalk toward Goldman's. Two women passed him going the opposite direction, heels clicking in unison. One dabbed her eyes with a handkerchief while the other chattered in Spanish, making sweeping gestures with her hands. As he approached the building, several circles of people stood huddled together; they looked his way, whispering.

A figure dashed toward him.

"Reverend!" Doyle Thomas's gruff voice and bushy red beard were unmistakable. He wove his way through the idling cars, thick black glasses glinting in the waning sunlight. "I saw it! I saw it with my own eyes, God blessit!" He skidded to a stop before Clark, shirt collar drenched with perspiration. "Just don't ask me to explain."

A horn sounded, and someone muttered an obscenity. Car exhaust stung Clark's eyes, and he squinted at the burly man before him. "What're you talking about, Doyle? What happened?"

Thomas pushed his glasses back up the bridge of his nose and said, almost matter-of-factly, "Marcella Amaya's boy came back to life."

Clark shifted his weight and looked sideways at the man. "Huh?"

Suddenly Mr. Thomas lunged at Clark, seized his shoulder, and spun him toward the mortuary. "He sat up in his flippin' coffin!" Thomas barked, stabbing his finger that direction.

Clark brushed his hand off and smirked, trying to make the words register. Then he laughed—a single, pronounced, incredulous snort of laughter, which turned heads and elicited scowls from those nearby. He cringed at the attention, then peered at Thomas and whispered, "He did *what?*"

Thomas smote Clark with a steely gaze.

"C'mon, Doyle, don't—who put you up to this?"

"I know what I saw, Ian. The kid came to life, back from the dead, however you wanna say it. He's with us now. If you don't believe me, go see for yourself."

A petite woman wearing white gloves and a plain blue dress approached Mr. Thomas's side and slipped her arm in his. Erin Thomas glanced at Clark without greeting him, whispered something in her husband's ear, and together they walked away. Thomas called over his shoulder, "Go ahead. See for yourself."

Another officer arrived, positioned himself near the intersection, and waved the motorists along. The line of cars stretched down Rivermeer, disappearing over the hill. Loud music thumped in several vehicles, adding to Clark's emotional dissonance. Small groups of people remained clustered along the sidewalk in front of the chapel in various stages of debate and anxious interaction, fanning themselves and rolling their eyes heavenward. Near the entrance a policeman scribbled on a pad of paper as Ira Goldman dabbed his forehead with a handkerchief and spoke to the officer.

Clark rubbed the sweat off the back of his neck and adjusted his glasses. Did he really want to see for himself? Maybe he should turn around, drive to Keen's, finalize the deal, and never look back. Clark stood squinting as the gears of his mind turned— only now they were doing double-time. Doyle Thomas was far from gullible. Yet how could this be? Corpses didn't just come to life.

He swayed at the thought, caught himself, and started toward the chapel with a slow, robotic gait.

A tall, unshaven man with dark sunglasses leaned against the hearse chomping gum. The mortuary doors were propped open, revealing worn, gold carpet littered with loose paper and trampled flowers. Two paramedics emerged and brushed by the police officer with a sharp nod. Clark approached the man, who glanced at him and closed his tablet.

"What's goin' on here, Brad?" Clark gazed through the open doorway, into the dark corridor. "There been a crime or something?"

The officer tapped the notepad against his palm. "This isn't a crime scene, Reverend. At the moment, I'm not sure what this is. But it's not a crime scene." He looked in Clark's eyes for a moment, just long enough to reveal apprehension, and then pointed his pen in the direction of the doorway. "Go see for yourself."

Clark hesitated. Running had become a way of life. His heart thundered in his chest. One more cowardly retreat wouldn't matter. Or would it? *No! See for yourself.* He stared at the open doors, caught between trepidation and wonder, and then lurched forward.

Three steps into the doorway Clark stopped so his eyes could adjust. Voices rose and fell, and a cobalt sheet of incense hovered above the pews. He scanned the room and froze.

Balanced precariously near the front steps of the altar was an empty coffin, twisted halfway off its stand.

He stepped back and fumbled for a pew to steady himself.

Candle stands stood on each end of the coffin, with one angled sideways. The flames cast a pulsating yellow luster over the satin interior. Near the head of the casket, flower stands lay toppled. Roses, carnations, and baby's breath jumbled together in a kaleidoscopic heap. An empty easel leaned against the steps of the altar, and a poster board filled with snapshots rested at its feet. Above the droning organ tracks rose sniffles, moans, and unbound laughter.

In the first pew sat a young Hispanic man in a rumpled black suit, with a mop of curly black hair. Twenty-plus jubilant witnesses encircled him, all teary-eyed and rosy. He appeared flushed, embarrassed.

And completely alive.

How could this be? Clark stared back out the doorway, trying to locate the cop. No doubt the authorities were collecting the facts, some rational evidence—they'd get to the bottom of this. He turned and wiped his clammy forehead with the back of his hand, but the exultant group seemed oblivious to his dismay. A tall, thin woman clutched a rosary to her bosom. At her shoulder stood a woman with bleached hair, mascara trails coursing her rouged cheeks, her head thrown back in laughter. At her side, a young, well-groomed boy in a silk vest stood with his lips curled and eyes locked in glazed disbelief.

This was madness! Maybe he should join the crowd, raise a shout of victory, and do laps around the mortuary. Better yet, he should curse the fools, storm off, and seal his indignation. *Get a grip, Clark!*

As his mind waged war, Marcella Amaya, veil rent from her face, spotted him from within the circle. She beamed. Her swollen eyes glistened as she pointed toward the front corner of the mortuary. He reluctantly turned to see a small cluster of people huddled around a woman in a gray suit. Two figures faced her with hands folded and heads bowed, mumbling inaudible words. A man genuflected and caressed her right hand. An elderly woman knelt and kissed her shoes, leaving steamy lip prints evaporating on the shiny black surface.

The object of their worship was someone he recognized.

Ruby Case stood like a statue, leaning left, indigo eyes filled with dismay and fixed on him.

Chapter 6

Ian Clark came to his senses at eighty-five miles an hour.

He'd left the mortuary and driven out of Stonetree Valley in a daze. The highway rose steadily before him into twilight skies, leveling out into the long, open stretch that led to Benjamin Keen's. The sweeping road cut through farmland, a two-lane asphalt runway unimpeded by traffic lights and urban sprawl. Because of the number of deaths incurred, some folks called it the Highway to Hell. At the moment he could care less about the superstitions or the statistics.

With both windows down, evening air whipped through the cab. The leather jacket fluttered on the passenger seat as though it would leap from the vehicle any moment. Tears scraped across his cheeks from the pounding wind. He finally came to himself and eased off the accelerator.

Barns and silos loomed on the dusky eastern horizon, and night birds took to the air, spiraling after moths and mosquitoes. But their shrill cries and the rich, fragrant smells of the upper country failed to engage him. In fact, they seemed insignificant.

The real world was upside down—or inside out—unfolded and shaken like a dusty quilt, revealing a tapestry of color and design heretofore unseen. A homemaker, an ordinary woman with two small kids and a bum leg, living in a quiet coastal town raised a dead boy to life, and suddenly Clark's world no longer made sense. He'd been intellectually broadsided, and his mind reeled.

Maybe he should pull to the shoulder of the road to regather his senses. Yet no amount of sitting and thinking would help him grasp the events of that evening. Still, he decelerated, veered onto the gravel, and stopped. The dust cloud caught up and swept over the vehicle, swirling into the cab and leaving a thin, gritty film on his glasses. He turned off the ignition, kept one hand on the wheel, and closed his eyes.

The sounds of the open country awoke in the gloaming. Grass rustled in steady waves mixed with a chorus of crickets. A swath of freshly tilled farmland stretched away to the foothills on his right. A dog barked in the distance, and an engine droned farther off. If only he could fill his body with this solitude. He drew a deep breath, hoping to do so.

Once he believed in miracles. But that was before the collision, before the heartbreak, before God became deaf and dumb.

So why now? Why on the way to Keen's—*the very road to Clark's defection*—would this happen? Why after years of waning faith and unanswered prayer would he be faced with the possibility of a genuine miracle? He ground his teeth and wrung the steering wheel with his hand. *Figger it out, Clark!*

An engine bore down from behind, rising to a crescendo, overwhelming the serenity, until it roared past and rocked the Jeep, jolting him back to reality. He opened his eyes as the diesel sailed past, silhouetted against the dying blue. A line of cars followed it, imprisoned behind the big rig, each one splashing him with red taillights and exhaust fumes as it passed.

He removed his glasses, placed them in his shirt pocket, leaned across the seat, and popped open the glove box. His wallet fell out and dropped into his hand. With his other hand, he pawed around for his cell phone before realizing he'd left it in his briefcase back home. He clucked his tongue and retrieved a water bottle. Then he removed the cap and drank deeply.

This is what he needed, something to steady him, something like water and fresh air. He took another drink, capped the bottle, and placed it back in the glove box.

But he held the wallet in his lap, thumbing its edge.

If he needed something real, something to steady him, all he had to do was look inside the soft, black leather wallet.

He'd done it a million times, and he needn't do it again. Leafing through the faded pictures had become punishment, something he did when he was feeling nostalgic or adrift. It was the two photos sandwiched together, one hiding the other, which tore at him: Stacie's high school graduation picture and, behind it, Cynthia, his ex-wife, before she'd stopped smiling. He didn't have the heart to trash the photos, though he'd been inclined many times. But with the plaque in the garbage can back home, maybe it was about time.

He tapped the wallet with his thumb.

Headlights approached the opposite direction, forcing him to look away as the vehicle raced past. Turning back to the road, he gazed into the distance. The highway dipped into a series of rolling hills and disappeared in the dusk. Fog seeped into the crags and ditches, and the smell of manure and cool, wet earth blanketed the ground.

Maybe he should turn around, give himself some time to investigate, try to make sense of it all. He could phone the professor when he got home, apologize and reschedule. As it stood, he was late for the meeting and completely unsettled. This was hardly the way to reacquaint himself with his old professor. Besides, Keen would only scoff at his duplicity.

And Clark had plenty of that.

He tapped his wallet again, rolled it over with his fingers, and placed it back in the glove box. Then he removed his glasses from his shirt pocket and blew the dust off. He put them on and gazed down the highway, a dark funnel into the unknown.

If the resurrection was a fraud, a quirk, a natural phenomenon, he had nothing to fear. But if a miracle had occurred, it could validate the very things he was running from; if a miracle had been performed, it meant that God—*the same God who took his sister and let his marriage collapse*—was very much alive. At the thought terror streaked across his mind like a fiery comet torching the landscape. Yet within that gray topography a shoot of hope lay just beneath the cracked facade.

Whether through fear or hope, he knew not which, Ian Clark started the ignition, turned back onto the asphalt, and drove forward into the growing dark.

By the time Ruby arrived, the powder blue sky had turned to twilight. She pulled her RAV into the driveway, her mind lost in thought. Suddenly she gasped and punched her brakes.

The cat stood frozen in her path, his back arched, wide eyes sparkling in the headlights.

Her heart raced, not just because of the jolting stop but because the stunned animal reminded her of Mondo.

Sitting up in his coffin.

Startled.

Eyes wide open and glistening in the candlelight.

She exhaled sharply as Sandy ambled across the driveway and ducked under Jack's truck.

Now she was shaking again. Ruby parked, turned off the engine, and sat wringing her hands, trying to subdue the trembling.

The wild peacocks yowled in the canyon below, as they did every evening. Their sad cries reminded her of a child calling after a mother who would never return.

Just as Ruby had done for thirty-two years.

She glanced at the front door. Maybe the boys hadn't seen her pull up. If so, that would give her a minute to compose herself. But after what happened at Goldman's, she feared she'd never be composed again.

She turned on the dome light and inspected her pantsuit. Other than the lingering funeral smell, it looked fine. Then she snatched a tissue out of the box in the console and started wiping the lipstick off the back of her right hand.

The hand she touched Mondo with.

She dabbed at the marks with the tissue, smudging the wine-colored lipstick across her knuckles. How many people had kissed her hand? Between all the hugs and handshakes, she'd lost count. Fear and confusion rattled inside her. The claustrophobia swooped out of nowhere, and her breathing quickened. She tucked the tissue in the console and fumbled for her keys and purse. She had to take a shower. The smell was driving her crazy.

As she grabbed the handle, she paused. What would she tell Jack? He would be concerned, maybe even a little angry, wondering what took so long. She'd purposely not told him about her fainting fit that morning. He would have blown a fuse. But there was no way she could hide this. No way! She had to tell him the truth—as incredible as it sounded. And why not? It really happened! But just how did one go about that? *Hi, hon. I'm home. Sorry I'm late. But when I touched the dead kid, he came back to life. After that, I kinda lost track of time. I apologize. It won't happen again.* She rolled her eyes at the absurdity of it all.

That's when it struck her: *This is only the beginning.* What would happen when the paper got ahold of it? Or the church? Or her kids? Her mind reeled at the onrushing possibilities.

The kitchen curtains spread, and the silhouette of a small head peered between them.

"Lord help me," she sighed, now at a complete loss.

She dropped her keys in the purse and got out of the SUV. The air was calm. Clusters of stars sprinkled the cloudless twilight sky. She walked around Jack's truck, passed the planter dotted with daffodils, and climbed the steps to the porch—*hitch, step, hitch, step*—just as the door opened.

"Mommy!" Sean piped.

"Heyya, baby," she said, opening the screen door and walking in. He seized her legs in a manic hug, and she gripped the door to keep from falling over. "Whoa. Did you miss me or what?"

The television pulsed in the corner, casting a strobe across Brian, who lounged on the sofa with the changer in his hand. He glanced at her. "Some people called for you."

"Oh?"

"Dad got mad and stopped answering. They left messages." He changed the channel and glanced at her again. "A bunch of 'em."

Ruby furrowed her brow. Who would be calling? Could word have spread that fast? She'd turned off her cell during the funeral and was almost afraid to turn it back on again. She patted Sean's back, and he loosened his grip and beamed a mischievous smile up at her. She wrinkled her nose at him and crossed the hardwood floor into the kitchen. Without bothering to turn the light on, she set her purse on the tile countertop near the stove and looked at the answering machine. The red light pulsed like a silent alarm.

No. It's already started.

The floor creaked as someone approached from the hall. She turned as Jack entered the kitchen and switched the light on. Ruby squinted.

He stood barefoot in his jeans and T-shirt, his wavy hair matted to one side. He cast a brief, piercing glance at her then looked away and rubbed his hand up and down his forearm. "Vinyette called," he said, biting back a yawn.

"Mmm, hmm." She glanced at the wine lipstick stain on her right hand and nonchalantly brought it to her side, shielding it from Jack's view.

"She heard about"—he glanced into the living room and then looked straight at her—"what happened at the funeral." He studied her with unflinching, uncharacteristic poise.

What did he know? Was he confused? Happy? Jack didn't have the best poker face, but she couldn't read him, and that amplified her insecurity.

Ruby clenched her jaw and fastened her gaze upon him, unsure how to proceed, ready to defend herself if necessary. Then Jack shook his head and smiled—a weak, sincere, compassionate smile—and her defenses withered. She stumbled into his outstretched arms, and her emotions unraveled.

"I just t–touched him," she sobbed. "I don't—I didn't expect to..." Her chest heaved, and he drew her into himself.

Jack's broad shoulders and strong arms enfolded her. The chaos and confusion of the funeral home seemed distant, miniscule to the moment. Jack held her, and right now that was all that mattered.

Sean wrestled his way through the tangle of legs. "What's wrong?" He looked up at them with wide, green eyes. "Can I help?"

Ruby laughed, wiped her cheeks, and knelt down and hugged him. As she did, Jack turned into the living room, blinking back tears. Ruby watched him. *The last time he cried was...* She couldn't remember. She patted Sean's back and gazed at Jilly's picture on the fridge, which seemed to glisten with a magic all its own.

Reverend Clark hunched forward, peering over the steering wheel. In his right hand he held the directions to Professor Keen's, and, in the glow of the dash, he glanced at them. In the open country, at night, there wasn't much to go by. So he stayed near the shoulder looking for landmarks.

The glare of the Jeep's headlights forced the landscape into immense, indistinguishable forms. Cool, sweet air swept in as he passed a flower farm. On his left was a massive archway made of timber rose, arrayed with horseshoes and antlers. Another half-mile, a dirt road branched off the highway, cordoned by a ragged barbed-wire fence that disappeared in the dark. Farther down, an upstairs light peeked through a grove of trees, and a dog barked as he clipped the gravel. Steadying the Jeep, he laid the directions aside and sat up straight. The next house should be Professor Keen's.

Several cars passed him, gunning their engines for emphasis. As they sped eastward, their headlamps revealed twisted oaks, logs, and boulders marring the open terrain up ahead. The luminescent fans slashed the darkness, rising and falling with each successive hill, diminishing in the distance. The road was all his.

He steadied his gaze until the high beams captured a tall, pale shack tilted to one side, looming on his right; next to it a water well squatted among dead grape vines.

This was it.

He turned onto the shoulder and slowed. The outline of a sprawling single-story house appeared, surrounded by wooden fence, set slightly back from the road. A large black mailbox tilted forward, buttressed at its base by a black crystalline rock—obsidian, no doubt—etched with strange symbols. He drove up to the mailbox and turned off the engine.

A bird screeched as it passed overhead, and something rustled in a nearby tree. The engine crackled as it cooled, and the darkness came alive with insect chatter.

He rolled up the windows and climbed out, peering at the shadowy structure. Then he retrieved his wallet, slipped on his jacket, and locked the vehicle. A large tree formed a pitch umbrella in front of the house, its branches rambling almost to the fence. At the far end of the building a solitary light shone behind a blanched orange shade. He circled around the mailbox to the fence, the sound of crunching gravel magnified in the open air.

Clark located a wooden gate across a dirt driveway, went there, and called out. His voice echoed off the foothills, and the insect noises stopped. There was no response. He called out again, fumbled for the latch, and, keeping his eyes riveted on the black porch, nudged the gate. It swung open on uneven hinges before scraping to a stop in the dirt.

He stood deliberating.

He'd spent the last year plotting his move to reconnect with Keen, but the vision of the empty casket burned in his brain, making him hesitate. Blast his indecision!

Taking a deep breath as if hoping to replenish his resolve, Clark marched through the entrance.

A path wound toward the front of the house, which he followed, crackling dry leaves with every step. As he passed beneath the tree, the starry sky disappeared and a chilling shadow enclosed him, as if he'd crossed some invisible barrier. He stopped, letting his eyes adjust to the shroud. Gooseflesh rippled his arms.

A coyote yelped in the distance. He turned toward the sound, and something skittered in the dry carpet of leaves near his feet. Clark leaped sideways to avoid it, struck his shoulder against the massive trunk, catapulting his glasses off his nose. The leaves rattled overhead from the concussion, and several acorns fell. He squatted, groping the earth in search of his glasses.

Faint laughter rose ahead of him.

Clark snapped his head up trying to locate the sound. A small light flickered on the porch, the dying yellow gasps of a doorbell shorting out. Next to it a figure stood in the entry, silhouetted by pale red light.

"Lost your way, stranger?"

Chapter 7

CLARK FUMBLED FOR HIS GLASSES, PUT THEM ON, AND peered at the figure in the dim red doorway. "Professor Keen? Is that you?"

The man chuckled. "You've met the black oak, I see, and Doire, the tree spirit."

Clark glanced up into the branches then strode to the porch and up the steps. His shoulder smarted from its collision with the oak, and he rubbed it as he stared at the shadowy figure.

"If I believed that stuff, I'd be worried," Clark said with a nervous grin, wiping perspiration off his forehead.

"Oh, but it's true. The tree fairy is quite mischievous. Would you two like to get more acquainted?"

The leaves chattered as a breeze swept through the branches. Clark readjusted his glasses and looked nervously into the ominous shroud.

"Forgive me," Benjamin Keen said as he stepped out of the house, took Clark's elbow, and drew him through the doorway. "The open country does that, you know. Everything is bigger out here—the sounds, the smells."

The frazzled gray afro and wispy goatee were unchanged. For a man his age, Keen's build remained lean and sturdy. Years of travel and rugged exploration kept the professor fit. He wore cargo shorts and a loose-fitting shirt with a slit neckline and sequined trim. Each ear contained several rings. His thin, chiseled face and deep, charcoal eyes fixed on Ian Clark.

"The old hound is probably out chasing rabbits. She'd have let me know you were here." He shut the door and turned back to Clark. A floor lamp in the far corner with a tubular, red shade projected a misshapen swath overhead and cast a ruddy glow across the room. "I assumed you weren't coming. Get caught up in traffic? Or maybe tangling with other, more oppressive spirits?"

"I'm sorry, Professor. I should've called. Something unexpected came up." His mind flinched at the thought of the incident at Goldman's.

Keen nodded. "That tends to happen. But here you are." He put his hand on Clark's shoulder and studied him. "So glad you could make it, Ian. What's it been, two...three years?"

"Just before you left the seminary."

"Ah, yes. Mallor. *Ground and Pillar of the Truth.* Isn't that how it goes? Bah!" He brushed his hand dismissively through the air.

Clark shook his head and smiled. "That's how it goes."

"You've been receiving my correspondence, yes?"

"Every one of them. And the gifts, they're–they're cool. Really unusual. Obviously, you've become quite the world traveler."

"Yes," Keen chuckled. Then he motioned to a nearby hallway. "Let's go to the study, shall we? Mr. O will prepare us some tea. We can chat there, get caught up on things."

A pungent musky aroma stung Clark's eyes. Two windows, each draped with khaki cloth, cordoned the front door. Dark, wood-paneled walls rose to a high, flat ceiling, making the alcove appear much higher than it was wide. He turned to follow the professor but stopped mid-stride.

Tribal masks lined the walls overhead, forming an odd tapestry of shape and color. A jigsaw of rectangles, ovals, and octagons clad with cloth and hair blended into abstract ambience. He stood with his jaw slack and set his gaze upon each face. Some stretched in laughter, mouths wide in mockery or delight. Others contorted in pain or misery, eyes bleeding blue gemstone or jade. Hair of stick and straw sprang wildly from black husks and taut leather. There were browns and burnt umber, bright yellows and dirty white. Some wore clay beads or shells; others had metal studs and bleached bone. Stripes, swirls, and jagged bolts joined the confluence of color. Warriors, banshees, seers, and priests looked on with empty eyes.

They all looked down upon Ian Clark.

"Ah, you've found the family," said Keen, returning from the hallway in search of his guest. He spread his arms, scanning the walls with a satisfied smile. "And each one has a story."

Clark nodded, still surveying the menagerie.

"But don't we all have a story?" The professor allowed Clark a moment and then said, "The study is this way."

They passed several dim, cluttered rooms before entering a library. A bank of dark wood shelves overlaid one wall and rose to the ceiling. Volumes with opulent leather and peeling spines rested at various angles. A thickly woven rug stitched with vibrant birdlike forms stretched before them, and slender figurines with elongated faces guarded each corner. Four black leather chairs with intricately carved handles circled a spacious marble table veined with beryl. Upon the table sat a dull metal box, an ashtray with a thin brown cigarette perched inside it, and an open book. The professor motioned him toward a chair and sat down.

Clark's eyes watered now from a heavy scent of spice. He removed his coat and prepared to sit when a shrill cry burst from the corner of the room. He bolted to his feet, bumped the table, and sent the objects clattering to one side.

The professor cackled and slapped his knee. "It's the chamber ward." He pointed across the room. "The chamber ward!"

A large parrot perched beside a plush burgundy curtain. It shrieked again, and Clark dropped his head to his chest and heaved an embarrassed sigh.

"Mr. Clark," Keen said, "meet Jade, ward of the library, guardian of the most arcane imaginings."

The bluish-green parrot ruffled its feathers, drawing a leg up under one wing, as if in response to its name. A scar slashed one eye, and several bald spots interrupted the bird's otherwise beautiful appearance.

"Jade was almost soup until I rescued her. Parrot is a delicacy in some parts. Its feet and entrails are said to have magical powers."

The bird stamped its perch and made a soft guttural sound.

"No, of course not, dear," Keen purred.

Clark sat down, shaking his head and smiling.

"So," the professor said, settling back in his chair. "Has the Wandering Soul found his way home, hmm?"

"Well, let's say I'm getting closer.

Keen peered at him. "The lore of youth is not easily discarded, is it?"

A figure emerged from another room and padded to the professor's side without acknowledging Clark. The dark-skinned man wore a skullcap and plain linen robe. He had a smooth oval face and small, sunken eyes. "Some tea, Mr. O," Keen said. The man tipped his head, pivoted, and left the room.

"Mr. O's ancestors traverse the island of his birth," Keen said. "For centuries his people have been immersed in the crudest of rituals—sacrificing to the gods of wood and stone, paying homage to the spirits of the hill country who, they believe, watch over them. Quite pagan, trust me."

Keen sunk further back in his chair, stroked his goatee, and peered across at Reverend Clark. "Is O mistaken, Mr. Clark? Will he be banished from paradise, cast into outer darkness, as so many of your cohorts suggest, for *his primitive views*? Are the customs and history of his tribe simply fodder for the fires of hell? Please, can you say?"

Clark conceded a wry smile. "It's good to see you haven't changed, Professor."

"Well? You still call yourself a minister, don't you? A *Christian* minister?"

The question knifed through Clark. He lowered his eyes and massaged his aching shoulder.

"Forgive me," said Keen. "My forthrightness is not becoming."

"No, Professor. I'd be lying if I said I was resolved, either way."

"In the netherworld, eh? Between faith and—"

"Unbelief? Yes."

Keen nodded, rose from his seat, and walked to the bookshelves. He wrestled a sizeable book from a stack, approached Clark, and extended the volume.

"Faith and unbelief *is* the question," Keen said, turning the cover toward Clark. "This is for you, Ian."

Clark moved to the edge of his seat, accepting the book and scanning the cover. "You did it! Congratulations, Professor." He rubbed his hand reverently over the book. "*The Myth of Religion* by Benjamin Keen."

"The university dragged their feet, or it would have been printed last year. Alas, the editorial gods must be appeased." He patted Clark's shoulder and walked back to his chair. "I've taken the liberty of signing your copy."

Clark opened the book and leafed through several pages. He stopped and ran his finger across the inscription. *For the Journey...and Its End. Your Friend, Benjamin Keen.* Clark looked at Keen, then back at the book. "Thank you, Professor. It's an honor."

"The sales have been mediocre. No one's interested in what an ex-seminary professor, anthropologist, world traveler, and first-rate chef has to say."

"Don't forget one of the forerunners of contemporary syncretism."

"Mustn't forget that."

"But a first-rate chef?"

"I make a mean marsupial stew."

Mr. O swept into the room carrying a tray with two cups. He set the cups before them, slipped the tray under his arm, and stood unmoving. Keen waved his hand, and the manservant left. Clark set the volume on the table and, as they drank, inquired of the black, astringent tea.

"An infusion of root and berry," Keen said between sips. "You'll not find this at the café in Stonetree."

"No, but I can get a latte there."

"That you can. But this particular recipe belongs to the Illuaco. Very special, indeed." Keen swirled the liquid in his cup. "They're just one of many indigenous tribes in the Peruvian Amazon—completely isolated from the industrial-technological world, quite primitive. Prehistoric, you could say. Hundreds, they say, perhaps thousands of tribes inhabit the remote stretches of the Amazon River Basin. Missiologists claim that the only unreached people groups in the world live there. And each one"—he set the cup down and wagged his finger at Clark—"each one has a unique set of myths and traditions dating back long before the time of Christ.

"My stay with the Illuaco was enlightening, to say the least. But enough about me. What of your quest? Where do you find yourself these days?"

Clark sipped the volatile mixture and winced as vapors seared his nostrils. He set the cup down and settled into his chair. The site of the empty coffin flashed into his mind again—would he ever get it out of his head?—and he wavered. How much did Keen need to know? Maybe Clark could ease into it, feel Keen out on the subject. But restraining his turmoil would be difficult.

"You know my reservations, Professor—organized religion, absolutist claims—those really haven't changed."

"Yes. Truth is neither ancient nor modern, festooned in any particular religious cabinet. It is for all, accessible to any who seek it, and resident in many, many diverse minds and systems. Perhaps you are not as far off as I feared."

"I'll concede that truth transcends any particular belief system, that all religion is rooted in myth, and that all myth is rooted in some truth. Although lately"—Clark paused—"lately I've been reconsidering."

Keen peered at him and then said coolly, "Something's prompted these second thoughts."

Clark traced his fingertips along the cup's ornate, polished handle. "You've said it yourself, Professor. Christianity is not completely wrong. Nor is Hinduism or Judaism. They're small pieces of a bigger puzzle." Clark took the cup and stared at his reflection in the black liquid. "It's just—I'm thinking I may need to examine these pieces more carefully." Then he chugged the remaining liquid.

Keen sat stroking his goatee. "Three years of seminary wasn't enough? Maybe the regents of Mallor should join you in your study. They had no problem dismissing my research for their ironclad assumptions." He brushed his hand through the air. "I want no part of their school or their brand of religion for that matter."

Labeling Keen a heretic had seemed a bit drastic. Yet his morphing theology and animosity toward orthodoxy had forced the bigwigs at Mallor Theological Seminary into a corner. The hearings were swift, with Keen resigning before they could terminate him. He'd relocated on the West Coast, where his florid beliefs blossomed. Now as a professor of religious anthropology at the nearby university, he had become an integral part of a growing interfaith community, one that sought to reconcile divergent strands of mythology and religion and integrate the ancient East with the West. Yet Keen's resignation from Mallor now appeared to be more than a sore spot—the wound had festered.

"Mallor did you wrong, Professor. I'll grant you that. But they have traditions and beliefs to uphold, agree with them or not. Besides, you can't indict all believers on the basis of your treatment at the seminary."

"You are correct," Keen said. "Faith stands or falls on other grounds. However, the Savior's followers will have to appear more saved if I am to follow Him."

"Well, if you're looking for perfect followers—from any religion—you're not going to find them. And you can start with me."

Keen's features became a study in concentration—with Clark his object. The professor's eyes drew into razor-thin slits. He calmly stroked his slender beard. "So, you've become an apologist for the church again, I see."

"No." Clark shook his head. "Hardly. It's just—" He ran his fingers through his hair and with an exasperated sigh said, "I don't know how to say this. Something happened tonight that has...rattled me."

Other than a raised eyebrow, Keen remained unmoved. "Tell me, Ian. What is it that troubles you?"

Clark leveled his gaze with the professor's and said, without flinching, "A member of my church—a lady—apparently raised someone from the dead."

Chapter 8

THE LIGHT ON THE ANSWERING MACHINE PULSED. RUBY strummed her fingernails on the porcelain tile countertop and stared at the phone. If anyone could help her get a grip on the incredible events of that evening, it was Vinyette. Her homespun logic and frank honesty had steadied Ruby plenty of times. It didn't feel right not calling her best friend, but at the moment, nothing felt right. She pursed her lips and unplugged the phone.

With the boys tucked in, she and Jack could finally talk. She peeked into Sean's room on her way down the hall. He had already kicked his race car blankets off and lay spread-eagle on the bed, snoring. She gently pulled his door shut and crept into her bedroom.

Jack sat on the end of the bed in his lounge pants with his shirt off, waiting. When they first married, he was lanky. But after years of construction work, his frame had given way to defined arms and upper body. Ruby still wished she shared his predisposition toward leanness.

"Brian knows something's up," Jack said.

She shut the door and stood with her back to it. "How do you know?"

"He heard some of the messages, and I got a little agitated talking to Vinyette. He knows."

"What'd you tell him?"

"I said we'd talk to him later, that it was nothing big." He looked at her and shrugged. "What else could I say?"

She screwed her lips up and shook her head. Then she walked to the closet and slipped off her loafers. Prints and tearstains clouded the surface of the shoes. She removed the blazer of her pantsuit, draped it over the foot of the bed, and plopped next to Jack with a heavy sigh.

"How'd Vin hear about it?"

"She didn't say." Jack stood and started pacing. "If she did, I don't remember."

"I can't believe word spread that fast. I mean, the whole city probably knows by now."

"Ya think?"

"Yeah. And who knows what they're saying. If the reaction at Goldman's is any indication, it can't be good."

"What do you mean?"

"I don't know. It was a circus. Half of them were"—she looked away with a flush of embarrassment—"worshiping me. The other half ran like I had the plague or something. It was...it was a madhouse."

"I think I know how they feel."

Ruby shot a defensive glance at him.

He stopped pacing. "No. I mean, it's weird, Rube. C'mon. Kid comes to life; we should be happy. But it seems so...so creepy. The dead reborn? It's like something from a horror flick." He resumed his march in front of the bed. "Besides, do you know for sure he was actually..."

"Dead?"

"Right. I mean, what if the doctors check it out and find something...I don't know. Maybe he just passed out. Or was hypnotized—in a coma, ya know? Maybe he forgot something and had to come back for it."

"Jack!" Ruby glared at him. "This isn't a joke."

"Sorry."

She crossed her arms. "Oh, I'm sure everybody'll have some sort of opinion."

"Well, then, what exactly happened? Vinyette said you kinda waved your hand over the body and said some type of command."

"Huh? Who told her that? No! Not even. See, that's what I mean about people twisting everything." Ruby slumped forward, weary at the thought of replaying the event. "If you would've come, I wouldn't have to explain."

Jack stopped and looked down, apparently struck by her

indictment. He approached, sat next to her, and took her hand in his. He'd developed calluses from the lumberyard, and the tough skin and firm grip bolstered Ruby's innate resilience.

"I was sitting on the end," she began. "You know, like I always do. The service ended and people started lining up to view the body, pay their last respects. So I got in line."

"Well, what did you feel like? I mean, did you know something was gonna happen? Did you, like, get goose bumps or have a premonition or something?"

Ruby looked sideways at him. She hadn't told anyone about the vision, and until that moment, she had not connected it with the resurrection. Maybe the vision was an omen—a warning or something. Still, what did a dead tree have to do with a boy climbing out of his coffin? She shook her head. "I didn't feel anything, really. I was sad for Marcella and the girls. I remember thinking about God's timing. You know, why Mondo? Why now? He was a good boy; his family really needed him. It seemed so...so outta whack."

"Kinda like my mom," Jack muttered.

"God can't be explained, but He can be trusted."

"Lemme guess—another famous quote from your father."

"Well, it's true."

"Yeah, maybe the *God can't be explained* part."

"But He *can* be trusted."

"Anyway," Jack huffed, "back to the story. What happened?"

"OK. So I was in line, just kinda praying and thinking. Really, I was tired and wanted to get home. Then it was my turn. I stepped up to the casket and stood there. Then I reached out and touched his arm—"

"Ugh!" Jack let loose an exaggerated shiver. "Touching dead people? That's disgusting!"

"It's just a body, Jack. For heaven's sake. You have one. I have one. You're not gonna touch me when I'm dead? Live with me all these years and just drop me in the ground?"

Jack scrunched his forehead. "Heck, Ruby, that's different."

"See, Daddy used to say that our body is like a Christmas

present—the good stuff's on the inside. When we die, it's God's way of unwrapping us."

Jack heaved a sigh. "Do we really need more quotes from your father? C'mon. So, what happened? Did his body start shaking or something?"

"Don't be so dramatic." Ruby let go of his hand, leaned forward, and squinted, retracing the mental footprints. "I had my hand on him, and I bowed my head. Then I prayed something simple, I don't know, took my hand off…"

"And?" Jack sat gaping.

"And someone screamed. Shrieked. It was horrible. I looked around, and people were freaking out, falling all over, shouting. Someone knocked over a bunch of flowers, and Mr. Goldman was trying to calm everyone down. And Mondo was sitting up in his coffin—just sitting up!—wiping his face and licking his lips. Ugh, he kept licking his lips; they were dry…and blinking, and looking surprised."

She grew quiet and twisted a lock of hair that had sprung free from her clip.

After a moment of silence, Jack shook his head. "That's weird."

"I don't remember much after that," Ruby continued. "The priest didn't know what to do. Marcella ran up and helped Mondo out of the coffin—almost knocked it over. He was all wobbly, could barely walk. She helped him to the front row and made him sit down. People started kissing him and crying. It was real noisy and hectic. Folks were hollering and shouting. Some were arguing and trying to get out, like there was a fire or something. It was crazy."

Ruby stood and started pacing in front of the bed.

"I just stayed there by the coffin, kinda lost. They were looking at me funny, putting two and two together, I guess. Trying to figure out what happened and what to do with me. Then this lady came up and took my hand. My right hand." She stopped and held her hand out. Turning it over and back. "This was the hand I touched him with."

Jack leaned back a little, his eyes wide and his face pasted with curiosity and wonder.

"She kissed it," Ruby gazed at her lipstick-stained hand, "and held it and said some things I didn't understand. Then some other people came up, thanked me, and started crying. Some man—one of Mondo's relatives, I think—wanted to give me some money. Do you believe it? He wanted to pay me."

"You're kidding."

"I told you, it was crazy. He handed me some folded up bills and tried to stuff them in my hand."

"Did you take it?"

"For what? I didn't do anything. And even if I did, I wouldn't want any money for that."

Jack appeared to ponder the implications, and she started pacing again.

"After a couple minutes the police showed up. Then the paramedics. They came busting through the doors like there was a big emergency. The police started asking questions, and eventually one of them took me aside."

"What did you tell him?"

She shrugged. "What could I tell him? I told him what happened. He wrote it all down, looked at me funny. Then he sent one of the paramedics over to check me out. I said I was fine, but they took my pulse and blood pressure anyway and asked me some questions. And that was it. They tried to take Mondo to the hospital, but Marcella refused. She said her son was healed and they were going home. So the paramedics packed up and left.

"Marcella came over—bless her heart—and hugged me and cried. She was so happy, Jack." Ruby smiled and joy swept over her spirit, bringing unexpected refreshment. "She promised to bring Mondo over."

"Over here?"

"Yeah. You afraid of him or something?"

"Afraid? Well…"

Ruby frowned. "There were people standing in the back, just watching, glaring really. Mr. Goldman didn't look happy."

"He's probably worried you'll take business away from him."

"Right. Anyway, that was it. Some people walked away happy, and some went away angry and bent out of shape. No one knew what to think. We left the place in shambles."

She shrugged and turned to him. He sat hunched forward with his elbow on his thigh, massaging the stubble on his jaw, his brow furrowed in thought.

She peered at him. "So, whaddya think? What's next?"

"I dunno. What can we do? We just go on with our lives, I guess."

"Like nothing ever happened? You didn't see it, Jack. The looks on their faces. The shock. The fear. We'll never, ever, be able to *just go on*."

The pulsating answering machine was a harbinger of things to come, haunting Ruby's thoughts. Their lives would never be the same, and she knew it. She walked to the bed, sat next to Jack, and leaned against him.

"What else are you gonna do, Rube? Put your life—our lives—on hold until everything calms down? You have to roll with it...face the consequences. I mean, what's the worse that can happen? So the newspaper wants a picture, someone wants an autograph. Hey. So you nod and smile and play the little game. Then it all blows over, and this time next year no one remembers a thing. Worst-case scenario, they erect a statue of you in the center of town and change the city's name to Rubyville, USA. I can be mayor and—"

"Oh, shush."

She closed her eyes and massaged her temples with her fingertips. *Face the consequences.* It sounded easy enough. But then again, the thought of all those people gawking, inspecting her with their eyes, worshiping her was almost overwhelming. She continued kneading her temples.

"Reverend Clark was there," she said out of sudden recall. "That's right. He must've come afterwards."

"What was *he* doing there?"

"I don't know. He just kinda showed up. And you should stop being so critical."

"Critical? That guy deserves a beat down."

"Jack! He's a minister."

"He's a man. At least, he might've been one once. He's a puppet for those guys. The way they run that church is a sin."

She leaned back and looked at him with her eyebrows raised.

"They don't really help people, don't get involved in the community." Jack spoke as if he was beginning to run down a list. "They drove off old man Lawrence."

"You mean, *Reverend* Lawrence."

"Yeah, Reverend Lawrence. They made him leave just because he started tellin' the truth about you folks. And then those self-righteous morons—"

"Jack!"

"That's what they are, Ruby. And if you're too...if you're too gullible to see it—"

"I'm not gullible!" She glanced at the door and lowered her voice. "I'm just not like you. I can't throw it all away just because *something* went wrong or *something else* doesn't make sense. Maybe a little more gullibility—more *faith*—would do you good."

Jack turned away, sulking.

She hadn't intended to be so bold or come off as being holier-than-thou. She'd played that card before, and it got her nowhere. Something special was happening, and she must handle it with care. Ruby hesitated then reached up and ran her fingers through his hair. "Let's not fight. We need each other right now."

Jack nodded and nudged his shoulder into her.

Someone tapped on the bedroom door. They cast puzzled glances at one another. Jack rose and went to the door. Ruby leaned over far enough to see Sean in his pajamas, rubbing his eyes, wobbling in the hallway.

"Somebody's outside my window," he mumbled.

"Huh? It's the wind," Jack said. "Go on. Go back to bed."

Sean nodded and shuffled back to his room.

Jack closed the door and started back to Ruby.

"Wait," she said. "It isn't windy."

He squinted at her for a moment, then flung the door open and marched into the hall.

Ruby sprung up and followed him to Sean's room. Jack yanked open the blinds and peered outside, his face pressed against the glass. Then he pushed away from the window, brushed past her, and raced into the living room without a word. Ruby kept her distance, watching from the hallway as Jack opened the front door and dashed outside. The screen door careened off the house and slammed shut.

What now? She couldn't handle any more drama, not after what she'd already been through. She inched toward the front door, her heart poised. Maybe it was Mr. Besbeck. Or perhaps a possum had wandered up from the canyon again.

"What is it?" Sean poked his head out of the bedroom door, rubbing his eyes.

"I dunno. Go back to bed, baby."

Through the screen mesh she watched Jack's tall shadow roaming about the yard. Suddenly he charged toward the oleander hedge and disappeared. Muffled voices rose—voices she did not recognize.

She looked to make sure Sean had returned to his bed, which he had. Turning to the screen, she watched as the tall shadow moved back across the lawn. Jack walked within range of the porch light, climbed the steps, and opened the door.

"It's someone for you," he said calmly and nodded toward the bushes. "It's all right. They just want…you."

Ruby stepped back with her mouth open. She looked down at her socks and then cast a puzzled look at Jack.

"It's all right." He opened the screen and walked past her. "I'll stay here."

She didn't move.

"It's all right," he reassured, placing his hand on her back and steering her to the door.

She took a deep breath and stepped outside. The night sky was crystal. Not far from the porch, just outside the reach of the light, a large, misshapen figure huddled. Ruby turned to Jack, and he nodded for her to go on. She walked down the steps and started along the grass. As she approached the dark form, she discerned two figures, one standing.

Ruby stopped as her eyes adjusted to the darkness. The dry grass crunched as one of the figures stepped forward. A frail, elderly man wearing overalls and a baseball cap moved into the light. Beside him, a crumpled figure sat in a wheelchair, head lolling to one side. The man mumbled something and extended his trembling hands toward her.

And she knew exactly what he wanted.

Chapter 9

KEEN'S DARK EYES DID NOT FALTER, NOR DID HIS MOVE-ments betray anxiety. The parrot made a garbled, throaty sound, and Clark glanced there, then steadied himself under the professor's cold, unrelenting gaze. The cat was out of the bag. Clark blew his cover, and now the strange case of Mondo Amaya was center stage.

"And you saw this?" Keen finally asked. "You saw the boy raised to life?"

Clark cleared his throat. "Well, no. I didn't actually see it."

"Blessed are those who have not seen, yet believed."

"I dunno. There's plenty of evidence for this one."

"Such as?"

Clark pushed himself to the edge of the chair and jabbed his finger toward the west. "There's an empty coffin in Stonetree, Professor. How's that for evidence?" Then he flung himself back and sat grinding his jaw.

Keen sat for a moment and studied him. Then he said, "You have something invested in this, yes?"

Clark looked away, flushed with embarrassment, and bit at the inside of his lip. The incident at the mortuary had pushed him to the brink, seared his emotional retina. Did he even know what he believed anymore? Either way, his nerves were officially out of control.

The professor leaned forward, took the thin brown cigarette from the ashtray, and tapped it on the table. He removed a lighter from the metal box, lit the cigarette, and settled back into his chair. The tip blazed and silver threads of smoke unfolded about his etched features. "Just last year, up north if I'm not mistaken, a man came to life after being pronounced dead. Don't remember the details, but he woke up in the morgue—his vital signs had apparently been misdiagnosed. Pity the mortician that found him. But this is not uncommon."

He drew off the cigarette, and his lids fluttered at the crackling ash. "In the 1700s, coffins were made with a pedal at the foot. Attached to this, a bell. Quite fascinating. The bell remained above ground after burial. Why? Seems there was an unusually high amount of premature burials at the time. So if a person was buried before their time, the newly revivified simply stomped on the pedal and rang the bell. In this case an attentive gravedigger would rush to their rescue. If not, they suffocated. Such was the ineptitude of early medicine."

Keen dragged on the cigarette and gestured toward a globe near the bookcase. "Many third world countries purport resurrection events. Often in the backwoods, shamans plying their trade. However, evangelistic crusades, revivals, are the most common. Of course, verifying the accounts is another story. In most cases, the facts are skewed. You see, people are so eager to believe, they will believe anything."

Keen peered at him. "You know these things, Ian. Do not lose your critical skills."

A thin blanket of smoke wafted overhead, and a sharp clove-like scent struck him. Keen was right about the need for investigation. There were other possibilities here, other avenues to explore. No one religion had the corner of the market on miracles. Clark had jumped the gun. He'd spent the last year formulating reasons to leave the church. So why did he jump so quickly to its defense?

"I sense you're still troubled," Keen said. His eyes glistened as he appraised Clark with unnerving poise. "You're conflicted about your sister's passing. It has poisoned your soul, crippled your faculties."

The statement pierced Clark with surgical precision. He slumped forward and said with a weary whisper, "You're right. I'm terribly conflicted."

"It's hard to let go—of our companions, our beliefs." Keen tapped a thick barrel of ash into the beveled glass tray and sunk back into the chair. His gaze became distant. "I've never told you—it may help, I don't know. My mother was a devout believer. It was a small, country church. All the bells and whistles—starched robes, pay-per prayers, and a smug, two-bit preacher who had no qualms about milking little old ladies out of their life savings. She went to every meeting, sang in the choir, worked the food pantry. Didn't miss a single day. She always dreamed I'd follow her lead, become the second coming of John the Baptist or something." He paused, squinting at a passing ribbon of smoke. "She died right before I graduated seminary, a slow, brutal death.

"That was the early eighties. They'd given her three months to live. But she was a fighter. She hung on for nearly six months, waiting for some elusive miracle. I'd sit at her bedside and read from the Bible, but before long she didn't even recognize me. She died one morning while I was away—never got to see young Reverend Benjamin."

"I'm sorry, Professor. I had no idea."

"No. Don't be sorry. That was the beginning of my salvation."

Clark peered skeptically at the professor.

"I was born again, you could say. Enlightened to the broader world. All the childhood fantasies of pie-in-the-sky, heaven and hell crumbled at my mother's grave. I was at a crossroad. The same one you're at."

He took a long drag, exhaled the smoke out his nostrils like an old dragon, and tamped the cigarette out in the ashtray. "It is this primitive notion of a loving, all-powerful God that's causing your conflict. How can such a God strike someone as lovely, as kind as your sister, in such a heartless manner? This is your conundrum."

Keen pointed to a picture propped on the far end of the book-shelves. "Look, there."

Clark scanned the cluttered archives until he spotted the grainy photo. In its center Benjamin Keen stood in khaki shorts and a dingy, white shawl, surrounded by dark-skinned men in loincloths and decked with crude jewelry.

"The Illuaco believe the earth has a soul, just like ours; that all its seasons, cycles, ecosystems are part of an organic chemistry. Similar to ancient druidism. The earth groans under the weight of pollution, grieves over deforestation and urban sprawl—just as my mother agonized over the cancer gnawing away at her insides. Still the earth gives, blesses us with rain, fruit, blossom." His eyes quivered in a type of passing rapture, and he uttered something in a foreign tongue. "The soul returns to elements—earth, air, fire, water. Death is just a cog in the machinery of the universe, Ian, not something to fear as we do in the Western world."

The sequins in his shirt sparkled, and his tone was almost reverent. "Once every year the Illuaco offer a sacrifice to the earth."

Clark dipped his head and peered over the top of his glasses. "You don't mean...?"

"It is an honor to die for the tribe. That one death replenishes the land, atones for the sins of the tribe. Regenerates the people."

"A human sacrifice?"

The professor's stare was cold. "It is an ancient way and one rife with power."

He eased back in his chair, and his tone relaxed. "In some strange way my mother's death was sacrificial. She entered the earth cycle and ascended, became one with all life. She was freed from the infernal orthodoxy that'd bound her. Her death replenished me, summoned me forward, and liberated me from the illusion."

Clark stared at Keen as his mind swung from intrigue to incredulity. This was nonsense—a retread of pagan beliefs and practices. *Tribal sacrifice? Earth cycle?* Keen's eccentricities had become madness; he'd gone off the deep end. But was it any different from Clark's duplicity and deception? He'd long ago conceded that myth foreshadowed truth, however crudely; primitive tales framed a childish scaffold around grander realities. But discarding the baser elements of the pagan mind was necessary, perhaps even an essential part of societal advance. One might esteem the sun a father, but killing his firstborn was still barbaric. No one in his or her right mind would dispute that. Apparently except Benjamin Keen.

The impulse to flee—to run from there as he'd run from the mortuary—tugged at Clark.

Mr. O entered the room and stood motionless near the table.

"Would you care for more tea, Mr. Clark?" Keen asked.

Clark pushed his glasses up the bridge of his nose. "No. No, thank you. It's delicious, I agree. But I think I'll stick to my lattes."

Keen laughed, motioned the servant to remove the setting, and Mr. O swept out of the room.

Clark shifted in his chair. Perhaps he could play the middle. "You're suggesting that Stacie's death actually serves me, that my reservations about organized religion are nothing more than a natural process of—"

"Evolution. Correct! You understand, Ian, I'm not trying to trivialize her suffering but to help you see it as part of a grander scheme. It is the transmigration of the soul, its journey to divine consciousness. Stacie has become part of that cycle and is summoning you forward." He scooted to the edge of the seat, his eyes rapt with concentration. "Your soul is fighting to ascend, Ian. But to do so, you must discard the religion of your youth. Even now it is strangling the life out of you."

The parrot snapped seeds and looked sideways at him. Clark pursed his lips. *Strangling.* Yes, that's what was happening. This morning he had stood at the pulpit, strangling on his doubt and indifference.

"I understand your struggles, Ian. Believe me. But many have taken this journey and overcome great obstacles to do so—good men, from all walks of life. You're not alone."

Clark nodded, but the words blurred past him.

"I've spoken to you before about our fraternity, yes? A community founded upon the tenets of contemporary syncretism. This is not some Skull and Bones affair, I assure you. Please, let me introduce you to them. You will find their stories illuminative."

Clark lowered his eyes and went back to biting his lip. He'd come here to distance himself from the church, but along the way, his plans were interrupted. Not far from here, Armando

Amaya was living and breathing. If it was a mistake or a natural phenomenon, as Keen suggested, Clark had nothing to fear. But if, perchance, it was God's doing, then nothing—not even Professor Benjamin Keen—could stand in the way.

"Yes," Clark finally said, "I'd like to meet this fraternity, Professor. Maybe they *can* help."

Keen slapped the arms of the chair. "Excellent! I'll tell them about your interest. The discussion is quite lively. We're meeting here this Wednesday, on the new moon. We'd love to have you."

Then Keen leaned forward and removed the lid from the metal box. He dug inside it and brought forth a small object wrapped in brown paper, which he extended to Reverend Clark.

"Another gift?" Clark shook his head. "No, please. The book is enough."

"I insist," Keen said, stretching across the table.

Clark took the object reluctantly, peeled away its brittle wrapping, and held it in his palm. It was an ivory dice with tiny, peculiar symbols etched into its sides. He took his opposite hand, plucked the die, and held it aloft, rotating it in his fingertips.

"These are the same symbols as the ones on the pendant, the necklace you gave me when we last met."

"The amulet," Keen whispered. "You have the amulet?"

Clark reached under his shirt collar and revealed the braided necklace and the diamond-shaped pendant. "I wear it all the time. It reminds me of you and the promise I made."

Keen eased back, stroking his goatee, with a glimmer in his eye. "Indeed, Mr. Clark, you *are* the Wandering Soul."

Chapter 10

RUBY REACHED HER FINGERTIPS TOWARD JACK. HE LAY with his back to her, breathing shallow and erratic. She held her hand inches away from his bare skin. If only she could heal him of his bitterness and cynicism, that would indeed be a miracle. Not wanting to disturb him, she withdrew her hand and lay motionless on the bed.

Her head ached from lack of sleep. Adrenaline lingered in her body like a hangover from the outrageous events of yesterday. Dark, brooding shapes had punctuated her restless sleep, and since Ruby was not much of a dreamer, she wondered if the vision had opened some floodgate inside her. Outside, Greyhorn sounded its shrill, familiar cry, marking the break of dawn. The majestic owl was probably seeking one last meal before retiring in the canyon.

Ruby slipped out of bed and Jack snuffled. He was not a light sleeper like her, but she wondered how he could sleep at all under these circumstances. Sean's nightlight cast a faint glow across the hall. She closed the door to her bedroom, walked across the cool hardwood floor, and entered the kitchen.

The light on the stove washed the room in a soft bluish haze. Monday morning and, for the life of her, she could not fathom facing the world. Ruby went to the window and pulled back the top of the tiered curtain. Another foggy morning. The rows of eucalyptus lining the canyon across the street were nothing more than slender opaque panels hedging in the asphalt. She craned to see the spot where Mr. Estwyler had knelt beside his wife's wheel-chair last night.

The old man had called Ruby the *Godsend*.

She shivered, looking into the gloom. Yet as she turned away, she glimpsed a dark object squatting on the front lawn.

Ruby yanked the curtain back and pressed her forehead against the cold pane. Her breath frosted the glass, obscuring the view. She clucked her tongue and swished her fingertips across the condensation, making the window bleed water. Now she couldn't see at all.

She tiptoed into the living room and unlatched the front door. After glancing down the hallway, she unlocked the handle and pulled the door halfway open.

Cool, damp air seeped across the floor and entwined round her ankles, sending a chill rippling up her legs. The daffodils in the planter coated the air with an intoxicating scent. Several houses up, a car idled, probably Leighton Huebry getting ready for his Monday commute. She held the screen open, poked her head outside, and peered into the gray curtain.

A small, shadowy form tilted in the center of the lawn.

Was it Sandy, stalking field mice again? Or maybe a piece of trash blew into the yard sometime overnight. A big piece of trash. She angled herself through the door and stepped onto the porch. Cool concrete pierced her socks, and she squeezed her pajama top together at the neck. She curled her toes over the edge of the porch and leaned forward. It looked like a stick figure or even a small skeleton.

"What're you doing?"

Ruby spun around, clutching her chest. "Jack! You scared me."

"The door was wide open. What was I supposed to do?"

"Shhh."

Jack stuck his head out the door and glanced up and down the street. "What's wrong? What're you doing out here?"

Ruby tapped his shoulder and pointed at the mysterious object.

"What is it?" Jack squinted then brushed by her and raced down the steps. He stalked to the form, chest out and knuckles clenched—his typical protective approach. Then he knelt before the object.

Three houses up, the dome light of Mr. Huebry's car glowed like a tiny lighthouse on a distant shore. If he saw Jack hunched in the front yard, in the fog, at this hour, he'd ask questions. Next door, the Besbecks' lights were still off, thank goodness. They'd begin an interrogation if they stumbled upon this scene.

Ruby yanked her socks off, laid them on the porch, and edged into the wet grass. Jack crouched in front of the figure with his jaw slack. She approached, placed her hand on his shoulder, and he stared up at her.

"What the heck's going on?" He turned back to the strange figurine.

It stood knee high, a conglomeration of parts and pieces assembled into the shape of a nightmarish gnome. Bound with fiber and strips of sackcloth impaled on a stick, the humanoid carcass sagged forward. Dry white cornhusks encircled the waist, forming a crude skirt. A rib cage, apparently from a sizeable animal, formed the torso, and draped over it was a necklace of withered herbs. Perched above the ribs a small orange gourd jammed into the spinal stick, comprising the head, and attached to it, the lower jaw of an animal with razor teeth hung wired into the shell. Atop the tiny skull rested the hollow lid of a canning jar, snipped and twisted into a jagged crown. Two shiny black rocks, embedded in the gourd, stared at them like empty eyes.

Ruby stepped back once, twice, and brought her hand to her mouth. A chill bank of fog swept by as Jack retrieved a note from the base of the doll. He studied the stilted handwriting.

"*Thou shalt have no other gods before me*," he read. "Then there's a letter, or symbol. Is this a joke?"

A car door slammed, and Ruby jumped in response. Mr. Huebry revved the engine, and his brake lights glowed.

Jack bounded to his feet. "I'm callin' the cops."

"Wait!" Ruby stepped forward and seized his arm. "We can't leave this thing here. The neighbors will see it and start asking questions."

Jack leaned forward and glared at her. "Ruby, we need to leave it and call the cops. This is weird. I don't care what the neighbors think. Somebody snuck into our yard and—" He shrugged off her hand, and his eyes narrowed. "Those people last night, would they do this?"

"Mr. Estwyler? No. Why? Why would he do this?"

"How should I know? The old kook lives in a shack. Who knows what goes on up there? Maybe he's a cultist or something."

"Right." Ruby grimaced at the effigy slouched at her feet. Greyhorn shrieked in the distance, and she turned toward the sound, peering into the impenetrable mist.

"What did they want anyway?"

"I already told you. They were hoping I could heal Mrs. Estwyler."

Mr. Huebry backed out of his driveway into the street, and the headlights pressed into the fog. Mist roiled before the beams as the car started forward.

"C'mon," Ruby said, snatching Jack's arm and steering him back to the house. "Leave it." They climbed the porch as the car crept past. She retrieved her socks. "You're right. We should call the cops. What's a little more attention anyway?"

❦

Ruby pressed her palms against the warm ceramic mug as the policeman finished scribbling on his notepad. *Officer Bean*, the nametag read, a pudgy man with soft features and kind eyes. Behind him, the picture on the refrigerator spread like a surreal reminder of the events of yesterday.

The front door opened, and Jack walked back in with the second police officer, the smell of dampness clinging to their clothing.

"Is it gone?" she asked.

"Yes, ma'am," the man said, readjusting his belt as he entered the kitchen with Jack. His nametag read, *Officer Ivan*. A small man with a swagger and firm, confident eyes. "We took some pictures and packed it up. We'll take it to the lab, and Beeko will take a look at it."

"I doubt it's anything to worry about." Bean flashed her a reassuring smile.

"Nice way to finish up our shift, though," Ivan said with his thumbs hooked in the front of his belt.

Brian poked his head around the corner and looked at the officers. "Can I come out yet, Dad?"

"No," Jack said. "You can start getting ready for school, like I said. Excuse us." Then he escorted Brian out of the room.

The officers nodded and returned their attention to Ruby. "So, you're the lady from the mortuary," Ivan said, casting a skeptical glance her way.

Ruby rolled her eyes. "I'm the one."

He peered at her, grinned, and nodded. And kept nodding, like he had some opinion he was dying to voice. "You gotta lot of folks talkin', Mrs. Case. Including the guys at the precinct." He glanced at his partner, apparently seeking confirmation.

Bean closed his tablet and jabbed his thumb toward the front yard. "I wouldn't worry too much about this. We find those things around here once in a while—in the groves, up at the old graveyard. Chief Gramer thinks it's those college kids. They call themselves neo-pagans. Build bonfires and dance around them, burn effigies, dress kinda weird."

"We think they're in on those abductions," Officer Ivan interjected. "Those missing university girls."

"Most likely they're just pranksters." Bean frowned at his partner. "Fooling around with spells and religious mumbo jumbo, trying to find themselves. You know how kids are. I wouldn't worry about it." He stepped from the room and signaled his partner to follow. Ruby got up and walked them to the front door.

"Now you're sure that Mr. Estwyler had nothing to do with this?" Officer Ivan asked again.

"No. I mean, yes. He wouldn't do this. He just wanted me to..."

"To perform a miracle," Ivan said with a smirk.

"Mmm, hmm."

Ruby opened the door and thanked them. She stood on the porch and watched them get in their car, cruise up the narrow canyon road, and disappear in the haze.

The fog had turned the landscape a pasty monochrome. Sandy

crept from the bushes and sniffed the spot where the stick man had been. Ruby hissed and swiped her hand at the cat. It leaped sideways and then sauntered across the yard toward the back of the house. The Besbecks' kitchen light was on, which meant they'd probably seen the cops. It was only a matter of time before they were over asking questions. And if they'd heard about the incident at the mortuary, like everyone else, they would be over even sooner. She backed into the house and shut the door.

Water ran in the front bathroom, and Brian's bedroom light slanted across the hallway. Sean still had another hour to sleep. She returned to the kitchen, sat at the table, and curled her fingers around the warm mug.

Thou shalt have no other gods before me.

What did it mean? And why her? This time yesterday morning the vision of the old tree blazed inside her. But that was only the beginning. Mondo Amaya sat up in his coffin, and if that wasn't enough, now a pagan stick man gets dropped off in their front yard. This puzzle wasn't getting any clearer.

The floorboards creaked, and Jack stepped into the kitchen, buttoning his flannel.

"I don't think I'm going to work," Ruby said, staring at her interlocked fingers.

He shot a stern glance at her. "You can't run from this, Rube." He took the baseball cap from beside his lunch box, put it on, and pointed to the phone. "I plugged it back in. You got a buncha messages there."

She tapped her toe on the linoleum, slid out of the chair, and went to the answering machine. She paused for a moment, pressed the button, and erased everything.

"Sean can stay home with me. I'll call the preschool. I just need some time to be alone."

"Vinyette called. And Marje. And Marcella. People wanna talk to you. Are you just gonna avoid everyone?"

"Not now, Jack. I was up half the night. This stuff is freakin' me out. And now I wake up to some—some voodoo doll in the front yard." She went to his side, put her arm around his waist, and leaned into him. "Stay home with me, babe."

He stroked her hair, and they stood snuggling for a moment. Finally he said, "I can't, Ruby." Jack disentangled himself and stepped away from her. "The police were right. We shouldn't worry about that thing. It was probably just a prank. Somebody heard about that stuff at Goldman's and wants to–to scare us."

"But why?"

He shook his head in a blank gesture.

She shuffled to the table and slunk down into the chair. She sat and clicked her fingernails on the Formica.

"I'm getting ready for work," Jack said, "and I suggest you do the same." He stepped to the table, leaned across it, and made eye contact. His green eyes hadn't lost their luster—or their ability to look right through her. "You'll get through this." His lips curled at the edges, and he winked. "You're a warhorse, Rube." Then he touched his chin and feigned confusion. "Or is it a battle-axe?"

She smiled and swiped at him as he turned and left the room.

Chapter 11

THE ANSWERING MACHINE CLICKED ON AT EIGHT-OH-ONE. Ruby inched up the volume enough to hear Vinyette's voice.

"Hello? Ruby? Are you listening? What's going on? And why aren't you returning my calls? I texted you, left a voicemail. Don't you dare try avoiding me, girl, or I'll—"

Ruby snatched the phone and clicked it on.

"Hello? Ruby, is that you?"

"It's me."

"Ruby, what is... I thought you were acting kinda weird yesterday. My gosh! It's all over town. Marje's called me, like, four times. She's beside herself. We can't—I mean, did you know something was gonna happen?"

"Uh..."

"Well, why didn't you just come out and say it?"

"Look, I'm sorry. I...things have just gone crazy. After last night, and this morning, and—"

"Whoa. Listen. I don't need to know everything. I just wantcha to know I'm here, hon. Whatever happens, whatever you need, I'm here."

Ruby slumped against the countertop, cradling the phone between her ear and shoulder. Why had she been so secretive in the first place? Her independence and stubbornness would be the death of her.

"I appreciate that, Vin. It means a lot."

"Well, *you* mean a lot. Besides, this could be just what we've been prayin' for. You know, maybe the start of something big, a revival, or awakenin'."

"I hope you're right."

"I'm gonna be at the office today. Probably till late. Why don't we get together? We can talk to Reverend Clark. In fact," she cleared her throat, "I've been meaning to, um…"

Ruby eased away from the countertop and squinted. "What is it? What's wrong, Vin?" As the line grew quiet, she pressed her ear to the phone.

After a moment of strained silence Vinyette drawled, "Oh, nothin'. This ain't the time. Why don't you come by when you get off work?"

Now it was Ruby's turn to hedge.

"If you don't," said Vin, "I'm comin' after you. I promise."

"Oh, all right," Ruby conceded. "I just…I'd hate to see this blown out of whack."

"For heaven's sake, Ruby. Someone come up from the dead! It's gonna be a tad hard corrallin' that one."

"I know." She sighed. "All right. I'll be there after four."

"Atta girl."

"And you're OK?"

"Yeah. We'll talk."

She clicked the phone off and stared at it in her open palm. Vinyette's feelings were rarely a mystery. Years of drug rehab and an agonizing divorce had congealed into a brutal honesty. One didn't have to guess where Vinyette stood. Her outspokenness and transparency were refreshing to Ruby, which made their brief conversation even more troubling. Maybe Vinyette had some secrets of her own. Welcome to the club.

Sean shuffled into the kitchen.

"Where's Brian?" he asked, blinking out the sleep, his hair a mop of curls.

"They left already. You're staying home with me today. OK? No preschool."

Sean's eyes widened, and he scampered out of the room. She smiled, picked up the phone, and prepared to dial work. Livery's kilns fired early, and Mr. Svenson normally arrived by seven. But what would she tell him? She couldn't lie or keep pretending nothing had happened. Yet the truth was so incredible, no one would believe her. She held the phone in her hand, pondering her options. Maybe Jack was right—she couldn't run from it; she had to stand up and face the consequences. She'd ask for a couple days off just to get her head on straight. Mr. Svenson would understand. She exhaled and punched in the number.

Blaine answered the phone and put Carl Svenson on the line.

"Ruby, you're just the person I wanted to talk to."

"Oh?"

"I heard about your performance at Goldman's last night. Didn't know you had it in you."

"Uh, neither did I."

"Things are probably gonna get mucky for a while. You may want to take a few days off, just to let it die down."

"Yeah, I was thinking about that."

"The last time this happened it threw everyone for a loop. But I doubt you'd remember that."

Ruby braced herself on the counter and stood rigid. "What do you mean, 'the last time this happened'? Are you—are you telling me someone else…? In Stonetree?"

He chuckled. "Why don't you come on in for a few minutes? I've got something to show you. I think you'll be surprised."

Clark swung his briefcase onto the desktop, clicked the tabs, and the lid popped free. The large book jammed inside was a tapestry of color against the plain black leather. Unusual symbols stitched the cover like an exotic quilt. According to Professor Keen, each symbol represented the name of God in a different language. There were waves, corkscrews, arrows, and octagonal eyes. Clark pawed about in the side pocket in search of Keen's latest gift. He removed the ivory dice and carried both items to the far end of the bookcase.

He hoisted the volume to the second shelf and laid it flat. Small, handcrafted objects, similar to the one in his hand, cluttered the ledge. He nudged the dice between a fluted piece of leather and a lock of coarse black hair. Tiny figurines, boxes, and beads made of wood and bone lined the shelf. Rarely a month went by without correspondence from Professor Keen, be it letter or package. After two years the assemblage of artifacts had grown into a mini museum of oddities.

He returned to his desk, reached into his briefcase, and removed his resignation letter. Did he really want to go through with this? Surely no one at Canyon Springs would object. The professor would be overjoyed: another trophy for his mantel. After last night Clark was more confused than ever. Was the resurrection of the boy a coincidence, a natural phenomenon, or evidence that other powers were afoot? He stood staring at the envelope in his hand.

Suddenly the door to the front office clicked, and someone came in.

He fumbled the letter, yanked open the bottom drawer of the desk, and shoved it behind a brown leather pouch. Then he jammed the drawer shut and quickly pretended to be busy inside his briefcase.

Keys jangled, then a soft thud, and Vinyette poked her head through his doorway and tapped on the jamb.

"Come on in," he said, closing his briefcase and setting it beside the desk. His hands trembled from the sudden interruption.

Vinyette sprang into the room with two strides, her long, brown hair sweeping behind her. She wore bell-bottom jeans and a light, long-sleeve polyester blouse. Her wide hazel eyes gazed at him, face flushed and vibrant. "You've heard about everything, right?"

"Uh, yeah. I have, Vin."

He cleared off his desk, trying to play it cool. Was there a way to ease into this without coming across as a total naysayer? If it was anyone else but Vinyette, he might be able to snow them.

"I don't know all the details yet," he said, hoping to cut her off at the pass, "and until I do, I'd prefer not to speculate. I'm sure people will have all kinds of opinions, and they'll want to talk—"

"The message machine is full." She bounced on her toes.

"Yeah, I saw that. But at this point I haven't talked to Ruby or the family of...um..."

"The boy that God raised?"

"See, I don't know that." He sounded like such a cad. "There's all kinds of possibilities here, Vin. We can't just start jumping to conclusions, you know, calling this a miracle. Especially if it's not. I think the best thing to do—and this is what I need from you today—is to tell folks we're looking into it. That's it. We'd be very, uh, excited if this was an act of God. We just don't know if that's the case."

Vinyette lowered her eyes and stopped bouncing. "I don't understand, Reverend. What else could it've been?"

The question slapped him. *Yeah, what else could it have been?* He marched around the desk and brushed by her on his way to the door. She always smelled like lavender. Lavender and lemons. He stood with his hand on the door. "I don't know. And until I do, I'd prefer downplaying this."

She looked back over her shoulder, eyebrows raised in an incredulous, gaping stare.

Clark stayed at the door, tapping his foot. This looked bad, but what else could he do? He couldn't concede a miracle without some investigation. Besides, there was nothing he hated more than blind faith. Of course, his overreliance on logic and evidence could prove equally fatal.

Vinyette turned and slunk back into the front office. "OK, Reverend. I'll do my best to"—she glanced at him—"*downplay this.*"

"Just give me the messages that're important. Call and tell the others we'll schedule something for later this week."

"OK," she droned.

"I'm going to the police this afternoon."

She pivoted and peered at him.

"Just to ask some questions about what happened. Maybe there's something we haven't heard, something that will help clarify this. And if Ruby calls—"

"I talked to her this morning." Vinyette's eyes regained their radiance. "She'll be by this afternoon. She wants to talk to you."

Fear lanced through him. "Well then, I'm sure we'll have plenty to discuss."

It was shortly after nine o'clock when Ruby pulled her RAV into Livery Ceramics. If it was up to her, she would have broken all contact with the outside world. She'd read enough of her text messages to know that the story had legs—or tentacles—of its own. In response, Ruby powered off her cell phone, buried it in her purse, and envisioned leaving it there till, well, hell froze over. But instead of retreat, here she was being drawn into an ever-thickening plot.

Livery Ceramics had been in the Svenson family for three generations. The original kilns still existed, a tiny appendix to the tall, plain buildings that ran parallel to Rivermeer. It was now part of Stonetree's historical society, one of the city's most popular tourist destinations.

Ruby parked in the back lot with the other employees' cars, unbuckled Sean, and they walked to the office. Mr. Svenson's statements had left her mystified. It wasn't conceivable that a resurrection occurred in town before. No way. Still, she had rushed from the house without a shower, throwing on some jeans and her favorite sweatshirt, eager to hear what her boss had to say.

Sean held her hand and turned his head as metallic taps and bursts of air echoed inside the building. They passed several large crates, and Ruby quickened her pace at the sound of the approaching forklift.

The clean, yellow lift barreled around the corner with its empty forks rattling. Sean jerked at Ruby's hand and stopped to watch, bringing her to a standstill.

Chris Hewitt always looked wild-eyed, and he drove that thing way too fast. If he wasn't one of Svenson's relatives, the kid would probably be demoted by now. When he spotted Ruby, he slowed and nodded her direction. Ruby returned the nod, yanked at Sean, and continued to the office door.

The forklift slowed and puttered across the parking lot. It crept along behind them until Ruby finally turned. The kid's bug eyes followed her from under the bill of his ball cap. He gunned it, and the forklift rattled into the warehouse.

Was there anyone who didn't know? And what in the world were they saying? It's not like she murdered someone or robbed a bank. Maybe dead people don't come back to life without someone paying the price.

Ruby opened the door and walked into the room. A counter separated them from the workspace—three desks, two with flat-screen monitors, one with a telephone and stacked letter trays. Down the hallway light shone in Mr. Svenson's office, and the familiar strains of big band music played in the background.

"Mom," Sean whispered, "where do you sit?"

"Same place." She pointed toward one of the desks. "We're not going there. C'mon."

Water ran in the tiny kitchen adjoining the office, and a woman with limp hair and droopy eyes leaned out holding a coffeepot. "Ruby?"

"Morning, Gerry."

"I heard about Marcella's kid." She looked like someone bracing for a head-on collision. "And you! I just...I can't believe it." She set the coffeepot down and hustled back out, wiping her hands on her plaid skirt. "I gotta hear about this."

"Uh, listen." Ruby looked down at Sean, who seemed fascinated with the woman's dramatic flare. "I'm here to see Mr. Svenson."

"You're not staying?"

"No. I'm taking a few days off." She started down the hall. "I'll fill you in when I come back."

Gerry grumbled something, and Ruby yanked Sean, who stood ogling. She led him down the hallway, peeked into the office, and tapped on the door. Hunched over the filing cabinets sat Mr. Svenson, his bald scalp shining under the fluorescents. A large-bottomed man with a friendly demeanor, he spun about in the chair, holding a yellowed newspaper folded in half.

"Ruby. And the little one."

"It's Sean," her son interjected, studying the colorful ceramics lining the walls.

"That's right. Sean. Now I remember. Come in, sit down." He motioned toward the two black vinyl guest chairs in front of his desk. The music warbled from a cassette player as if the tape was stretched from age or overplay. He swiveled around and lowered the volume.

She helped Sean into the chair and, as she turned to sit, noticed a newspaper open on the desk. She glanced at Mr. Svenson.

"Nope. You didn't make today's paper. Not yet. They probably got word too late, plus it was Sunday night. But believe me, they'll get the scoop." He looked at his wristwatch. "Romaine or Gilquist will be here by noon, trust me."

"Gee, that's encouraging."

"Oh, it's just the start of it, dear heart. You'll be a celebrity before you know it. Just like Aida Elston." He reached across the desk and handed her the newspaper.

She opened the brittle bundle, and dust motes wafted into the air. "The *Bridge River Beacon*," she read and glanced at Mr. Svenson. "This is almost ninety years old."

"That's right. The first newspaper to come out of Stonetree—or Bridge River back then. The building's still standing up in Old Town." He motioned for her to continue reading.

"Loggers rebut Conservationists."

"Further down."

She scanned the dingy page and found a small, washed-out picture of a young girl standing at attention in a long, lacy dress. She read the caption. "Local girl nearly buried alive."

"That's it."

Ruby stared at the page, took a deep breath, and started reading. "Some called it a miracle." She strained to follow the faded print. "Others, a close call. Moments before she was to be buried, seven-year-old Aida Elston climbed out of her coffin, creating near bedlam at Bridge River Mortuary."

Ruby caught herself gawking and glanced at Mr. Svenson, who motioned her to continue.

"Victim of the fever sweeping cities along the coastal loop, the young girl was pronounced dead two days previous. Her sudden recovery was not a surprise to Midas Shay, an attending physician, who examined the girl following the incident. According to Dr. Shay, catatonic states are symptomatic in fever victims. However, he was quick to dismiss attributions of religious nature.

"Others were not. Reverend Giles, officiate of Miss Elston's funeral, proclaimed the event a modern-day miracle. One eyewitness called it 'the sign of the prophet Jonah,' referring to the Jewish prophet who, according to the Bible, was swallowed by a whale and regurgitated.

"As the residents take sides and this bizarre tale unfolds, only two things appear obvious: young Aida Elston is alive, and Bridge River will never be the same."

Sean wriggled off his chair and stood at Ruby's side, gazing at the paper and riffling its ragged edges. Ruby looked at Mr. Svenson, who leaned back in his chair studying her.

"I've never heard about this. What...how did she...?"

Svenson retrieved the newspaper and set it on the desk. "There was a farmer named Aaron," he said, as if anticipating the question rumbling inside her. "He was kind of a loner, a real serious fella. Supposedly he touched the body, and that's when it happened."

He leaned back in his chair and shook his head. "Poor guy. The paper was right, though, about the city never being the same. Once word got out, Aida Elston became a legend—a curiosity, really. People came from all over to see her." His gaze became distant, and he rubbed his palm in circular motions over his shiny head. "The farmer didn't have it that easy."

"What happened?"

"Well, they called him the Godsend."

Ruby gasped. "That's what Mr. Estwyler called me."

Svenson nodded. "It was some belief that had rattled around amongst the early settlers. A gifted one, they said, a miracle worker who would rise up and summon the divine. Townsfolk took sides. Churches squabbled over the incident—if you can imagine that. Folks became mighty upset over the whole affair. Some of them called the farmer an angel. Some called him a devil." He stared off and rocked in the chair. "In a way, I think we're still paying the price."

"How? What do you mean?"

Svenson stopped rocking and looked at Sean, who was fidgeting the other direction. "They found him dead under the old oak. Hanging."

Ruby sat, letting the information distill. Then she leaned forward, her voice almost a whisper. "Suicide?"

Svenson smiled, picked up the paper, and swiveled with it to the filing cabinet. He placed it in the bottom drawer and slid it shut. "No one knows. At least, there's half a dozen different stories. Some reckon he was murdered—a sacrifice for the fever that was killing off the town. Others say he took his own life. It's the Stonetree curse. It's a mystery." He leaned back again, smiling. "A mystery you'll have to uncover on your own."

"Well, what happened to the girl? Aida?"

"She's still alive—in her nineties now—living up in Old Town. Her health is failing, but I'm sure she'd love to talk. Maybe you should pay her a visit."

Chapter 12

RUBY PULLED THE CAR OUT OF LIVERY'S AND TURNED onto Rivermeer. She squinted as the morning sun crested the canyon and ignited the haze. A shopkeeper with a green apron swept his storefront, while another arranged wrought iron chairs and tables. Monday mornings always seemed like a dull hangover compared with the tourist-infested weekends. Several locals sipped coffee in sidewalk cafés, their newspapers spread across tables, and the smell of fresh bagels clung to the dissipating gloom.

Ruby craned her neck, blinking against the bright sky, trying to catch a glimpse of the cursed tree perched on the hill.

The vision and the resurrection were parts of a bigger story—a story that stretched much further into the past. Yet how in the world had she come to play a role in this tale? It definitely wasn't something she earned or coveted. It didn't help that the last incident had caused such a stir and ended so tragically. Ruby sighed, struck by the sense of an inevitable, mounting destiny, one that she could not avoid. The image of Aaron, the anguished healer found dead under the Sailor's Oak, haunted her. Did she really want to begin an investigation, like Mr. Svenson had suggested?

She turned off Rivermeer and circled past Canyon Springs on her way home. The sign tilted out front, a testament to the church's indifference. Between the camphor and avocado trees the white stucco and red Spanish tiles gleamed. The bell tower rose above the green canopy like a watchtower. She could only guess the last time it had sounded—or something occurred worth ringing it for.

The parsonage sat back on the property, entombed in ivy-covered walls. The thought of facing Reverend Clark this afternoon sent a pang of anxiety hurtling through her. He had stumbled into the mortuary last night looking lost and befuddled, as if he'd been thrust into a nightmare. How was he handling all this? Surely he wasn't a terminal pessimist like her. Maybe he stayed up all night, bubbling with exuberance. More likely he tossed and turned, grappling with the implications. Somewhere inside those green walls she suspected her minister was entombed in a world all his own.

The car rumbled over the bridge, and Sean simulated the sound, flapping lips and flinging spittle, as he always did. They turned up the street, and Ruby's heart leaped. A car was parked across the street from her house—a car she did not recognize—and two people stood in the front yard.

She took her foot off the gas and glanced in the rearview mirror, calculating ways to avoid more attention—until she noticed it was Marcella and Mondo.

The gloom that had descended on her after the conversation with Mr. Svenson suddenly dissipated. She pulled into the driveway, flung her door open, and rushed to them.

"Thank you!" Marcella wrapped her in a bear hug and buried her face in Ruby's shoulder. "Thank you. Thank you. God bless you, Ruby Case."

Marcella's body quaked, and her tears tumbled down Ruby's sweatshirt. Ruby wanted to laugh—or dance, if her leg would allow it. Maybe it was worth it after all. Her confusion and stress were a small price to pay for the joy of this simple woman. Her son was dead, and now he lived. And for the first time the wonder of the event swept over Ruby. She stood amazed—even grateful—that she'd been chosen to play a part in the miracle.

After a moment she separated herself from Marcella, wiped her cheeks, and turned to Armando. He stood back, his typical shy self. He wore dress slacks and a sweater vest—obviously, he dressed up for the visit—and a lock of black curls covered one eye. He extended his hand, and Ruby took it.

"How are you feeling?" she asked.

"Um," he grinned. "I feel fine, Mrs. Case." He glanced at his mother then back at Ruby. "I just want to…you know, thank you."

She smiled, pulled him toward her, and hugged him. It was

almost impossible to believe that a person this solid and warm—this alive—had been lying in a coffin yesterday evening, pale and stiff and altogether absent.

"Lemme out!" Sean chirped from the car. "Lemme out!"

They laughed, and Ruby went to the car and unbuckled him from his car seat. As Sean bustled from the vehicle, Ruby noticed a car idling at the top of the hill. It was black and wide and low to the ground. Two figures sat inside and stared down at them.

She walked to Marcella, hoping not to betray her unease, and invited them into the house. She unlocked the door and held the screen open as they entered. As she did, the car coasted down the street. It was a black Hummer, the wide, older models, with several rust stains, a gray Bondo patch on the front fender, and mud splashes up its side. Ruby stepped into the house, turned, and peered through the screen as the car rumbled by. The two figures stared forward. Both wore dark sweat jackets with hoods pulled tight over their heads.

She'd never seen the car before—it wasn't easy to miss—and the two hooded figures added to a sense of foreboding. Were these the people who placed the stick man on the front lawn, or were they just more busybodies wanting to catch a glimpse of the woman with the magic touch? Maybe she should call the cops again and report the strange vehicle. No doubt, Officer Ivan wouldn't mind returning to see the show. But more than likely she'd be drawing needless attention to herself.

Ruby shut the door and turned back to her guests. Sean went to his room to play, still overjoyed to be free of school, and she prepared coffee for her and Marcella. Armando sat without speaking, smoothing out his pant legs and tapping his foot, while the two of them talked.

Ruby discovered she wasn't the only one under the microscope. Marcella said she had been flooded with calls and visits from friends and relatives, as well as a few strangers inquiring about the unusual events and wanting to see the boy. Despite the rabid opinions of many, Marcella insisted this was a miracle and that God had some special plan for Ruby and Mondo.

Nevertheless, Ruby was clueless about any plan.

At one point she considered telling them about Aida Elston, but in the end, she felt it would only distract and complicate matters. Right now her joy for Marcella overshadowed the looming mystery of the Stonetree curse.

As Marcella finished her coffee and prepared to leave, a knock sounded at the door. Ruby flinched. Maybe the two hooded figures had returned in search of the miniature scarecrow. Or perhaps something more sinister was afoot. Either way she was far too edgy.

Ruby rose and went to the front door.

A short, round man with a khaki vest and a camera strapped over his shoulder stood on the front porch.

"Mrs. Case?"

"Yes?"

"I'm Romaine with the *Stonetree Sentinel*. We heard about the incident last night at Goldman's Mortuary and were interested in following up, maybe taking a few pictures."

Ruby glanced over her shoulder at Marcella, who smiled and nodded.

"I'm sorry, I have some guests now. Could you come back later?"

"Well, I'd rather—" The reporter leaned to his left and peered into the house. "Isn't that the Amayas? Perfect! Maybe some pictures with the three of you…and the folks outside."

"The folks outside?" Ruby pushed the screen door open and nudged her head out.

The reporter stepped back, allowing her to see a small group at the curb. A half dozen people gathered there, bearing flowers and gifts. At the sight of her a cry went up, and they surged forward.

Ruby ducked into the house and stood with her back to the door, knowing this was only the beginning.

Chapter 13

THE LIMESTONE BLOCK BUILDING REMINDED CLARK OF A military institution. Well over seventy years old, the Stonetree Police Department headquarters remained untainted by the city's downtown renovation. The original jail cells still occupied the basement, while the courthouse on the second floor had been gutted in favor of office space.

Reverend Clark found a parking spot in the civic complex. Before leaving his Jeep, he glanced at the note Vinyette had given him. Coy Barkham, the chairman of the Board of Elders, called an emergency meeting for this afternoon. No doubt he was stressing over yesterday's incident. While Clark wanted nothing more than to resolve his past and get on with his life, the Board of Elders had a bigger agenda. And neither he nor God seemed to fit into their plans.

The broad, weathered steps rose, and Clark began the climb. Unlike many of his ministerial brethren, he'd stayed in shape. But in Stonetree he didn't have much competition. Compared with Reverend Moss and Father Terry, Clark was Mr. Universe. His weekly jogs and hikes along the coastal trails allowed him to sprint the steps with ease.

Flanking the entry, two ornate stone columns rose and, between them, a tall bank of windows and oxidized bronze doors. The door ground open, metal to metal, and he stepped onto polished marble floor.

"Well, well," said the officer at the front desk. "I bet I know why you're here."

"I'll bet you do too, Gayle."

A dark wood barrier, topped with similar marble, separated the entryway from several desks and filing cabinets. A tanned woman with graying blonde hair rocked in her chair. Clear blue eyes and bright smile offset her aging features.

"Everybody's talking about it, Reverend. Let's see." Officer Gayle Jay swiveled forward and glanced at a swath of sticky notes on her desk. "Mr. Goldman wants an official statement. As does the *Sentinel*. Romaine has already been down here nosing around. We've got"—she counted on her fingers—"seven different calls from residents inquiring about the incident, including Renny. Bradley took the day off. He's shaken up, and Chief Gramer thinks he might need psych time. And to top it off, I just took a call from *Rippington Weekly*."

"The *Rippington Weekly*?" Clark lowered his head and looked over the top of his glasses. "The tabloid?"

"You got it." She leaned back in her chair and started rocking again. "They're sending a journalist...well"—she rolled her eyes—"a *reporter*, tomorrow. Looks like Stonetree's going national."

"You've got to be kidding. How did they find out?"

"Probably someone from the *Sentinel*. Hey, just think what *Rippington* could do with a story like this." She spread her hands across invisible headlines. "'Space Aliens Raise Boy From the Dead.' Or, 'Homemaker Becomes Hometown Healer.'"

Clark shook his head. "Please, Gayle."

Another officer emerged from a side door, handed her some paperwork, and left. She glanced at it and placed it to the side. "Which reminds me—this morning we sent a dispatch to the Cases' house."

Clark leaned across the countertop, squinting at the officer. "Why? What happened now?"

"They found one of those scarecrows in their front yard. Like the ones we found at Shepherd's Ranch and the old graveyard. What'd you call them?"

"Druid dolls?" He fought to conceal his puzzlement.

"Yeah." She furrowed her brow. "They put hexes on people, right?"

"No, not exactly. They're similar to totems, tribal fetishes, like those used by some Native Americans. They usually represent a personal spirit or an animal helper, like a deer or wolf. Or it could serve as some elemental archetype, you know, a mineral or vegetable. I'm just guessing."

Gayle looked on, puzzling over what he'd said but clearly wanting more.

He shifted his weight. "Primitive people identified with the earth, the animals, respected them as part of a sacred order. Sometimes they believed the spirit of an ancestor or an animal guided or protected them—even became part of them. So they'd make an image of the creature or a combination of creatures out of wood or stone, herb or grain, oftentimes part of their own crops. And it would serve as a guardian, a symbol of tribal identity."

She squinted, bringing to life finely stitched wrinkles in her flesh. "So why did somebody put one in the Cases' front yard?"

"I don't know. Sometimes totems were used to mark the territory of a spirit or delineate its tribe. A village would adopt, let's say, a hawk. They'd make a replica of it and place it near their camp or fishing hole or a clearing to mark that spirit's turf. I don't know. Maybe someone believes that this area—this city or valley—is someone's turf."

Gayle stared then shook her head. "Sounds awfully weird." She gathered some papers and stacked them to the side. "I think I'll stick with the chief on this. It's probably those kids up at the university, the ones into that gothic stuff."

"Hmm. This doesn't sound like Goths. But..."

The phone buzzed and she reached for it.

Clark held out his hand to stop her. "Is Dr. Beeko here? I know Mondays are—"

"Yeah, he is. Go on back." She picked up the phone and waved as he opened the door in the counter and slipped behind it.

He walked through the workspace past a series of offices that intersected a wide, sloping corridor. He followed the cool passageway as it descended into the belly of the building. A bleak, poorly lit basement warehouse stretched before him. How in the world could Dr. Amon Beeko work in this dungeon? Block walls leaching lime rose above pockets of shadow. The combination of formaldehyde, cardboard boxes, and mortar coalesced into a dank, musty chill. The least they could do was douse the place with disinfectant once a month and mount some better lights.

He passed between rows of metal shelves, catalogued with items from crime scenes past and present. At the end of one aisle, a door stood open, emitting a long, narrow shaft of light. A sign above designated the lab.

This was Beeko's world.

Clark had crossed paths with the Nigerian doctor under difficult circumstances. A local family requested a minister, and though new to the area, Clark obliged. It was the third of three abductions along the central coast. Their daughter's body was found burned and partly decapitated in an artichoke farm along the inland highway. Beeko, a forensic criminologist employed at the university just north of Stonetree, had the case. The doctor's background in sexual assault and criminal profiling, as well as his offbeat insights, intrigued Clark, much as Keen did. Monday mornings had become a regular stopover on Beeko's south county sweeps, and Clark was anxious to quiz the doctor about the recent bizarre goings-on.

A lamp hung low over a stainless steel lab table in the middle of the room, casting a brilliant oval beam on a potpourri of bones and feathers arranged there. Clark stepped through the doorway, peering at the puzzle.

"Animal parts, mainly." Beeko's slight British accent was unmistakable. He stepped out of the shadows and stuck a pencil behind his ear.

"Dr. Beeko." Clark shook the man's hand. "I was hoping you were in town."

"Seems things are heating up in this little city of yours." He wore a white lab coat and dense, black-rimmed bifocals. The jumbo specs perched precariously on his small nose. "Found another one of your mannequins, they did." He nodded toward the remains on the table. "We've got us some animal bones—maybe fox or possum—feathers, a squash, corn husks, and a necklace of sage.

And two obsidian eyes, just like the rest." He shrugged. "Nothing criminal about it, really."

"Criminal? No. Maybe some type of Wiccan or pagan practice—possibly Native American. Or a combination of all three. Harmless, unless you believe that stuff."

"I suppose. But if someone's killing animals for the parts, there's no telling what they'll do next." He snapped some surgical gloves on each hand and placed the items in a large, ziplock plastic bag. Then he sealed the bag, placed it on a shelf, and stripped off the gloves. "There's been a resurgence up north in what they assume is a satanic cult. Last week I visited an abandoned cabin outside Lucia. Someone had built a crude altar and was apparently using it for ritualistic purposes. No sign of foul play, just wreaths and staves—druidic paraphernalia. They insist on calling it satanic, but it's different, part of this new paganism gaining in popularity. Nevertheless, prevailing wisdom is that these are the culprits behind the abductions. I disagree, but…"

The doctor stepped on the pedal of a tall cylindrical wastebasket, tossed the gloves in, and the lid clanked shut. He removed the pencil from his ear, turned to the desk, and scribbled something on a tag. "Oh, and we also found this on the critter." He handed Clark a note.

Clark took the tattered slip of paper, squinted, and read the uneven handwritten words. "'Thou shalt have no other gods before me.' Huh? It's a quote from the Bible, the first commandment. But what's this symbol?"

"I was hoping you could tell me." Beeko leaned against the desk with his arms crossed. "Appears religious, the note 'n all, and that's your specialty, eh?"

Clark glanced at the doctor and then traced the symbol with his finger. "A letter, or pictograph maybe."

"Could be a signature of sort."

"Or a warning. Can you copy it for me? Maybe I can dig something up on it." He handed the paper back to the doctor, who hunched over his desk and reproduced the image on a nearby notepad.

"By the way," Clark said, "have you had a chance to read the reports on the...the, um..."

"The reviving boy?"

Clark nodded, embarrassed to be bringing the subject up and not wanting to disclose his trepidation.

"Yes, I have."

"Well, what's your assessment?"

"My assessment?" He handed the paper to Clark and studied him. The thick lenses looked like submarine portholes inflating the doctor's misshapen eyes. "My assessment is that the boy is alive."

Clark squirmed. Was there any way to discuss the issue without appearing to be a complete unbeliever?

"Look, Reverend," Beeko continued, "if you want me to validate the miraculous, you're out of luck. And if you're after some clinical explanation to this, I'm sure you'll find some. But until the investigation is complete—reports from the coroner, medical records, and such—you've got an incident which can go either way. Even when all the data's sifted and an official statement's issued, in the end people are going to believe what they want."

Clark squeezed the back of his neck and winced. "I have an emergency board meeting to be at in a couple hours. People are scared, excited. They have questions. Gayle told me the newspaper already has hold of it. Look, Doctor, I need something—something *rational* to tell these folks."

Beeko arched his eyebrows. "Do you want me to make something up for you, Reverend? I'm not daft enough to guess or dead certain either way. Let me tell you how it is; I've seen it too many times: the naturalists, they'll take one side, and the super-naturalists, they'll take the other. Each group will slug it out, convinced that their position is the right one. Statistics and anecdotes will be cited; holy books, historic figures referenced. There will be claims of enlightenment and charges of narrow-mindedness. Along the way converts will be made and lost. It happens every time. But me?" He locked his hands at his chest and steepled his index fingers. "I'll stay in the middle. And I suggest you do the same."

Clark adjusted his glasses, fighting to restrain a growing grimace. Staying in the middle was natural for him. Of course, it cost him his marriage and his first church, but in this case, jumping to conclusions was the greater of two evils.

"You're a religious man," Beeko said. "You believe in the power of faith and all that comes with it. Is there some reason this couldn't be an actual resurrection?"

"You don't really believe that, do you, Doctor?"

Beeko's jaw slackened then his lips bent into a derisive smile. "Do I detect some skepticism? A bit of a doubting Thomas, are we? How unusual, a man of God with misgivings…"

"I didn't say I didn't believe."

"No, just everything but." Beeko looked away from Clark and nodded to himself. "Maybe what they say about Stonetree is true."

"What do you mean?"

The doctor peered at him, as if debating whether to proceed. When he did, his words were measured. "They say this place is a dead zone."

"A dead zone? Stonetree? What's that supposed to mean?"

The doctor walked to the stainless steel table and cocked his head toward the overhead light. His lenses sparkled as he switched it off. Shadows engulfed the room, leaving only a desk lamp to provide illumination. "They say some places have more light than others. I'm not sure if it's true, but it's a novel theory."

"I'm lost, Doctor. Who—what do you mean?"

"Some folks in the Central Valley have it down to a science. Course they're"—he leaned forward and said with a wink—"religious fanatics. Very interested in this evangelism jazz. You know, takin' it to the streets, etcetera, etcetera. Well, it seems they're mapping the continent—spiritually speaking."

"Spiritual mapping? I've heard of it." How did Beeko know this stuff? Clark's fondness for the man's arcane knowledge was coming back to bite him.

"They describe it as a metaphysical climate," Beeko said. "Say every city's got one, every region, every nation. An identity, a narrative that shapes or defines that area. Take the American

South with its history of racism. Its present has been scarred by its past, a stigma they cannot shake. Auschwitz, Treblinka are terrible places, stained with an inescapable memory of evil. Frisco's got a certain feel. So does Beverly Hills and Shanghai. But where does that feel come from? Is it purely cultural, you know, demographic? Or do ideals and beliefs and actions and lifestyles become living things—a spirit, if you will?

"You've been around, eh? East Coast, traveled the States. Lotsa places along the way. Think about it: some cities are diverse, free-wheelin', while others are segregated and penned in. The atmosphere is a manifestation of cumulative events or a series of historic concessions; the residents build a bridge to the discarnate, in a sense. Some cities are characterized by crime or poverty, others by snobbery and elitism. Is it purely sociological, some herd mentality? Or is something, someone, molding them, influencing them? Are they emulating a reigning power? You got some places right receptive of the Good Book; others, as cold as a morgue. Every city's on the spiritual map—and it seems Stonetree's on the dark side of the spectrum."

Clark stood befuddled, unable to wrap his thoughts around the implications.

"You really don't get it, do you?" Beeko pushed his glasses up his nose. "Let me ask you: Canyon Springs Community—you all believe in miracles, right? Your God can part oceans and give sight to the blind; He is unbound by condition or circumstance. Is that so, Reverend Clark?"

"Listen, I—"

"Angels and devils—you believe in them, right?"

Clark swallowed and stared on without offering an answer.

"Blast it! You believe God speaks, don't ya, man?"

Clark remained silent.

Beeko sighed. "Then tell me, Reverend, when was the last time He spoke to you?"

Clark ran his fingers through his hair and gaped. How had this happened? It was hard enough dealing with his guilty conscience. Now a forensic criminologist had him on the spot.

"This is really unfair," Clark managed to say. "I'm struggling with this, just like everyone else."

"Yeah. The strugglin's true. But you've got three churches in this city, and from what I understand, none of them get along. They talk about love and unity and truth and blah-de-blah. Fact is, they spend more time swapping disgruntled members and bad-mouthing each other than doin' anything constructive. And all the while, the poor remain unclothed and the hungry remain unfed."

Clark mumbled, "We have a food pantry."

"Reverend Clark," Beeko chuckled, "you have the largest church in town, and we're here debating whether or not God can perform miracles."

"Listen, I'm not about to start a praise-a-thon because of some freak incident."

"Yes, well...I can't blame ya. Still, it lends credence to the theory." Beeko walked to the desk, leaned against it, and folded his arms. "They say something evil's over Stonetree—something ancient, unnamed. By inference, you all are under its shadow."

Something ancient, unnamed? The doctor was as mad as Keen!

"They can say what they want," Clark grumbled. "Nothing's forcing me to believe what I do. Besides, I thought you were middle-of-the-road. You know, uncommitted."

"Yes. So I am." Beeko sighed and eased up. "You've got something there about not goin' ga-ga over the unproven. Lotta bandwagon believers. But when it comes to religion, it's not always cut and dried.

"When I was a boy, growing up outside Bwari, a traveling evangelist came to town and stirred up a bunch of hoopla. His tent meetings attracted big crowds, and many claimed to be healed. Newspapers and TV crews came asking questions, and all kind of wild stories emerged. 'Course, none of it could be verified.

"Until one night a woman from the outback brought her dead son. Said the boy'd died that morning. She traveled all day to get there, and when she walked to the platform carrying him, he started shaking and coughing. They said he came to life. Of course, nothing could be substantiated. Still, the crowds came, and the stories continued. The lady went back to her village and converted every last one of them. To this day that small village is a Christian village. And it can all be traced back to that one little boy and his mother.

"Did he rise from the dead? Was it a miracle or a medical curiosity? Perhaps they struck a deal with some tribal deity. Who's to say? For me, I'll stay in the middle."

Clark shook his head. He'd given up trying to contain his skepticism. "Part of me wants to believe in miracles. Really. But there's so much abuse. Heck, ninety-nine percent of what people label miracles or healings is probably emotionalism or just wishful thinking."

"Yeah, but there's still that one percent."

Clark looked at the floor. It was clean and cold—like him. He had no more rebuttals. The end of his rope was fast approaching.

"Look, Reverend Clark." Beeko seemed to sense his turmoil. "There's a lot of chicanery in religion. And mystery. Even in my field, with all the advances, some things still go unexplained. Maybe this is a case of hysteria. Or maybe someone made a mistake, and there's a reasonable explanation. However, there's another possibility which you and I must face—as uncomfortable and messy as it might be. Maybe—just maybe—we have a miracle on our hands. A modern-day miracle. If that's the case, no word-swapping or mental gymnastics will change that fact. If something—someone—is invading the dead zone, we'd best stop debating and get out of his way."

Chapter 14

CLARK PACED THE BOARDROOM, GLANCING AT THE CLOCK as it approached four o'clock. The church elders would be here any minute. This wasn't going to be pretty. He debated announcing his resignation to the board, but after the meeting with Beeko, his head was spinning. Could it be possible the entire city was cloaked in some invisible darkness? If so, how had it affected him? And what part did the resurrection play in the whole affair?

Voices rose in the front office, and his internal deliberation came to a screeching halt. Vinyette opened the door and leaned into the boardroom.

"Reverend, they're here."

He motioned, and she stepped aside as two men entered.

The first approached Clark, shook his hand, and rendered a stern nod. "Reverend."

"Mr. Millquint, how are you?"

Stark white hair framed his flinty eyes. "I'm not sure. I'll let you know after the meeting." Did the man ever smile? Clark may have mixed feelings, but at least he could still laugh. Millquint, on the other hand, was incurably constipated. Doyle Thomas walked around the long walnut table and sat, detached and brooding. Yesterday's funeral had thrown him for a loop, and it showed.

More voices and a soft thud sounded in the outer office. Vinyette opened the door again, and Oscar Hayes shuffled in behind a small, wiry man.

"Coy isn't here yet?" piped the small man.

"When is he ever on time?" Millquint grumbled, settling into the chair next to Thomas.

"I didn't get the message till noon, so I had to leave early and rush over." He shook Clark's hand vigorously. "Wonderful message yesterday, Reverend."

"Thank you, Mr. Easton."

"One of my all-time favorite parables. Faith like a mustard seed—indispensable!" He scanned the room with his chest out, slapped his hands together, and wrung them. "Well, it sounds like we've got an old-fashioned revival on our hands, gentlemen. A hand-clappin', hallelujah-ringin' revival."

"A revival?" snorted Coy Barkham, striding into the board-room. "Either that or a serious case of fanaticism." For a man in his fifties, Barkham stayed in remarkable shape. His impeccable posture amplified his six-foot-five frame, and his shaven head made him even more intimidating. If not for his usual business attire, the chairman could be easily mistaken for a biker or professional wrestler.

"I want the minutes on this meeting, Kevin," Barkham said. He picked a seat near the head of the table and plopped into it with a heavy sigh. He loosened his tie, slipped it off, and unbuttoned his collar. "I was out of town yesterday evening. Sue called me in Oakland and told me what happened, so I came straight down." He folded his hands on the table and scanned the participants.

Barkham was a master of diplomacy, and no doubt he was sizing them up. If they were puppets, Barkham was the puppeteer. He knew how to pull strings—and he had strings on each of them. Although Clark's felt more like a noose.

"Oscar, how is Luz?"

Hayes looked at Barkham, glanced side to side, and shook his head. "She doesn't have much longer. All the hospice nurse does is wash her...keep the IV going." He blinked his puffy eyes, as if trying to recoup lost sleep. "She doesn't even acknowledge me anymore." He hung his head and slouched forward. Mr. Millquint reached across and squeezed his shoulder.

"I'm sorry," Barkham said. "And we appreciate you coming. We really do."

Hayes looked up with a sudden flicker in his eyes. "Has anyone spoken to Ruby? She promised she'd be by this week, and I was hoping…"

They looked at one another with collective apprehension. Clark had resumed his pace, but he stopped, cleared his throat with a cough, and said, "Yeah. I mean, I saw her yesterday. After the funeral service."

Barkham glanced at Easton, who sat next to him with a narrow ledger. "Gentlemen, I think we should begin this meeting. Reverend." He motioned toward a chair, and Clark seated himself. "All right. This board is officially convened."

Barkham kept his hands folded atop the table and surveyed the men. "My family has been part of this city, and Canyon Springs, for three generations. We've weathered many difficulties, as you well know, but none quite so fantastic as this." He had a flare for melodrama and was sure to milk this for all its worth. From high school quarterback to successful businessman to protector of the flame—he knew how to run the huddle. "I know for a fact that multiple versions of this story are floating around town; some of them are quite spectacular. Eventually they're gonna make their way back to us, and when that happens, I think we should be prepared."

"My wife's folks attend First Baptist," Mr. Millquint said, leaning forward. "They're already talking about us down there, saying we turned Pentecostal and all, that we're teaching our people to seek signs and wonders. If we don't quell this, we'll become laughingstocks."

"Ha!" Mr. Easton pushed the ledger forward. "What would First Baptist know about a resurrection anyway? They're about as dead as a—"

"Resurrection?" Millquint snorted. "Does anyone at this table know for sure that that boy was raised from the dead?" He glared at them, folded his arms, and sat back in his chair.

"Well," Barkham said, "that's what we're here to find out. From what I understand, Doyle, you were there."

Thomas had sunk into his chair, beard resting on his chest. He pursed his lips and straightened. "Yeah. Erin and me were there."

"Well," Barkham coaxed, "can you tell the board what happened? Maybe we can dispel some of the rumors."

Thomas stared at the table, as if laden with some colossal weight. "I'm still trying to figure it out myself. Erin's practically in shock. I mean, you don't go to a funeral expecting that to happen."

Millquint scowled. "Someone said Mrs. Case put on a show, like some type of TV evangelist or faith healer, all kinds of theatrics."

"No." Thomas glared sideways. "That's ridiculous. Ruby Case? C'mon, Frank. Do you really think that she would put on a show, try to impress people? If that's the word going around, then it needs to be stopped."

"Easy, Doyle," Barkham said. "Then why don't you tell us what did happen."

Thomas sunk back into himself, as if the recollection was painful. "I've been through it a hundred times already." He heaved an exasperated sigh. "All right. But it happened so fast." He stared at the tabletop again and knit his brow. "We were sitting near the back, and so people were kind of blocking our view. It was the end of the service. Erin had bent over to get her purse, and I was standing, watching the line up front. Out of the corner of my eye I caught some commotion." He scratched his beard, and his fingers disappeared in the bushy brown whiskers. "Someone screamed, and I saw the boy sitting up—in his coffin—just sitting up! I almost keeled over. After that it just turned into a madhouse. People were crying, falling all over, trying to get out. And that's what we did: we got out." He looked at them and shrugged. "That's... that's all I know."

"What about Ruby?" asked Millquint with narrowed eyes. "Bea's folks said she touched the kid, and people were bowing down, worshiping her. If that's the case—"

"I don't know. I saw her up front, but after that it was pandemonium."

Kevin Easton tapped his pen on the ledger in slow, methodical beats.

Barkham squinted at Thomas. "Hmph. Well, has there been an official statement? Has anyone spoken to someone in authority?" He glanced at Clark.

"Yeah." Clark cleared his throat again and thrust his hand in the air like a schoolboy. "Yeah, I went to the police and spoke to Dr. Beeko. But I'm afraid he wasn't much help. It'll take them awhile to finish all their investigations. And until then—"

"Until then," Millquint growled, "we've got a confused congregation, a city on edge, and a member being called a miracle worker."

Clark bristled. Millquint had never been on his side. Had any of them? Besides, Clark was on his way out, so he might as well take a few parting shots. "Well, Frank. That's something we just might need to put up with."

Easton tapped his pen.

"Are you suggesting we shouldn't correct false doctrine, Reverend? The devil can perform miracles too. As an elder in this church, I refuse—"

"No one's talking about tolerating false doctrine, Frank."

"Gentleman." Barkham pressed his hands forward. "Reverend, we do need to consider the implications of this. Now, what exactly did Beeko say?"

Clark's irritation was about to bubble over. "He basically said that more info is needed—"

Millquint nodded with a smug, I-told-you-so gleam.

"—but that we shouldn't rule out the possibility of…of a medical miracle."

Millquint huffed. "And this is a doctor?"

"He's a forensics specialist."

"He's a fanatic tied in with those nuts up north."

"Easy, Frank," Barkham said.

"This is borderline heresy!" Millquint jumped to his feet, rocking the table and startling everyone. "The fact that we're sitting here entertaining the thought that–that common people can raise the dead is preposterous! We have God's Word. We don't need hocus-pocus." He fell back into his chair, face flushed, tapping his chest. "I for one refuse to put up with this."

They cast pensive glances at one another. The lines were being drawn; Clark had seen it a million times.

Easton cleared his throat and broke the uncomfortable silence. "I'm interested in hearing more of what the reverend has to say about this. Is it true that you were there, at the funeral? And if so, what's your opinion of all this?"

Clark scratched at the choker under his shirt collar. *Yes, what is your opinion, Reverend?* Did he really know himself? He'd defended himself against the professor's attacks last night. But that was Keen's MO, part of their typical banter. Clark had no intent of becoming an apologist for the church. But here he was again, pushed into a corner.

"Yes. I was on the way out of town, noticed the commotion, and stopped."

"So you were there too?" Millquint whined.

"No. I mean, I walked in after it happened."

"So you didn't actually see anything."

"Frank." Barkham was tiring of Millquint's hostility. Everyone eventually did. "Let the reverend talk."

"Yeah. You're right, Frank. I didn't actually see anything." Clark's sarcasm was intentional. "Just an empty coffin and a boy— who was dead minutes before I got there—alive, surrounded by people who loved him and were thankful that he was breathing again. And I saw folks who were afraid and confused because something weird, unimaginable, barged into their little, hermetically sealed world and disrupted their theology and their boring existence."

Millquint pointed at Reverend Clark and looked around the table. "Next he's gonna tell us that Ruby Case can raise people from the dead."

"No. Not Ruby."

Millquint huffed and leaned back in his chair, shaking his head.

"So," Easton drew out the word, "let me get this straight, Reverend. You believe that this was a miracle."

"Of course he does," Millquint said.

"I didn't say that." Clark settled back, playing the middle like Dr. Beeko had told him. "But I don't think we can rule it out."

Millquint snorted again, Easton resumed tapping his pen, and the men cast furtive glances at each other.

Oscar Hayes, who'd watched the exchange with interest, said to no one in particular, "If somehow Ruby can heal, then maybe she can heal Luz."

Easton froze and looked at Barkham. Millquint maintained his scowl, but Clark's caustic tone softened.

"Oscar, none of us can fathom what you must be going through." Clark's words were measured. "Even if Ruby was gifted with some kind of power, there's no guarantee she can do this again."

Oscar lowered his eyes, apparently grappling with the obvious.

"Reverend's right, Oscar," Barkham said. "We should be cautious about getting our hopes up. We've no idea exactly what happened yesterday and would be misguided to expect this could be duplicated."

Millquint squirmed in his seat, probably wanting to say something sharper, but refrained. Movement sounded outside, voices, and then came a tap on the door. Vinyette poked her head through, beaming.

"Reverend, Ruby's here." She stepped in and opened the door far enough to show Ruby Case, with her hands folded, standing politely in the front office.

The men straightened their posture and pasted smiles on their faces. Reverend Clark rose, as did Oscar Hayes, nearly toppling the chair behind him.

"Vinyette," Clark whispered as he approached the secretary, "we're right in the middle of a meeting."

"I know," she matched his tone. "I just thought you might be interested—"

"Ruby," Millquint called, "come in, please."

Clark scowled at Vinyette.

As Ruby walked in, Clark made eye contact with her. She

looked pretty with her hair down, though she rarely wore it that way. There was a sweet simplicity about this woman, and Clark could see why she was chosen. Her limp seemed worse, maybe aggravated by the stress of the last few days. A slight smile passed between them—one of pain, confusion, understanding. They were two souls in opposite orbits, hurtling toward different galaxies. Yet they'd been yoked by a wondrous event. In her eyes Ian Clark saw himself. Or maybe he saw what he could be.

And for that he feared for her.

"We've been talking about you," Millquint said in his cold, calculating way.

Oscar Hayes smiled and did an awkward near curtsy.

"Oh," Ruby said, looking away from Hayes's rabid eyes to Millquint. "I imagine a lot of people are talking about me now."

The men chuckled politely.

"Yes," Millquint said. "We're sure there are. And not all of the talk is good."

"Well, I can't control that."

"What Frank is trying to say," Barkham interjected, glancing at Millquint, "is that there's a lot of wild stories going around about what happened yesterday. We're worried that some of them may put you, and us, in a bad light."

"Well…"

"And we kind of want to head this off at the pass. Of course, we'd be elated if God was behind this."

"Really?" Ruby creased her brow.

"That's if God was behind it," Millquint interjected. "And I have my doubts about that."

Ruby leveled her gaze on him. She wasn't known for her outspokenness, but Clark sensed that was about to change. Millquint deserved everything he got, and Clark hoped Ruby would give it to him. She didn't flinch but stood silent, glaring.

Vinyette stepped forward, breaking the tension. "Reverend, Ruby just wanted to speak to you and was hoping you could find time in your schedule for her."

Clark wandered back to his chair and stood over it, grasping the back. "Uh-huh. Yeah. As soon as we're done here, we'll schedule something."

Vinyette took Ruby's shoulder and drew her back. "Sorry for the interruption," Vinyette said, and the two turned to leave.

"I'm sorry." Hayes stepped toward them, bumbling and oafish. "Ruby, you promised you'd come by and see Luz this week." His hands trembled as he wiped spittle from the corner of his mouth.

Ruby cocked her head, as if sending up a spiritual antenna. She pulled away from Vinyette and approached Hayes. He withered before her, and his eyes pooled with tears.

"I haven't forgotten," she said, taking hold of his pudgy hands. "I will, Oscar. I've been thinking a lot about the two of you." She squeezed his hands and smiled. Then Vinyette drew Ruby back, and they left the room.

Oscar stood stunned, fumbled for his chair, and fell into it. At least one of the elders still had a heart. The door shut, and Easton began tapping his pen again.

"Gentleman," Barkham said, turning back to them, his thick forearms crossed on the table. "I'm afraid we're not going to endear ourselves to some people. But I fear we're on the verge of seeing things unravel."

"Agreed," Millquint growled.

Barkham ignored the comment, his features engraved with a businesslike sterility. "We've been elected to serve and protect the members of Canyon Springs Community. While we rejoice with the Amaya family and appreciate that God has, at least, allowed this to happen, I am not convinced that this is His doing. Consequently we would be remiss to attach such labels until we have further evidence."

Millquint and Easton nodded, while Thomas and Hayes sat unmoving.

"I am fearful for Mrs. Case," the chairman continued. "If it's even assumed she has some type of healing power or can duplicate this feat, she will be inundated by misguided miracle-seekers. I'm afraid there could be an outbreak of emotionalism, even fanaticism. People will turn away from the church to her...and we cannot allow that to happen."

Barkham contorted his features, his Neanderthal forehead over-shadowing his stony eyes. His tone was callous. "My suggestion is that, for her sake and ours, we neutralize this. Downplay it."

"For heaven's sake, Coy," Thomas retorted. "Some kid climbed out of his coffin, and we're supposed to downplay it?"

Oscar Hayes nodded and looked at Barkham.

"I didn't say lie, Doyle. We can be appreciative without throwing our hat in the ring. Perhaps someone is behind this. I don't know. I have my doubts, like some of you, but until all the facts are in, we can't start jumping to conclusions. I'm afraid we'll have to remain noncommittal...and hope some type of revival doesn't break out in the meantime."

He settled back in the chair. "And we must dissuade people from attaching some special power to Mrs. Case."

The men sat, brooding and introspective, pondering Barkham's statements. Did they understand the implications? Maybe all too much. Barkham was pulling strings again, challenging them to cross him. Which was unlikely.

Easton raised his hand. "I agree with the chairman. I can't get behind this until I know more."

Clark rolled his eyes. Gee, what a surprise. Easton was the ultimate toady. Clark couldn't remember the last time the twerp disagreed with the chairman of the board.

Barkham grunted and surveyed the others.

"Of course." Millquint raised his hand, and an icy smile cracked his lips.

Thomas and Hayes agitated, glancing at each other, in some type of behind-the-scenes standoff.

Finally Doyle Thomas shook his head. "It just doesn't fit, Oscar. I'm sorry." He turned his head away and raised his hand.

Oscar Hayes sat looking lost. It wasn't enough his wife lay dying of cancer; now they wanted to snatch away his last remaining hope. "I guess I wouldn't want people to get the wrong idea." He raised his hand with a timid shrug.

As if on cue, they all looked at Clark.

He leaned upon the chair and straightened as the elders stared at him. *Follow your dreams.* What dreams? Any dreams he had were buried with Stacie. What did God care if he marched lockstep with the other blind men? Straight into the ditch. What did God care if he raised his hand and turned his back on the obvious? He'd been doing that the last five years.

They watched him—the insecure, empty eyes dissecting every twitch and bead of perspiration. Dissenting from the board would be quite satisfying. Nevertheless, conceding a miracle was not something he relished. So, without a word, Ian Clark raised his hand.

The dead zone, huh? Maybe this was ground zero.

Chapter 15

THE GRAINY, YELLOWED NEWSPRINT OF YOUNG AIDA Elston was engraved in Ruby's mind. She lay on her back, as she had most of the night, fidgeting and twirling a lock of hair as she mulled yesterday's events. Somewhere, not far from here, the old woman lived, summoned from the grave long ago. And overlooking the city, the haunted tree, its branches raised in solemn disregard, marked the spot of the wounded healer.

Just days ago, the Stonetree curse was a fable, superstitious mumbo jumbo, remnants of bored, simple, small-town antiquity. Now, Tuesday morning, she was part of the legend. Could it be that the resurrections were bookends of a much bigger story? If so, how'd Ruby come to be a player in the tragic tale?

She caressed Jack's bare shoulder, and he muttered something but did not wake. The news about the prying reporter had angered him, and he demanded she stop entertaining strangers—even if it was to help them. Had she told him about the black Hummer or the hooded figures—especially the elder board's rudeness—he would have flipped out. Keeping things to herself was becoming a way of life.

The sun had not yet risen. The reflection of Sean's nightlight in the hallway cast a pale sheen through her doorway. Careful not to wake Jack, Ruby slipped the covers back and swung her feet out.

Something warm and solid lay huddled on the floor.

She gasped and yanked her feet back, rocking the bed.

Jack murmured and tugged the blankets over his bare shoulder. She craned her neck to peer at the dark shape at her feet. It was Sean in a fetal position. She exhaled and slumped forward. He called this his *'fraid spot*. It looked like she wasn't the only one getting weirded out. Maybe the little guy was more perceptive than she gave him credit for. She bent, scooped him into her arms, and laid him in the warm crater she'd vacated next to his father.

As she tiptoed into the hallway, the fragrance of roses struck her. The aroma hung thick, invoking memories of the funeral, and she shivered. She passed into the living room, and the pungent sweetness hovered like a pall. Three bouquets lined the mantle, wilting.

She couldn't recall exactly how many people had come yesterday—twelve, maybe fifteen. They were simple folk who just wanted to see the miracle worker. But when Jack arrived, he shooed them off. Ruby felt she had nothing to offer them, but Jack thought they were plain kooks.

Still she wondered how they heard about Mondo—or better yet, how they found her house. How many more were on the way? After the *Sentinel* broke the story today, there'd be no telling.

She peeked through the kitchen curtains into the front lawn. The spot where the stick man had been yesterday morning was vacant. She pursed her lips and turned away. But as the curtains fell into place, she glimpsed a soft flicker of light outside.

Bolting from the window, she stood with her hand over her chest. Maybe the farmer's ghost had tracked her down, or the hooded men were waiting at her door with another surprise.

She carefully peeled back the curtain and angled for a closer look. A mellow, orange glow pulsated outside, near the front of the house. The light seemed to come from the porch, but she could not identify its source.

Stepping away from the window, she returned to the living room and looked down the hallway. With everything going on, opening the front door was not an option. Maybe she should wake Jack. Or wait. He would be up soon. He could handle this.

She paced in front of the door, glancing from the window to the handle, and back down the hall. Her heart continued its torrid tempo. After a few minutes she stopped and flattened her ear against the front door. As her cheek pressed the cold wood, she hissed and recoiled. Then more gingerly, she put her head against the surface and strained to listen.

No sound. No voices. Nothing.

Maybe the stress was catching up to her. Her mind was playing tricks. She unlatched the door and curled her fingers around the cold handle. Clamping her eyes shut, she pressed her ear against the chill surface again.

The floorboards creaked behind her, and a tall, dark figure skated from the hallway. She sprang from the door, bumped into the end table, and fumbled to catch her balance.

"What is it?" Jack pounced on the door and glared at her. "What're you doing? Is it out there again?"

"No. I mean, yeah—something is."

The bed had turned his wavy hair bouffant. He scowled. "I'm getting tired of this, Rube. You're up for ten minutes, and you're ready to go traipsing outside. What's wrong with you? If somebody's been fooling around out there, I'm callin' the cops again. I mean it."

She shrugged, embarrassed by her own impetuousness.

He unlocked the handle and yanked the door open.

A warm yellow light pulsed from outside, illuminating him as he stood motionless, staring through the screen. Ruby went to his side, slid her arm in his, and together they peered at the shrine on their porch.

Jack shook his head. "Please, tell me this isn't happening."

Ruby nudged the screen open, poked her head out, and surveyed the street. The sky was crystal, without fog for the first time in weeks. The eastern horizon had become a pale blue, outlining the edges of the rolling hills. The fragrance of jasmine and oleander intermingled. Greyhorn screeched in the distance as Ruby stepped onto the porch. Her pajamas were bathed in the undulating light.

Five tall vigil candles clustered in the corner near the far post, fluttering in a gentle breeze. Huddled about them, gifts and trinkets lay like offerings at an altar. Ruby knelt to examine the strange collection.

"Don't touch anything," Jack growled. He had his hand on his hip, elbow cocked out.

"It's all right."

He curled his lips and stood in the doorway, a picture of disgust.

A rosary draped over a picture of two children. She set aside a bouquet of wildflowers, took the picture, and angled it toward the porch light. Scrawled across it were the words, *Pray for my grandbabies, Casey and Sundance.* Ruby smiled, set the picture down, and fingered through the assorted items.

Jack heaved an exaggerated sigh. "C'mon. That stuff is dirty. Who knows what kinds of diseases those people have. I'm gettin' a trash bag, and we're dumping this crap."

"No. Just leave it. It's not hurting anything."

"You won't say that when those candles burn down the house."

"It's all right. These people are hurting…they need something."

"Well, you can't give it to them."

Ruby glanced at him.

Then she continued scanning the collection. There was a wood crucifix, two stuffed animals, and a plaque engraved with praying hands. She picked up a jewelry box, opened it, and a tune emerged, mingling with the crickets and birdsong. A necklace coiled inside and sparkled in the candlelight. She lifted a card and a tiny photo fell out. On it was a picture of a boy and scribbled overtop, *In Memory of Lucas, Beloved Son. Pray for him.*

"C'mon. Get in here." Jack held the screen open. "If you're leaving that junk out there, at least don't let anyone see you rummaging through it like a bum."

She rose, stepped inside, and stood next to him. For a moment they stared at the unusual stockpile of gifts. Their porch had become an altar, and Ruby's mind flitted between fear and wonder. Last week she was plain Jane, normal, run-of-the-mill Ruby. Now everyone wanted a piece of her.

"I wish I could help them."

"I know you do." He took her hand. "But you're not God—and you can't pretend to be."

Ruby finished making Jack's lunch as Brian walked into the kitchen, slung his backpack over a chair, and prepared a bowl of cereal.

"Sean's not in his bed," he grumbled, sliding the bowl along the tabletop as he took a seat.

"He's in mine."

He rolled his eyes. "What a baby."

Even as an eight-year-old, Brian still demanded a level playing field.

Ruby wiped her hands on a dishtowel, walked to the table, and bent over. "You know, Bri, we haven't told you everything that's going on. Something—something pretty weird happened the other day, and it's got a lot of people shaken up, including me and Dad."

He looked away and slowed his chomping to a chew.

"We've been waiting to talk to you until—"

"The kids at school said you're a witch."

She stopped, straightened up, and stared at him. Then she swallowed hard and clenched her jaw. "What? Who would say that? How do they know—?"

"They said only freaks can do stuff like that." Brian kept eating, staring into his bowl.

Ruby stood dazed; anger and confusion coursed through her, vying for supremacy. To some she'd become a saint, a spectacle, and to others, she was a witch. The middle ground was shrinking.

She turned away, unable to look her son in the eye. What had she done to hurt anyone? All she wanted to do was remain faithful, finish the race set before her.

"It's all right, Mom," Brian said, crunching cereal. "I don't play with those kids anyway. But they're right."

Ruby cast a puzzled look over her shoulder.

"You are weird," he said, flashing a smile.

Tears welled in her eyes, and she walked to his side and hugged him. He had his father's sense of humor. They could bring a smile into the darkest situation. What a perfect match: somber, serious Saint Ruby and the twin jokers.

Jack came thumping up the hall in his work boots and turned into the kitchen, buttoning his flannel shirt. Ruby stood, wiping her eyes. He glanced at her, then did a double take.

"Are you all right?"

Ruby nodded and went to retrieve Jack's lunch box, making sure to angle away from him while she blinked back moisture.

"You haven't been sleeping, have you?"

She set his lunch box on the counter by the stove. "I made you a couple of sandwiches." Then she walked back to the sink. "And no, I haven't been sleeping."

"I can tell."

She pretended to busy herself with a washrag and asked, with her back to him, "Did the guys at work say anything yesterday?" She turned to face him. "About me?"

Brian watched the exchange with interest.

Jack's eyes narrowed, and he studied her. "What does it matter?" He glanced sideways at Brian. "You don't expect something like this can happen without people saying stuff, do you? If they want to base their opinions on hearsay, that's their problem. Just don't let me catch them talking trash."

Brian scooted off the chair and started to leave.

"The bowl," Jack ordered, without looking at him. Brian slunk back to the counter, took the bowl to the sink, and cantered out of the kitchen. Jack returned his attention to Ruby. "You're letting this stuff get to you. I mean, what happened to Miss Stand-On-My-Own-Two-Feet? C'mon, Rube, buck up."

She pursed her lips and turned away from him. The chinks in her armor were starting to show. She stood with her back to him, arms crossed, staring at the apricot tile.

He shuffled up from behind and took her shoulders in his hands. "Look, I'm sorry. This has gotta be tough. But you can't control what people say, and you can't feel obligated to help everybody."

"There's more going on than you know, Jack." Her words were cold, shorn of emotion.

He stood without speaking and then stepped away from her. "Like what? What do you mean?"

"It all happened before. All this." She stared off and spoke without passion, as though revisiting some unavoidable, predetermined script. "A resurrection, controversy, people taking sides. Almost a hundred years ago. It happened before. Someone even died because of it."

She turned to see Jack with his brow creased. He started to say something, refrained, and started again. "What're you talking about?"

"There's a woman living up in Old Town." Ruby maintained her grim composure. "I need to see her, Jack. Can you take me? Tonight? Please."

Brian stepped into the kitchen, retrieved his backpack from the chair, and hoisted it over his shoulder. "I'm ready, Dad."

Jack nodded without looking at him. "Go on, I'll be out. And watch out for that stuff on the porch." Then he peered at Ruby as if trying to decipher details etched in her eyes. No doubt the information was bubbling in his brain. *Another resurrection?* He shook himself from the speculative gaze and said slowly, "All right. On one condition. No, two conditions."

She folded her arms and looked away in childish stubbornness.

"One, do not leave this house till we come home—for anything. And two, that junk is off the porch by tonight."

"It's not junk."

"All right then. Those gifts, donations—whatever they are, we're getting them outta here."

She kept her hands folded and managed to nod. Next to being treated like a cripple, she hated being told what to do.

"OK. There it is." He took his lunch box from the counter and, to her chagrin, kissed her on the cheek as he passed.

Chapter 16

THE LARGE VOLUME LAY FLAT ON THE BOOKSHELF, JUST where Clark had left it. He lifted the hefty book with a slight grunt and walked across his office. Maybe Keen's expertise would be good for something. He hoisted it onto the desktop, and the book thudded open. Vinyette's note skittered across the cluttered workspace, and he snatched the paper before it fell to the floor.

Clark glanced at the secretary's list, and anxiety surged inside him again. Tuesday morning, and he already had a full slate...and none of it was good. Despite the board's desire to deflect attention and downplay the incident at Goldman's, they could not quell the flood of attention. The *Sentinel* requested an interview with Clark. Reverend Moss and Father Terry issued lukewarm praise, while outlining numerous theological reservations. And the number of church members demanding information and needing to talk continued to grow. He stared at the handwritten outline of scheduled appointments, fending off waves of panic. What in the world could he say to these people? He'd been sucker punched, and his only retort was complete bewilderment.

Luckily he was able to put off meeting with Ruby until tomorrow. Yet the anticipation of that encounter gnawed at him.

He set the list aside and from his briefcase retrieved the image Beeko had copied for him. Spreading the paper out on top of the desk, he studied the crude pictograph. It was a long shot, but if anyone's work could reveal the meaning of the mystical symbol, it would be Keen's. His knowledge of religious myth was encyclopedic—a summary of the man's life as much as the subject it covered. Clark studied the bizarre symbol: two vertical lines stood parallel, like an equal sign on end, and adorning the symbol at its top and bottom were wavy lines, each one possessing a fluted head. How could he even begin to make sense of this?

He removed his glasses and rubbed his eyes. The image was there, imprinted in his mind. For all its peculiarity, it looked like the Roman numeral 2. Or the English letter *I*—a capital *I*. What did he have to lose? Clark put his glasses back on, turned to the index, and began tracing subjects under the "I" category. *I Ching. Ichthyomancy. Iduna. Illuminati.* He thumbed through pages of maps and symbol sketches, pictures of gods, primitive tribes, and colorful flora. The weighty book seemed to exude a magical aura, like an ancient treasure chest, unearthed, yielding its contents to awestruck eyes. Keen's understanding of science, esoterica, and the occult arts was amazing, if not downright unnerving. How far the man had wandered from his conservative religious upbringing.

Clark scanned the pages, yet nothing matched the pictograph. It would be impossible to identify the symbol. Most likely it was just the scribbling of some loners harassing the townsfolk with their juvenile pranks. *Immaculate Conception. Incas. Inti. Ishtar. Isis.* Until *Itzcoliuhqui.* He stopped.

He was unfamiliar with the word and followed the index until the book lay open on a picture entitled "The Wall of Skulls." Row upon row of human skulls filled the page; stacked like brick they rose into an immense ivory embankment. Then Clark's breath caught in his throat, for notched into the clay embankment next to the dreadful monument was the fluted wavy line, similar to the ones on the pictograph.

He stared, almost incredulous, from book to paper. It was the same! No doubt about it. Opposite the image, the section "The Gods of Ancient Mesoamerica" began. Clark pulled the chain on the brass banker's lamp, the light came on, and he hunched over the volume, studying the text and the strange photograph.

Gods? Ancient Mesoamerica? What could any of this have to do with Stonetree? Or with the stick figure placed in Ruby Case's front yard? A faint chill skulked up his spine, threatening to yank his mind into irrational panic. *Get hold of yourself, Clark!* He inhaled deeply and then continued forward until he found the word he was looking for. Embedded in the text was the symbol, nearly identical to the one found on the note, and its definition.

> Itzcoliuhqui—Part of the pantheon of Mesoamerican gods and, along with Hun Came and Vucub Came, one of the principle death gods of Xibalba, the Mayan underworld. Also called, the "Twisted Obsidian One," or "Master of the Curved Obsidian Knife." A god of earth and stone, Itzcoliuhqui ruled over darkness, terrible cold, fog, fire, and natural disaster. According to legend, Itzcoliuhqui was blinded and cast down to the earth, where he now lives to spread darkness, wreak destruction, and misery. Also called Itzlacoliuhque, he is alternately identified with, or an aspect of, Quetzalcoatl or Tezcatlipoca, the supreme Aztecan gods.

Clark stared from text to picture. The original note in Beeko's lab quoted the first commandment: *Thou shalt have no other gods before me.* But what did ancient death gods have to do with Stonetree? Or the first commandment?

Without a doubt the city attracted a diverse religious crowd. Crystal shops, aromatherapists, and avant-garde apothecaries sprinkled the downtown arts colony. People came great distances to purchase dragon's blood resin or rare white sage from some dude in sandals, frock, or tie-dyed regalia. But every city had its religious fringe. Even Windayven, with its well-to-do, white-collar establishments, had its share of hole-in-the-wall psychics. Clark had prepared himself for the "fruits and nuts" of the West Coast, so Stonetree's occult underbelly was not a great surprise. Nevertheless, Mesoamerican death gods were a far cry from herbalists and astrologers.

He turned and looked at the chunk of obsidian on his file cabinet. Its barbed glassy surface splashed tiny refractions of light across the ceiling. About the size of a softball, he'd found it during one of his hikes along the granite cliffs that framed the Stonetree Valley. The rock was plentiful in the craggy volcanic landscape. *Twisted Obsidian One, or Master of the Curved Obsidian Knife.*

He bit his lip. Was it pure coincidence, or did the shiny mineral link the city to some mythological Aztecan deity?

"Pfh!" He rolled his eyes at the preposterous thought. Keen was getting to his head. Clark closed the book and carried it back to the shelf. Whoever *Itzcoliuhqui* was, the resurrection of Mondo Amaya had apparently disturbed him. If that was the case, then the two of them had something in common.

In anticipation of the warmer weather, Ruby unearthed her white capri pants from their winter hiding. Between the banana slipons and yellow print blouse, she was hoping to counter the gloom that had crept into her spirit after her conversation with Jack. She finished washing dishes, wiped down the counter, and prepared to sit at the table with a cup of green tea when the first person arrived.

"Hello," a faint voice called from outside. "Hello."

She pulled back the curtain just enough to see two figures at the end of the driveway. A small, hunch-backed woman waved and tugged at the elbow of the person next to her. Ruby let the curtains close and heaved an exasperated sigh. Barely eight o'clock and the pilgrimage had begun. "What do you want from me?" she whispered.

Sean shuffled into the kitchen, rubbing his eyes and yawning. "Who you talking to?"

"Hello. Hello," the voice prattled outside, now with increased urgency.

"Myself. Listen, why don't you go in your room and play for a little bit?"

"But I'm hungry."

"I'll make you something in a minute. Just, for now..." She nudged him in the direction of his bedroom, and he straggled there with a scowl.

She went to the front door and stood deliberating. If she opened it, she'd be breaking her promise—and that wasn't like her. It also wasn't like her to turn someone away. If she'd been suddenly blessed with some special ability, shouldn't she use it? Ruby twirled a lock of hair and stared at the door handle. How is it that something as wonderful as a resurrection could make everything so complicated?

"Hello," the voice called. "Can you hear?"

Jack would understand. He had to. Ruby exhaled sharply and opened the front door.

After weeks of foggy mornings, a crisp, blue sky greeted her. She stepped onto the porch, careful not to trample the gifts assembled there. The dry air stung at her nostrils. Summer was on its way. The sun had crested the canyon, sending ribbons of light through the eucalyptus. A beam rested on her, illuminating the porch, and she stood in its glow.

Upon seeing her, the hunch-backed woman grew wide-eyed and agitated. "Can you help us? Please."

Ruby descended the porch, and the woman fumbled at her companion. An adolescent girl, tall and slender, with dark, stringy hair dangling before her pale face, lurched forward. She moved with terrible jerking motions, heaving her right side forward, swinging a limp, twisted arm. Her lips contorted with each step, as though the motions required great effort. Behind the dirty hair one eye was visible—just a small, milky slit.

Ruby stopped in her tracks and brought her fingers to her lips. This was more than she bargained for.

"Ms. Kess? Ms. Kess." The little hunchback hobbled alongside. "Yes, hello. It's Celia. She's almost blind now." She spread the girl's hair aside to reveal pink, watery eyes quivering in the intrusive sunlight.

Ruby turned away, struck by the severity of the girl's condition, and noticed Sean perched at the kitchen window with his head resting in his hands, watching them intently.

"I believe in the miracle," said the woman. "Please pray for my Celia."

The girl trembled as the old woman let the hair fall back into place.

Ruby groaned from deep within. "I–I can't…"

The old woman took Ruby's hands in hers. "Please. For Celia. I beg you."

"No, don't. I..." Ruby gazed helplessly into the woman's pleading eyes. "OK. I'll try, but...OK."

The old woman smiled and drew Celia closer. Then she made the sign of the cross, bowed her head, and began mumbling in another language. The girl swayed, as if keeping time to an inaudible metronome, her crippled arm drawn into her side.

Ruby extended her right hand toward the girl's head. She touched the clammy flesh with her fingertips, and the girl flinched. The old woman's babbling increased.

As Ruby closed her eyes, a flush of warmth swept up her neck. The sensation reminded her of Sunday morning. A similar feeling had preceded the vision. Was this a sign? Maybe there was a formula, a divine pattern she'd stumbled upon. Confidence rose in her as she prayed. Maybe it *could* happen again. She'd heard about healers from the past, ordinary men and women suddenly blessed with a divine ability, thrust into the spotlight and forever revered as saints. Perhaps she was one of them. Her fingers tingled with the thought. The event at the mortuary couldn't happen again, could it? She peeked at Celia.

The girl remained twisted, tongue lolling out one side of her mouth.

Ruby plunged back into prayer, refusing to surrender. Maybe she needed more passion, more sincerity—*more faith*. Televangelists and healers always emphasized faith. Yes! That's what she was missing. *Faith!* She squeezed her eyes shut again and spoke with calculated precision. "Dear Lord, touch Celia's withered arm. Open her eyes. I believe. *We* believe!"

The old woman's voice had become a frenzied, high-pitched warble. Ruby slipped open her eyes.

The girl remained unchanged.

Again Ruby bowed her head, vesting each word with added urgency. With her brow furrowed in concentration, she implored God for a miracle. Eloquent phrases and dramatic scenarios unfolded in her mind—far more eloquent and dramatic than

anything she would normally venture. The tingling in her fingertips seemed to intensify. This was it! If anyone deserved to be
healed, it was this poor young girl. Yes! It *could* happen. She must
believe! Ruby remained steadfast, focused only upon the twisted
figure before her.

Yet despite her newfound zeal, nothing changed.

Who in the world was Ruby kidding?

Frustration swelled inside her. She took the girl's head in both
hands and glared into the pale fluttering eyes. "Be healed! I–I
command you!"

The old woman sobbed, and the young girl shrunk back,
wincing at every word.

"Please!" Ruby began crying. "Please!"

But there was no healing.

Ruby let go, dropped her hands to her side, and staggered
backward. The girl burst into tears and hugged the old woman.
Shame pierced Ruby's heart. She should have stayed inside like
Jack wanted, turned her back on them. What a fool to think she
had anything to offer. What a fool to think she was anything
but a very average person. By the looks of it, she was doing more
harm than good. Yet even more puzzling than her own impotence
was God's inaction. Why would He use her and then abandon
her, give her power and then take it away? Maybe this was part of
the curse. Maybe this is what drove the old farmer mad.

"I–I'm sorry," Ruby choked back tears. "I'm so sorry."

Upon hearing the words, Celia looked up and tilted her head,
as if tuning in to some high-pitched frequency. Beneath her
swollen eyelids the dull whites pattered side to side. Then she
wobbled forward, stretched out her good arm, and groped toward
Ruby. Their hands met.

A warm spring breeze rose up the canyon, and the eucalyptus
leaves chattered with its passing. The scent of wildflowers and
ocean air followed and buoyed the moment.

"Thank you," the girl whispered. "Thank you, Miss Ruby."

Ruby's anger deflated. She hugged the crippled girl and, in that
embrace, wondered who was in more need of healing.

Chapter 17

BY NOON A STEADY STREAM OF VISITORS HAD COME TO SEE
Ruby. Each one had a unique story—a reason for the short
pilgrimage. She listened carefully, encouraged them, and laid her
hands on their twisted limbs and pallid flesh. Yet Ruby had abandoned hope for another miracle.

As the day grew hot, she placed a lawn chair under the shade
of the porch. The Besbecks went from peeking out the window to
peering out their front door. By late afternoon they carried a tray
of lemonade onto their patio and sat fanning themselves, smiling,
watching the cars go by and the strangers climb the driveway
with their gifts and prayer requests.

Mrs. Besbeck brought the morning paper over and proudly
displayed the photo of Ruby and Mondo on the front page.
"You're famous, dear." She was beaming.

"Bizarre Events at Mortuary" read the headline.

> Late Sunday afternoon, just hours away from burial,
> Armando Amaya climbed out of his coffin in full view of a
> packed house of stunned, frightened mourners. "I've never
> seen anything like it," said a shocked Arthur Goldman,
> owner of the Goldman's Mortuary. "And I hope I never see
> anything like it again."

Ruby didn't bother reading the entire article. She handed it
back to Mrs. Besbeck.

"You don't want to keep it?"

Ruby wrinkled her nose and shook her head, hoping not to
come off as impolite. She already had an idea about the word
around town. Still, she wondered if the *Sentinel* knew about the
first resurrection almost ninety years ago. Maybe if she told them,

she could deflect some attention. But the way things were going, it would only make matters worse.

By late afternoon, the pile of gifts had grown, transforming the front porch into a cluttered altar. Flowers, statues, and handwritten notes were heaped upon the steps. Jack was going to kill her.

Sandy huddled under the oleander, jittery, watching the goings on with suspicion. Sean stayed at the kitchen table, where he could see Ruby through the window. He looked out every now and then, waved, and returned to his coloring book.

The sun soon gave way to a cool breeze. The looky-loos and miracle-seekers thinned, and Ruby found enough time between visitors to slip inside and lie on the couch. The lack of sleep caught up to her and she dozed, until Sean padded out from the kitchen.

"Mom, 'nother customer."

Her eyes snapped open, and she lay staring at the ceiling. Jack would be home any minute, but she'd already resolved to stand her ground. Besides, facing his anger would be easier than turning away all the hurting souls. Maybe her dilemma was part of some divine plan. Ruby could only hope.

She stepped out the door as a woman with a billowy red beehive hairdo and stiletto heels pulled a boy along behind her. Ruby rubbed her eyes and squinted in the sunlight.

"Are you the lady in the paper?" The woman peered through horn-rimmed bifocals. "You are!" She wobbled up the driveway in her heels, looking like a space alien out of Brian's comics, still tugging the plump boy.

Meanwhile, a blue compact sporting a spare doughnut tire on one of the front wheels pulled onto the shoulder across the street.

Ms. Beehive approached, chattering. "I've taken him to one doctor after another. James!" She barked at the boy and yanked him forward. "He's got a terrible case of acne." The boy stood sulking, with his arms folded. "It's so demeaning—just look at it—and nothing helps. We've seen an herbalist, but she went outta business, and acupuncture didn't seem to work. Ya know, they say that stuff is connected. Psychosomatic and all. Anyways,

Jean next door read about you in the paper—it's just crazy what you did!—and suggested we buzz on over. James!"

A man and woman left the blue compact and crossed the street. The man held a shoebox under his arm and whispered to his companion as they climbed the driveway. They looked sour and frumpy and stared expectantly at Ruby.

Ms. Beehive glanced over her shoulder and stepped between Ruby and the approaching couple. The boy shook his mother free and stood with his arms locked atop his belly, scowling. "Could you just touch him, or pray, or whatever it is you do, and we'll be on our way. And if you need a donation or something, well—" She patted a petite pink leather handbag and stepped sideways.

The Besbecks returned to their porch, this time with a plate of cookies. Mr. Huebry drove by, did a double take, and swerved onto the gravel. The Besbecks waved at him, and he cruised up the street, craning to see the commotion. Just as Ruby turned her attention back to the obnoxious woman, another car pulled across the street. The neighborhood had become Grand Central Station.

The car had the look of a generic rental. As the cloud of dust swept by, two men quickly emerged. One of them reached into the back seat and retrieved a bulky item, and the two men marched into the front yard. Everyone turned to see this odd couple.

A man with a photographer's vest wrestled a camera over his neck, veered off, and began snapping pictures of the five of them. Ms. Beehive yanked the boy to her side, adjusted her glasses, and did her best to strike a modish pose. The other man strode toward Ruby.

"Wilflee, ma'am." He extended his hand. "Mace Wilflee."

He wore wraparound sunglasses, the kind that looked very cool or very trendy, depending on one's hipster IQ. His hair was short and spiky with bleached ends; his polyester shirt was unbuttoned enough to expose a tanned chest draped with excessive jewelry.

"Excuse me?" Ruby squinted at the stranger. "You're—"

"Mace Wilflee. *Rippington Weekly*, ma'am."

Ruby reluctantly shook his hand. "*Rippington*? The tabloid?"

He flashed brilliant, bleached teeth. "We prefer to think of ourselves as an *alternative news* outlet."

Ms. Beehive gasped and fluffed her red mop. Ruby was unsure whether the lady had the hots for Wilflee or actually believed a career in modeling was unfolding before her eyes.

"Uh, how can I help you?" Ruby asked the reporter with intentional skepticism.

The Besbecks leaned together, waving for the photographer, as he clicked away. The frumpy couple swung around the other side of the woman, who was now preoccupied with the reporter from *Rippington*, and the man drummed on the shoebox, waiting for Ruby's attention.

"We're interested in your story, Mrs. Case. Very interested! Got the *Rippington* staff buzzing crazy-like. The kinda thing that rewires *reality*. We're prepared to purchase exclusive rights and can have a contract to you by this evening."

"I'm sorry, Mr.—" She cleared her throat and peered harder at the man.

"Wil-flee, ma'am. Mace Wilflee."

"Mr. Wilflee, this stuff is personal. I don't think *Rippington* could handle this in a way I'd be comfortable with."

"Now, ma'am, I can personally vouch for *Rippington*'s handling and can guarantee the utmost care. We value our features. 'Course, as you probably know, we are not a hard news entity. Our stories lean toward the...*fabulistic*. And your story definitely fits that category."

The photographer squatted in the middle of the yard, his lens pointed toward the shrine. Sean was back on his elbows, face plastered against the glass. And Mr. Huebry stood in his driveway three houses up, briefcase at his side, gawking.

"I'm sorry," Ruby said. "The Amayas are friends of ours. I wouldn't want this blown out of proportion, exploited, or something."

Wilflee leaned closer, and with him came a heavy scent of cologne and breath mints. He glanced at Ms. Beehive and the couple with the shoebox and lowered his voice. "It looks like it's already being exploited, Ruby. May I call you Ruby?" He lifted his sunglasses, revealing electric blue eyes. Then he stepped back and let the glasses fall into place.

"Look. *Rippington's* prepared to offer a sizable amount of money. Quite sizable. It's yours just for letting us tell your story. That's it. No strings attached. You and the husband can do what you want: take a vacation, save for the boys' college fund. Start your own healing crusade if ya like, travel the country. It's up to you. But I can guarantee any inconvenience you may incur will be well offset by our lucrative offer."

Ruby shook her head, incredulous. Was this guy for real? "You know what, Mr. Wilflee?" She folded her arms. "I'm not interested in selling my story. I'm gonna have to ask you to leave."

She took a step back and prepared to pivot, when the reporter countered her move and blocked her exit.

"Whoa! Hold on now, Mrs. Case. I'm not easily dissuaded. Nor will I entertain incompliance lightly. I always get my story. And I reckon this here's mine. Tell ya what. You name your price. That's right. Whatever it is…of course, within reason. It's not our usual policy, mind you, but in your case we feel this is a story the American public needs to hear. And *Rippington* is the perfect fit.

"Just last month we broke the story on the Plains Prophet. You may've heard. Listen, this guy can summon UFOs—or at least these weird colored lights—with just his mind. Trip out! He's got a huge cult following. Says it's a sign of the coming apocalypse— the end of the world.

"We've been charting it for a while now, all over the world, strange phenomenon, like this here in Stonetree. Phantoms, ghost ships. And miracles. A few months back we did a feature on Nedna the Swamp Witch—that woman in the bayou who can talk to animals. She's a"—he leaned closer and whispered— "hermaphrodite. Communicates telepathically. Her head's twice the size of a normal human's. Talks to dogs and cats, has a ferret that runs the house. And they all say the same thing: 'the storm's coming.'"

Ruby caught herself with her mouth open, staring in stupefied disbelief. A surreal, nonsensical circus had descended on her front yard, and she was the ringleader. How'd it come to this? She drew her fingers across her lips, partly to make sure she hadn't drooled while gawking at the reporter. "This is weird. I don't believe in that stuff, Mr. Willflee. Phantoms? Ghost ships? And anyway, how's this connected?"

"You don't see a connection here?" He glanced at Ms. Beehive, who appeared anxious to nod in agreement. "Ya don't think zombies are part of the apocalypse? The walking dead?" He stiffened, raised his arms, and did a brief Frankenstein impersonation.

"No. Huh-uh. This is not about that." She pointed to the street. "I want you to leave. Now! Or I'm calling the police."

"It's in the Bible, Ruby. When Jesus comes, the dead will rise. Maybe this is it—the start of some huge, cataclysmic zombie-thon. Stonetree: *The Beginning of the End.* Or *The City That Death Forgot.*"

She clamped her jaw and glared at the rabid reporter. Just as she was about to march into the house and call the authorities, Jack drove up the street in his truck. He pulled into the driveway, gaping at the scene in his front yard. He parked the truck, opened the door, and stepped out, his face flushed and the veins in his neck straining. Brian climbed out the other side with his backpack and scampered to Jack's side.

The photographer stopped shooting and let the camera dangle at his chest. Inching closer to Wilflee, the two watched nervously as Jack marched toward Ruby with his nostrils flaring. He stopped in front of her, lifted the bill of his baseball cap, and surveyed the crowd. He cast a curt smile at the Besbecks, who were on their porch waving, and then glanced sideways at the reporter and the redhead. In a sharp, unemotional voice he said, "Ruby, what is going on? You promised me—"

"Pardon the interruption, Mr. Case." The reporter stepped toward Jack, and the jewelry about his neck jangled with the abrupt motion. "It is Mr. Case, hmm? Mace Wilflee. *Rippington Weekly.*" He thrust his hand out.

Jack glared at Ruby, then reluctantly shook the reporter's hand.

"As I was telling your lovely wife, we'd like to purchase the rights to her story. We think there's real potential for a lead, and the financial remuneration would be substantial."

Jack furrowed his brow, looking more puzzled than angry. "The rights to her story? What story?"

"Jack, I want him out of here."

"Why, *this* story." Wilflee motioned to the shrine, Ms. Beehive, her pudgy, scowling son, and the Besbecks. "We can pay well, Mr. Case. Trust me on that. And I can guarantee the story will get the treatment it deserves."

Jack lifted the hat and scratched his head. Then he jammed the cap on and his eyes darted back and forth between Ruby and the reporter.

"Make him leave, Jack." Ruby had her hands on her hips. "This isn't right. He's rude and—and I won't be a part of it. I'm not about to be used by these people."

"Excuse me, Mrs. Case," Wilflee's smile became a sneer. "But you already *are* being used."

"All right, bro." Jack turned toward the reporter with his chest out. "That's it! She wants you outta here, and so do I. Pack it up. Now!"

Brian dashed from beside Jack to Ruby, and she pulled him close. Ms. Beehive yanked her son back, and the frumpy couple coddled the shoebox and retreated with a look of dread.

Wilflee stumbled away from Jack and motioned to the photographer. "All right, all right." He lifted his hands in surrender and backed toward the street, glancing over his shoulder, chattering all the way. "But you're missing the opportunity of a lifetime. Trust me. It's how celebrities are born. Seen it a million times." He teetered on the curb and leaped awkwardly onto the street. "There's somethin' more going on here. Believe me. And I'm gonna get the story." He skidded to a stop, and Jack, who was on his tail, almost ran over him. The reporter glared at Jack. "I always do."

Jack flinched, as if cocking to throw a punch, and Wilflee fled to the car with the photographer at his heels. The rental car tore out, sending pebbles ticking across the asphalt and a bank of dust rising into the air.

Jack turned to the visitors, who stood dumbfounded. "Show's over, folks! Mrs. Case is closing shop. Time to leave."

Ms. Beehive threw her head back, huffed, and snatched the boy. She stormed down the driveway in her stilettos in spastic, jerking motions, looking as if she might break an ankle any second. The frumpy couple stared at each other, then at Ruby, and skulked to their car.

Ruby stroked Brian's shoulder, and the boy looked proudly at his father. The cloud of dust floated up the street, and she watched it, pondering Wilflee's words. The goofball was probably right—a storm was coming.

Chapter 18

RUBY GAZED OUT THE CAR WINDOW, WATCHING BOULDER-laden hills and timberline sweep past. The drive to Old Town took twenty minutes, yet this evening it seemed much longer. Getting Ivy to babysit the boys was easy enough. Convincing Jack to take her was another story. She twisted a lock of hair as he sulked and glanced at her in between curves.

"I don't know why I'm doing this," he finally grumbled.

"I said I'm sorry."

"Yeah, well, if we're gonna get through this, I suggest we work together."

He had a point, even if working together wasn't her strong suit. "You didn't have to throw those things away."

"Ruby, those people are nuts. I know they mean well, but bringing junk—"

"It's not junk."

"All right then, coming to a total stranger's house and—and expecting a miracle, that *is* nuts. Between them and that clown reporter—"

She continued twirling the dangling blonde lock. "I can't just ignore them. They need something. They need hope. It wouldn't be right. And I didn't do it to defy you. I still don't think you should have thrown that stuff away."

He exhaled and glanced out of the corner of his eye. "I didn't. It's on the side of the house in a trash bag." He tapped his fingers on the steering wheel. "I figured I'd let it accumulate and use it for kindling next winter."

She suppressed a grin. Maybe Jack did get it after all. He was just trying to protect her and, in his own way, help her figure things out. After all, he wouldn't be driving her to Aida Elston's if he didn't care.

The SUV's tires squealed as the car took a hairpin turn.

"Slow down!" Ruby seized the overhead grip.

"Highway to hell, babe. Woo-hoo!"

"Cut it out! And watch the road."

The single-lane highway climbed out of Stonetree Valley, winding inland. She couldn't remember exactly how many people had died on this death trap, plummeting down the pass or skating out of a turn into the gravel shoulder. The superstitions never seemed to bother her…until she was on this road.

Jack slowed enough for her comfort, and she let go of the handgrip. Below, between redwood groves and rock outcroppings, ramshackle houses and abandoned cars sprinkled the valley floor.

"There!" Ruby pointed as they came out of a wide turn.

Buckshot riddled the sign, but the words *Old Town* were still visible. Jack turned off the highway onto the narrow asphalt road. It coiled down the mountainside before spilling into a sloping green plain, disappearing amidst trees and a layer of haze.

"What a dump. Smells like burnt trash. Are you sure you wanna talk to this lady?"

As she scanned the blighted valley, Ruby asked herself the same question. Mr. Svenson suggested she start her investigation here—though she didn't consider herself much of a detective. And looking at this place only fueled her misgivings.

At one time Bridge River was a thriving logging and mining town, a center of commerce. But that was almost a hundred years ago. The residents had chased the resources into more fertile terrain, relocated nearer the coast, and renamed themselves Stonetree. Old Town, the historical epicenter, now stood rundown and tawdry, the butt of jokes and home to the not so well off. By the looks of it, Aida Elston would be a toothless hag, a backwater bumpkin spinning yarns about a fabled, long-forgotten miracle.

But if there was any chance the old woman could provide clues to the resurrection of Mondo Amaya and its connection to the curse—as well as Ruby's role in the crazy event—she was more than willing to endure the inconvenience and embarrassment.

"Yeah. I want to talk to her."

Jack huffed. "OK," he said in his you'll-be-sorry voice.

The setting sun struck the far hillside, tinting the basin in gold and umber, casting a dull sheen atop the blanket of haze. The road leveled, and they passed small, rustic houses made of stone and log, nestled beneath ancient redwoods.

Ruby patted the dash and retrieved the directions Mr. Svenson had sketched. "Straight ahead, second light."

"Oh, they have stoplights here? I thought they'd still be using torches or lanterns."

"Ha-ha. They're not *that* far behind."

As they entered the shadow of the canyon, the air grew cool. Blue jays darted overhead, and, between the trees, the town became visible. Several streets, consisting of nothing more than crumbling asphalt, trailed into the woods. They drove through the first intersection, passed a market, a Laundromat, and a gun shop with a dead neon sign. A group of men leaned against the storefront and stopped their conversation, glaring as the SUV drove by. Behind the buildings and the forest, sheer granite cliffs rose like a vast curtain. Ruby spotted one of the mines, bored in the mountainside, evidence of a once vibrant economy.

"Here. Turn right." She pointed to the next set of lights.

Jack scanned the town square and mumbled to himself. Across a freshly painted, two-story house with checkered curtains hung a limp, yellowed banner. City Hall, it announced, in calligraphic script. In front of the house, blanketed by pine needles, stood a life-size statue of a grizzled woodsman with an axe slung over his shoulder. Except for a few cars, a woman carrying a paper sack, and a shopkeeper sweeping his storefront, the streets were empty. On the corner sat a wooden barrel, stenciled with the words *Bridge River*.

Jack shook his head. "Next time the boys think they got it rough, I'm sending 'em here."

They turned down a road hedged by forest. The dying orange sky peeked through the canopy, mottling the windshield with shadows and shards of light.

"It's on the right side," Ruby said. "A white house, with a white, wood-paneled station wagon out front." She set the paper on her lap and raised her eyebrows. "No address."

"Oh, it shouldn't be too hard to find. White, wood-paneled station wagons are up there with Bigfoot sightings. Pretty rare."

"Cut it out."

"Well, you got enough pressure on you. Why don't we just drop this whole thing—get on with our lives?"

"Tell that to the folks coming by the house. Just keep driving."

The houses sat back, a stone's throw from the main road, bordered by dirt driveways and sagging fences. Ruby drew a deep breath. She'd grown nervous in anticipation of meeting Aida Elston. How had the miracle changed the old woman and the people around her? Was it anything like Ruby's ordeal? And what of the farmer and his mysterious death? Shadows loomed in the forest, creating a sense of foreboding.

"There it is!"

Jack jumped and tapped the brakes, snapping their heads forward. "What's wrong with you?" He pulled the car onto the dirt shoulder, crunching pinecones, parked, and turned off the ignition. "You nervous or what?"

The solitude of the forest crept in, and Ruby sat rigid, staring forward.

"You *are* nervous." Jack studied her. "C'mon, Rube. It's just an old lady."

"We need to pray."

He leaned back in his seat, as if stunned by her words, and looked out his window. "Go ahead. Just keep me out of it."

"No. *We* need to pray. Both of us."

"I told you before—I'm not ready. That's your gig."

They'd had this conversation so many times before. Jack had made a clean break from the church, vowing never to return. He said God had let him down—if there even was a God—and he wasn't shy about voicing his objections. Yet he still had a soft spot. As headstrong as she was, and as much as she'd love to confront him, Ruby knew this was holy ground. So instead of pressing the issue, she reached across and took his hand. "OK, then you sit there."

He pursed his lips and sat stiffly.

She nodded, closed her eyes, and sighed. "Lord, thank You for all Your blessings. I don't understand everything that's happening or why I've been chosen. I really, really need Your help. Place a covering over us, the boys too. Deliver us from evil." Jack became so still, she could feel his pulse throbbing. "Give me wisdom about the...about Mondo. And that old curse. And give me the strength to handle the consequences, whatever they may be. Amen."

She opened her eyes, squeezed Jack's hand, and tried to let go. But he didn't. He held on, kept his head bowed, and for a second, she thought he might pray. Her heart thrummed as she gazed at him, awaiting his next move.

"You're scaring me, Rube."

Before she could respond, he looked up and gave her a stern glance. "You didn't tell me this was about that stupid curse. And what kinda danger could we be in? There's something you're not telling me, isn't there?"

Well, there's the vision, the black Hummer, the hooded figures, and the dead farmer.

She reached for the door handle. "I'll tell you after the meeting. OK?" She gave him her best puppy dog eyes, and he backed down.

"OK. But like I said, if we're gonna get through this thing, we need to work together."

She nodded and opened the door. Cool mountain air rushed in, sending a chill through her. Jack came around the other side, and they stood together, looking down the dirt driveway into the gloom. A bare bulb burned in the doorway of a small white house. In front of it sat the grimy, white wood-paneled station wagon. A massive, unkempt woodpile flanked the house. Along the length of the property ran a low-lying stone wall and, leaning against it, some wooden milk crates, two bald tires, and an axe.

Something pinged off the hood of the car, and an acorn

ricocheted between them. Ruby glanced into the trees, took Jack's hand, and they started down the driveway.

Twilight pressed between the interlaced conifers. Pockets of fog wrapped the redwood groves, and once again, Ruby caught herself battling unnamed fears. Next door a ribbon of smoke rose from a cottage. On the porch an elderly couple sat unmoving and watched them with narrow eyes.

"I guess they haven't seen humans in a while," Jack said under his breath.

Ruby jabbed him with her elbow and quickened their pace.

They approached the house and followed a cobblestone footpath to the front door. The porch light illumined a thicket of cobwebs, layered with insect husks, draped like fishing nets above the shabby green door. Several yellowed newspapers lay unopened at their feet. Jack let go of Ruby's hand, pulled back the screen, and rapped on the weathered door. It drifted open.

A thick greasy smell wafted onto the porch. They waited, and then Jack knocked a second time. Footsteps thudded inside, and a gangly teenage boy wearing a knit beanie poked his head out.

"Hey. Thought I heard something," the boy said in between chewing.

Ruby and Jack looked at each other, as though negotiating who would talk. Jack deferred with his eyes.

"We're looking for Aida Elston. Carl Svenson suggested I speak to her."

The boy nodded, chewing faster, and then gulped. "She's here." Black hair curled from under the Rasta beanie. He looked them over and smiled, showing braces. "And who're you?"

"I'm Jack Case." He stepped forward with his chest out, trying to sound masculine. "And this is Ruby. My wife had some questions about...I mean, something happened in town that, um..." Then he deflated.

"I work for Livery," Ruby said. "Mr. Svenson told me a little bit about Aida and said she might be able to help me with something."

"Grandma loves to talk, that's for sure." The boy ducked behind the door then back again. "Hold on a sec." He spun around, and his footsteps thumped back into the house.

The couple on the porch next door leaned back into the shadows, still spying on Jack and Ruby. A dog barked in the distance, and a blue jay bounded onto the wooden shingles overhead. It turned its head sideways and studied them, then skittered away as the heavy footsteps thudded inside again.

The boy opened the screen door, making the cobwebs flutter. "C'mon in. Pardon the mess. We don't get many visitors."

Jack went first with Ruby close behind him. They entered a dingy hallway, and a dense smell of nicotine struck them. Jack immediately started sniffling. The boy led them into a tiny square kitchen, cluttered with knick-knacks and unwashed dishes. On a grimy stove something sizzled under the lid of a cast iron skillet. Slits of twilight crept through heavy curtains, outlining large, jumbled shapes in an adjoining room. A trash can, piled high, stood next to a breakfast nook ringed with coffee stains and dotted with cigarette burns. A sticky, yellow film clung to the room, and Ruby shivered in response.

"Down the hall to your right. She's waiting." The boy turned to Jack and motioned to the breakfast nook. "Would you like some soda? Or fried bologna?" He showed his braces again.

Jack sniffled and glanced at Ruby. She flashed him a good luck smile and turned into the darkened hallway.

A faint light shone from the room at the end. Several pictures hung cockeyed on the walls, and a faucet dripped in another room. Someone coughed—a hoarse, dry cough—and phlegm rattled in the person's lungs. Ruby's eyes watered from the pervasive odor of smoke. She approached the doorway, tapped on the jamb, and peered into the room. A digital clock cast a thin, red glow atop indistinguishable forms.

"Hello?" Ruby spoke into the shadows. "Hello?"

The red barrel of a cigarette blazed, and she recognized a seated figure to one side of the room. "So, you work for ol' Buck," said a raspy voice.

Ruby stared at the misshapen figure. "Buck? Um, I work for Carl Svenson."

"We used to call him Buck. His folks lived down the street. They sold the place awhile back." She spoke with a Southern drawl, more prominent than Vinyette's. The figure motioned with the cigarette, leaving a red trail in the dark. "Sit down, hon. Please. Marty'll keep your boyfriend entertained."

"He's my husband."

"Oh. Uh-huh."

"His name's Jack, and I'm Ruby. Ruby Case."

"Ruby. That's pretty."

Marty chattered in the front room, and Jack sneezed. Ruby smiled. Her husband may not be as spiritual as she'd like, but he had been faithful and supportive. She hadn't made it easy for him, and with the thought came a pang of guilt.

She took two steps into the room and then wavered, fearing she may stumble.

"I'm sorry," the woman said. "You can't see, can ya? There's a lamp on the bureau, to your left. Just, if ya could, turn it the other way."

Ruby fumbled about on the dresser, found the lamp, traced her fingers up its side, and clicked on the light. An orange lampshade with embroidered flowers glowed. She tilted the shade toward the wall and turned around.

Across the room, in a wheelchair, sat a bony, birdlike woman with stark white hair and both hands clamped over her face.

Chapter 19

AIDA ELSTON HUNCHED IN THE WHEELCHAIR, HANDS clasped over her face, shielding herself from the glow of the lamp. A cigarette dangled from her fingers, trailing smoke to a discolored ceiling. The frail woman sat with her legs drawn together in a limp bundle. Her face, or what Ruby glimpsed of it, was narrow and stitched with wrinkles like fine burlap. Brilliant white hair, silky fine, disappeared behind her back.

"My eyes ain't what they used to be." She peeked from behind her palms, blinking against the light.

Ruby switched the lamp off. "I'm sorry. I can do without it."

"Thank you, hon. I 'precitate it. Here, come sit down."

Ruby heard the old woman pat the bed. She shuffled forward and sat, causing the springs to creak. Aida sucked on the cigarette and it crackled, illuminating a hawk nose and thin, weathered lips. Her eyes glistened in the red glow as she studied Ruby.

"Don't get many visitors out here. Used ta. So what brings ya to these parts? You a reporter? Come ta see the freak?" She twisted her body and ground the cigarette in an ashtray on the nightstand.

"A reporter? No. But I've seen my share of them lately." Ruby chuckled, attempting to ease her disquiet.

"Oh?" Aida wheeled herself closer, until the footrests grazed Ruby's shins. The old woman leaned forward and sniffed the air like a dog searching a scent.

Ruby tilted back, the bed squeaked, and she glanced down the hall. Marty jabbered away in the kitchen. Jack would be here in a heartbeat if necessary. Comforted by the awareness of his proximity, she turned back to the shadowy figure before her.

Aida gripped the wheels and rolled away from the bed. "Every coupla years or so, someone new comes: reporters, tourists, pranksters. Marty knows not to let the witches in. I reckon you ain't one of them."

"No. I'm not a witch."

"Didn't think so. They smell different, and I can see the black halo round 'em. The real bad ones, that is. You ain't got that. Sometimes they set up camp in the glen, make a terrible ruckus, leave junk layin' around. I had to call the police coupla times. But mostly, God sends an angel and drives 'em off."

Black halo? Angel? Ruby's stomach fluttered, and she ran her hands up and down her thighs. "I've never been bothered by them. At least, not that I know of."

"Well, if you live 'round here, you've been bothered by 'em, one way or 'nother. They got their fingers in a lotta pies, though most folks can't distinguish. Them reporters are about as much nuisance. They snoop around, asking the same old questions. *What happened? Who's ta blame?* Then they go spinnin' yarns in all kinds o' directions, like they always done. Lord knows what madness them ink slingers conjured these last ninety years." She laughed, a guttural laugh that rocked the wheelchair and made the phlegm rattle inside her. Then she grew quiet and returned her gaze to Ruby.

"But it's been awhile since a reporter came, or anyone, so I figger somethin's up. Is it?"

Ruby cleared her throat. "Well, Mr. Svenson—I mean, Buck— uh, he said you might be able to help me. You see…um, the other day…" She cleared her throat again. Where should she begin? The vision, the resurrection, the stick man, the pilgrims at her doorstep—it sounded so absurd.

"Sunday morning…"

She felt like a fool, fumbling for words, twitching like a nervous wreck on the bed of some strange old woman. *C'mon, Ruby. Spit it out!* "Um, Carl had a…a…" The flutter in her stomach became a knot. "He showed me the newspaper about the first resurrection. Yours. And how the church split and the farmer died. He said you might—that maybe you could—"

"What's wrong, child?" A bracelet shimmered in the pale red

light as Aida reached out and opened her hand. "Whatcha tryin' to say?"

Not until that moment, with Aida Elston's hand extended to her, did Ruby realize how empty and lost she had become. A collage of faces rose inside her: the board of elders, stern and critical; the news hacks clambering to scoop the next story at her expense; the sick and infirm yearning for a miracle. And all of them wanted something from her—all of them, except this old woman with an empty hand.

Her chest quivered; she grasped Aida's hand and slumped forward.

They remained in that position, interlocked between bed and wheelchair, for what seemed a long time. Aida stroked Ruby's hand and hummed a gruff, unfamiliar tune.

And Ruby rested there.

"You got a problem lettin' go o' stuff, don't ya?"

Ruby nodded, fighting the urge to pull away.

"Can't ya see? This one's too big for ya, Ruby."

The words penetrated her façade as a stone does the surface of the water, sinking into the depth of her being, sending ripples into the furthest corners of her heart. *Too big?* Was anything too big for Ruby? Maybe she'd finally met her match. Her stubbornness and self-reliance had become a millstone about her neck. She had to let go or sink.

Ruby's breathing settled, and a strange calm possessed her. "I've been on my own a lot. My mother died when I was young— just a baby really. I learned to get by. Had to. It's become second nature...a survival skill, I guess." She let go of Aida's hand and wiped her eyes. The unexpected show of vulnerability would usually embarrass her, but at the moment, it felt refreshing. "I know it's a problem. So does everyone else."

"Mmm, hmm." Aida nodded.

Ruby pushed a strand of hair out of her face and sighed. "Last Sunday morning, at my prayer group, I received a vision."

Aida cocked her head to one side. "Oh? Tell me 'bout it."

"That's just the beginning. There's more. That night, Sunday night, a boy was raised from the dead—through me. I mean, I touched him, and he...he just sat up. I don't know exactly how or what it means. But the last few days have been crazy."

Aida retrieved another cigarette and tapped one end on the nightstand. "It's been a long time comin', but maybe the stone tree will sprout after all."

Ruby scooted to the edge of the bed and peered at the shadowy form. For the last three days she'd kept the vision of the petrified oak to herself, shared it with no one. Not Vinyette or Marje or Jack. She peered at Aida Elston. "How'd you know?"

Aida sat there nodding, drawing the cigarette through her fingertips.

"The morning of the resurrection," Ruby said, "that's what I saw, inside me. It–it knocked me off my feet. Literally. Hit my head. I saw the stone tree sprouting."

"You ain't alone, hon. I've had that premonition many times." She raised the cigarette and clicked on the lighter. "Don't mind, do ya?"

Ruby shook her head and watched the woman light up. The flame swelled, illuminating gauzy gray pupils. Aida inhaled and blew out the smoke with a great, tired wheeze.

"This here place was meant to be like a tree, all right. But not a stone one. Like a tree planted by rivers of water, bringin' forth fruit in its season. At one time it *was*. Course now it's all dried up and dead—like the rivers and the Sailor's Oak and the churches.

"I been prayin' for the breakin' for seventy-some years and believin' I'd see it in my time. So I been waitin'. And waitin'. And here you come."

She took another drag and started coughing. Which turned into hacking. Ruby winced as the old woman's body heaved in the wheelchair, rocking it back and forth. The fit subsided, and she panted until her breathing steadied.

"Me and Marty go 'round and 'round. I told him I'm too old to quit. Been raised once, and I don't 'spect it'll happen again."

Ruby leaned forward with her elbows on her knees. "I don't understand, Miss Elston. How does it all fit? I mean, the vision and resurrection? Me and Mondo? And what kind of *breaking* are you talking about?"

"Why, the breakin' of the curse."

"I dunno...I don't think I even believe in the Stonetree curse."

Aida chuckled and nodded again, a swooping, exaggerated nod, as if she'd heard this all before. "There's more goin' on than you know, child. You're caught in the middle of somethin' big."

Ruby squinted against the smoke and asked hesitantly, "So is it true what people say about you?"

"Well, it depends what they say." She laughed, and Ruby hoped the woman wouldn't start hacking again. She didn't. "If it's about the healing, then it's true. God called me back from the grave." She sucked on the cigarette and blew the smoke in the other direction. The cloud roiled in the center of the room, inflamed by the digital light. "It's what came after that needed healin'."

"What do you mean?"

She angled the wheelchair further away from Ruby and spoke into the darkened room as if beginning a well-worn, painful tale. "Ya ever seen a revival, Ruby? I mean a real, Holy Ghost revival?"

"Um..."

"Well, that year was the great revival. Nineteen twenty-one. I was seven years old. It swept down from up north. And Bridge River got caught up in it. Churches were filled; people got saved. The industry took off too. Folks far and wide traveled here. It was a glorious time. But everyone wasn't happy about the spiritual awakenin'.

"The mines and mills attracted lotsa folks. Men could make a decent wage and feed their family, so they came in droves. The bosses hired a lotta migrants, Indians, gypsies, ya know, strangers to these parts. Basically, anyone who'd work got a job. But some brought more'n just a work ethic with 'em. They brought the religion of their people—ancient, tribal-like, devilish stuff. That's when the battle begun.

"Weird altars and shrines started poppin' up in the forest. Gertie found one near the quarry. An idol or effigy made of fruit 'n animal bones. A likeness of somethin'...somethin' not human."

Ruby gasped. "I found one! Or–or something like that. The day after Mondo came back somebody put one of those things in my yard. Bones and plants pieced together like a monster."

"Mmm, hmm. Then it's all comin' 'round again." She paused for a moment, then continued, "When it was found out, the churches came together, took a stand against it. Today ya gotta buncha spineless ministers 'fraid ta speak up 'bout anything. Not then. They weren't 'bout to waffle 'round while some foreigners took over. So we all joined together. But things got worse."

Ruby sat spellbound, forcing the information into her already overloaded switchboard, wondering where this was leading and dreading the implications.

Aida took a few drags, allowing things to gestate in Ruby, then resumed. "They tried scarin' us—painted threats around town, peculiar names and symbols in animal blood. We knew we had a fight on our hands. The kinda fight that's been ragin' ever since the beginning. Gods and demons; ancient things vyin' for supremacy.

"Well, the churches united like they never had. Believers put aside their differences, if you can believe it. That's when the fever broke out. It stopped the revival dead. People got confused; they lost faith. Heck, they lost family! Somethin' bigger'n us had been let loose by the evil, and none of us was ready.

"They'd summoned a dark angel, an ancient deity of sorts. A god of earth and stone. There was a war in the heavenly places. Principalities and powers squabblin' over property rights. And somehow, I got caught 'n the crossfire."

She grew quiet for a moment and stared off into the dark, grinding her jaw.

Ruby leaned forward, debating whether to probe. The conversation was taking her places she didn't want to go. Of course she believed in demons. Seeing the evil in the world, how could she not? But the notion that invisible superpowers raged over Stonetree seemed absurd. Sure, the spiritual realm was real…but not *this* real. Suddenly her faith seemed anemic, miniscule in light of the mounting possibilities.

"Twenty-seven of us in all," Aida resumed, "dead from the fever. All's I remember is layin' in bed, shiverin' somethin' terrible. Momma prayed, patted me down with cold water, and stood over me quotin' Scripture. After that, I only know what they told me."

She shifted in the wheelchair, swung her limp legs to the other side, and groaned. "I woke up in the coffin. Sat straight up. Lord, I was thirsty!" She chuckled, and the whites of her eyes quivered. "There was a man standing over me, a farmer named Aaron. He'd done the deed. Touched me and said somethin'. And then it happened. Poof! People was shoutin', raising a ruckus, fallin' all over themselves. Momma said it was a miracle and all. Said God had answered our prayers and raised me as a sign to prove His power over the evil. But some had their doubts.

"Bad men, I say they were. They called me the devil's child and got to wippin' people up. Others said only God could raise the dead, that ol' Mr. Aaron was a bona fide healer. The town split. A buncha' infightin' ensued, and we were forced outta the church. And I guess it sealed their fate."

Ruby sat staring at the old woman, lost in thought. "Why didn't they believe?"

"Well, it ain't the first time people resented a miracle. No, sir. The Good Lord was nailed to a tree for practicin' miracles, raisin' the dead, and all. Nothing like a miracle to spoil everyone's day. 'Specially when the roost is ruled by the hard of heart." Her eyes glistened, and her tone turned somber. "They near crucified my mother. Just for believin', mind you. I'd done come back to life, and all those holy men could do was strain at gnats and swallow camels. They said I really wasn't dead, just sleepin'. Said God don't do those things anymore... and He definitely don't use farmers to do 'em.

"Mr. Aaron, he got the worst of it. He lived alone. A widower. A simple man by all accounts, with simple faith—just enough to believe the impossible. But by the time news got 'round 'bout what happened, he became a spectacle. They called him the Godsend, a prophet o' sorts. A hero to some and a villain to others. But like a sheep is dumb before the shearers, Mr. Aaron was led away to slaughter."

Ruby gasped. "They killed him?"

"Mmm. Somethin' happened. Somethin' happened that no man's yet explained. Ya see, they drove him outta town, run him off like a dog with mange. Until one day we seen his body hangin' from yonder tree."

"He hung himself?"

"'Cept when they climbed the mountain, they found his body'd been taken down and all sliced up. And they found a black blade—a knife carved from rock found in them mines. A sacrifice or somethin'. Murder maybe. But that's the sum of it. It's a mystery, dear, just waitin' for the light o' day."

Ruby settled back, numbed by the knowledge. Images churned in her brain. The vision of the twisted oak, brooding over the city, flashed in her mind. And from its weathered arms hung the body of the healer, sacrificed for the sin of his people.

Aida ground out her cigarette and angled her chair back toward Ruby. "You ever wondered why the churches 'round here are so dead, so unbelieving? Always bickerin' and backbitin'? Why, they'd kick God Himself out if He happened to show up."

"I know I've wondered about my church and my pastor. We just can't seem to get going."

"It's the curse, Ruby. It's a blanket coverin' this valley, smotherin' all that's good. It's the black angel empowered by blood, wrestlin' with the heavenly host. It's Mr. Aaron hangin' over Stonetree, keepin' watch, cursin' 'em with unbelief—burning bad tidings into the lot of us, day after day. Waitin' for his blood to be avenged."

"Avenged? How? What do you mean?"

"With the curse comes a promise. Just as someone gave their life for the bindin', someone must give their life for the breakin'. It's laid law. Life and death are in the pow'r of the blood. Ya see, one day another healer will rise to undo the evil and free Mr. Aaron from his prison. Your vision—the vision of the tree—is prophecy, child. It's a forthtellin', a foreshadow of the real Godsend."

She rolled closer, and her nicotine-laced breath lapped at Ruby. "Somethin' was invited here, hon, and it ain't never left. No need ta. Instead of takin' a stand like we oughta, people been runnin'. Hidin'. Until someone stands up, it ain't ever gonna end. Could be you're the one."

Ruby hung her head and squeezed her eyes shut. Her normal, mundane life had been swept away by a supernatural tidal wave. *Gods. Black angels. Pagan sacrifices.* She was so far out of her league she could no longer see the playing field. The implications forced her into a stupefied silence.

Finally Ruby said, "What can I do, Miss Elston? Really. I hate to admit it, but I can barely stay afloat as is. Where do I even start?"

"You already started by comin' here."

Ruby ran her fingers through her hair. "What'd you mean that someone has to give up their life?"

Aida leaned back and grew still. Her labored breaths charged the silence, and she stared at Ruby.

"It's in God's hands, child. Just do what He puts before ya. The rest's up to Him. And don't be so glum. Your little bit of faith has got you into a world of hurt—probably more'n you realize. But the burden ain't yours alone, so don't try carryin' it. There's more folks 'n you realize that have a stake in this. And take heart; the stone tree may yet sprout."

Ruby sat without moving, measuring the gaunt, white-haired mystic. "I have a lot to think about, Miss Elston. Thank you for your time and the information. It was really..."

"Illuminatin'?"

"Yeah." Ruby grinned. "It was illuminatin'. Thank you." She leaned across and hugged Aida, who chuckled and wrapped her frail arms around Ruby's shoulders. In spite of the dreadful smell of nicotine, it was as close to a motherly embrace as she'd had in years.

Ruby rose and walked to the door as Aida wheeled behind her.

"And Ruby," Aida said, "keep an eye on that minister of yours. He's up to somethin'."

Ruby turned. "Reverend Clark?"

"Yes," Aida drawled. "Reverend Clark. He's got a part in all this, and I ain't sure whose side he's on."

"It's funny you say that. I'm meeting with him tomorrow morning, and I've had suspicions myself." Ruby shrugged. "Anyway, thank you again, Miss Elston."

In the kitchen, Marty was talking about the boring patterns of pine beetles while Jack sniffled in response. Aida leaned into the hallway and called after her. "Maybe next time I can meet that boyfriend of yours." The old woman laughed, and Ruby cringed when the hacking started.

Chapter 20

E HUNCHED OVER HIS DESK AND STUDIED KEEN'S BOOK. Clark adjusted his glasses and stared at the wall of skulls pictured there. The image haunted him last night, as did Beeko's discourse about spiritual mapping. What did it all mean? And was it somehow connected to the recent incidents in Stonetree? The logical part of him dismissed the concepts as superstitious hogwash, but try as he might, he could not shake the personal implications of it all.

A knock sounded at his office door and jolted him back to earth. He shut the book and carried it to the far end of the book-shelves. "C'mon in," he said, laying the book on the edge where it had been.

Vinyette stepped in, holding a pad of paper and a pencil. "You've got a full slate again, Reverend."

Yesterday he'd spent the entire day listening to people's concerns and deflecting criticism. He was getting sick of meetings—and even sicker of trying to tow the board's line. It was Wednesday morning, and the controversy was not going away.

"You ready?" Vinyette asked.

"Go ahead," he sighed, moping back to his desk.

"First appointment, ten o'clock, is Ruby. And that's in fifteen minutes."

He nodded but fought to conceal his unease. Did Ruby have any idea about the potential scope of this thing?

"After lunch," Vinyette read, "Mr. Barkham will be here."

"Regarding?"

"Didn't say. He left a message on the phone last night."

A surprise visit from the chairman of the elder board did not bode well. If Clark survived the meeting with Ruby, he had Coy

Barkham to look forward to. This was getting more disturbing by the second.

"At two, Mrs. Hertz."

He grimaced. Things were going from bad to worse. Evelyn Hertz couldn't get along with anyone. Especially her own husband. Clark should tell her the truth for once and stop beating around the bush. Of course, the Hertzes were some of the biggest financial givers in Canyon Springs, and that wouldn't sit well with the board. Vinyette watched him wrestling inside, and he cursed his transparency.

"Go ahead," he said. "I'm sorry."

"At three, Willis wants to run Sunday's song selection by you." She looked up. "And he said he's got something else important he wants to speak to you about."

"Another fire to put out? When will it end?" He let loose an exasperated sigh.

Vinyette winced at his words and looked back down at the paper in her hand.

Shame flecked his conscience, and he felt an embarrassed flush wash over him. Here she was, elated about the miraculous goings-on, and he couldn't even muster a shred of optimism. All he could do was bring her down.

"Time out, Vin. Listen. I'm sorry...I'm sorry for the way I've been acting lately. My attitude's been rotten. I–I've been on edge. I guess we all have."

She glanced up from the paper with a look of surprise.

"I was curt with you the other day at the board meeting," he continued. "I apologize. This is new to me. I mean, I've never had a member raise somebody from the dead. It's not the kinda thing they prepare you for in seminary, ya know?"

She swept the hair out of her face, and a smile creased her lips.

Maybe he should have apologized a long time ago—confessed his pessimism and relentless introspection. He'd smothered the poor thing...just like he had Cynthia.

"I'm just trying to get a handle on all this, like everybody else, I guess. Forgive me?"

"You know I do. And I understand. What with all the hubbub, I couldn't imagine. You must be under tons of pressure. But I just know everything will work out."

The door in the front office opened. Vinyette stepped back to see who'd entered. She smiled at someone and looked back at her notepad. "And don't forget, tonight you have another meeting. Did you say with a professor?"

"Oh. Yeah...thanks."

Vinyette walked into the front office. He'd forgotten about the invitation to Keen's group and had purposely avoided details with the secretary. The spark of faith kindled by her words evaporated. The two opposing forces tore at him. On one side, the simple faith of Vinyette and Ruby, their willingness to forgo answers and cling resolutely to their beliefs, haunted him. On the other, Benjamin Keen's stolid intellectualism and enlightened mysticism beckoned. The professor was onto something; Clark couldn't deny it. So many religions and faiths—they shared so many commonalities. But did that make them all right? At some point, despite the incongruities or lack of evidence, one must concede belief. But where that point was, and what was required of him, was becoming increasingly unclear. In that middle ground Clark twisted like a spiritual invertebrate.

Muffled conversation rose in the front office as Clark paced the room, wrestling with his melancholy.

Vinyette poked her head into the room. "Reverend? It's Ruby."

He stopped and nodded.

Ruby walked in and stood with her hands clasped at her waist. She wore jeans and a long-sleeve button-up shirt with fine embroidered neckline and cuffs. Her hair was pulled back to one side with a rose-colored barrette. Vinyette whispered something to her and turned to Clark.

"I've gotta run up front, Reverend, dig up something in the storage room. If anybody calls, just let the answering machine get it. I'll only be ten minutes or so."

"Gotcha. Thanks, Vin."

Vinyette winked at Ruby and left the room, pulling the door

halfway shut. The door in the front office closed, and Ruby turned to him.

Clark cupped his fist over his mouth and cleared his throat. "I'm sorry we couldn't have met sooner. I've been really swamped."

"Me too. I mean, I'm sorry we couldn't meet sooner."

Dark pockets framed her eyes, and he sensed great fatigue in her words.

A moment of uncomfortable silence passed. Where did he want this conversation to go? Should he tell her about Beeko, about the mythological obsidian god? Maybe he should come clean about his own doubts and disbelief. But what good would that do, other than dig him into a deeper hole?

He cleared his throat again. "So, did you walk here?"

"Yeah."

"Looks like it's starting to cloud up, huh?"

She nodded. "They say we might get some rain in a day or two."

"Really? Yesterday was beautiful."

"Oh, yeah."

Clark tapped the desktop. "I'm sorry. Here, sit down." He motioned to one of the leather chairs near his desk. She walked to it—her limp was noticeably worse—and sat down. "Would you like something to drink? We have some coffee or—"

"No, I'm fine, Reverend. Thanks."

He rearranged items on his desk.

"You know," he said, "I talked to the police on Monday."

She looked surprised.

"No." He waved her off. "No, nothing's wrong. I just wanted to go over the details with them. You know, get some more info. Not that I don't trust you or the other witnesses."

"Well, there were plenty of other witnesses."

She sounded defensive. This was already heading in the wrong direction.

"Yeah, I talked to some of them. Look, folks are pretty shaken up, Ruby. They're confused by all this. It's not every day that someone is...that something like this happens."

She looked away and tapped her foot on the carpet.

"And about yesterday, I'm sorry for the inquisition. Board meetings can get a little rough, and you happened to walk in on a rough one."

She looked impatient then turned and fixed him with a steely gaze. "I'm not the devil, Reverend Clark."

"Well, I—"

"I didn't plan this, and I sure didn't ask to be chosen. I'm just a housewife, a mother. My life's pretty simple, pretty bland. I'm not a saint or a–a miracle worker."

He leaned back, clamped his jaw, and prepared for a lashing.

"I don't want to hurt anyone," she continued. "I don't want to start some big controversy or divide the churches. And I definitely don't want to disgrace the name of Jesus. I just want to know what He wants and follow it through." She looked into her lap, and her tone became less defiant. "Something's happening here. Something bigger than both of us."

She leaned back in her chair and heaved a great sigh, as if the words had sapped strength from a diminishing reserve.

Clark shifted in his seat and attempted to collect himself. He started to say something, stopped, and started again. "You've been a faithful member of this church since I arrived here, Ruby. I probably don't thank you enough for your prayers and your support. People like you. They respect you. And that makes this all the more confusing."

"Do you believe in the Stonetree curse, Reverend Clark?"

He sat, stunned, and started fidgeting with items on his desk again. "Well, I haven't given it much thought. Nowadays people—"

"I hadn't given it much thought either, until all this happened. Then yesterday I spoke to Aida Elston."

"Aida who?"

"Aida Elston. She lives in Old Town. Mr. Svenson told me about her, showed me an old newspaper with a story about her."

"Oh?"

"She was raised from the dead almost ninety years ago."

Clark adjusted his glasses and fought to contain his astonishment. He wanted to ask her to repeat the statement, but he'd heard it clearly. *The world is full of wonders*, as Keen would say. But another resurrection? Here?

"I know it sounds ridiculous. But something evil—a spirit of some sort—is at work in this city. Some type of invisible war is going on, and we're involved."

He glanced at Keen's book on the shelf, fighting the urge to haul it down and join her investigation. But she didn't give him a chance.

"It's here for a reason." Ruby peered at him with an innocence that made his heart quell. "Evil things don't stay around unless they're wanted. Or invited."

"Ruby, that's a big subject."

"Well, yeah."

"I mean, *evil spirits?*" He tried not to sound sarcastic.

"But if people don't know they're there, don't believe in them, how do you ever get rid of them?"

He shook his head. "It's too cut and dried. An invisible war? Listen to what you're saying." He leaned back in his chair. "Where're you going with this, Ruby? And what does it have to do with Aida Elston, the resurrection, and everything else that's been going on?"

"Can't you see? The devil's here, in this city! It goes way back. The graveyard and the Sailor's Oak. The missing college girls, the bars and shops downtown. Those silly stories about the Highway to Hell might be part of it too. There's a history around here—of bad things. This was once a place for families, real homey, traditional. But not anymore. Did you know they sell tarot cards and spell books at those shops downtown?"

"Oh, I'm sure they do."

"Those places are gateways to darker things."

"So are lots of places. Does that mean there's a devil in the city?"

"No. But it could mean the churches are too indifferent to care."

His jaw dropped slightly. Her words were like a slap in the face. He gathered himself. It was his turn to be defensive. "Every city has its warts. But to suggest it's the result of some *demon* is a stretch. I mean, what're we supposed to do, burn those stores down? This is a free country. And besides, there's a lot of different religions. If people want to experiment with magic or mysticism, that's up to them."

"Well, the least we can do is love them, tell them there's another way. Pshh! Our church can't even get along! How can we ever expect to help others?"

Clark sunk into his chair, stung by her indignation. Had she spoken to Beeko? This seemed more like a conspiracy every minute. Either way, the death gods had him bound and gagged.

"Someone's trying to get our attention," she said somberly. "To wake us up, separate the wheat from the chaff. I'm not sure how I'm involved—or you. I just know we've got to stand up and fight."

"Slow down, Ruby. Come back to earth." A sour taste suddenly filled his mouth. He coughed and tugged at his shirt collar.

Before he had a chance to continue, a faint crackling danced in the air, and a sheet of static electricity rippled through the room, making his skin bristle. A parched, rancid smell suffused the atmosphere, and his throat constricted. He wheezed and grew rigid.

Ruby seemed to sense it too. She ran her hands up and down her arms then grew rigid and stared toward the bookcase with her mouth gaping.

Ian Clark turned just enough to see Mr. Cellophane hovering in the corner.

Chapter 21

OISTURE POOLED IN CLARK'S EYES AS HE STARED forward, refusing to acknowledge the apparition. The air tingled, energized by the ghostly presence. Ruby gawked in stunned silence.

He had to give her credit. The first time he saw Mr. Cellophane, he about jumped out of his shoes. He had bolted from the chair spouting Bible verses, commanding the spirit to flee. But not Ruby. She sat peering—first at the specter, then at Reverend Clark—back and forth, as though both were anomalies.

"You've seen it before, haven't you?" she whispered, wheezing and blinking back tears.

"Ever since I started here." It sounded like a terrible confession.

"What does it want?"

He remained focused on her, refusing to look at the phantom. "Want? I don't know. It's just a lost soul, a spiritual echo or something. I usually just ignore it, and it goes away." He pushed himself away from the desk. "Maybe we should leave."

"Does Vinyette know about it?"

"No. At least, I don't think so." He didn't bother trying to hide his annoyance. "Look, let's talk about this somewhere else." He rose from his chair.

"Reverend!" Ruby glared at him, forcing him back into seat. "There's a demon in your office, and you want to leave? What's going on?"

Clark tugged at the collar of his sweater and wiped his eyes. He was cornered again. His little secret was finally out of the closet. He turned to the writhing form at the end of the bookshelves.

Mr. Cellophane floated in the corner, its gauzy outline undulating in midair. Beneath the opaque shell, colorless organs and sinews throbbed. The figure rose until its head touched the ceiling. The familiar high, flat cheekbones inset with large, sad eyes turned down at him, brooding.

"It's not a demon...at least, I don't think it is."

"Well, it ain't an angel."

"I don't know for sure. I tried confronting it at first, but nothing happened. Demons aren't neutral. They'll counter a challenge. This is something different. It's here for a reason; I just don't know why."

Ruby squinted at him. "You know more than you're letting on."

"Let's just say I've drifted from my roots."

"Have you tried...communicating with it?"

"Talk to it?" Clark glanced at the apparition. "That hasn't crossed my mind."

"Well then, let's try."

Ruby stood, and as she did, Mr. Cellophane spun toward her. Its body had become a hazy broiling mass, not much more than a cloud. The globular bundle swirled, and its eyes fixed on the approaching woman.

Clark leaped from his seat, toppling the pencil holder, spilling pens across the desktop. This woman was mad! "Ruby! Wait!"

But she ignored him and hobbled toward the phantom.

So this was the type of person who raised the dead—someone bold and reckless and defiant. Someone with faith. He should have done this a year ago, stood his ground and refused to tolerate the spectral visitations. Instead he surrendered to the haunting. Now he stood paralyzed, impotent to act, and watched as this crippled homemaker slowly approached the gauzy figure. *Clark, you're a wuss!*

With her head tilted back, she drew her hands into fists. "Who are you?" Her voice cracked as she spoke. "Why are you here?"

The spirit towered over her, looking even more immense and inhuman. Its crystalline skull rested on the ceiling and stared down upon her, apparently unmoved by the questions.

"In the name of Jesus," she commanded, "tell us who you are."

The spirit did not respond.

As if things couldn't get any worse, a soft thud sounded in the front office, and he knew it was Vinyette. Clark glanced at his door, which stood propped half open. She would hear the ruckus and come bursting in any second. How could he have let it come this far? And how would he ever explain it?

Yet this was way beyond explaining.

Ruby took a step closer, her chin set resolutely to the monster, and stood four, maybe five feet away. The murky sheet fluttered before her, as if she sent forth invisible waves. Goose bumps covered his arms. His breath caught in his throat. Clark swayed, wanting to whisk her away from this evil.

But Ruby didn't need rescuing.

She clenched her fists and shouted. "Why are you here? And what do you want?"

With that, a long, slender appendage rose from the foggy mass. At first he thought it a root or tree limb. It took the shape of an arm—a gaunt pale appendage webbed with gray veins—and sprouted a claw, then a hand, then a single finger. With that finger, Mr. Cellophane turned and pointed at Ian Clark.

Ruby, her face deathly pale, stared at Clark.

As his mouth opened and then closed, he reached for his desk and backed up.

Three knocks—more like rapid punches to his brain—sounded on the door, and it drifted open. "Is everything all right?" Vinyette stood just outside the office.

The ghost lowered its head and descended upon Ruby like a heavy mist. She grew limp, her chin dropped to her chest, and she swayed as if buoyed by the swirling mass. The tendons, eyes, and organs become a fleshy fog, with Ruby cocooned in its center.

Vinyette remained just outside the door. "Reverend? Is everything all right?"

Clark glanced at the door and fumbled for the desk to keep from keeling over. As Vinyette opened the door, the spirit vanished, taking the parched static with it.

Ruby crumbled to the carpet near the bookcase.

Vinyette walked in and stopped in her tracks. "What's going

on? Is everything—" She sniffed the air and curdled her nose. Then she spotted Ruby and scrambled across the room, pushing the chair out of her path. "What happened?" She knelt, cradled Ruby's head in her arms, and glanced at Clark.

"She passed out. I dunno." One more lie wouldn't matter. Clark's world was full of them now. He scanned the room to make sure the spirit had left and struggled to keep his heart from pounding out of his throat. "She got up and passed out." He shrugged.

Vinyette felt Ruby's forehead. "She's cold."

Ruby mumbled something, twisted her body, and sat up. "I'm– I'm OK, Vin. Don't." She brushed Vinyette's hand aside. "I'm just...tired." She looked at Clark, pursed her lips, and looked away. "I think I blacked out for a second."

"She hasn't been feeling well," Vinyette said to no one in particular. "Don't get up too fast. Here, let me get you some water."

As Vinyette rushed out of the room, Clark went to Ruby, took her elbow, and helped her up. She grasped his shoulder and stood. Her grip was strong, but an airy, delicate fragrance bathed her skin and disarmed any notion of toughness or masculinity. She let go of his shoulder and took his hand. Was this the healing hand? The same hand used to summon the dead? Maybe it would work on him.

He led her to the chair, and she plopped into it, sweeping the hair away from her face, looking foggy.

Clark took two steps back. What could he say after that? Things were unraveling quickly. Maybe he could impose a vow of silence, keep the incident between the two of them. After all, he wouldn't want Vinyette finding out. But why draw Ruby into his lies? Besides, he'd already been exposed as a fraud. No use dragging this thing out. He might as well just take his licking and slither out of town.

Vinyette hurried in with a paper cup and knelt beside Ruby's chair. "You've got the flu or somethin'. Did you go to the doctor like I told you?" She felt Ruby's forehead again.

Ruby took the cup. "I'm all right, Vin. Please."

Clark wandered back around his desk, glancing at the corner. Mr. Cellophane was gone, but the damage was done.

Ruby sipped the water. "I've been…stressed. Haven't slept. And with everyone comin' over and asking questions…" She glanced at Clark again. "I didn't mean to cause such a problem."

"Don't be silly." Vinyette squeezed Ruby's hand. "You ain't a problem." She turned back to Reverend Clark. "I'll bring my truck around."

"I'm all right. Really. I can walk."

"Sit your butt down! Be back in a sec." Vinyette rushed out with her car keys jangling, and the door in the front office closed.

"Ruby, I'm sorry," Clark said. His apologies were becoming routine.

"Reverend." She leaned over and set the cup down. "It's a boy, a young man." She glanced in the corner and quavered. "He was murdered. And somehow, you're part of it."

Clark swayed and gripped the desk. *Murder?* He might be dishonest, unbelieving, but he was not a murderer. He dropped into his chair.

She looked at him, but without condescension or rebuke. "Before this is over," she said, "someone else is gonna die."

Chapter 22

He PARKED IN THE EAST LOT, TURNED OFF THE JEEP'S ignition, and sat wringing the steering wheel. The resignation letter in his desk drawer and the years of festering grief suddenly paled. It was time for Clark to do some investigating of his own.

He climbed out of the vehicle and scanned the town square. Civic buildings clustered to one side, interspersed with trees and park benches, while across the street the marketplace emerged from its morning slumber. Downtown Stonetree. Not-so-Grand Central. Or as Beeko called it, a dead zone.

Clark glanced at the overcast sky, rubbed his jaw, and winced. Ten minutes grinding his teeth, and his mouth felt like a rusty bear trap. At this point, he didn't care what Ruby told Vinyette. He'd been implicated for a murder he knew nothing about. In front of a member of his congregation. By a ghost, no less! Trying to distance himself from the supernatural was becoming a losing battle.

He gazed across the asphalt parking lot, past the complex, to the main intersection. Pedestrians strolled through the crosswalk at Rivermeer and Sun as automobiles idled. The sidewalk cafés had a sprinkling of lunch guests, and the easels were up in the arts colony. He spotted The Purple Maze and SpellWind near the Green Man Pub and eyed them. Nothing unusual about the shops. At least from his perspective. Still, Ruby's words rang in his ears. *Those places are gateways to darker things.* He put his cell phone in the pocket of his slacks and marched across the asphalt parking lot. As he climbed the steps to the police station, he pulled his sweater to his face and smelled it. A faint burnt residue lingered. Mr. Cellophane had been his secret for a year now. Yet one by one his ghosts were being dragged into the light. And Clark along with them.

Yet something other than shame stirred within him.

Reaching the top of the steps, he stood with his heart thumping, but not because of the climb. A surreal scenario, much bigger than he could conceive, was unfolding around him. The resurrection of the boy, the baggage of his past, and the ghastly ethereal finger aimed at him converged like a car wreck in his brain. The powers of reason and logic were useless here. Someone had a hand on Ian Clark, and this time he could not squirm free. And, in a way, he didn't want to.

He flattened his palm across his chest, willing his heart to slow. Then he glanced to the heavens again—and stepped into the Stonetree police station.

The glass door grated shut behind him. A man in a tan leather jacket leaned on the counter facing the opposite direction. Clark approached, his footsteps echoing off the marble floor, and the man turned. Wraparound sunglasses perched atop the stranger's bleached, spiky hair, and a hollow black plug, the size of a cork, punctured one ear. The guy was either a rock star or doing a terrible impression of one. He tipped his head to Clark, who then did a double take. Mr. Hollywood had bright blue eyes, and he winked one at Clark.

Gayle Jay poked her head from behind the man. "Well, well. I figured you'd be back."

Clark saluted her and flashed a nervous grin, feeling strangely unsettled by the stranger's icy wink.

She slipped Mr. Hollywood a business card with something sketched on the back. He thanked her and sped across the lobby, staring at Clark on his way out. The door ground shut.

"And who was that?"

"That was Mister Mace Wilflee," the officer announced, showing her glorious smile. "With *Rippington Weekly*."

"So the wheels are turning."

"You betcha. We're a hotspot. It's official." She stamped the desk with her palm. "So, what brings you out again, Reverend? Someone else climb out of their coffin? Or maybe you need some info 'bout the end of the world."

"Not today."

"Well, that's what Mr. Wilflee's here for." She leaned forward, looked side to side, and lowered her voice in mock secrecy. "That thing at Goldman's is connected to something catastrophic…or catalytic. Something like that. At least according to Wilflee."

"Is that so?"

She nodded. "I guess Jack Case ran him off. Now the guy's snooping around town looking for some kind of story. He's convinced something unnatural is up. And, by golly, he's gonna get the scoop. So I helped him along, gave him just enough leads to keep him chasing his tail. But if you've got questions about zombies, Wilflee's your man."

"Um, no questions about zombies." Clark rested his elbows on the countertop. "But I do have a few other questions for you."

Footsteps thumped down the hall. Chief Gramer emerged, his massive frame filled the doorway, and he scowled at Clark.

"The last thing we need is another religious war, Mr. Clark," he grumbled. Gramer never called him *Reverend*. The chief marched to the front desk, handed some papers to Officer Jay, and then glared at Clark, his thick, black eyebrows furrowed. "And I'd suggest you people keep things down." Gramer harrumphed and stormed back down the hall, his boots thumping out indignation.

Clark and Officer Jay exchanged surprised looks.

"What's that supposed to mean?" Clark asked.

"The man is never happy. Now he's getting it from all sides. The incident at the funeral home has stirred up a hornets' nest, and Gramer ain't used to being on the hot seat." She swiveled back, clasping her hands behind her head. "So, what kinda questions you got? I'm all ears."

"After that I'm not sure I want to ask."

"Pfhh." She brushed her hand in the chief's direction. "Go for it."

"Well, I've got some questions about—this is embarrassing—about the Stonetree curse."

She raised an eyebrow, and a mischievous smile creased her

lips. "Now it's getting interesting. Pull up a chair, Reverend. This is a long, dark tale."

"I don't have a lot of time. Can you give me the abbreviated version?"

"OK. Thumbnail. Stonetree made a pact with the devil." Then she leaned back and twiddled her thumbs in her lap.

"No kidding."

"Well, it's something like that. It goes back to the early twenties, to Bridge River. Some fella hung himself on the Sailor's Oak in exchange for the fever."

"Now I've heard about that. I mean the fever."

"Yeah, it took a lotta lives. Though some folks dispute the suicide; they say the guy was murdered. Anyway, after that, the fever stopped. Supposedly it was a pact with the devil, some kind of agreement. That's where the Watcher's Woods got its start and all that hokum about ghouls in the graveyard."

"The Watcher's Woods?"

"That's what they call East Basin, you know, the forest outside Old Town. Near the mines. Rumor has it something lives out there. Somethin' inhuman. They've found altars, you know, pagan type stuff—bones, jewelry, flowers, candles, rock rings. Every month or so, without fail, someone calls to report an incident. Strangers creeping around in the woods or loud noises. Once in a while, dead animals. Ritualistic stuff."

"Serious?"

"Oh yeah. It's getting so none of the guys want to go out there anymore. Just last week a couple of officers were called up. Someone reported a ruckus near South Wall, and they found evidence of a bonfire and occult items. The usual things."

"Beeko told me there'd been some reports, but I had no idea..."

"It doesn't make the headlines, but it's been going on forever. It's all part of the legend. And then you have White Creek Chapel."

He massaged his chin with his fingertips and squinted. "I've heard something about it. It's around here?"

"Well, it was. Till it burned to the ground. See, I told you this is juicy. Sure you don't wanna sit down?"

"I've got a meeting at one."

"Right. Well, White Creek is part of the curse too. That's what they say, anyway. It used to be the main church in Stonetree, old-fashioned, folksy-type chapel—I saw pictures once. Right in the middle of downtown." She pointed in the direction of the city square, but the cloudy plate glass on the door afforded little view. "That was back in fifty-something. Late fifties. Then one night it caught fire. They never determined the cause. Nobody was hurt, but the church never recovered. The building was razed, they put up a plaque or something, and that was that."

"So what makes it part of the curse?"

"The going theory is that the church was trying to fight it— you know, trying to break the spell—but they ran into something bigger than they could handle. I guess that's why most folks around here don't like to discuss the subject. Wouldn't want to rile up any werewolves or vampires."

"Right." He hoped the sarcasm would hide his growing unease. *Something bigger than they could handle.* Like an ancient death god maybe? If that's what happened to those who meddled with the curse, he'd better think twice about his Ghostbusters shtick.

"If you really wanna know more…"

"Uh, sure."

"…you might try the library while you're here. Check the city records. They have a lotta stuff filed and on microfiche. Course, that's about all they have."

Footsteps thumped down the hall, Gramer turned the corner with some papers in his hand and glared at Clark again.

"Thanks for the help, Gayle. I appreciate it." Clark spun and left with Gramer staring holes into his back.

Chapter 23

Gayle's all-too-eager info dump left Clark feeling more shaken than empowered. He descended the steps of the police station and peered across the concrete colonnade to the town square. Hard to believe that such a laid-back community could harbor such dark secrets. Even harder to believe, he'd lived here a whole year and never suspected a blessed thing.

Along with the police station, the civic complex consisted of a courthouse, city hall, and library. Immense, staggered magnolias populated the interconnected walkways, leaving white saucer flowers scattered like overturned boats along the concrete plain. Clark maneuvered his way through the trees and park benches to the Stonetree Library.

It was a single-story, octagonal-shaped building that, like the rest, appeared sorely in need of modernization. Tall cypress lined the entrance, and on each side, two window-sized marquees announced reading events and playhouse presentations. From last Christmas.

Warm, stale air accosted him as he entered, and several guests glanced his way. He would burn up in this crypt. Clark approached the counter and stood, airing out the neckline of his sweater, waiting for acknowledgment. A bearded man wearing a black velvet Jewish kippa thumbed through index cards and glanced at the anorexic girl on the other side. "How can I help you?" she asked.

Heavy blush accented her gaunt cheekbones, and Clark fought to keep from staring. "Um, I'm kinda new to the area and doing some research on the city. Can you direct me to your historical records?"

As if on cue, they looked at each other, then back at Clark. The man returned to his index cards as the girl stalked from behind the counter with long strides. She padded along the blue carpet toward a computer bank at the far end of the building.

"Anything in particular?"

"Yeah." He struggled to keep up with her swift, robotic pace. "Something on White Creek Chapel and the fire."

"That's not exactly one of our historical highlights." She glanced over her shoulder and flashed a smile, which stretched the skin so taut over her cheekbones she appeared skeletal. She chugged forward with her head swiveling side to side like an overgrown praying mantis on the hunt. "We keep those records downstairs."

They passed the computers—oversized monoliths from another era—and came to a double-wide passageway. Without hesitation she descended, clicking her heels like a ball-peen hammer on the cement steps. But Clark hesitated. The dim passage disappeared in a cellar far below. What more secrets did the city hold?

He entered the stairwell, craning to see the layout below. Cool air rushed up the dungeon, bringing refreshment along with mystery. He continued down the steps and stopped at the bottom. A vast, low ceiling stretched over an empty chamber. Except for a ring of large wooden cabinets in the center and crates and discarded office furniture around the periphery, the room was empty. His footsteps echoed off the polished cement floor as he approached mantis woman, who stood waiting at the wooden cabinets.

"That'll be archived in this section." She waved her hand like a game show hostess. "You'll find entries back to the early teens. Clippings, documents. Just look for the year you want. White Creek Chapel fire was in fifty-six, I believe. Maybe fifty-eight. We've been trying to get these records scanned and stored in an online database, but, as usual, the city is trying to stay one step behind the twenty-first century. The historical society prefers to keep this info…underground." She flashed an emaciated smile again. "Anyway, if you have any more questions, my name is Tam, and I'll be at the desk."

She blinked her large lids and, without waiting for his reply, whisked back across the vacant stretch of floors and clicked up the stairs. Maybe she was in training for land speed librarian of the year award. If so, she had his vote.

"Thank you, Tam," he said to the space she'd vacated. Then he went to work locating the file labeled 1956.

The cabinets consisted of flat rollout trays, each one baring a typed insert on its face. *Early James' photos, Loggers Mill 2, Coastal Trail Loop, East Wall C Shaft, Silver!*

Up and down the Stonehenge-like cabinet ring he went, scanning the labels, until he spotted the one titled *White Creek Chapel, 1942–58.* He slid the deep tray out, and the sound was swallowed by the cellar. The dusty chill of the place had him biting back shivers. *So much for burning up in here.*

A jumbled compilation of photos, newsprint, and clippings was scattered in the drawer. He sifted the material until spotting a drab laminated newspaper with a picture of a half-burned building. Charred beams tilted against a crumbled plaster façade, and several clusters of people stood on each side, surveying the remains.

The caption read, "Historic landmark destroyed. Mystery fire is to blame."

Clark angled the laminate sheet away from the glare of the overhead fluorescent. *Stonetree Sentinel*, April 3, 1958, and the White Creek Chapel fire made the front page headline.

Nearly seventeen years after Cecil Byrd erected White Creek Chapel, it lies in smoldering ruin. Byrd, longtime resident of Stonetree, founded and led the church since its inception in 1942. During that time, the small congregation has endured endless legal battles and internal strife, only to see the historic structure demolished by fire the night of April 2—an ignominious, some would say fitting, end to its troubled past.

Members were quick to state the church's intention to rebuild, but with legal expenditures mounting, the chapel faces a long, arduous road.

Long the center of property disputes with local artisans and entrepreneur and developer Cade Barkham, Byrd has repeatedly fought to retain what the church considers rightful ownership of the prime business parcel.

Clark adjusted his glasses and reread the name. *Cade Barkham.* Everyone knew the Barkhams' roots sank deep into the city. In fact, Coy went to great lengths to jog the board's memory—or rub it in, as the case may be. Most likely Coy Barkham was related to this man, a note that struck discord in Clark's spirit.

He continued reading:

> No doubt the mysterious nature of the fire will only add to the controversy. While authorities have yet to determine the cause of the blaze, some were quick to call it an act of arson...or something even more insidious. What's certain is that the White Creek Chapel fire is sure to become a lasting controversy amidst already heated combatants.

Clark's upcoming meeting with Coy Barkham invoked unease. He shook off the disquiet and leafed through several more documents and old photos, most relating to the development of the downtown area. Seemed '58 was a boon for developers, with the demo of the church leading the way. As Clark prepared to close the drawer, a picture of a stout gentleman shaking hands with a man in a suit caught his eye.

> Cade Barkham acquires long sought-after property. Church is razed amidst promise of downtown redevelopment project.

Square jaw, Neanderthal forehead, and muscular build—this had to be a relative of Coy Barkham. Behind them, the corner of Rivermeer and Sun was filled with scaffolding, hardhats, and possibility. Exactly how much of downtown Stonetree did the Barkhams own? And what kind of help did they get along the way?

Clark stiffened as another chill raced up the back of his neck. His investigation had taken an unexpected turn. Perhaps he should worry about his own dirty laundry, concentrate on evicting Mr. Cellophane and resolving his own existential plight, and leave the PI gig to someone more qualified. But sticking his head in the sand hadn't solved anything.

Muffled classical music rose somewhere nearby. He turned, trying to spot the source, before he realized it was his cell phone. He dug in his pants pocket and answered it.

"Reverend," Vinyette said, before the signal became garbled.

"Hold on, let me—" He jogged across the shiny cement, footsteps slapping off the walls as he made his way to the stairwell. "Vin?" He scampered up the stairway into the library and was socked by the stuffy air.

"Are you there?" he said, his palm cupping the phone.

"Yeah. Hello?"

"Go ahead."

"Reverend, Mr. Barkham's here. He's been waiting."

"He's early."

"Not by much. You'd better hurry."

"I'm on my way," he whispered, thinking about the open drawer down below.

"Someone else called."

"Oh?"

"A woman named Cynthia."

He froze and the air left his lungs.

"She said she's your ex-wife."

Chapter 24

ROM RIVERMEER, CLARK COULD SEE THE CHURCH'S BELL tower rising above the trees. It disappeared from view as he tore up the driveway in his Jeep. He passed Barkham's car in the lot and groaned. No doubt the elder was waiting impatiently. Of all days to come early, Barkham had to pick this one. During the frenzied trip from the library, Clark resumed his teeth grinding. Any personal momentum he'd gained during his brief investigation had fizzled on the way.

He parked, climbed out, and wiped his palms on his slacks. Word of Cynthia's call had him reeling. It'd been two years since they last spoke—and that just to finalize divorce papers. What could she want? And why was she calling now? Either way he'd have some explaining to do.

He entered the offices and found Vinyette leaning over her desk writing something. She straightened, marched over, and, without making eye contact, handed him a sticky note with a phone number on it. "Mr. Barkham's waiting."

Clark stared at the paper as Vinyette returned to her desk. She plopped into her seat and inspected her fingernails. "Not to be nosey, but shouldn't the congregation have been told about this?"

He brought his hand down. "Listen, I'm sorry. I can imagine how this looks. It was the board's decision, more or less. I objected at first, but they insisted. They said God was forgiving, you know; there was no need to dig up the past. I was free to discuss it when asked, it's just...no one did."

She crossed her arms, stared across the room, and crimped her lips.

"Look, Vin, I never intended to hide it, though I guess it could look like that."

"You're right—it does." The tension in her face eased, and she made eye contact. "It just seems like something you'd want to be up front about. People trust you. Now to hear this..."

"I understand, believe me. The board seemed like they were in a hurry to hire someone. I was still smarting from the whole thing—the divorce, I mean—so I didn't really protest. It was a poor choice on our part."

She nodded, and he went back to staring at the note in his hand.

"Did she happen to say what she wanted?"

"No, but she sounded nervous. Or worried." She uncrossed her arms and stared at him. "Are you all right? You look pale."

"I'll be fine. It's just we hadn't talked in a while. It kinda caught me off guard."

"Well, she sounds like a sweet lady."

He didn't have time for a rebuttal, so he shrugged. "Maybe someday we can talk about it, Vin."

"I understand."

He started toward his office and then stopped. "What about Ruby? Have you... how is she?" He studied Vinyette's movements looking for clues.

"I don't know." Her eyes narrowed. "She hasn't been herself lately, that's for sure. With everything going on, I guess I shouldn't expect her to be. But..." She shrugged and then motioned toward his office. "Mr. Barkham's waiting."

Clark placed the slip of paper in his pants pocket. "Wish me luck," he said under his breath.

As he trudged to his office, his thoughts became a mental thicket. Barkham knew how to mount an offensive, keep his detractors on their heels. No doubt he'd scheduled this impromptu meeting with that in mind. Clark's compliance had established a pattern, which Barkham would surely exploit. But after his research at the library, Clark had some ammunition of his own.

Coy Barkham stood at the bookshelves examining the curios and turned as Clark entered the room. "This is quite a collection you've got."

"Different, isn't it?"

"Yes. And every time I see it, it's a little bigger."

"You can blame Professor Keen for that."

"Professor..."

"Keen. Benjamin Keen. He's a friend, an anthropologist. Lectures at the university. Always bringing something unusual back from his trips. Pendants, pottery, incense, it's all there."

"That must be where you get all the funny jewelry."

"Yeah." Clark pulled back the arm of his sweater to reveal a black leather bracelet. "Kinda reminds me of college—my hippie, bohemian phase."

"Something I'm glad you grew out of."

Clark brushed the jab aside, closed the door, and walked around his desk. "Have a seat?" He motioned to one of the guest chairs across from him.

"This won't take long," Barkham said. "I've got to be back up in Oakland this evening."

As Clark sat, he glanced at the spot Barkham vacated near the corner. Two times in one week was a record for Mr. Cellophane. Clark cringed at the thought of Ruby encased in the swirling bag of bones and returned his gaze to the church elder.

Barkham wore dress slacks and shirt and swaggered to the chair where he sat down and gazed at Clark. The square jaw, broad shoulders, granite dome. This was the man in the photo at the library. With the wrecking ball behind him.

"I hear you met with Ruby today."

So the chairman had done some snooping of his own. Had he spoken to Vinyette? Or Ruby? If so, what did he know about the last two days? Clark rearranged the pens in his pencil holder, hoping to appear unnerved. "Yeah, we've been trying to coordinate our schedules. We just wanted to talk about what's been going on."

"Quite a bit going on, that's for sure."

"You know, Coy"—Clark removed his glasses and set them on the desk—"Ruby's been under a lot of pressure."

"I can imagine."

"And I don't think our handling of the situation has helped matters."

Barkham folded his hands on his lap. "Frankly, I'm more concerned for the church as a whole. Besides, I thought we already discussed this."

"Well, if you could call it a discussion..."

He studied Clark with unflinching eyes. "So I take it you're having reservations?"

"About everything."

"Then my hunches were right. Millquint and Easton both expressed concerns to me privately. We feared you weren't on board with this, that you may do something rash. Look, the last thing we need is the senior minister of Canyon Springs speaking to reporters, claiming some miraculous power is at work and that some woman in his church is a healer."

Clark shook his head and stared at the desktop. "I'm just looking for the truth, Coy. Something I've been avoiding since I got here."

"The truth? If you're referring to the incident at Goldman's..."

"I'm referring to the resurrection."

A moment of silence passed. Barkham's hands remained folded on his lap while Clark fought to keep from fidgeting. The game of chicken had begun.

After a long, appraising stare, Barkham said, "Is that what that was? A resurrection? I thought we agreed not to use that label—at least until we get more credible evidence to the contrary."

"I'm not sure what more credible evidence we need. But whatever you want to call it—resurrection, resuscitation, magic act—it's opened up a can of worms."

"Really? Is there something else that I—that the board—needs to know?"

Clark put his glasses back on and glanced at the corner. Where was Mr. Cellophane when he needed him? Perhaps the creature could make another grand entrance and scare the wits out of the chairman of the board.

"Coy, when I was hired, a lot of things got swept under the

rug. Well, right now, that rug's coming out from under me. My ex-wife called here today."

Barkham raised an eyebrow.

"Vinyette knows," Clark said. "We can't pretend I didn't come without some baggage."

"You were free to discuss your history with anyone you chose. Either way, it isn't terminal. We'll process everyone and move on. It's not like you're a murderer or something."

Clark gazed at Barkham. *Murder?* Maybe he did know about the ghost.

"No," Clark said, "but it's a breach of trust. For my part I just wanted to settle down. I intentionally didn't ask a lot of questions about the church and the city. But with everything going on, a lot of questions have come up."

"For instance?"

"For instance…the Stonetree curse. You never told me about the stories, the history—the hanging at the old graveyard or White Creek Chapel or the Watcher's Woods. None of that stuff."

Barkham seemed unfazed. "Every city's got its skeletons, and we didn't need to parade ours before the new minister. Most people put little stock in those fables anyway. Besides, you were in no condition to understand or care."

Clark sunk back into his seat. That much was true. At the time he couldn't have cared less about curses and haunted mines. He just needed a rest.

"Well, things have changed," Clark said. "I think someone is using this to get my—no, to get *our* attention. There's more than a few folks who think that the incident at Goldman's is part of a much bigger picture, that something's been going on a long time. Frankly, that something is being hidden."

"I'd be careful about believing everything you hear, Reverend. There's people who would love to see us falter." He raised his eyes and looked to the wall behind Clark. "Do you see that picture?"

Clark nodded without turning. The elders demanded that the enormous photo of the church, ensconced in its gaudy gilded frame, remain mounted through each successive minister.

"That picture was taken in nineteen fifty-eight. The church hasn't changed much, has it? Canyon Springs has existed peacefully here for over fifty years. We have faithful membership, a wonderful facility, strong leaders." His gaze turned frigid. "I'd be careful about looking for bogeymen and snooping around in things that don't concern you. You're being paid to perform a service, and that's the limit of your obligations. We don't need a detective."

Clark gripped the arms of the chair and yanked himself to the edge. "My obligations are to seek out the truth, and if that means being a detective, then that's what I'll be."

The chairman sat stunned, his mouth frozen in mid-speech. This wasn't Clark's usual spineless compliance, and it took Barkham a moment to recover. Then his eyes narrowed, and a thick grin crept across his face. "You're sounding more like Reverend Lawrence every day."

"I was down at the library doing some research," Clark said, ignoring the comment. "Trying to piece all this together. And I came across an article on White Creek Chapel and a picture of a man named Cade. Cade Barkham."

The chairman maintained his smug demeanor and appeared unruffled. "Like I said before, Ian, I'm third generation."

Clark settled back in his seat, his jaw clamped like a vice. So much for his offensive. He'd hoped to catch Barkham off guard. But he didn't have enough to indict him in any wrongdoing, much less some occult conspiracy. The church burned down, and one of Barkham's relatives bought the property. So what? That's what businesspeople do. Maybe Clark *had* been looking for bogeymen.

"White Creek was behind the times." Barkham crossed his legs and unbuttoned the top two buttons on his shirt. "The city was growing, and the church held some prime acreage. Of course, they wouldn't give it up. Until the fire. Then they had to."

"Some people say it was arson."

"I know what the stories say. From what I understand, that building was so old, the wiring so outdated, they were lucky the thing hadn't burned down long before and taken the whole congregation with it. After some negotiations, my father bought the property straight up."

"Cade Barkham."

"Yep. And this city's been better off for it. Downtown development took off. Business owners were brought in, Stonetree landed on the map. It was a simple case of survival of the fittest. And White Creek Chapel wasn't very fit."

"And the curse?"

"Folklore, Reverend Clark. Good old, homespun, urban legends." He rose from the chair, brushing the wrinkles out of his shirt. "It's kid stuff. I mean, c'mon, do you really think the graveyard is haunted?"

Clark's skepticism uncoiled. He must sound like a lunatic. Did he really believe an invisible puppeteer ran the city, pulling strings, manipulating details? Barkham had summoned Clark's unbelief like a snake charmer does a serpent. And the inner war began again.

"I'm not sure what I believe anymore." The rigidity left Clark's body, and his shoulders slumped. "Something's going on, Coy. And I can't be at peace until I know what it is."

Barkham approached Clark and stood looking down at him. Despite the elder's hulking frame, his tone was not hostile. "This is a critical time for our church, young man. We need your undivided attention."

Clark gnawed the inside of his lip. Then he rose and tried to match Barkham's gaze. The man seemed even bigger this close. Clark did not back down. "You're right, this is a critical time in the life of our church."

They measured each other with their eyes, neither yielding. Then Barkham tipped his head. "I must be going. If anything comes up while I'm away, feel free to phone Millquint or Easton."

Barkham extended his hand, and Clark looked at it. They were far from peace, but a temporary truce would keep the dogs off his heels. So Clark shook his hand.

Barkham left Clark's office, commenting on Vinyette's lime green leather chair as he passed. He always called it *flashback furniture,* and, as usual, she chuckled at that. Clark followed Barkham to the entrance, where the chairman opened the door and stopped.

"We're counting on you, Reverend."

Clark pursed his lips and nodded. Barkham cast a slow acute glance at him then left. With a heavy sigh, Clark slumped with his back against the door. He closed his eyes and listened to the pounding of his heart.

"Reverend? Are you—"

"Yeah. I am." He gathered himself and opened his eyes then moseyed to Vineyette's desk. "I want you to cancel the rest of my appointments."

"Huh? Now?"

"I know it's late notice, but I'm—I'm behind on Sunday's message. And I'm driving to—I mean I've got a meeting this evening and need some time alone."

"OK," she drawled.

He meandered back to his office. When he reached the doorway, he turned to her. "One more thing. Would it be possible to track down Reverend Lawrence's address for me? I think it's time I pay him a visit."

❧

He unfolded the note with Cynthia's phone number on it and checked it against the one in his phone book. Sure enough, she'd moved again. To what part of the country was anyone's guess.

To the best of his knowledge, after they separated, she'd done the same thing as he—wander. He paced the office, glancing at the strip of paper on his desk, mulling over possible conversations, before he finally picked up the cordless and called.

The phone rang once. Twice. If an answering machine picked up, he would not leave a message. Third ring, and he looked at the clock: 4:30 p.m. Even if this was an East Coast number, the hour was reasonable. Fourth ring, and he prepared to set the phone in its cradle.

"Hello?" a female voice answered, sounding tired.

"Cynthia?"

"Hello? Who is it?"

"Cynthia. It's Ian."

Electronic waves lapped at the earpiece as the person on the other end bustled about.

"Cynthia? You all right?"

"Ian. Something's wrong. I think..." She mumbled away from the phone. "I think you're in danger."

"What do you mean? Where are you?"

"I don't have time to explain. Do you have a cell?"

"Yeah. What is—?"

"Give me the number. Hurry."

More electronic waves. Either she was running a track meet or in the middle of an electric storm. He gave her the number, protested again, but she interrupted.

"I'll call you sometime tomorrow. Please, stay close."

"Wait."

"I'm sorry."

She hung up. He stood numb, then dropped the phone to his side and listened to the dial tone wailing like a distant siren.

Chapter 25

WITH HIS SLEEVE ROLLED UP TO HIS BICEP, CLARK PLUNGED his arm into the trash can. He pushed past a layer of pasta and wet coffee grinds, probing deeper into the moist, rancid clutter. Then his fingers struck something solid near the bottom. He clasped the object and slowly brought it up out of the metal receptacle, unearthing brown lettuce leaves and damp newspapers along the way.

"Ugh!" He finally exhaled and stood with a milky substance coating his forearm. It didn't matter—he had Stacie's plaque.

After jamming the lid on the can, he hurried through the back door, white slime dribbling down his arm. Laying the plaque on the countertop, he went to the sink, cranked the water on, and shoved his arm underneath the stream. He scrubbed with soap, lowered the pressure, and rinsed off the wooden plaque.

Follow your dreams.

He traced his fingertips across the curvature of the carved letters.

It seemed like so long ago. All he wanted was to help people and be a truth seeker. Instead he'd become a fount of regret and unbelief.

He swept straggling beads of water off the plaque.

He'd tossed the thing Sunday afternoon, but the pain didn't go away. Maybe it never would. His questions were no different, but he could not escape the reality. No matter how fast he ran, he could not run away. And deep down inside he didn't want to.

There was only one thing left to do.

He turned off the water and patted the plaque dry with a dish-towel. Then he carried it into the living room and hung it on the empty nail over his desk. A wet swatch stained one side. His dreams had been buried under years of debris. But like Stacie's masterpiece, they could be salvaged.

Clark stood staring at the plaque, drifting in thought. Only then did he realize how tired he had become. Five years' worth of regret and bottled-up anger gnawing away at the bones of his being had left him emotionally gutted, a ghost of his former self. The kinetic wonder that had once driven him lay shipwrecked on the shoreline of his personal failings. The Wandering Soul had meandered into a ditch.

Standing there in contemplation, Clark received no special insight, no revelation. But he didn't need one. He knew what he had to do.

Clark locked the parsonage, tossed his leather jacket into the Jeep, and prepared to climb in. He paused with his foot on the step side. Meeting with Benjamin Keen's mysterious fraternity might leave him unnerved, but forgoing it would be even more unnerving. If he balked, it would be another concession to indecision and incompetence. He had to do this for himself and Stacie.

Overcast skies blanketed the Stonetree Valley, and cool air swirled through the Jeep as he drove inland to Keen's ranch. The setting sun was hidden behind a vast umbrella of gray. The panoramic vista, once captivating, had turned to a sea of monochrome.

He passed the timber archway with the mounted antlers on his left—the first landmark. Next, the bleached wooden shack tilted near the water well, and then a small, unkempt vineyard stretched toward the purple foothills. Ahead, a handful of cars lined the dirt shoulder, and the ranch house sat overshadowed by the massive black oak.

Clark pulled to the side of the road and parked near the mailbox. Crickets chirped in concert, and night birds pealed across the plain. A chill breeze crept through the open window and with it the scent of rain.

Clark stepped out of the Jeep, put his jacket on, and eyed the ranch. Did malevolent forces hunker there? Was the professor's research an innocent quest for knowledge or an invitation to something more sinister? The seminary had downplayed the existence of spiritual powers; unseen entities that tinker with the affairs of men were little more than fodder for conspiracy theorists. Between the psychobabble and historical revisionism of his old school, Clark had come to believe, like the rest of them, that demons posed little threat for the twenty-first century. Yet the unfolding events had suggested otherwise. But who was Clark's adversary in all this? Coy Barkham? Benjamin Keen? Himself? Or was something unnamed and ancient really at work in Stonetree?

Either way, he had made his mind up—for once. He could no longer deny his misgivings about organized religion, the nagging philosophical questions that remained unanswered, and pretend to be a man of God. But neither could he deny the absurd, amoral ramblings of Benjamin Keen. There must be a middle ground without selling out to either side. But he must distance himself from Keen, give himself room to think, to dream again.

The gate stood open, as did the front door. The red lamp burned inside, tainting the entryway in its glow. Clark found the footpath, followed it under the oak, and plunged into its shadow. He reached the gnarled trunk and skidded to a stop. The canopy of twisted branches and riffling leaves, like monstrous lungs, undulated overhead. A chill rattled up his spine. *The tree spirit!* He walked briskly to the porch. Either Keen was right and something lived in that tree, or Clark was way too spooked.

Exotic music, full of sitars and cymbals, emanated from inside the house, as did the hum of voices. A musky, exotic scent mingled with the sweetness of pipe tobacco and filled the air.

Clark stepped in and glanced at the wall of masks overhead. Laughter burst from another room. He spun around and hurried down the hall toward the study.

"Good evening," a voice thundered from an adjoining room to his left.

Three men in casual dress stood holding drinks, studying him. A tall man with a handlebar mustache stepped forward. "Can we help you find someone?" He had an Irish accent and walked with a limp.

"Professor Keen. Yes. I'm here on his invitation."

The other two men glanced at Clark and whispered to each other.

"Keen's in the study," said the tall man. "Can I see you there?"

"I'll manage. Thank you." He turned on his heel and continued down the hall. Laughter burst from the room behind him again, no doubt at his expense.

What did he expect—a welcoming committee?

Clark entered the study, and Jade, the gnarly parrot, announced his arrival with a hellacious squawk that startled everyone. The men stood clustered in four or five groups amidst smoke and thick spice, staring at him.

"Mr. Clark," exclaimed Keen, opening his arms in welcome. He wore a green sarong with his unruly afro pulled up in a ponytail. Only Keen could make such absurd fashion statements and remain dignified.

The professor strode to Clark with arms outstretched. "Gentleman," he announced to the room. "I'd like to introduce to you, Mr. Ian Clark, the Wandering Soul."

The professor chuckled and embraced him, and throughout the room, drinking glasses were raised and cordial gestures ensued.

Keen stepped back as a jovial-looking man with red cheeks and a broad, pink forehead seized Clark's hand and shook it enthusiastically.

"Nice to meet ya, son. Nice to meet ya."

"Thank you, sir. I wasn't expecting such a welcome." About now he wished he could hit the rewind button and do this privately.

"Big welcome. Big." He cackled and slapped Clark's shoulder. "Heard lots about you, we have. Good to have ya on board. Good to have ya."

The man ambled back to his group, and the others there eyed Clark.

"So glad you could come, Ian." Keen stepped to his side and motioned to Mr. O, who stood like a statue near the far doorway with a towel draped over one arm. He nodded at Keen's beck, wove through the crowd, and arrived in seconds before them.

"Would you like something?" the professor asked. "Some juice, tonic, or some of O's tea?"

Clark waved him off. "I was still buzzing the next day from Mr. O's tea."

They laughed, except Mr. O, who retained his normal stony glaze.

"Thank you," Clark said, "but I'm fine."

Keen motioned, and Mr. O bowed and swept back to his spot. Moving to Clark's side, Keen surveyed the eclectic group with an obvious sense of pride. "We call ourselves *Orbis of Scientia*, Latin for 'Circle of Knowledge.' The group is incredibly diverse. We've some professors, some clergy, Mr. Gruenwald is in television, and Simon Paine oversees several literary agencies. The circle encompasses a wide spectrum—all adherents of the basic tenets of contemporary syncretism. At its root, all are united. Forging unity between religion and myth—demolishing barriers and distinctions that separate humankind, bringing us under one banner—is our ultimate aim. Every new moon we gather to discuss issues pertaining to the broader world of metaphysics."

Clark watched the professor's animated presentation with growing disquiet. He'd come here to break ties with Keen, only to land smack dab in the middle of *Orbis of* whatever. How would he get out of this one? Maybe he should save his defection for a later date, relax, and enjoy the highbrows.

"Here, let me introduce you to some of the members." Keen placed his hand on Clark's back and steered him toward two men conversing in a corner of the room. They turned as Keen approached. "Mr. Clark, this is Hale Gooden from the university."

A man with intense dark eyes and a jet-black, razor-thin goatee extended a hand. "So, you're the next victim," he said in a rich, humorless voice.

Clark managed a nervous smile.

"And this," Keen said, motioning to the man opposite Gooden, "is Gavin Commons. He's from up north, a Silicon Valley brat, in technologies—"

"Cybernetics," the man interrupted, shaking Clark's hand. "Or, as these gentlemen say, video games."

Keen laughed. "Really, now, it's all in jest. Mr. Commons is on the cutting edge of synthetic intelligence."

The man took a hurried sip of brown ale and turned to Clark, wiping foam from his lips. "The synthesis of neurophysiology and computer science, men and machines. It's amazing, really." He wore wire-rimmed glasses and a wrinkled dress shirt. He rushed another sip and used his shirtsleeve to dab at the residue. "We've implanted microchips in human subjects and successfully interfaced their brains with a computer network. Thus far they've developed the ability to manipulate robotic arms with just their thoughts."

"Cyborgs?" Clark looked skeptically over the top of his glasses.

"Amazing, isn't it?" Keen gushed.

"In the future," Commons continued, "everyone will have cybernetic implants. The blind will see. The deaf will hear."

"So that's the secret to your handicap," Gooden croaked, tapping his temple with his forefinger.

"Sorry, Hale. The golf skills are all natural."

They burst into laughter.

"So, tell us about yourself, Mr. Clark," said Gooden, as the laughter subsided. "What brings you to the circle?"

Clark cleared his throat and shifted his weight. Where was the courage he'd sought for? And who was he trying to kid anyway? He'd look like a fool trying to slug it out with these brains. "Well, actually..." But he already looked like a fool, so he might as well go all the way. "I think God brought me here."

They cast puzzled glances at each other.

"Is that so?" Gooden's eyes were dark slits. "Hasn't He brought us all?"

"I suppose. But I'm here to tell Professor Keen I won't be joining the group."

Keen snorted. "Last we spoke, you were interested in learning more."

"I know, and I'm sorry, Professor. No malice was intended. It's just, the incident I spoke to you about has challenged me, forced me to reconsider things, take a closer look at the... forces at work in my life."

"And what exactly is the incident we're referring to?" Gooden asked, looking from Clark to Keen.

The professor glared at Clark and made a sweeping gesture with his hand. "Take it away," he said, sulking.

Clark cleared his throat. "A member of my congregation raised a boy from the dead."

Gooden and Commons stood stupefied. Then Commons stepped forward, sloshing ale down his mug.

"In whose name?"

Clark adjusted his glasses and squinted at the man. Was this a trick question? What other names were there? He shrugged and said matter-of-factly, "In the name of Christ."

The conversations in the room grew hushed, and several craned to observe the interaction between the four men.

"You're west of here. Stonetree, right?" asked Commons.

"That's correct, Gavin," Keen said, rousing from his funk.

"But that valley is governed by Vucub Came and the other Mesos, is it not?"

Keen placed his hand on Commons's shoulder, as if to silence him.

"Do you mean he doesn't know about the Pantheons?" Commons glanced back and forth, from Keen to Gooden, with a look of incredulity. "I thought he was privy to the circle?"

"In due time, Mr. Commons," Keen said, patting the man's shoulder.

"What do you mean, 'the Pantheons'?" asked Clark. "One of them wouldn't happen to be *Itzcoliuhqui*, would it?"

A palpable ripple of surprise swept through the room. Chatter rose, and the man with the broad, pink forehead, stood watching and smiling, jabbing his thumb in Clark's direction.

Finally, Keen stepped forward. "Well, then, maybe your God did bring you here, Mr. Clark. And if that's the case, we'd like to meet Him."

Chapter 26

EEN LED THE THREE OF THEM THROUGH THE SMOKE-FILLED study while the roomful of men watched, swirling drinks and whispering among themselves. What new magic was up the professor's sleeve? They stopped before the lush burgundy curtains that draped behind Jade, and Keen pulled back the musty shroud and motioned the men to enter. Gooden and Commons ducked inside. Clark hurried past the parrot as the bird skittered across its perch, chattering.

He pulled up short of the entryway and looked at Keen. The professor extended the veil and tipped his head. His lips were drawn into a cold seam, his charcoal eyes like dark portents. Clark's confidence balanced on a tightrope of disconcertment. Each step took him farther out on a limb of presumption, deeper into Keen's madness. Was someone orchestrating all this, or was Clark reaping the fruits of the whirlwind he had sown? Was Clark walking boldly into battle or willingly into a trap? He swallowed—a dry, wrenching gulp—and stepped behind the curtain.

The thick fabric ruffled shut behind them. Keen walked ahead, his footsteps clicking across an open stretch of hardwood floor. Then the professor swung his arm in a wide arc. "Mr. Clark, welcome to the Temple of All-Father."

Clark took two steps forward, blinking as his eyes adjusted to the dim light, and his jaw grew slack.

He stood on the shore of an oblique oval-shaped room. Tapestries with indistinguishable ciphers hung from an octagonal ceiling that ascended in all directions to a black vent, a chimney, in the center. Beneath the charred flue, in the center of the room, on a round, elevated stage, sat an altar. It was nothing more than a massive stone slab, notched and scarred, that rested atop four squat, leg-like columns. Inscribed in each column, winged animals with inhuman faces wove in picturesque disarray. A circular set of stairs rose to the altar. On both ends of the stone table stood ornate bronze lampstands, huge torches, capped with massive bowls. In each basin a blue flame throbbed, sending a thin flume of smoke into the burnt funnel overhead.

Clark gawked in disbelief. "This is...how did you...?"

"It's taken years," Keen said. "Collecting, planning. But now my vision has become flesh. Hundreds of temples are represented here—Orissa; Dakshinaarka, the Sun Temple at Gaya; Dendara; Angkor Wat; Amon; and Apollo. Bits and pieces, an amalgam of the world's shrines."

Keen pointed to the outskirts of the room, and, for the first time, Clark noticed glass casings around the perimeter casting shadows across the ceiling. Each display case housed artifacts, caches of herb and tiny relics—a virtual museum in the bowels of the ranch.

Clark shook his head, stupefied by the richness of the secret chamber. He'd only seen a small portion of the ranch, but standing in the repository piqued his interest. And unnerved him. What other wonders could be found here? And what else went on behind the thick burgundy veil?

He glanced at the professor, who ambled toward the altar, surveying the place. Colorful banners with arcane symbols draped the walls, and strange figurines lurked in the shadows guarding fluted vases on pedestals. A smell of salts, oils, and exotic spice stirred intangible sensations.

"The constellations are Nordic." Keen raised his hands. Engraved in the ceiling an elegant celestial chart, almost imperceptible, stretched. "The metalwork is Egyptian. And Mesoamerican themes are throughout—hieroglyphics, headdresses."

"It's...incredible, Professor. Really." Clark's gaze flitted from one station to the next, while Gooden and Commons watched, looking impatient.

Keen climbed the steps of the altar. "As you know, *All-Father* was the term used for Odin, or *Óðinn*, whom the Vikings considered the greatest of the northern gods, the ultimate authority within the Pantheons, the ruler of Asgard. And this is why I find Odin so compelling, Ian." He pointed to a band of intricate carved plates embedded around the edge of the altar. "According to myth, Odin sacrificed himself upon *Yggdrasill*, the World Tree, in order to gain the secrets of the runes. These runes tell that tale."

Keen straightened, his ratty ponytail glowing in the eerie torchlight. "It is the age-old myth, the dying god that runs through all cultures, predating even Christianity. It is the one bridge, the sinew that connects all religions, the belief that in death is life, that through one's sacrifice, we ascend."

Commons cleared his throat and shifted his weight.

"Yes, yes." Keen glanced toward him. "The young man should know. He's been summoned here, isn't that what you said, Ian? Called by your God?"

Clark drew his attention away from the eclectic surroundings and gathered himself back into the ensuing debate. "Well, yes. I'd say that."

Commons stepped forward, the empty mug dangling from his fingertips. "Then tell us, Mr. Clark, about the resurrection in Stonetree. I'm surprised we've not heard anything about it." Commons glared at Keen, who compensated.

"Provided you explain this"—Clark pointed to the altar—"and this talk of gods and the nature of this group of yours."

Keen descended the steps. "Nothing you and I haven't already discussed, though we'll accommodate your interest. But before that, tell the gentleman a bit more about the incident in Stonetree."

Clark stared at the hardwood floor. He was still grappling with the resurrection himself. *Someone's trying to get our attention,* Ruby had said. *To wake us up, separate the wheat from the chaff.* He peered into the jumbled shadows. "The seminary taught that these types of things didn't happen anymore. The age of miracles is passed; we don't need signs. That was their line of reasoning."

"Basic dispensational theology—we're well aware of it." Until then, Gooden stood stroking his micro-fine goatee, brooding. Now he stepped forward, his voice rich and eyes icy. "We've no need of a discourse on cessationism. Tell us who the miracle worker is."

Clark shrugged. "It's a woman in my congregation. A mother, homemaker, for the most part. She leads a small prayer group in the church."

"And you're sure about this?" Gooden asked.

"Well, I saw the boy alive at the funeral home, if that's what you mean. The empty casket. I've talked to a half-dozen eyewitnesses, and it's all over the newspapers. As far as I can tell, it's legit. But what it all means..." Clark shook his head, then straightened himself and gestured toward the altar and the flickering torches. "Now, tell me about all this. Your secret order. And why the resurrection is of such concern to you."

Gooden lowered his gaze upon Clark and deferred to Keen.

The professor cleared his throat. "Well, the circle is hardly secret. If it were, you'd not be here. And the resurrection? They're not really that unusual, Mr. Clark. There's many reported incidents. Some Indian gurus have supposedly performed them. Revivalists, especially in third world countries, routinely claim to see the dead raised. In the States and other industrialized nations, it's rare. But thankfully the rest of the world isn't shackled by the Western worldview."

Keen sauntered along the base of the altar, hands clasped behind his back, sarong flowing over his sinewy frame. The silver ribbons of smoke trembled in response to his movement.

"Human history is marked by spiritual conflict, an ongoing battle between fire and ice, the clash of elementals—it's the struggle of the Pantheons. Gods of mammon, materialism, technology; gods of earth and air, agriculture. Your own Bible teaches this, doesn't it? Jehovah versus Baal. Yahweh versus Moloch. Christ against Satan. Spirit against flesh. There's a battle all around us, isn't there?"

Clark squinted. Keen was baiting him. "Well, yes. But are all gods real? And if they are, are they all good?"

"Ah!" Keen raised a bony finger and resumed his stride. "Yet they rule. Real or not. Good or bad. Your so-called pagan deities govern two-thirds of the earth's inhabitants. Look at the East, with its ancestral shrines and bodhisattvas by the bushel. Where is the Almighty? And of course, there's Shiva and Kali with their incessant death grip over the Hindus. They've ravaged that land for centuries. Then there's Allah, stern and cold. America's got its own unique set—designer deities for the most part. These are the same golden calves the Jews worshiped ages ago. The gods never died. They're alive and well."

"Apparently some people believe so," Clark said. "The day after the resurrection someone placed a druidic totem—an effigy of some sort—on the woman's front lawn, with a symbol, *Itzcoli-uhqui,* on it." Clark glanced at the three men and issued a faint grin. "This isn't the type of thing the Circle of Knowledge would do, is it, Professor Keen?"

Keen laughed, followed by Gooden and Commons, their voices merging in mock crescendo.

"Yes, Mr. Clark," Keen said with a raspy chuckle. "Yes. We've nothing better to do than skulk about old women's houses, planting wreaths and statues. Please, spare yourself the embarrassment."

Clark clamped his jaw, and perspiration erupted on his forehead. "Then who would do it? Tell me that. You're the one talking about gods. Are you suggesting it's a coincidence?"

Keen's sneer faded. "It's a fair question, actually—one that sheds light upon the nature of your city."

"We're not the only such group in this area," Gooden droned.

"Nor were we the first to recognize the Pantheons," Commons added.

Clark adjusted his glasses. "What're you saying? What other groups are there?"

"This area is rife with practitioners of the occult sciences," Keen said. "Of course, none as refined or cosmopolitan as *Orbis of Scientia*—haven't you noticed? We've charted druid, Wiccan, neo-pagan sects all across the spectrum. Most are grassroots, decentralized, and rather unsophisticated. But the area's become a mecca of sorts. No doubt, the resurrection you speak of will only add to the attraction."

"I know about the shops downtown, but this? It's a lot bigger than I imagined."

"Really, Reverend, you must get out more. Anyone with a rudimentary grasp of metaphysics can discern the ruling powers. It's the basest, most elementary of all human impulses. Born into a cold, vast universe. Are we alone, existentially adrift, left to our Sisyphean plying? Or are we being watched, steered toward some appointed end? And, if so, who are these unnamed?

"Is it any wonder that we, as a species, should seek to identify and define the powers? Myth and religion—whether primitive or advanced—grapple with the same end. In their own crude ways, these groups and individuals recognize and serve the gods of the valley…even if it means bedecking lawns with replicas of their lord."

"So you want me to believe that you people, that these groups, have identified a god—or, gods—that govern the Stonetree Valley."

"You can choose to believe what you want," Commons snorted, appearing agitated. "But facts are facts." Then he turned to Keen. "Why are we wasting our time, Benjamin? He's not ready."

"And now he knows more than he should," Gooden snarled, glancing about the sanctuary.

"Gentleman. His questions are valid. None of us became initiates overnight." Then he walked toward Clark.

"Long before we'd arrived in these parts, a cluster of Mesoamerican deities were summoned here. The history is sketchy." He passed Clark and went to a glass case on the far wall. He opened the top hatch, reached in, and produced a crude black blade, curved, maybe twelve inches in length. The professor balanced the instrument in his palm. "Obsidian. From the records I've gathered, it's similar to the one used near East Basin. At the tree. For the sacrifice."

"You don't mean—"

"Yes."

"A human sacrifice?" Clark peered at Keen, turned back to the other men who looked on without emotion.

Keen took the knife by its butt and approached Clark. "Immigrants from South America, it appears, full of fear and superstition. They worked the mines and struck an obsidian vein. To them, it was confirmation." He stood in front of Clark and extended the knife on his palm. "*Itzcoliuhqui*—the Twisted Obsidian One."

The chiseled blade glistened in Keen's hand.

"A blood sacrifice opened the door. *Tlaloc*, *Xipe*, the Came twins. We're not certain who all came—the entire family of death gods, perhaps. A struggle ensued, which is always the case, and the Mesos won. To this day they remain unchallenged."

Clark's jaw opened and closed, but he could find no words. He drew his hand across his forehead, and a wave of fatigue tore through him, causing him to sway. He shook himself, attempting to regain his equilibrium. "What about the churches? We have an impact, don't we? I mean, we can force the spirits to leave."

"Jehovah's followers are impotent, Mr. Clark. Yes, they drove the old religion underground with their inquisition and witch hunts. But it was only a matter of time. Complacency set in. Arrogance. And they call us a Christian nation? Bah! Absorbed in their affluence, hypnotized by the American zeitgeist. The churches in Stonetree have relinquished their power. They squabble and bicker, handcuffed by their pettiness. I'm afraid you and your ministerial peers pose no threat to the Pantheons."

Keen returned the blade to its case. "For our part, we are just spectators in this great war, rendering honor to the victor. We've no stake in this, other than to identify the ruling power and comply."

Clark swallowed hard again. His mouth felt sapped of its saliva. The potpourri of fragrance had become a psychotropic cocktail, intoxicating, sending his thoughts arcing wildly. Could his agnosticism be the outworking of a much more insidious plan? Was he nothing more than a pawn to be sacrificed in an unseen game? He shifted his weight as the concepts tumbled inside him.

Clark stared up into the dangling banners and the Nordic constellations and drew a deep breath. Then he crossed the room, came to the foot of the altar, and gazed at the scorched stone in the throbbing torchlight. This elaborate shrine wasn't just for show. It had been used.

He turned around and faced the men. "Resurrections may not be that unusual, Professor. But they are in Stonetree. And I think this one means something."

"Perhaps," Keen said halfheartedly.

"Well, then, *perhaps* it means this Twisted Obsidian One, this–this family of gods are losing their grip."

"Ian, I'm not talking about a theory or a caricature in some seminary textbook. We're dealing with an entity, an ancient spirit, a presence unconstrained by morals or mortality. Millennia spent meddling in human affairs, gorging on blood and power. You can't just waltz in, sprinkle some holy water, and shoo these things off like gnats."

"Professor Keen, I can't go on like this." Clark was trembling now, not out of fear but conviction. "You've helped me and been an encouragement during some extremely difficult times. I'm indebted. Really. I've been up front with you about my questions and reservations. Maybe I should've never became a minister. But this"—Clark motioned to the lush, mysterious environs, the sooty altar, and the celestial map stretched overhead—"this is too much. I mean, where do you stop? Before long we're all drinking goat's blood and dancing around in loincloths, worshiping the sun or some other nonsense. I can concede elements of paganism without becoming one."

Keen stood silently smoldering.

"No. I don't have the answer," Clark sighed. "But I know this isn't it. I'm sorry. But people I love are getting hurt. Whatever it is—a cosmic spiritual struggle or a–a medical anomaly—I've gotta follow my heart."

Keen stepped toward him, his charcoal eyes pleading. "I don't know what you're thinking, Ian. But challenging the powers...they've been here for decades. They're here for a reason. And they will not yield without a fight."

Clark's heartbeat sent tremors through his limbs. Keen was spot on. Were there, at this moment, malevolent eyes watching them, plotting against them? Was this the same power that leveled White Creek Chapel? If so, Clark's defiance would surely have consequences. He bit back the acid rising in his throat.

"You're right, Professor. I don't understand everything. I still have a lot of questions. I'll just have to take my chances. Thank you, gentlemen. Professor Keen." Clark bowed—a slow, sincere gesture—then rose. "But consider me officially out of your Circle of Knowledge."

Chapter 27

THE DOOR BURST OPEN, AND BRIAN STORMED PAST RUBY with his backpack slapping his shoulder. Cool air swooshed into the living room as he marched down the hallway scowling. She tossed aside the quilt and bolted from the couch.

"Bri? What's wrong?"

A thump sounded in his room, and the bedsprings crunched in response.

She rushed to the front door and pushed it shut just as Jack crammed his lunch box through the opening. "Whoa!" He poked his head in and frowned at her. "What's the big hurry?"

"It's freezing. And what's wrong with Brian?"

"I dunno. Somebody was teasing him or something." Jack stepped into the house. "What's with all that trash in the street?"

Ruby shut the door and tightened the sweater around her shoulders. "Those kids are still giving him a hard time, aren't they? We've gotta talk to someone, Jack. This isn't right." She started walking toward the hallway.

"Leave him. He'll get over it." Jack went into the kitchen, work boots thumping across the linoleum, and emerged tugging on the sleeves of his flannel. "Why's it so cold in here?"

"The pilot's broke again." She crossed her arms and pouted her lips. "I can't stand this. I feel like a prisoner here. And if that keeps up," she pointed toward Brian's room, "he's staying home with me and Sean."

"Sure, let's all just take the next year off." He marched down the hall, knelt before the wall heater, and removed the bottom panel. "I told you all along we needed to gut this out. It'll turn into a circus if we let it." He rolled up his shirtsleeve, doubled over, and probed inside the old unit.

"Yeah, but you're not the one having to deal with all these people. It's Thursday already, and it still hasn't let up."

"More people come today?"

"Yeah. Plus some. That's what all that stuff in the street is. Some guy was out there ranting for most of the morning, passing out tracts or something. I felt like calling the cops."

Jack snapped the panel back on, rose to his feet, and approached her, dusting off his hands. "You stayed inside, right?"

She nodded sheepishly.

"Ruby?"

"I talked to one lady this afternoon, on the porch, that's it."

Jack put his hands on her shoulders and gazed into her eyes. Flecks of sawdust sprinkled his wavy hair, and the scent of pine and fir clung to his clothing. She loved that smell, and combined with his sympathetic demeanor, she couldn't help but wilt. Jack's grip was firm. "The more you give to these people, the more they'll take. You can't keep feeding their fascination."

What was going on behind his green eyes? Was someone hammering away at Jack's heart, or was she the only one on the anvil?

"I can't turn them away." She touched his hands and separated herself. Then she went to the front window and inched the curtains open. "What if it happens again? A healing or..." She let the curtains slip shut. "There's so many others. Why Mondo? Why would it happen just once?"

"Maybe it's a test."

She glanced over her shoulder at him.

"So what did the weirdo out front have to say?" Jack rolled his eyes.

Sean scampered out of his room with a blanket wrapped around his shoulders like a superhero. He prattled something as he swept by and did a sharp turn into the kitchen.

"Oh, I don't know," Ruby said. "Something about false prophets and false miracles, the devil looks like an angel of light and other stuff. A newspaper guy took his picture."

Jack threw his hands in the air. "Unreal. This is unreal! If I was here—"

The phone rang in the kitchen.

"Well, I'm glad you weren't. The last thing we need is you in jail for assaulting a street preacher." Then she called to Sean. "Don't answer it."

"Yeah," Sean said, ambling back into the room with the cordless at his ear. "Do you wanna talk to her?" He handed the phone to Ruby. "For you, Mom."

She scowled at him, took it, and tapped him on the head. "Hello?"

"Ruby, it's Vin. I'm on my way over."

She stepped away from Jack and lowered her voice. "Is everything all right?"

"I'm not sure," Vinyette said. "Reverend Clark asked if we could meet him at the church. He's been gone all day, called on his cell. Said it's important."

Ruby glanced over her shoulder at Jack, who stood with his arms crossed, squinting at her. "Yeah, uh, should be all right."

"Be there in ten minutes."

Ruby clicked off, walked into the kitchen, and hung up the phone. She came out and found Jack in the same position, arms crossed, one eyebrow raised in a quizzical slant.

"Vinyette's picking me up. I guess Reverend Clark wants to meet with us." She started to the bedroom, dragging her fingertips across his chest as she passed. "You're all right with the boys?"

"Mmm, hmm."

She passed Brian's room and glanced inside. He lay across the bed, head resting on his hands, sleeping. Pulling his door shut, she continued to her bedroom. Jack followed and stood watching as she removed her sweater and retrieved her heavy wool coat.

He leaned against the door jamb, staring.

"If you don't want me to go, just say so."

"Oh, don't let me stop you." He folded his arms.

She put on the thick black coat and fluffed her hair from under the collar.

He watched her with a smug nonchalance.

She finally cracked and scowled. "What?"

"Oh, nothing. I just don't wanna see this thing dragging on forever. I mean, you guys met yesterday. C'mon. How long is this gonna go on? You're already stressing. And I hope—I really hope to God—you're not obsessing over that stupid curse and that tree up there."

What was that Aida told her about needing to let go? Still, for the life of her, she couldn't imagine Jack carrying some of the load. How could she explain the ghost in Reverend Clark's office or the prophecy about another healer who would break the spell? *It's a test, all right.* But thus far, she'd failed.

She pulled the sleeves of the coat over her wrists. "Believe me, babe, I want to get over this too." She hugged him. But Ruby knew things were far from over.

Vinyette's truck, like her, was not glitzy. Maybe *durable* was the word, Ruby thought, as she climbed out and heaved the door shut. An older model Chevy, faded red, replete with pings and nasty rust wounds. Vinyette always parked in back of the church, knowing the more esteemed members of the congregation frowned on her earthy, tomboyish bent.

"Don't get many passengers," Vinyette said apologetically, her door emitting a metallic yawn before thumping shut. She circled around, yanking her shirtsleeve down over her tattoo.

"Aren't you cold?" Ruby glanced at the inverted ocean of gray rolling up the canyon, tightening its noose about the city.

Vinyette jangled through the bulky key ring and stopped to look at the ominous sky. "Now that you mention it."

Ruby hurried to keep up with Vinyette's frenetic pace.

"D'you see the doctor?" Vinyette asked over her shoulder.

"I'm all right, Vin."

Vinyette stopped at the base of the steps. "What is wrong with you, woman? You're bound and determined to run yourself into the ground, aren't you?"

"I'll be OK. I promise." It was getting harder to sound convincing.

"Of course, rushing out like this probably doesn't help." Vinyette shrugged, turned, and marched up the steps with Ruby in tow.

A figure in a navy blue Windbreaker waited at the top of the steps. "Marje?" Ruby cast a puzzled look at Vinyette. "What're you doing here?"

Marje stood with her back to the massive wood doors, shivering, clinging to her tiny, tan purse. "I'm freezing right now, that's what I'm doing." She looked at Vinyette with wide eyes. "You must be crazy."

Vinyette unlocked the door of the church and pushed it open. "Sorry, ladies, some of us just idle hot."

"Oh brother. Just get us inside." Marje pushed her way in behind Vinyette.

The foyer provided little warmth.

The three of them stood huddled in the center, Ruby and Marje moving about, trying to get warm, while Vinyette turned on the lights.

"Can't we meet in the office?" Marje hugged herself and jogged in place as the chandelier blinked to life.

"It ain't much warmer in there, let me tell you. Besides, he wants to see us in here." Vinyette motioned toward the sanctuary.

"What does he want?" Ruby asked.

"I don't know, but he's sure been acting strange. I'm starting to get bad vibes." Vinyette stared off, her hazel eyes fixed on some distant point.

"About what?" Marje continued her Eskimo shuffle. "I thought people were jazzed about Mondo. That's what we've been hoping for, isn't it? Miracles and revival. Now it comes, and everbody's...Has something else been going on?"

Ruby looked away, wringing her frigid fingers. This was going to bust wide open.

"Yeah. You woulda thought there'd be a shindig," Vinyette said sarcastically. "Instead, there's been a whole lotta confusion." She shook her head, led them to the sanctuary doors, and pushed one open.

The three of them stepped in, and their footfalls echoed in the dreary, cavernous room. The tall, stained glass windows lacked their normal luster, deadened by the overcast skies. Fingers of blue and orange mottled the empty pews, transforming languid dust motes into abstract pockets. They stared into the silent, shadowy chamber.

Suddenly Marje hissed and grabbed Vinyette's arm, who grabbed Ruby's. Marje tilted forward, her massive gold hoops shimmering in the dimness, and pointed toward the front of the church.

"I see them." Vinyette craned forward, and Ruby followed her gaze.

A figure sat hunched, motionless in the front pew.

Marje motioned back to the foyer and started there. But Vinyette held up one finger, took a step away from them, and cleared her throat. The sound died in the room.

The figure remained bent and still.

Marje tugged at Vinyette, but she took another step forward and cleared her throat again, this time much louder.

The person sat up and, without turning, said, "It's me."

Marje heaved a sigh. Vinyette motioned them forward and started up the aisle. "I thought you were still on the road."

Reverend Clark put his glasses on and turned around. "I've been here for an hour."

They walked to the front of the church, formed a semicircle, and stood looking at Ian Clark.

Maybe Ruby wasn't the only one dangling by a thread. His unshaven cheeks and bloodshot eyes betrayed great fatigue. Clark's choker shown through the rumpled, unbuttoned shirt. He ran his fingers through disheveled hair but did not look at them as he spoke.

"I'm sorry. I should've told you, Vin. I got back about an hour ago. I parked at the parsonage and walked over. I've been sitting here thinking."

He adjusted his glasses and looked at them, his features gaunt and haggard. His voice quavered in a weary monotone.

"For the last year—really, since I arrived—you ladies have been faithful to pray for us, for me. But there's a lot I haven't told you, or told anyone. It's time I come clean. And I figured this would be the best place to start."

He's got a part in all this, Aida had said about Reverend Clark. *And I ain't sure whose side he's on.* Ruby angled her head, and her baloney detector revved to life.

Clark left the pew and walked to the base of the altar steps.

"A long time ago someone died, and it's haunting me. And I'm afraid something terrible is upon us because of it."

Chapter 28

VINYETTE AND MARJE STOOD FIXATED AT RUBY'S SIDE, watching Reverend Clark trudge up the steps of the darkened altar. Ruby tightened the coat around her shoulders and scanned the sanctuary. Perhaps the ghost in Clark's office wasn't the only one. She peered into the shadowed pews, but the thought of the swirling apparition with its large, sad eyes sent chills up her arms. She shivered and thrust her gaze back upon the tortured minister.

Halfway up the steps Clark sat down. He locked his arms around his knees and angled himself toward the stained glass windows. Refractive rainbows sparkled in his wire-rimmed glasses.

"About five years ago," he said, "my sister, Stacie, was decapitated. I've been at war with God ever since, and it's eating me alive."

Marje gasped and glanced at them. Vinyette put her hand over her mouth, and Ruby peered at Clark, hoping for a serious dose of discernment.

"She was so full of life," Clark continued. "Bound and determined to become a missionary. She wanted to go to Darfur and serve in the refugee camps. She had a heart for those kids, wrote letters back and forth, and kept pictures of them up on the fridge. She worked after school at the corner market bagging groceries and mopping floors, saving money to go overseas when she graduated. Even started learning the language."

He heaved a sigh and stared into the ranks of empty pews. "The night before she was supposed to leave, on the way home from a farewell party, a car jumped the divider and peeled off the top of her car. She died instantly. It was some old man—a nice guy, really. He'd been working overtime to pay for some hospital bills. Fell asleep at the wheel."

Clark stared into the desolate sanctuary, detached, as if emotion had long since been shorn from his memory.

"I'd just finished seminary, gotten married, and began ministering. It was my first church. But everything just caved in. She was like my own personal cheerleader, constantly prodding me forward. I just couldn't grasp the meaning of it all, why God would let something like that happen. I gradually lost faith and drifted off. Cynthia—my ex—tried her best to stick it out, but I was gone. She eventually divorced me, the church let me go, and I wandered, until I came here. The ministry was all I'd dreamt of, but I guess I got lost along the way."

He picked at something on his pant leg and sat grinding his jaw.

Ruby toyed with the thin silver bracelet on her left wrist and studied him. *Everybody's a little crippled.* She believed that now more than ever. Reverend Clark hid his pain behind the ministry, dragging around that emotional ball and chain one sermon to the next. She'd heard somewhere that brokenness prepared people for service. If that was the case, the whole lot of them were on the verge of something great.

He pointed to the red carpeted steps with a pained expression.

"Do you know how many people have gotten saved at this altar in the last year?" He didn't look at them or wait for an answer. "None. And do you know why?" He glanced at them with a look of disgust, jabbing himself in the chest with accusatory force.

"Reverend," Vinyette began, "you shouldn't be—"

He held up his hand. "Don't, Vin. You don't know the half of it. Does she, Ruby?"

Vinyette and Marje turned toward Ruby with owl eyes. Ruby opened her mouth but had no reply. She shrugged and played dumb and prepared for the dam to burst.

"I'm not what I appear to be," he said. "Although I'm sure I appear to be a complete fool. The resurrection of the boy has changed something, I'm not sure—in me, in us. It's brought things to light, and I can't run any longer."

"Reverend." Vinyette cleared her throat, clearly attempting to understand the disclosure. "If you need prayer, we'd be happy to pray for you."

Marje nodded with enthusiasm.

"Oh. Believe me, Vin, I need prayer. But before this is over, I might need a mortician."

Marje's countenance plunged.

"I don't understand," Vinyette said. "Why?"

He stared at the ground for a moment then looked at them, eyes tired but stern. "Listen to me carefully. What I'm about to say may sound crazy. I don't fully understand it myself. But a spirit, a demon—something ancient—is at work in this city. It was summoned here through a human sacrifice a long time ago and will try to destroy whoever challenges it."

Ruby sighed. "And the resurrection is the first challenge."

Clark looked at her, and his surprise melted into an acquiescent nod. "Now it's just a matter of preparing for battle."

The silence of the room lapped at the four of them, the stillness magnifying the moment.

"Is that what Reverend Lawrence told you?" Vinyette finally managed.

Marje gripped the tiny purse at her waist. "Reverend Lawrence? Eugene Lawrence? Our old pastor?"

"Yeah, Marje," he said. "I drove up the coast this morning. He lives just outside Santa Cruz, works part-time at a church up there, and does some consultation for another. Wonderful man. Said to say hi to you all."

"We started the prayer group because of Reverend Lawrence." Marje beamed a proud smile.

"It was terrible how that all went down." Vinyette frowned and tapped the carpet with the toe of her boot.

"That's one of the reasons Jack ended up leaving," Ruby added.

"Yeah, well, that's how these things work." Clark rose, ascended the remaining steps, and took the pulpit, where he looked down at the women with his shimmering specs. "The board forced him to resign. They didn't like his talk of revival. It was too fanatical, they said. He kept trying to unite the other churches, bring the community together, and that didn't sit well. Plus, he was snooping around in the city's history—like I've been doing—and found some disturbing things."

"Mr. Barkham? Mr. Millquint?" Marje pinched her face into a skeptical squint. "I voted for them. Why would they force Reverend Lawrence to resign?"

"And what did he find out about the city that was so disturbing?" Vinyette asked.

Ruby sighed again, as if she had no choice but to come clean. "There was another resurrection. A long time ago."

"Huh?" Vinyette put her hands on her hips and glared at Ruby. "How do you know all this?"

Reverend Clark motioned for Ruby to continue.

She shuffled to the pew and dropped into it. "I wasn't sick Sunday morning, Vin. I had a—a vision. I dunno what to call it. A premonition or something. And that night Mondo was raised."

"I thought something was up," Marge said.

Vinyette crossed her arms and cocked her hip. "Why didn't you tell us?"

"I know." Ruby nodded. "I'm sorry. It was just too weird at first. So I kept it to myself, tried to think it through."

Vinyette rolled her eyes. "Gee, that's new. So what was it? I mean, your vision?"

"It was the Sailor's Oak, up by the old graveyard, all gray and dead—sprouting a new leaf. I didn't know what to make of it. That night Mondo woke up. The next day Mr. Svenson told me about the last resurrection. Aida Elston is a sweet old lady, ninety-some years old, who lives up in Old Town. She was raised from the dead."

"Two resurrections?" Vinyette wondered aloud.

"Bookends to a bigger picture, I think." Reverend Clark bent over with his elbows across the lectern. "Some type of struggle is going on—been going on for a while. Some people call it the Stonetree curse, but it's much bigger, deeper, more complex. And from what I gather, we've been brought together to fight it."

"Uh, what exactly are we fighting?" Marje scrolled her eyes back and forth, looking paranoid.

Clark stepped away from the pulpit and pointed to one of the stained glass windows on the west side of the church. A ray of sunlight, piercing the overcast outside, awakened the prisms on that side of the sanctuary. At the window's highest point, an angel clothed in a breastplate and military girdle, wings unfurled overhead, stood thrusting a golden sword toward several skeletal figures at its feet, driving them into a swirling gray abyss.

"The ancients believed that demons exist in ranks, like angels. Remember Michael and Gabriel?" He motioned toward the glowing glass. "They were archangels, leaders of the heavenly army. According to medieval theologians, angels were organized into three 'choirs' or 'hierarchies.' Archangels were near the top of that list.

"Well, the same's true of demons. The holy books describe them as principalities, powers, and rulers—it's military terminology. The idea is that these spirits rule by rank, sometimes by region. In the Book of Daniel, for instance, Michael tangles with the prince of Persia and the prince of Greece, two demonic superpowers over those cities. Many cultures and faith traditions believe that a land can become defiled, entire cities polluted by idolatry or immorality, geographical areas immersed in a type of spiritual darkness."

Vinyette hooked her thumbs through her belt loops and gazed at the fading stained glass angel. "I'm pretty dense about stuff like this. I mean, it's interesting and all, Reverend, don't get me wrong, but how exactly do you fight something like that? Can't we just pray?"

Marje nodded her agreement. "The devil must flee when we come in the name of Jesus. He cannot stand!" She thrust her fist in the air.

"Preach it, sister." Vinyette and Marje exchanged a high five.

Ruby smiled and shook her head.

Clark descended the steps and stood before them. "Have you ever heard of White Creek Chapel?"

They glanced at each other with quizzical looks.

"This is the kicker, and it's why I called the three of you." Clark rolled up his shirtsleeves and began pacing. "Reverend Lawrence researched it; in fact, that's what got him in trouble. White Creek used to be the main church in Stonetree, right in the middle of town. In the old days the center of town defined the makeup of the city, its identity. That's why churches were often one of the first civil structures built.

"Anyway, they learned about the curse and began speaking against it, poking around and starting controversy. At first they received strange threats and warnings. Then a series of bizarre accidents occurred. Some members were stricken with a mysterious fever. People started leaving. There were accusations. One night a fire broke out in the cellar. The church burned down. It's a sad story. The pastor became ill, they were forced to sell the property, and the congregation disbanded amidst the scandal."

Ruby sat hunched forward, with her elbows on her knees, twirling a lock of hair. "All because they tried to challenge it?"

"It sure looks that way." Clark resumed his pace, his demeanor calm but driven. "Lawrence is convinced that's why he got ousted."

Vinyette's tone was guarded. "So you're saying we can't just barge in on this thing."

Clark nodded. "Yes. But, in my mind, we also can't turn and run. I've been doing that for the last five years, Vin, since Stacie's death, and I'm tired. If I don't stand up and fight, I'll just get rolled. I'll be denying everything she lived for…everything she believed about me."

"So how do we start?" Marje asked, minus the exuberance.

A breeze rattled the side door and moaned through crevices in the tall windows. The sun disappeared, and the sanctuary faded into gloom. They glanced at each other, and Ruby clenched the coat around her shoulders.

"Remember what you told me, Ruby?" Clark stopped pacing and looked at her, as if trying to enlist her in his cause. "You said some places are gateways to darker things."

She stopped twisting her hair and sat up.

"Well," he continued. "Can you think of any places like that in this city?"

"That old graveyard up there always gives me the creeps." Marje bounced on her toes and looked sideways at them.

"The forest near Old Town," Ruby said. "Where they say the witches meet."

Clark nodded and kept staring, as if trying to extract something else from them.

The sanctuary doors rattled, and drafts crept along the floor, sending chills up Ruby's legs.

"Those shops downtown," Vinyette murmured.

Clark stepped forward, his eyes transfixed with resolve. "The exact place where White Creek Chapel used to be. Instead of a house of God in the center of Stonetree, there are psychics and spell shops. And do you know who owns that property?" Wind whistled through unseen cracks, gnawing at the silence. "Mr. Coy Barkham."

Marje gasped. "The chairman of the elder board?"

Vinyette peered at Clark. "You're saying an elder in Canyon Springs owns occult stores?"

"No, doesn't own them. According to Reverend Lawrence, he's got some kind of agreement with them. It's been in their family a long time. When Reverend Lawrence found out and confronted Barkham, he was promptly forced to resign. He said he's been hoping someone would come along to press the issue. And I guess I'm it."

The impending storm set the old building rattling, groaning in unseen apertures and creaking across its massive timbers. Despite the disturbing revelations, this was want they'd wanted all along. Ruby had spent the last two years yearning for something more. So she wasn't about to miss her chance.

She cleared her throat. "Well, don't forget me."

Clark laughed—something Ruby couldn't recall seeing much before. He slid into the pew and hugged her.

"Count us in too." Vinyette turned to Marje and winked. "And if the church burns down, we'll just rebuild."

They turned to Vinyette in unison, their eyebrows arched in incredulity.

"Kidding! I'm just kidding."

"We need a plan of attack." Clark sprung from the seat and resumed his pacing, this time with a skip in his step. "But we need to keep this to ourselves, ladies. Be bold, but be wise."

"Reverend Clark?" Ruby rose from the pew and looked up at the stained glass angel and the three dark figures huddled at its feet recoiling from the golden blade. "I'm not sure we have to go too far."

"What do mean, Ruby?"

She lifted her eyes to the altar and the five ornate chairs lining the back of the stage, designated for the elders of Canyon Springs.

"Maybe the gateway is right here."

Chapter 29

RUBY AND MARJE CROSSED THE THRESHOLD OF THE CHURCH and stepped into the chill breeze. Vinyette pulled the heavy door shut and locked it behind them. She turned, and together they watched Reverend Clark walk back to the parsonage. Ruby shoved her hands into the deep pockets of her coat.

"Maybe that explains why he's been acting so strange."

"You got that straight." Vinyette clamped the bundle of keys in her fist. "I feel sorry for him. And mad."

Marje yanked the zipper of her Windbreaker as far up as it would go. "Why's that?"

"He should've told us about that stuff a long time ago—about his sister and his divorce. It's not right that the church didn't know."

Ruby watched Clark follow the path along the property and pass between the olive trees. He'd conveniently avoided mentioning the ghost in his office, and she wasn't about to bring it up. Nevertheless, its absence from the conversation seemed none too significant. Was this what Aida had warned her about?

Clark plunged into shadow and disappeared from Ruby's view. What part did he play in this thing? And was there something else he wasn't telling them?

"Do you think those things are true?" Marje stared up into the lazy charcoal sky, batting her eyes against the breeze. "That there's really some kinda demon spirits around here?"

Ruby and Vinyette gazed upward with her. Leaves swirled across the steps like a solemn warning, a precursor to a brooding tempest. They huddled together with their eyes to the heavens.

"Do you remember that guy, Fittwater? Leon Fittwater? I told y'all about him." Vinyette's hair wafted about her shoulders in the gusty air. She stared into the sky.

Marje snapped her fingers. "Oh, um...yeah. He was that nutty neighbor of yours."

"That's him. He was part of some church that met out in the boonies. They raised rattlesnakes as part of their religion."

Marje forced an exaggerated shiver. "Snakes? Ugh!"

"Yeah, well, they believed God would protect them, make 'em immune to poisons and venom. Ol' Leon used to get ta rantin', said they had power to tread on serpents and scorpions and over all the power of the enemy, that nothin' could by any means hurt a real child of God."

Vinyette folded her arms and stared into the distance, eagle-eyed. Ruby followed her gaze along the sloping hill, through the camphor trees, past the tilted church sign, down the winding asphalt driveway that spilled onto Rivermeer, toward downtown Stonetree.

"What're you thinking?" Marje sounded suspicious.

A mischievous smile blossomed across Vinyette's face. "I think it's time we do some treading."

Vinyette's truck rumbled to rest in front of Bloom Moon. Billows of purple statice, baby's breath, and plump sunflowers adorned the sidewalk. An aromatic mélange flooded the cab of the truck. Next door, fruits and vegetables from local growers rose in columned crates at the produce stand. A man with a black beanie filled a paper sack with tangerines and glanced at the three women sitting in the faded red Chevy.

"Are you sure we should be here?" Marje stared across the brick intersection.

"We live here, don't we?" Vinyette pointed to the shops along Sun Street. "That's it, the block where the chapel was."

Ruby craned to see past a street vendor selling hot pretzels from a cart. "That whole row of shops is—"

"Creepy." Marje let loose an exaggerated tremble. "I don't know if we should go in there. Really."

"What're they gonna do?" Vinyette yanked the handle, and

the door groaned open. "Kick us out for lookin'?" A jean jacket hung over the seat. She retrieved it, put it on, and swept her hair out from under the collar. "C'mon, girls, let's see what we're up against." She heaved the door shut, walked around, and met Marje and Ruby as they slid out of the truck.

Vinyette marched ahead of them, cowboy boots clicking on the concrete, chestnut hair flowing atop her angular shoulders. She had a strut about her, not of cockiness, as Ruby had learned, but from being so downright full of life. How the woman had survived all the garbage—the drugs and bruises and with-drawals—and managed to remain so light-hearted was a glorious mystery. Ruby would've sunk long ago if not for Vin's incessant encouragement.

They crossed the street and angled toward Bapho's, the corner gallery anchoring that section of shops. Just who or what Bapho was remained a mystery—a mystery that had not affected business. People up and down the coast, with cultlike fervor, cele-brated the bizarre art gallery. Bapho's shipped as far away as Paris and had catapulted several local artists into acrylic and watercolor stardom.

"I haven't been down here in a long time." Ruby cocked her head as subtle strains of world music piped through unseen speakers. Tiny white lights twinkled in the magnolias along the walkway, brought to life by the overcast skies.

"Just remember"—Vinyette turned to them as they approached the gallery—"wherever the sole of your foot treads, it's ours. Got it?" She shrugged. "So let's just see what happens."

Rows of easels displayed paintings, and two men roosted out front on stools, scratching out charcoal sketches. Marje lagged behind, and Ruby tried to look nonchalant, until she noticed the first canvas. A female form, wrung like a wet rag, shrieking in agony between two oily serpentine hands, announced their entry to Bapho's gallery.

Vinyette stopped, and the three of them gaped at images of horns and hoofs, collages of peeled lips, lidless eyes, and monstrous appendages. Between sculptures of dolphins and shells—the common coastal fare—were grotesque forms and sensual images. Marje sucked air through her clenched teeth, and Ruby shivered as they surveyed the exhibit.

A gust of cold wind sent some nearby chimes tinkling.

"Can I help you?" A middle-aged woman, with dyed-black hair and one eyebrow full of rings, pushed herself off a counter and sauntered toward them, chewing gum. Thick black eyeliner, like that of an Egyptian priestess, swirled out from her lids onto gaunt pale cheekbones.

Vinyette leaned toward Ruby and Marje and whispered, "Lemme do the talkin'." Then she turned back to the approaching woman. "Yes, could you tell us what this particular piece symbolizes?" She gestured to the image of the reptilian hands and the wrung-out torso.

The woman cast a dubious glance at them, her multi-ringed eyebrow at attention, then at the picture. "It means anything you want it to mean, dear."

"Hmm." Vinyette squinted and stroked her chin. "It's awfully dark."

The woman glanced back at the picture. "Yeah? Well so's life."

Vinyette cocked her hip and scanned the place. "In fact, there's a lotta dark stuff here. Depressing."

A man wearing a skin-tight turtleneck, perched at a nearby easel, stopped sketching and glared at them.

Ruby cleared her throat, and Marje mumbled something.

The wannabe-Egyptian priestess blinked slow enough to display lids full of silver glitter. "Are you guys looking for anything special?"

"No, no." Vinyette tilted her chin up and casually surveyed the marketplace. "Just seeing what's going on in downtown Stonetree."

The priestess chomped her gum, spun on her toe, and swaggered back to her spot at the counter. The man returned to his sketching and peeked at them from behind the canvas. Ruby started walking, grabbed Vinyette by the belt loop, and tugged her along. "What're you trying to do?"

"Just observing."

Marje scowled. "You're trying to start something."

"Well, if Cleopatra wasn't such a snob, I'd have been nicer. All right. I'll be good."

They rambled down the street with Vinyette strutting in the lead. Marje straggled to one side, and Ruby limped on the other. To their left, hardcore music throbbed from deep inside a tattoo parlor. A bearded man with black leather pants and a shiny shaved head leaned in the doorway smoking a peculiar-smelling thin black cigarette. Next door a naked mannequin wearing a Robin Hood cap was propped in front of an antique store, and after that, the Green Man Pub, one of the more fabled college hotspots. Then, one after the other, like an unholy trinity, Purple Maze, SpellWind, and Mars, three of the most popular occult shops in Stonetree.

Marje slowed her pace and straggled behind, her hands jammed in the pockets of her Windbreaker. "I don't know, Vin."

Vinyette reached back, took Marje's arm, and tugged her forward. "Hey, remember? Power to tread on serpents and scorpions?" She held up her hand for another high five.

Marje grinned, plucked her hand from her pocket, and gave Vinyette a reluctant tap.

"Over there." Ruby pointed to an oxidized bronze plaque embedded in the brickwork in front of the Purple Maze. They walked over and gathered around the memorial.

"White Creek Chapel," Vinyette read. "1942–58. Historic marker." She looked up with raised eyebrows. "That's it?"

Ruby squatted and traced her fingers across the raised letters. An anarchy symbol, scrawled in black ink, defaced the bland monument, and dark, syrupy sludge pooled at its base. She looked up at the large plate glass windows stretched across the storefront, painted solid lavender. In flowing, sixties-type psychedelia, the words *Purple Maze* swept across the length of the glass, adorned with paisley swirls and multicolor flowers.

"What's that smell?" Marje tipped her head and sniffed the air. "Something's burning."

Ruby lurched to her feet and did a three-sixty on the sidewalk. The memory of the bubbling specter in Reverend Clark's office and its stench unfurled in her mind. Cold creeps danced atop her scalp. Was the invisible hand nearby, waiting to snatch her back into the Sunday morning dream world?

"It's coming from in here." Vinyette leaned back and scanned the shop, reciting the words in her Southern drawl, "Purple Maze." She leveled her gaze at them. "Shall we?"

"I don't know, Vin." Marje stood plastered to the sidewalk.

"What're we going to do when we get in there?" Ruby looked to Marje for support.

Vinyette leaned in, appearing perturbed by their reluctance. "We're gonna look around. That's it. Besides, this is a public place. What're they gonna do?"

"They might put a hex on us," Marje said, gazing at Ruby. They were officially tag-teaming.

"Or summon a devil." Ruby scratched her tingling scalp.

A gust of wind flung trash from the gutter, and a group of laughing college kids ambled by, casting glances at the three women.

"Listen now." Vinyette's eyes sparkled. She was in her element. As she drew closer, the breeze whipped her hair, and it brushed Ruby's cheek. "We've been praying for two years for this city. And now that things start bustin' open, you guys are afraid? Where's your faith? We're stronger than the Purple Maze and Miss Mesopotamia over there.

"And Ruby." The edges of Vinyette's lips curled into a slight, knowing smile. "You're blessed, woman. Seeing visions and raisin' people from the dead. I could only wish. Things are gonna change forever because of you."

Vinyette stared at Ruby with that faint smile, exuding confidence.

The burden ain't yours alone, so don't try carryin' it. Aida was adamant about that. *There's more folks 'n you realize that have a stake in this.* Vinyette and the old woman might as well as have been twins. Maybe Ruby wasn't alone after all. Maybe she could finish this crazy race set before her. Even if it cost everything.

She gulped and looked up at the kaleidoscopic purple swath. "Okay, Vin. Just promise us you won't start anything."

"I promise." Vinyette winked and strode toward the door.

Chapter 30

A SHEET OF BLACK BEADS DRAPED THE ENTRYWAY TO THE Purple Maze. Ruby ducked as she followed Vinyette through the dark curtain, and Marje stumbled after. The veil swayed and rattled with their passing.

Ruby wrinkled her nose, struck by a convoluted mixture of scents—a smell so heady she could taste it. She kept a close eye on Vinyette. No telling what that wild thing would do. Classic rock emanated from a back room, as did a faint whistling sound. Vinyette took a few steps in, scanning the place, and Ruby followed close by.

"I don't know." Marje crept behind them, peeping over Vinyette's shoulder.

Much like a warehouse, the building rose into open beam rafters. Corrugated metal, air ducts, girders—everything overhead—was painted solid black, like an inky night sky. Entwined around each beam tiny white Christmas lights blinked, and in the corners, bare black lights descended and splashed the areas with an eerie fluorescent sheen. An oval cashier's counter sat vacant in the middle of the store.

"Now look at that." Vinyette pointed to a bank of books, maybe ten feet tall, filling the far wall. A frail wooden extension ladder perched against the shelves. "Betcha they don't have Mother Goose over there."

Ruby surveyed the colorful, ragged spines. "Probably spell books."

"Shh." Marje was practically on Ruby's back. "What's that smell?"

"Which one?"

"I don't know. It smells like . . . weeds. Sweet weeds."

Vinyette pointed. "It's that." She veered into a narrow aisle containing an assortment of stout canisters and florid bottles. Heavy parchment unfurled overhead, bridging the displays. "Herbs and oils." Vinyette read the calligraphic lettering. "Let's see, we've got rose petals, sandalwood chips, tansy, dried jasmine flowers, orrisroot. Wow. Half this stuff I've never heard of. Balm of Gilead buds. Mojo Wish Beans. You've gotta be kidding."

"This isn't a health food store, that's for sure." Ruby glanced at the tiny lights twinkling against the ebony expanse. "This is for witches."

Marje squeezed between them, her big gold hoops trembling along with her. "You don't suppose there's one here, do you?"

The whistling in the back changed pitches, becoming a subsonic twill, and a rhythmic metallic ticking started. Vinyette glanced at them, stretched on her tiptoes to eyeball the place, shrugged, and turned to the opposite side of the aisle.

Herbal oils lined the shelves in colorful array. Cruets, flasks, and decanters, from the elegant and dainty to the squat and plain, stretched before them. Lotus oil, patchouli, musk amberette, and absinthe. Ruby licked her lips, but she couldn't taste her clear lip gloss. The smell of the place overwhelmed everything. They'd stepped into a time warp of sorts, a medieval alchemist's parlor— in the middle of town. No wonder she'd stopped shopping down here.

"Check it out." Vinyette lifted a fine red bottle shaped like a winged serpent. "Dragon's blood resin."

"Don't touch it," Marje hissed.

Vinyette clucked her tongue. "I ain't afraid." She carefully wedged the bottle back into place.

"Storm's coming."

They spun about in unison to see a plump, big-bosomed woman with short, unevenly cropped pomegranate hair and wearing an oversized tie-dyed shirt. She stood at the end of the aisle drying a head of collard greens with a paper towel.

"You ladies finding everything?"

"Um." Vinyette cleared her throat.

Ruby nudged Vinyette with her elbow. "No. I mean, yes. We're just looking. Thanks."

"If you need anything, just holler. I'm feeding Crank. He's fidgety, for some reason." Her fingernails were painted neon green and filed into points. She strode off and called over her shoulder, "Our crystals are on sale. Gotta big selection."

They looked at each other for a brief, blank moment.

"Who's Crank?" Ruby asked.

"You mean, what's Crank?" Vinyette jabbed her thumb toward the corner, where the woman was shredding the leafy greens into a bowl in front of a massive driftwood chunk beneath the black light.

"I don't want to know." Marje tugged at Ruby's sweater. "Let's get outta here."

"Hold on a sec." Ruby peered at a row of crude figurines near the white driftwood trunk. Something about the color and shape looked strangely familiar. She wandered out into the main aisle, captivated by the odd icons, and headed toward Crank's estate.

The whistling in the back of the store changed pitches again. Behind an oval doorway draped with more black beads a large figure passed, unsettling the veil, and the metallic clinking started. More intricately shaped glass bottles and sculptures cluttered the back room. The burnt smell was coming from there. But Ruby's eyes were set on the tiny images, and she continued there.

Vinyette came thumping up behind her in her cowboy boots. "What're you doin', hon?"

"I just—" Ruby stared ahead. "I've seen those things before."

Marje bustled up on the other side, looking twitchy.

The shopkeeper set the bowl of greens at the base of the wooden perch and looked side to side. "Crank baby," she warbled. "Cranky." She lumbered off and began hunting through the aisles.

Ruby kept on walking. They passed a row of candles, incense burners of all shapes and sizes, censers, and magic lanterns. The counter in the middle of the store housed an array of ceremonial knives, daggers, and scimitars. Behind the counter a life-sized suit of armor stood guard.

Against the wall rose three shelves of crystal balls. The translucent orbs rested atop plush burgundy fabric. Next to them—and dangerously close to the twisted trunk—was a crude cabinet made of stitched fiber, husks, and hewn limbs, upon which the small colorful images were assembled.

Ruby approached the cabinet, gawking at the miniature characters, with Vinyette and Marje right behind.

"What is it?" Vinyette peered over her shoulder. "What are those things?"

The shopkeeper returned, clearly flustered. "I can't find him. He usually ain't afraid of folks." Then she squinted at them. "You didn't bring something with you, did ya?"

Vinyette patted her pants pockets and looked at Ruby, then Marje. "Nope. Just us." She cast a smug smile at the woman.

Ruby motioned to the family of figurines. "Excuse me, but can you tell me what these things are?"

The woman kept glaring at the girls, her red hair doused vibrant purple in the black light. She glanced at the shelf. "They're Gatekeepers."

Ruby tilted her head, wanting more.

"You know, like archangels, territorial guardians." After a momentary silence she rolled her eyes. "They represent protective spirits. The local seers make them." The woman squatted with a grunt, hands spread on her thick thighs, eyes roaming to and fro. "I gotta find my baby. Pardon me." She heaved herself up and continued her search.

They stood bathed in the luminous sheen, perplexing over the exchange. The low whistling snapped on in the back room, accompanied by grinding guitar riffs from the unseen radio.

"C'mon. Let's get." Marje unzipped her Windbreaker halfway and started fanning herself with her hand. "I've seen enough of this place."

Vinyette watched the shopkeeper hunting the aisles, clearly amused by the woman's agitation.

"All right," Ruby said. "Just let me look at these real quick."

The objects stood five to six inches tall, a collection of shells, pebbles, feather, and twine, assembled into upright animal-like forms. Each had a moniker carved in its wooden base, names likes *Glyph, Genghis,* and *Djinn.* Ruby fingered through the items, which released a faint herbal aura that she tried not to inhale. Then she removed one from the collection. Holding it up to the multicolor light, she inspected the critter.

It wore a skirt made from strips of husks, and a dried dwarf squash perched atop the wooden spine. Two black stones embedded in the cranium formed eerie unblinking eyes. At the figure's side leaned a thin, pointed spear, and on its base, the word *Goliath* scrawled.

Ruby gasped. *It was the stickman!* The same type of figure they'd found perched in the front yard the morning after the resurrection. She dropped the creature on the shelf and stumbled backward, taking Vinyette with her.

"Whoa." Vinyette braced Ruby from behind. "What's wrong?"

An army of Gatekeepers, pint-sized spirit guides, stood in mocking array, with tiny heads and lidless eyes sneering at Ruby.

She was on their turf now.

"Something ain't right." Marje gripped Ruby's arm. "We shouldn't have come here. I told you guys."

The three of them backed away from the corner, preparing to jet, when the black bead curtain parted and the largest man Ruby had ever seen ducked under it and emerged.

The face shield is what made them stop.

A tinted full-face welder's mask covered the man's features, and from behind it, dreadlocks bundled into a ponytail dangled down his back. The cuffs of his denim shirt were rolled up enough to reveal solid tattooed forearms. He wore a welder's apron and biker's boots and, by Ruby's estimate, approached the seven-foot range. The smell of smoke came with him.

He pulled his gloves off, oblivious to the three women, flipped the mask up, and bellowed, "Gwen. Gwen, that lizard's back here."

"Lizard?" Marje yelped and seized Ruby's arm.

The giant man turned to them, and a smile spread across his

grimy cheeks. In a thick voice he said, "Pardon me, ladies. Didn't mean to scare you." A tongue stud flashed behind several missing teeth.

"No. Pardon us," Vinyette said, sounding as if she was trying to compete with the behemoth's burly tone. "We were just on our way out."

Marje nodded, and they backed down the aisle, staring at the man.

Gwen marched past them going the opposite way, wiping her pointy neon fingertips on the tie-dyed shirt. "Now what's he doing back there? He's gonna break something, Clive."

But Clive seemed interested in the women.

His dark eyes followed them as they bumbled their way toward the exit, casting nervous glances over their shoulders.

"Excuse me," he called, his thunderous voice stopping them in their tracks.

Vinyette whispered, "See? I didn't do anything."

Marje moaned, and Ruby swallowed hard as they turned to face him.

Clive put his hand on Gwen's shoulder as she attempted to pass him and spun her about. She scowled up at him and then looked at the three women with a suspicious sideways glare.

"Aren't you the lady in the paper?" He squinted at Ruby and waved his finger. "The one who raised the kid."

Ruby heaved a tired sigh, swung her bad leg forward, and stepped in front of the girls. *Power to tread on serpents and scorpions.* Even though her stomach churned, she believed it. *And nothing shall by any means hurt you.* Not witches, warlocks, or giant welders.

"It is her!" The pomegranate-haired woman's mouth gaped. "I'll be! I knew you brought something with you." Her eyes blazed, hair radiating from the overhead spectrum. "They're *Christians,*" she hissed.

"You got that straight." Vinyette sprung to Ruby's side. "And we did bring something with us. Somethin' more powerful than all these weeds and spell books and little"—she wiggled her fingers in the direction of the Gatekeeper collection—"voodoo dolls combined."

Ruby nudged Vinyette with her elbow. Couldn't the woman back down for a minute?

Clive chuckled, a low rumble that rose from his gut into churlish laughter.

"Yeah?" Gwen put her hands on her hips. "Is that so?"

Marje mumbled behind them, pleading to forgo the confrontation.

"That's right." Vinyette shook her hair back and set her chin. "We attend Canyon Springs Community, and we're proud of it."

Clive and Gwen gawked at each other. Then in unison they burst into laughter.

But Vinyette appeared unruffled, and her eyes retained their gleam. She winked at Ruby and turned back to the couple. "We ain't afraid of you. We got God on our side."

The shopkeeper wiped tears, smearing black mascara across her chubby cheeks. "Yeah? Well if your God is all that, then how come she can't walk?"

Ruby instinctively touched her hip.

Vinyette glanced at Ruby; the gleam in her eyes waned. Her lips compressed into a cold vise, and the tendons in her neck trembled. Suddenly she lunged forward.

Ruby caught her wrist and yanked her back. "Don't, Vin." Ruby cast a weak smile at her friend and turned back to the smirking couple.

A clammy rush of fatigue swelled inside her. The sleepless nights, the rancor and dissension, and the colossal mystery of it all swept across her frame. How many eyes were watching? How many vile spirits had turned their gaze upon her? How much weight could she carry? But alongside the fatigue, in another compartment of her soul, a sense of assurance swelled. *God can't be explained, but He can be trusted.* Daddy believed that all the way to his grave. And so would she. Without knowing why, Ruby began walking toward the couple.

"C'mon, Ruby," Marje pleaded from behind her. "Just leave it."

"I'm coming too." Vinyette clomped to her side with renewed vigor.

The welder tugged off his mask and shook out his dreadlocks, which thumped his shoulders like dark tentacles. He raised one eyebrow, maintaining his toothless grin, as the women approached.

"I suggest you *Christians* go back where you came from." Gwen raised her hand, palm out, neon-nailed index finger doubled over, and waved it in a circular motion, chanting unknown words.

But Ruby and Vinyette advanced.

The Gatekeepers came into view, clustered on the shelf, silent spectators to the clash. *Goliath.* Yep, that was its name. Probably the same spirit too—the one that motivated the big blowhard thousands of years ago—the one little David, the shepherd boy, toppled. It was Brian's and Sean's favorite Bible story, and Ruby smiled at the thought.

She limped forward, stopped, and stood before them with Vinyette at her shoulder and a strange confidence brewing.

Gwen made another hasty hand motion, jiggling the flab of her underarms, and babbled some words. But nothing happened. Clive's grin disappeared, and he towered over them, grinding his teeth.

Ruby didn't have a sling and a stone, but she felt as brave as ever. With placid self-assurance she said, "This is our town."

The words had barely left her mouth when Marje shrieked, jolting everyone.

Ruby and Vinyette spun around to see Marje dancing in the aisle with one hand over her mouth. She jabbed her finger toward the back room. As if on cue, everyone turned.

The head of a monstrous iguana peered from between the black bead curtain.

"Crank!" Gwen cried with affection, creeping toward the reptile with her arms extended. "C'mon, baby. Don't be frightened by the Christians."

The creature's head was the size of a bowling ball, grizzled and white with age. A studded leather collar clasped its neck, and a pink tongue protruded between its jaws. Its icy eyes did not leave Ruby.

She found her arm wrapped in Vinyette's, and together they started walking backward.

"Come on, Cranky." Gwen inched closer. "Here we go."

Crank sucked its tongue back in and rose on its claws, spikes bristling along the arched spine.

"I've got a torch on back there," Clive growled. "Don't let it—"

The iguana reeled, its tail sluicing through the curtain, sending black beads scattering across the floor. The woman barreled after it and disappeared behind the rattling curtain.

Clive clenched his fists, turned, and glared at Ruby. "Get out. Now!"

Glass shattered in the back room, and the woman cursed, followed by a series of thuds.

"OK, we're leaving." Vinyette held her hands up, unable to restrain a smile.

The giant thumped toward the room, hit a puddle of beads, and went skating into the crystal balls with his arms flailing. The impact reverberated through the room. One of the braces snapped and the shelf tilted, dumping the entire row of balls on the floor with successive thuds.

A great whooshing sound burst from the back room, and the lizard skittered through the curtain, aimed at Ruby. Crank tore down the center aisle with its tail whipping the air. Vinyette jumped to one side, Ruby the other, and they let it pass like matadors. The thing was at least six feet in length—a regular dinosaur. Marje shrieked again and tangoed down an aisle as the creature headed for the front door.

"Fire! Clive, hurry!" Gwen yelped, skidding through the curtain. "The trash can's burning. Get the extinguisher. Quick!"

Clive thumped past Ruby, reached under the counter, and pulled out a fire extinguisher. He dashed through the curtain as the extinguisher sputtered and spat to life. White smoke rolled into the shop, washed neon by the black lights.

Vinyette had Ruby's hand and pulled her along as fast as she could go. *Hitch, step. Hitch, step.* Marje joined them, and they dashed for the door.

"Crank!" screeched the shopkeeper. "My baby!" She shoved them aside and lumbered through the black curtain.

Ruby ducked as they passed through, Vinyette in the lead, chattering along the way. The fresh air struck Ruby like a revelation. She inhaled, and the oxygen burned her nostrils. Only then did she realize how intoxicating and oppressive the herbal atmosphere had been. They stood before the storefront, collecting themselves in the twilight.

A horn blared. Then another. Someone shouted, and Ruby looked up just in time to see the iguana racing along the storefronts with the woman waddling after it, crying. Pedestrians scampered from the sidewalk, dropping their bags and shouting obscenities. The lizard scurried past the naked mannequin, causing it to teeter and fall facedown, sending the Robin Hood hat spiraling into the gutter.

Vinyette had their hands and jogged them across the street, laughing with abandon.

The whole marketplace fixated with fear and amusement on the unfolding scene. Someone shrieked as Crank clambered over wrought iron railing and leaped into the art gallery, sending an easel reeling. Cleopatra flew into a rage, hurling profanities as Gwen chugged by. The lizard burst into the street, causing an eruption of car horns and skidding vehicles along Rivermeer.

The girls arrived at the truck breathless. Marje playfully slapped at Vinyette, who leaned against the cab doubled in laughter, while Ruby tried her best to keep from joining the delirium.

Chapter 31

VINYETTE YAKKED THE WHOLE WAY HOME, BUT RUBY DID her best to downplay the incident at the Purple Maze. Of course, this wasn't the first time she'd played the role of wet blanket. She always liked to think of her perpetual pessimism as the upside of being even-keeled.

After dropping Marje at the church to pick up her car, they drove to Ruby's.

"Did you see them running?" Vinyette asked, as she pulled to the curb and turned off the ignition. "That'll teach those weirdoes."

"Well, we're lucky the place didn't burn to the ground."

A wry smile slithered across Vinyette's face. "Maybe it should've."

A stiff, cool breeze rose up the gulley, nudging the old truck. The wild peacocks yowled in the canyon as night descended. The front light came on, and Jack stepped out and began clearing items from the porch, his routine the last three nights. He placed a picture, some candles, and several smaller objects into a black trash bag. By tomorrow it would be full and join the other two on the side of the house.

Vinyette stared out her window. "What's he doing?"

"People have been, um…" Ruby played with her bracelet. "They're coming by and leaving things."

"What kinda things?" She kept staring out the window.

"Gifts, tithes." Would it ever stop sounding so weird? Ruby shifted uncomfortably in the worn vinyl seat.

"You're a saint to them."

"I'm no saint."

"Saint Ruby." She turned and smiled. "They believe you can heal 'em, help them get closer to heaven."

"Well, I can't."

The rap on the side window startled them both. Vinyette rolled it down with an ornery smile.

"If it isn't the church secretary," Jack chided.

"And if it isn't the best youth group leader Canyon Springs ever saw and the husband of my all-time best friend."

"Sorry, my youth group days are over, Vin."

"Well, you got youths." She waved to Sean and Brian, who stood huddled in the doorway, waving. "Now all you need is to get back to church."

Vinyette's forthrightness was refreshing, especially after Ruby had spent the last year tiptoeing around the issue.

Jack glanced at the boys. "Yeah, well—" He looked away. "So you guys gonna sit out here?"

"We're just chatting. Girl stuff, ya know. I gotta get home, get something to eat. We had a busy evening, didn't we?" She patted Ruby's thigh.

Ruby winced, hoping Vinyette wouldn't reveal too much about their escapades downtown.

"Just do me a favor, Vin," Jack said, "and don't prolong this." He held up the trash bag. "I think Ruby's had her share of excitement for one lifetime." He glanced at the sky and braced himself against a gust of wind. "Don't stay out here too long." He started back to the house and said over his shoulder, "It was good to see you, Ms. Church Secretary."

"Be good, Jack."

He half-turned and saluted, took the trash bag to the side of the house, and hustled the boys inside.

Ruby watched the door close behind them. "I can't tell if he's coming or going."

Vinyette cranked her window up. "Still hasn't got over that stuff, huh?"

"Between his mom's passing and Reverend Lawrence's resignation—"

"You mean termination."

"Yeah. He just, I dunno, flipped a switch."

Cool drafts chilled Ruby's ankles. She hunched forward with her hands sandwiched between her legs while Vinyette sat staring at the front porch, fogging the window.

"Why does it happen, Rube?"

"Why does what happen?"

"You know, some get healed and others don't. I mean, why Mondo? Why not Luz Hayes or Mr. Richter's wife?"

Or Celia, the blind girl, or any one of a dozen strangers that had been to her doorstep. Before Ruby had a chance to answer, Vinyette turned back with a guarded, almost guilty look.

"I've been meaning to tell you, just kept puttin' it off. But I guess now's as good a time as any." She fidgeted with her turquoise rings. "This coming July will be six years drug free."

"If Jeff could see you now."

"He still wouldn't want me." She laughed and kept fiddling with the rings, one after the other. "Anyway, you know, I got messed up in all kinds of bad stuff. Thank God, I quit. But I went through a stretch where I was"—she looked out the windshield with her forehead scrunched—"mainlining. Ya know, usin' a needle. Never made it to heroin, praise God. But I probably would've if I hadn't got busted."

Vinyette rubbed the inside of her arm, as if reliving the memory.

"During that time, I guess, I caught something."

Ruby sat stunned for a moment then started shaking her head real slow. *No! Please, God! No!*

"I've been feelin' fine," Vinyette continued. "Haven't lost a step. Last month I went in for my yearly check up. They got back to me. Ruby, they found somethin'. I got...I guess, I got somethin'." She cast a sweet, apologetic smile then turned away and stared out the window again.

The peacocks yowled in the canyon. Now, more than ever, it sounded like a child wailing for a mother who would never come home.

Vinyette turned back, wiping tears from her eyes. "Funny it should happen now, what with the miracle and all. I tried to tell you the other day, but...I ain't mad at God, mind you. He's blessed me. And you never know 'bout these things. I mean nowadays people are living a long time with it. They got medicines and..."

A gust rattled the truck, but Ruby sat numb, unresponsive. The jubilation of downtown's excursion had been sucked out of her; the cold hard reality of the here-and-now seemed to mock that brief, distant euphoria.

It all seemed so familiar.

"I've got things I haven't told you too." Ruby glanced at Vinyette, without smiling, and then stared out her window into the gloomy canyon. Her breath frosted the glass, and she unfolded her tale.

"Daddy called me a miracle baby. They all did. You know, I'm an only child. You can probably tell. Jack says I'm spoiled like one. But I don't blame my father for pampering me. He lost the love of his life because of me." She turned, and Vinyette sat with her glistening eyes frozen on her.

"I guess her labor was really hard. Something about her blood pressure and the doctors. It was a country physician, you know. Not like out here with all the medicine and machines. She worked hard to get me here. It just cost her everything. She died. And all I got was a bad hip out of the deal." She laughed, and snot was already puddling under her nose. Then she fumbled for Vinyette's hand.

"I don't think I can lose someone like that again, Vin. You're closer than a mother...than the one I never had."

Vinyette squeezed her hand.

"Why?" Ruby choked. "Why, Vin?"

"I should've told you sooner, hon. I'm sorry. I been meaning to make it official and all. I'll have to resign, I guess. I just hope folks will understand."

Ruby reached across and gathered Vinyette into herself, drawing the scent of lavender and lemon with her. Sweet and sour. How fitting. She buried her face in Vinyette's hair, her lips quivering.

"C'mon. I ain't dead yet, girl." Vinyette patted Ruby's thigh and wrestled free.

"God can heal you, Vin." Ruby sat up straight and extended her right hand. "I know He can."

Vinyette seized Ruby's hand and clasped it to herself. "Oh, I've already begged and pleaded. Shed enough tears to fill that canyon. I just reckon some things were meant to be. But I'm not going anywhere soon, so you can stop your bawlin'."

"He can do it again." Ruby yanked her hand away. "I know it. I *believe* it."

"Ruby," Vinyette scolded. "It's not on you, woman. Don't do this to yourself."

Ruby's voice rose with accusatory force. "Why? Why use me and then take it away? I don't— Let me pray for you, Vin. It can happen. I believe it with all my heart."

Vinyette released an exasperated sigh. "I know. Call me stupid, but I believe it too."

Ruby clutched Vinyette's hand, clamped her eyes shut, and launched into prayer.

If healing could be earned by sincerity, Ruby's would've surely ripped the dreaded disease out of her friend's body right then and there. But there was no magical aura, no vision, no hot tingling sensations. Her words were eloquent and exact. And full of affection. Yet when she finished, nothing seemed different. She slumped in exhaustion against Vinyette, convinced her friend's condition remained unchanged, that there'd been no miracle.

A series of rapid whacks on the window jolted them.

Brian peered through Vinyette's window, his hands cupped on the glass, while Sean pogoed behind him, waving his hands frantically.

Vinyette sighed and patted Ruby. Then she turned to the spastic boys. "Oh my goodness." She cracked the door open, careful not to topple them, and slipped out of the truck. "There's a coupla rascals." She squatted while they mauled her. "I got me a coupla rascals."

Ruby sat limp. The sad, eerie cry of the peacocks echoed again in the ravine. She wiped her eyes, climbed out of the truck, and slammed the door. She walked around and stood watching the three of them laugh and jostle in the grass.

Her ability to bounce back was obviously nowhere near Vinyette's.

After a few minutes, wherein Vinyette officially surrendered, Ruby shooed the boys inside. She faced Vinyette and they hugged. But something had changed, a boundary had been crossed, a precious vial of life had been drawn from Ruby's depleting reserve.

"Now don't go blabbin'," Vinyette said. "Not just yet. And cheer up. We're gonna win in the end."

Ruby stood on the curb watching Vinyette's truck rumble into the night. Her taillights faded and disappeared, just as did the elation of that evening.

Rain was in the air. A gust whipped her hair, and she stared up into the turbulent dark. Why she'd been chosen and what was required of her seemed more elusive than ever. The miracle had become a curse, a burden she could not carry, a noose tightening ever so slowly about her neck.

Somewhere in the night Ruby's sleep went from restless to tortured, for a shapeless figure, tall and forbidding, lingered at her bed.

At first she reckoned it was Clive, the mammoth, tattooed welder. Until a judge's robe became visible and it was Coy Barkham, gavel in hand, hammering out judgment with a vindictive sneer. Then the image roiled as the phantom in Reverend Clark's office took shape and gaped with its languid, sallow eyes. From that hellish limbo the horror faded…

…and gave way to a vision or dream, apocalyptic and haunting. Ruby stood on a gusty cliff, alone, under a blood-red sky. The rich earth parted, and a seedling burst forth, became a sapling, and sprung into a monstrous tree. She craned, watching it rise higher and higher into the heavens. As it stood in all its glory, a tiny figure—a mere mite—approached, pulled open the trunk, and wriggled inside the tree.

As the trunk sealed behind the figure, the great tree sagged, and, like a black shower, its leaves poured to the ground, revealing a gaunt scaffold of bare branches. Twigs and limbs crackled to earth, and the tree groaned and rested, a skeleton of its former self.

Clouds churned on the horizon, turning gold and red and black with the passage of time, and the tree withered, becoming a dead, gray icon. Until a light sprung from the sky, a single warm beam that descended on her. She stood before the dead tree, wrapped in that friendly ray. And within it a voice emerged.

"Who will rescue My beloved?"

And she knew the beloved lay entombed and the task to be hers.

"I'm weak," she said. "My thigh is crippled. And my husband says I'm a perpetual pessimist. He's probably right. But I'll do what You ask. It just won't be pretty."

And the voice inside the ray laughed—a resounding, unbridled joy that reached the edges of space and every particle therein.

As she rested in the warm, inviting ray, the tree groaned and stretched, as though rising from a deep slumber. The ground heaved, and she stumbled. Clods of parched earth rippled, and dark tendrils slithered forth, became tentacles, and entwined themselves round her feet. She stood immobilized as the hungry roots clambered up her legs, to her waist, groping, strangling, and sucking the life out of her.

Ruby jolted up, gasping, gripping the front of her nightshirt, and the dream scattered. The dark shapeless figure was gone, a figment of the dreamscape. She tossed the covers aside, swung her legs off the bed, and sat in the dark, panting. Over her shoulder Jack rustled but did not wake.

She slipped out of bed and padded into the kitchen. The stove light cast a faint glow about the room. *One thirty-six.* The ticking of the wall clock, amplified in the stillness, measured out the moments.

She removed Jilly's picture from the refrigerator and studied it in the dim light. The gray trunk, drawn with such precision by the little girl, tilted to the side, and on one branch, a bright green leaf.

This is what started it all, the revelation that knocked her off her feet and set the wheels in motion. She held the crayon masterpiece with reverence.

It's a forthtellin', Aida said, *a foreshadow of the real Godsend.* Ruby smiled at the memory of the old woman's Southern drawl. *With the curse comes a promise. Just as someone gave their life for the bindin', someone must give their life for the breakin'.*

With the words came an unusual peace. And there, early Friday morning in her kitchen, Ruby Case understood her calling and found the resolve to take the next step. Miss Even-Keeled was on a rescue mission that would surely take her life.

Chapter 32

"Y̶ou're in danger," Cynthia said.

Clark pressed the cell phone to his ear and squinted. In spite of her warning, hearing her voice bolstered his spirit. The last time they'd spoken, it was to seal the divorce. Now her voice gave him hope.

"I had a dream, Ian." She was always so intense, and that passion—that never-ending intellectual curiosity—had drawn them together. Her pointed phrases and husky timbre reawakened in him a better day. "I keep having it. I–I'm not sure what I should do, but...are you all right?"

He rocked back in his office chair. He wanted to say he still loved her. "I am. But..."

"There's a smell. It's like flesh. Burned flesh, Ian."

He glanced at the corner of his office, and the hackles on his neck rose.

"I don't know," she said. "I think it's a warning. You're in danger."

After hearing Keen's spiel and witnessing his museum of oddities, her concerns were hard to argue with. Clark tried to reassure her, but in the end, she had the last word.

"Please," she said, "be careful." And then a long silence, full of electronic showers.

He got off the phone in a semi-stupor.

Clark closed the laptop and rested his elbows on the desk. With Sunday's outline completed and now, having had a civil—if not, promising—conversation with his ex, a strange but welcome optimism greeted him. Even though the church's complacency and corruption in the elder board were partly his fault, he had a platform to make things right. After his sermon this coming

Sunday, he would make a few more enemies, but at least he'd be standing up for what he believed.

As he sat contemplating the implications of it all, someone knocked on his office door and flung it open. It was Vinyette.

"Reverend, Ruby's missing!"

"Missing? What do you mean?"

Jack Case strode in behind her. He wore a black San Francisco Giants cap speckled with water drops and sported a full-on scowl. "I got home from work, and Ivy was with the boys. She said Ruby called, needed her to babysit. Didn't say where she was going; she just took off." He lifted the bill of his cap and glared at Clark. "My wife has enough things to deal with, without you scaring her."

Vinyette took his arm. "Calm down, Jack."

"I ain't gonna calm down!" He yanked away and marched to Clark's desk with his shoulders squared and his eyes blazing. "You know as well as me, Vin, that this weasel doesn't care about you people!"

"Jack!" Vinyette fumbled for his arm. "Wait!"

Clark pushed back from his desk without thought of defending himself, rose to his feet, and faced Jack.

"He's been a puppet for these nimrods ever since they chased old man Lawrence outta town. And you know it! And now he's feeding Rube a crock and scarin' her silly." Jack inched closer, his breath pummeling Clark's face. "If you weren't a minister, I'd..."

Clark stood stolidly, almost wishing Jack would hit him. He deserved it. If not for his complicity, then for penance.

Vinyette tugged Jack away. "Cool it! Both of you!" She glared at them.

Jack muttered something, stepped away, and resumed his pacing.

"Maybe she went to the market," Vinyette said. "Or Livery's."

"You know as well as me, Vin, Ruby doesn't just leave the boys spur of the moment. It's talk about that curse that's got her freaked out." Jack cast a sore glance at Clark. "She's already got people breathing down her neck like she's some kinda celebrity.

And she ain't! And with you people tryin' to convince her she's got some type of power..."

Clark's tone was firm but not combative. "I haven't been trying to convince Ruby of anything."

"Yeah, well..."

"I'm still trying to figure this out myself. But you're right—I have been a weasel who hasn't cared about these people."

Vinyette and Jack turned, gawking at him.

"Listen, something's happening with Ruby," Clark said. "Something...fantastic. I haven't tried to scare her. But there's some things we *should* be scared about. I've been too wrapped up in myself, but..." Clark peered at Jack. "You think something bad's happened. Why?"

Jack shifted his weight and started pacing behind the leather guest chairs. "She was bummed this morning. Real bummed. She hasn't been sleeping. Oscar Hayes called last night and wanted her to come over. He's convinced she can heal Luz, some craziness. Ruby didn't go and then felt guilty about it."

"Maybe that's where she went," Vinyette offered.

Jack shook his head. "I called there. Oscar begged me to send her over. I lied and said she was sick." He dug in his Levi's pocket and produced a folded sheet of white paper that he handed to Clark. "And she left this."

Clark took the paper and looked at Jack, unsure of what new surprise awaited him. It was drawing paper, folded into quarters, which he opened. He read the elegant handwritten text aloud.

> Dear Jack,
>   Daddy used to say we're closest to God when we're at the end of us. I can only trust that God is very near, because I am very tired. I cannot understand why I've been chosen, but I will do my best to follow to the end. Please don't worry; I'm in good hands. Stand strong, my love. Ruby.

Jack resumed his pace. "It's all wrong."

"She won't do anything stupid." Vinyette folded her arms and tapped her foot on the carpet. "Not Ruby. She's just stressed. She needs some space."

"Yeah, well—" Jack stopped and pointed at Vinyette. "It was right after you guys talked out front."

Vinyette tapped her foot faster.

Clark turned the paper over and stared. "Will you look at this." A child's crayon sketch graced the back of the note with an image he recognized. A gray withered tree with bare branches filled the page, and from the stark plain limbs, a bright green leaf unfurled. "Look at this, Vin."

Vinyette hustled over to gaze at the picture, and a look of astonishment swept over her. "Isn't that—? It's the vision she had."

"Where'd she get this, Jack?" Clark displayed the crayon caricature.

"I don't know. Some kid at church, I think. She's always bringing stuff home."

Clark studied the picture again. In the lower left corner was a royal blue letter J. "Help me, Vin." He spread the picture on his desk.

Vinyette stood beside him, staring at the picture and mumbling to herself, before she said, "Jilly! Jilly Raynee. It has to be. Ruby teaches that age group. And Jilly adores her."

Clark reared up, stroking his chin. "Vin, would you please call Mrs. Raynee? I have a hunch that little Jilly might be able to help us out."

A fine mist blanketed Ian Clark's windshield as he pulled up to Mrs. Patricia Raynee's house. In the passenger seat Jack Case fidgeted. Their relationship was strained from day one. Of course, Jack had plenty of other issues brewing. But as far as Clark was concerned, Jack's resentment of him was well founded. Reverend Lawrence's resignation had angered more than a few members. So after Clark filled the vacancy, it was not a surprise he was automatically added to several hit lists. Such was the politics of religion. Of course, the way he'd acted the last year had not won

Clark any sympathizers. And neither he nor Jack had lifted a finger to heal the breach. The tension of that unspoken acrimony lay like a thicket around them.

Before the Jeep came to a complete stop, Jack had his door open. He lunged out, leaped over the curb, and strode to the front porch where Patricia Raynee waited, wiping her hands on a checkered dishtowel. Clark shut off the ignition and glanced behind the seat. His hiking boots and wool beanie lay in their usual spot. With the storm moving inland, he knew he would need them soon.

As he approached the house, a rich aroma of freshly baked pastry greeted him. Mrs. Raynee wore a cherry-stained apron and stood propping the screen open. "C'mon in, guys."

They stamped their feet on the mat and crossed the toasty threshold. The convergence of air masses made Clark shiver. Mrs. Raynee closed the door and stood with her back to it, wiping her hands on the towel and surveying the men. A tall, affable woman with stunning turquoise eyes, she taught art composition at the college and carried herself with the type of confidence that made insecure men dither.

"We've missed you at church, Jack." Her gracious smile eliminated any note of condemnation.

Jack looked away, then returned her gaze, tipped his cap, and said, "Thank you, ma'am."

"She was here less than an hour ago." Mrs. Raynee gestured toward the kitchen. "She wanted to see Jilly."

The little, blonde five-year-old sat at the kitchen table, legs curled underneath her, humming and coloring, surrounded by all the accessories of a budding artist.

Jack shifted nervously. "Did she look—I mean, was she all right?"

"Ruby's never one to show a lot of emotion, but you probably know that. She was quiet, yeah. Mainly wanted to ask Jilly some questions. Why? Something isn't wrong, is it?"

Clark unzipped his jacket. "We're not sure. She's been under a lot of pressure lately."

"I'll bet. I've been following the paper. Of course, they blow everything out of proportion. Jilly talks about her all the time."

"They have a special relationship?"

"Oh, yeah." A lavish smile graced her glowing cheeks. "Jilly's always been sensitive to spiritual things. I've learned to trust her, really. And she and Ruby—she calls her, Ruby Rainbow—really hit it off in Sunday school. Jilly's in Sean's class, I think." She looked at Jack, as if expecting confirmation, but he stood spacing out.

"Can we talk to her?" Clark nodded toward the little girl.

"Sure." Mrs. Raynee led them into the kitchen, untied her apron, and hung it over the back of a chair. The woman's artistic sensibilities showed in the décor—color-washed walls of cream and sunny yellow, a wrought iron corner piece with sweeping philodendrons and terra cotta vase bulging with Easter lilies. A cherry pie sat cooling on the counter, and the windowpanes sweat with condensation.

"Jilly, some folks are here to see you."

The little girl kept grinding away on a swirling light blue swath. "Hello," she offered, without looking up. To one side, two fig bars lay on a napkin next to a plastic cup half-full of milk. On her other side rested a cigar box with the lid open, full of crayons in various stages of wear.

"It's Reverend Clark, Jills. And Ruby's husband."

At that the little girl stopped coloring, turned, and looked at Jack with her big green eyes. "Ruby Rainbow's worried about you."

Jack glanced at Clark. "Well, I'm worried about Ruby Rainbow." The softness of his tone surprised Clark. Below the gruff, cynical exterior he had a kid's heart. Like most folks, Clark guessed, it got buried along the way. "I need to find her, I'm Ruby's angel."

"Oh no, you're not." Jilly turned away abruptly and sat staring forward.

Jack looked at Mrs. Raynee, who shrugged in response. "Oh yes, I am," he said, sounding extra diplomatic.

"Uh-uh. I saw her angel, and she's not like you."

Clark and Jack exchanged glances again.

"You've seen Ruby's angel?" Mrs. Raynee asked with a note of skepticism.

Jilly nodded and went back to coloring.

"Jilly, can you tell Reverend Clark what you and Ruby talked about a little bit ago?"

The little girl kept on coloring, tongue worming around in her mouth.

"Jilly?"

"We talked about the tree."

"This tree?" Clark slipped the picture from his top pocket, unfolded it, and set it on the table in front of the little girl.

"Mmm hmm," she said, without looking at the picture.

"What did she ask you about the tree?"

She set her crayon down, nibbled on a fig bar, and brushed the crumbs away from her masterpiece. Then she rummaged through the cigar box and came out with half a blue crayon and resumed her work.

Mrs. Raynee's voice was more firm. "What did she ask about the tree, Jilly?"

"She wanted to know about the pretty leaf."

Clark pointed to the picture. "This leaf?"

The girl nodded.

"What did you tell her about the pretty leaf?"

"That if she climbs the mountain, she'll find it."

"The mountain?" Jack asked, his tone laced with concern. "What mountain, hon?"

"The big mountain with the ugly tree. Mmm hmm. If she's climbs the mountain," her voice ascended in oscillating glee, "the leaf'll grow."

"Climb the mountain?" Jack hung his head. "Don't tell me she went up there."

But Clark was already folding the picture up and thanking Mrs. Raynee. Jack rushed to the door and fumbled with the handle.

"I'll be praying," Mrs. Raynee said. "Let me know if I can do anything."

"Thanks, Pat." He squeezed her hands. "And thank you, Jilly." He patted her head.

She nodded and kept on coloring.

Clark joined Jack at the door and stopped. "Jilly, when Ruby Rainbow left, did her angel go with her?"

"Oh, yes." She turned around and looked at them with her big green eyes. "And a whole bunch more was coming."

Chapter 33

CLARK FLIPPED OPEN HIS CELL PHONE, PEERED THROUGH the watery windshield, and turned the wipers up a notch. The craggy southern hillside that bordered Stonetree rose like a monstrous boundary before them, vaulting upward into the mist. He craned for a glimpse of the petrified oak but couldn't see it.

"I can't believe her." Jack shook his head. "And in this weather."

Clark auto-dialed the church office, and Vinyette answered. He rushed over the details but asked her to keep things confidential until they knew more.

"How's Jack?" Vinyette asked before hanging up.

Clark glanced at Jack, who sat turned to the window, staring blankly into the foggy pane. "Uh, not good. Gotta go." He clicked off. "You ever been up here?"

Jack shook his head without looking at him. "Once, when we first moved here, I came up with Brian. We didn't get to the top. I just wanted to see what the stories were about, but..."

After a minute of silence Clark said, "Should I call the police?"

Jack flashed him a let's-not-go-there type of look. "We ain't sure she's even up here. And if she is, we won't need them. Until after I'm finished with her."

Clark looked sternly over the top of his glasses.

"Kidding, Rev," Jack said. "Just kidding."

The single-lane road meandered along the foothills. Trails and gravel fingers branched off, snaking up the steep canyon in various degrees of difficulty. A huge orange boulder rested amidst shards of rock, remnants of a thunderous landslide.

"That's it," Jack pointed.

Clark veered onto the gravel, near the boulder, and spotted a dirt road zigzagging its way up the craggy face, disappearing in the mist. He sat there with the Jeep idling.

"She went up there?"

"It's not that bad. Level, for the most part." Jack peered forward. Tiny rivulets had formed from the thickening gloom, etching muddy veins in the clay. "But that was three years ago. There's switchbacks most of the way. Then a trailhead to park. Supposed to be about a fifteen-minute hike from there."

"And a graveyard's up there, is that right?"

"That's what they say."

"How'd they get... did they use horseback to haul the coffins up there?"

Jack rubbed his nose and sniffled. He turned to Clark, looking impatient with the quiz. "There's some old shacks, an abandoned mining town up there. I guess people lived on the mountain. A foot trail comes up from East Basin on the other side." He hung his head and exhaled. "I cannot stinkin' believe her."

"She's a tough one, huh?"

"You don't know the half of it." He glanced at Clark with a slight hint of warming in his expression.

"All right." Clark shifted into gear. "Hang on."

Broken glass littered the gravel along with crumpled beer cans and stained rocks. The place was a haven for the college crowd. Yet their affinity for environmentalism and earth worship didn't appear to have had any practical lifestyle implications. The tires skidded, caught, and they lurched forward.

The road traveled in a series of long switchbacks, just as Jack said, and they observed fresh car tracks along the way.

"That's hers." Jack pointed at a set of tracks clinging close to the mountainside. "I'm pretty sure."

"Then what're those?"

Another set of tracks wove atop the first, fresher by all appearance.

"Wide wheelbase," Jack said. "And deep. It's a big car." He bounced with the choppy motions of the vehicle. "Like someone was following her."

They glanced at each other, and Clark accelerated.

Jack hung his head again, pulled the bill of his cap over his eyes, and heaved a sigh. The poor guy was outgunned. He sat there quiet like, then yanked his hat up and composed himself. "I just hope the kid sends reinforcements."

They entered the mist, and Clark turned the wipers up another tick. The road jackknifed several times, and the grade increased. Jack braced himself against another turn as the tires spun and caught. A boulder with a spray-painted neon skull loomed before them. Clark tapped the brakes, slowed, and the dirt road emptied into a wide flat surface rimmed with rocks. Ruby's SUV, clods of mud clinging to the undercarriage, sat parked near a tilted wooden sign. Next to it was an older model, military style, black Hummer.

"Someone else is up there." Jack cracked his knuckles and studied the vehicle as Clark pulled next to it.

"Could just be kids," Clark offered, without much confidence.

They ground to a stop. Jack flung his door open and began marching around the tank and peering through its windows. Clark's loafers were no match for the muck, so he pulled the seat up and retrieved his hiking boots from the back, along with the wool cap. Never in his wildest would he have thought he'd be needing them for a manhunt. Between the black leather jacket, waffle stompers, and ragged wool beanie, Clark felt like a vagabond.

"What's this?" Jack leaned over the front windshield of the Hummer, squinting.

Clark laced his boots, yanked the beanie on, and locked the Jeep. He went to the car and leaned over the opposite side. A pendant on a braided leather cord hung from the rearview mirror.

"It's a pentagram." Clark looked across the vehicle at Jack, prepared to give further explanation.

But Jack had already turned and started an anxious trek toward the sign. "Let's go, Clark," he barked over his shoulder.

From the ragged wooden sign a path rambled upward until disappearing between boulders and mist. *Bridge River Cemetery, 1890.* Obscene symbols and names carved into the weathered wood disfigured the landmark, and a coil of human excrement lay nearby. Jack glanced at the sign and trudged up the path, not waiting for Clark to catch him.

He removed his glasses, now glazed with moisture, and plodded forward until he reached Jack. Clark shoved his hands in the pockets of his jacket and came up behind Jack, panting and light-headed. Clark had the hiking experience, but Jack was the one blazing a trail. It would be impossible to maintain this torrid pace.

Smooth boulders rose on both sides of the trail, granite crowns bursting from the rich earth, giant half-domes that formed a narrow canyon. Crunching gravel sounded in the tight passage, and the thinning oxygen burned Clark's nostrils.

Jack huffed and drove forward. "Do you have a signal up here?" he asked over his shoulder.

Clark wiped his glasses off, put them back on, and pulled the phone out of his jacket pocket. "No." He held the phone up and waved it around, watching the signal bars stay flat. "Nothing."

"Keep it handy."

A steady drizzle fell now. Jack's ball cap bled into another shade, and droplets fell steadily off the bill. He slogged upward, his work boots saturated.

Just as Clark was about to ask for a breather, Jack shouted. "Here! Hurry." He jogged forward, looking from side to side with his fists balled. The path emptied into a vast, level clearing.

Clark pulled up, shoulders hunched, hyperventilating. Before him spread an ocean of bright spring grasses and glistening wildflowers, blanketed by low-lying clouds. The path cut across the field and faded into a wall of murky misshapen forms less than a hundred yards ahead.

Now upon the mountaintop, the sky stretched wide, unfurling above them like a colorless tarp, a circus tent without end. Other than the drudging of their footfall, the air was still. Perhaps the death gods lived here. If so, they were most surely aware of Clark's arrival.

He stumbled forward. "Is that the—"

"It's the cemetery." Jack settled into a nervous stride, scanning the tombstones sprinkling the vast green field ahead of them. Suddenly he stopped, grew tall and straight, and raised his eyes to the northern edge of the plain.

At the cliff's edge, an immense specter loomed in the misty shroud, towering above the graveyard.

Clark wiped the moisture off his glasses—an almost futile endeavor in the steady sprinkle—and joined Jack. They stood side by side staring at the monstrous form.

An eerie calm seemed to possess Jack. "What'd the kid say? What was Ruby lookin' for?" Flumes of breath chugged from his mouth.

"A leaf. Something about leaves."

Jack adjusted his hat and gazed at the soaring silhouette, as if negotiating an approach.

Clark yanked the phone out of his pocket and flicked it open. Still no signal.

Jack glanced at Clark, groaned, and resumed his march up the path. Clark shoved the phone in his pocket and hurried to catch him.

As they went, the great stone tree became visible, more daunting with every step. Its massive gray limbs swooped over the flatland, trunk thrust from the bowels of the earth like an ancient pillar. Branches, long barren, stretched skyward, forming a tangled, empty web against the monochrome sky. Under its canopy timeworn headstones tilted like oversized acorns dropped from the hoary oak. Eighty or ninety feet in height, with girth to match, the wild tales about the cursed tree now seemed meager in the presence of the terrible vision.

Clark's eyes rose, and with each step, so did a great unease. It was as if they'd crossed a boundary, cracked open an invisible door, and wandered into a giant's lair. He searched the sky overhead, his ears peeled for warning, but a deathly stillness wrapped the mountaintop. His heartbeat reverberated throughout his frame.

As they slogged forward, a high-pitched cry slashed the air, forcing both of them to freeze. A hawk burst from the bowels of the oak, sending twigs showering. It swept across the cemetery with nary a wing beat, ascended and disappeared overhead, bleating.

That's when they noticed the hooded figures.

Jack seized Clark by the bicep, but the minister had already seen them. Two people wearing black, drawn hoodies surrounded a tombstone near the edge of the graveyard. One of them bobbed up and down, circling the headstone, while the other stood watch.

"Is that her?" Jack whispered. "What're they doing?"

"I don't know." If the pentagram in the Hummer was any indication, they weren't here paying respects.

"Well, let's find out."

Without hesitation Jack marched down the footpath, apparently unconcerned about the noise of his approach. He strode with his chest out and fists clenched, while Clark scurried behind. The ministry hadn't softened Clark that much. If necessary, he could handle a physical altercation. But by the looks of it, Jack wouldn't need his help.

The path cut through the middle of the graveyard, headstones randomly spread on both sides. Most of the markers were crude and unadorned, testimony to the early settlers of these parts. Weathered by time, they stood cockeyed, caked with gull droppings and bleached by the coastal sun.

But neither of them had time to appreciate the historic significance, for both hooded figures were now waiting for them.

Gnarled branches extended overhead as they passed under the tree's skeletal umbrella, and several logs, long decayed, crisscrossed the area. Heavy droplets pattered the ground around them, filling the path with pock-laden puddles. From here the trunk looked enormous, maybe twenty-five or thirty feet in diameter. It tilted north, extending over the cliff's edge before rising upright.

The hawk shrieked above as Jack and Reverend Clark approached the hooded figures.

At the foot of the grave a short stout man stood with his arms folded, hood drawn so tight that just a small oval of pale impish face showed.

"Afternoon, gentleman," he said in a high-pitched, nasally voice.

Without acknowledging the man, Jack scanned the area. As he drew a breath and prepared to speak, Clark stretched his hand out to silence him.

"Afternoon," Clark said. "Hope we didn't disturb you. We're looking for someone. You wouldn't have happened to see anyone else up here, would you?"

The man turned to his companion, a heavyset woman with locks of dyed red hair protruding from under her hood, who studied the intruders. Her nails were painted neon green and pointed—a detail that would have provoked more interest in another setting. She brushed a crumbly substance off her hands and shook her head. Turning back, the man replied, "Nope. Just us."

Jack agitated, glanced at the gnarled branches snaking over-head, and glared at them. In a semicivilized tone he said, "Well, you parked right next to someone."

"A lotta folks come up here." A grin crossed the man's plump red lips. He wore eyeliner, waterproof by all estimates, and a faint black mustache. His hands were large, disproportionate to his body, and he possessed the build of a wrestler.

That's when Clark noticed the ring.

A circle of rocks, from pebbles to boulders, encompassed the entire grave, and in the middle, upon a bed of fresh vegetation, lay a druid doll—a pagan stickman—identical to the effigy in Beeko's lab. It stared into the gray sky, stretched upon the mound like some lifeless, feral mutation.

Jack must have seen it too, for he stepped off the footpath and waded through the grass, pointing at the hideous doll. "Did you do this?"

The short man retained his grin and did not quaver at Jack's approach. His hands spread and poised at his side.

"You put one of those in our yard, didn't you?" Jack's fists balled, his knuckles white with tension.

"Jack!" Clark shouted and bounded off the trail into the wet grass. "Hold on!" He wove through several slumping gravestones and seized Jack's shoulder. "We don't know anything. Not yet."

The woman at the other end of the grave backed up, still brushing the powder off her pointy nails. "Leave us alone. We ain't hurting anyone. And we don't know where she is. So let us be."

Clark studied her. "I never said we were looking for a woman."

The hawk screeched overhead, and raindrops tamped the ground around them like hundreds of little feet marching to war.

"Where is she?" Jack hissed.

Clark tightened his grip on Jack's shoulder, knowing at any moment the guy would snap. Only six feet from the imp, Jack could be upon him in a wink.

Somehow the man retained his smug, unnerving grin, even with Jack in his face. Then he squinted and said, "You're messin' with things you have no business in."

"Listen, bud." Jack took a step closer, his jaw set. "As far as I'm concerned, you're defacing public property. And my wife *is* my business. So help me God, if you freaks have done somethin' to her—"

"She's no match for the Gatekeeper!" The woman plodded around the grave. "You can't fight the powers. You, your church, your piddly little prayer team. It's already been tried; you shoulda known that." She stood next to her companion and with a note of sympathy said, "She doesn't stand a chance."

Jack fumbled for words, and a tremor shook his body.

Clark tightened his grip on Jack's shoulder and tried to nudge him back.

"This is holy ground," the man said, "and I advise you gentlemen to back off." He spread his arms in a graceful, ballet-like motion. "Unless you need a little assistance." His grin gave way to a toothy sneer.

Jack's tremor became a roar. He yanked free of Clark's grip and lunged at the man.

Clark stumbled, slipped on the matted grass, and plopped on his rump.

As Jack dove, the man ducked and rolled backward with seeming ease. Landing in a crouch, he thrust his leg out, almost perpendicular to his body. The boot to the gut sent Jack catapulting onto his back. He slapped the muck, just missing a marble headstone, and gulped air as his breath left him. The man rose, brushing grass off his hood and shoulders, and stared calmly at Clark.

The smell of fresh spring grass filled his nostrils, but Clark had no time to enjoy it. He scrambled to his feet, eyes darting from the hooded dwarf to Jack, who was lying stunned, still sucking air. So much for Jack's physical prowess. Suddenly Clark's confidence in his own physical fitness withered.

The woman watched Jack writhing and tipped her head toward the man. "This is Breyven, the local warlock. He guards the gate, and right now, you better man up."

Chapter 34

E'D NEVER CONFRONTED A GENUINE WARLOCK, AND WITH one standing in front of him, Clark felt rather intrigued, as if discussing the man's religious history and upbringing might shed light on this problematic lifestyle choice. But seeing Jack writhing in the mud prevented any sort of meaningful dialogue with the hooded imp. Besides, what arrested Clark's attention at the moment was not Breyven and his haughty, puckish demeanor but Ruby limping toward them from behind the dead oak, bleeding.

Clark froze at the sight of the ragged woman weaving through the tombstones, looking as if she'd just dragged herself out of a foxhole in the middle of combat.

"Stop!" she shouted, slogging forward, jeans muddy and torn. Underneath the shredded fabric her left knee oozed blood. "No more!" Her hair dangled in wet strands before her face, her black wool jacket saturated and mud stained.

Jack rolled over, struggled to his feet, and glared at the warlock, who gave a curt nod in return.

The woman stood rigid and watched Ruby approach. "Breyven. Breyven! She's got some kinda magic. Her and her friends tore up the shop yesterday. Be careful."

Breyven turned to face Ruby, who hobbled to Jack and embraced him, burying her face in his chest. Then she pulled free of him, limped to the opposite side of the grave, and stared at the stick man and the ring of rocks.

"You can't fight them." Ruby cast a tired look at Jack.

"Watch me." Jack snatched up his hat, groaning as he bent over.

"No, not like that."

Jack put his cap on and hobbled to her side. "What were you thinking anyway? Are you hurt? Did these creeps do somethin' to

251

you?" He glowered at Breyven, as if ready for round two.

Ruby gazed at the tombstone and shook her head. "No. I slipped and skinned myself. I heard them coming and hid."

Breyven cocked his head. "And what, pray tell, brought you here?"

Ruby fell to her knees, wincing. She leaned over the grave and began wiping the face of the headstone. "I was sent to unlock the door and heal the tree."

The warlock hissed as Ruby's hand brushed the granite. "Oh, I think not." His nasal voice turned throaty.

The woman tugged at Breyven's jacket. "C'mon, man. It's not worth it. They can't beat 'em anyway."

Jack thrust his finger at the imp, eyes blazing. "Listen, bro, if she was sent to open the door and heal the tree, then that's what she's gonna do. Clark! Wake up! Call the cops! Somethin'! 'Cuz when I get through with this maggot—"

"Jack!" Ruby pleaded. "That won't stop him." She settled back on her knees, eyes distant and placid. "This will."

Then she grabbed the totem and twisted her body, as if preparing to heave it. The warlock bolted forward across the grave and seized her wrist. They locked eyes. Ruby struggled against his knotted, oversized-hand but couldn't budge. He lay on his belly, stretched in the mud, his grin replaced by a bestial sneer.

Breyven's tone descended several octaves, becoming a guttural growl. "Drop it."

The words had barely left his mouth when Jack reared back and booted the warlock in the jaw. The impact wrenched Breyven's head back with such violence Clark was sure Jack had rendered the man unconscious. His body twirled and splat into the soupy mess. Ruby tumbled backward, flinging the stick figure into the air. It fragmented into pieces as it arced. The effectiveness of the shot seemed to surprise even Jack, who stood stunned for a moment before huddling over Ruby.

"Breyven!" The woman made a garbled yelp and backed up.

The warlock groaned and heaved himself into a sitting position. Then he scrambled to his feet and assumed another crouch.

His lip was split; blood and saliva drooled down his jaw. He ignored the wound and fixed Ruby from across the grave with bestial black eyes.

"Leave 'em, Breyven!" the woman barked. "We don't need the cops up here again."

But the exhortation did nothing to alter Brevyn's stance. The stumpy warlock, guardian of the gate, remained squared off against the crippled, miracle-working homemaker and her husband.

Meanwhile Clark stood gaping, powerless, a spectator to the battle. If he'd kept his guard up, this would have never happened. Instead he had surrendered to the cowardice, entertained Keen's madness, become a channel for powers outside of his control. It was the law of life. *Whatsover a man sows, that shall he also reap.* If Ruby's life wasn't in the balance, he'd stand up and reap his punishment like a man.

But she had struggled to her knees and met the warlock's gaze with unflinching fury. They stared at each other like caged animals. Then, with slow, calculated movements, Ruby began plucking the stones from the rock ring and tossing them helter-skelter about the graveyard.

Thunder rumbled overhead, a rolling quake that spread across the open sky like a sonic tsunami. The death gods had them in their sights. Clark looked into the fomenting gray.

Somewhere in the valley, little Jilly sat coloring by steamy windowpanes, ensconced in the aroma of cherry pastries, praying for legions of angels. The thought brought a smile to his face and gave Clark an unusual reassurance—just enough to move him to action.

He lurched toward the grave, positioning himself between Ruby and the warlock. His voice cracked as he blurted, "I'm the one they want."

Breyven glanced at Clark and snarled. He crouched lower, looking even more like a wrestler—minus the eyeliner—his lip swollen and seeping bloody liquid. He opened and closed his gnarly-knuckled hands and sized up the minister. This wouldn't be a fair fight.

Breyven remained poised. "We've named 'em, ya know?"

"Named what?"

"The Pantheons, dimwit! The ones they brought here. We named 'em. And now they're gonna help me beat you beyond recognition."

After seeing the man's duck-and-roll maneuver against Jack, Clark was pretty sure the warlock did not need divine assistance to keep his word. At this stage Clark hoped only to die with nobility. At the least, lose some teeth. As he drew a deep breath and braced himself for the onslaught, the large woman bellowed.

"Stop! Look!" She yanked the hood off her head, revealing funky red hair. With wide eyes and mouth gaping, she pointed a neon nail at Reverend Clark.

The manic ferocity drained from the warlock's face, and he rose to his feet, brushing his hands on his sweat jacket. Joined by the woman, they stood peering at some point on Clark's chest.

Ruby continued dismantling the rock ring, now with Jack's assistance. The stones plunked the ground and skidded across the swamp as they cleared the grave. Yet they both stopped to see what had given pause.

Standing placid next to the grave and its strange bed of herbs, Clark looked down, patting his chest, trying to identify the object of their fascination. His fingers groped until resting on his necklace. It'd become such a part of him, such a normal part of his attire, he hardly remembered he had it on. Keen christened him *the Wandering Soul* years back and said the pendant would protect him until his journey was complete. Now, with the occultists cowering before him, eyes fixated on the crude ornament, Clark guessed the power was real and his journey wasn't over.

Breyven's face grew nausea white. Either Jack's boot had knocked some sense into him, or the warlock knew something Clark had yet to discover. "That's it," Breyven murmured. "The magician's amulet."

"He's the One," the large woman sighed, fog rising from her words.

Clark held the pendant out from his collar and leaned forward, like a vampire slayer fending off night creatures with a crucifix.

If the jewelry possessed some power, then he might as well use it. The sky rumbled again, and the steady sprinkle became a shower. He ripped his glasses off, perched them on his beanie, and watched the couple begin their slow retreat, backing out of the ancient graveyard, whispering to one another, until they turned and jogged into the mist.

Jack jumped to his feet and shouted after the couple, "And you better not touch those cars!" Then he massaged his lower back and groaned.

Ruby continued clearing the grave, groveling in the mud, casting rocks over her shoulder and removing the herbal bouquet.

Clark's pulse pounded in his throat, and the adrenaline rush hit him hard. He took his hand off the necklace and staggered away from the grave, drawing deep breaths.

That's when he noticed the single word carved in the plain granite tombstone—*Beloved*.

Jack stood over Ruby, looking befuddled as she scuttled around the grave, clearing debris. "Are you happy?" He stretched from side to side and grimaced. "C'mon, Rube. It's over. Let's get outta here before we die of pneumonia."

"No. It's not over."

Clark had his wits again, knelt next to Ruby, and rested his hand on her shoulder. "What is it, Ruby? What're you trying to do?"

She paused from her effort, looked through dangling strands of hair at Clark, then the headstone. "He's the first healer. The Beloved. They murdered him. This place is desecrated. Somehow—I don't know—they've kept him bound, kept his soul imprisoned with magic. It's part of the curse, a gateway of sorts." She hunched over, lugged a large stone aside, and it rolled into the slop.

The sky growled and the hawk screeched in response.

Ruby glanced through the barren branches to the heavens, her indigo eyes vibrant. "But the gate's open. Now the battle can start."

Chapter 35

CLARK REMOVED THE LAST STONE FROM THE GRAVE AND heaved it into the fog. Rain pattered the ground about them, draping the branches overhead with swollen droplets. Jack stood next to Ruby, massaging his lower back.

"Okay, Ruby Rainbow. Can we go now?"

Ruby rested on her knees and stared at the grave, now swept clean. "No. There's one more thing we need to do."

"Maybe fight some more dwarves? C'mon, Rube. Let's get outta here."

"We need to build our own circle."

"Huh? Why didn't we just use that one?"

"No. Not that kind of circle." She stood and extended her hands to them. "This kind."

Jack cast an apprehensive glance at Clark, moved in, and the three of them joined hands around the grave.

"Reverend, as a minister, you can reclaim this ground."

Clark needed no explanation—though he hardly felt like a spiritual leader. If a place could be defiled, it could be cleansed, metaphysically debugged. No doubt generations of wickedness branded the cemetery; blasphemy and evil invocations infused the terrain. Beeko had said it himself: *The land can be scarred.* But there were ways to make it right.

Mr. Cellophane had forced Clark to reopen his study of exorcism. He knew that the liturgical structure for an exorcism followed a certain classical arrangement: *exordium, narratio, divisio, refutatio, probatio,* and *peroratio.* There were five audiences in any given exorcism, three supernatural and two human, and each required a specific approach. Perhaps he could follow those stages here, address those audiences. Of course, mouthing some words and invoking powers he didn't fully understand couldn't rescind years of malice, but it was a start.

Ruby nodded to him. In a way she was leading the show anyway, and he couldn't complain. Clark returned her nod, and they bowed their heads together. Maybe little Jilly's angels erupted in applause at the sight of them—that is, if they weren't clashing swords in some nearby universe. As the rain fell, Clark spoke haltingly, doing his best not to sound like the canned, dorky minister of last Sunday. He renounced the unnamed powers and petitioned beings of light, but the primitive death gods were the objects of his thought. How could he expect to stand against such ancient, malevolent forces? In reality he still wondered whether those forces were even real. But at the moment he couldn't take that chance. Clark's words were not eloquent, but he still stood with a newfound sincerity, a genuine desire to see the land, the community, freed from the shroud that covered it. Yet whether or not their adventure on the mountain accomplished that was yet to be seen.

Clark concluded clumsily, but they agreed their job was over there and began their trek back to the cars.

Jack gave Ruby his hat, though by now they were drenched. He put his arm over her shoulder and set a decent pace. Her limp, aggravated by the bloody knee, did not appear to disrupt him. He'd embraced her handicap long ago.

Jack looked over his shoulder. "The high school kids call you Surfer Dude."

"I haven't surfed in years."

"Well, what's up with the beads? They did a number on the goons."

Clark brushed the diamond-shaped pendant with his fingertips. "I'm not sure, Jack."

The cars were untouched, for which Jack claimed credit. Clark agreed to follow them home, just to ensure no further problems. His cell phone signal returned near the foot of the mountain, and he buzzed Vinyette and, without going into details, told her Ruby was all right. The rest of the way he let the heater blast. He even burst into song at one point.

However, Ruby's ominous prediction that the battle could begin lurked in the back of his mind. Would something more be required of him? He'd taken a stand against Keen, admitted his failures to the girls, and helped Ruby cleanse the defiled grave. Surely he could now turn the page and begin his own odyssey.

Dark clouds settled in the valley, casting sheets of rain upon the land. His ruminations seemed to darken with the growing gloom. The wipers, set on high, beat over the Jeep's windshield like war drums.

They turned up Ruby's street, and Clark hunched forward, peering through the steamy glass. A cream-colored sedan sat angled on the lawn in the Cases' front yard. The SUV accelerated, casting a burst of spray behind it, and skidded into the driveway.

Time seemed to screech to a standstill. Clark's jaw hung limp as he pulled onto the shoulder across the street. Jack bounded out of the vehicle toward a large figure on the porch.

Clark ripped his water-stained glasses off and dropped them on the passenger's seat. Pulling his beanie down over his ears, he opened the door. Rain pelted the trees, releasing the aroma of the nearby eucalyptus. The damp chill swept into the Jeep and overtook it. Then Clark slipped into the downpour.

It took a moment for the unfolding scene to compute. Ivy, the Cases' babysitter, poked her head from behind the screen door and said something to Jack, who was marching up to the large figure on the porch. The two men exchanged words.

Clark jogged across the street in time to see it was Oscar Hayes and hear him say, "She promised she'd come."

Ruby limped out of the car, still wearing Jack's cap, and winced at the pummeling rain. Hayes brushed by Jack and approached Ruby with hands open. A ragged beard framed his sullen features. His scant comb-over lay plastered in black strands down the front of his face. He wore muddy house slippers and a dress shirt that clung to his belly. Blubbering something, he reached for Ruby.

Jack stepped between them, keeping Hayes at arms length. "Calm down, Oscar. Please."

Clark slogged around the sedan, eyes fixed on their exchange. He glanced in the car, skidded, and did a double take. The body of Luz Hayes stretched across the backseat, pale and lifeless.

"If you would've come," Hayes sputtered, "she m–might've made it. There's still time, Ruby. You can pray, like you did for Mondo. Y–you have the gift."

Clark rushed up behind him and took his shoulder firmly. "Oscar, I'm sorry. Please, don't—"

He shrugged off Clark and stepped closer to Ruby.

Jack pushed him back with a stiff forearm and yelled to the teenager. "Ivy! Stay inside." Then to Hayes, "Get back, Oscar. We're sorry about Luz. Really. But, so help me, if you lay a hand on my wife..."

Hayes stumbled back, his lips quivering.

"Wait." Ruby stepped away from Jack. "I'm so sorry, Oscar. Really. It's...it's been crazy. I meant to come, but—" She shook her head, battered knee now a muddy red swath down the front of her jeans. "I don't—I can't heal her. It's not for me to say." She thrust out her hand, as if trying to prove her point. "I'm not the one who chooses, I can't...I can't tell God what to do. Luz is in a better place, Oscar. Go home, bury your wife, give thanks...for all your years together."

He stood trembling, staring at her. A slight convulsion jolted his head, and his eyes rolled back into his skull. He shook himself back into cognizance. Then he reached into the pocket of his trousers and produced a pistol, which he held at his side.

Jack yanked Ruby back and stepped in front of her. "What are you doing?"

Ivy and the boys watched from the kitchen window, steaming it up, and disappeared at the sight of the gun.

In a stern but composed voice, Jack said, "Clark, call the police. Now."

Hayes kept the gun at his side, as if it was dead weight. "It's had the same bullets in it for the last ten years."

Clark dug in his coat pocket for the cell phone.

"Go ahead, Reverend," Hayes said in a soft, vacant tone. "By the time they get here, either Luz will be alive or I'll be dead." Then he gazed at Clark, looking very much like a frightened child. "Will God still let me in if I kill myself?"

In the movies, people lunge at gunmen and wrestle the weapon away. For some reason Clark began riffling through his mental archive for a film to pattern such a move after. When no such movie came to mind, conflicting possibilities arose instead, none of them promising. He had the phone in one hand, and with the other, he found himself stroking the pendant. If the necklace had the power to stop warlocks, maybe it could halt a deranged church elder too. But how does one logistically use a choker to stop a suicide?

"Oscar, get a grip, man!" Jack struggled to keep Ruby pinned behind him. "Clark, what're you waiting for? Call the cops!"

"Wait!" Ruby stumbled from behind Jack, arms flailing to keep her balance. "Oscar, you're not gonna shoot yourself. Do you hear me?" She limped to the car. "Let me see her."

"Ruby!" Jack implored, eyeing Hayes. "Get back here!"

A noticeable glint filled Oscar Hayes's eyes. "The door's open, Ruby."

Clark stood to the elder's right, the same side he held the gun. Suicide intervention seldom involved a physical offensive. Most training stressed engagement of the individual in nonconfrontational conversation, bringing them down to earth, helping them weather the onslaught of emotion until they came down from the ledge or could safely be corralled. Clark did not intend to attempt heroics. Still he violated the first principle by taking several steps toward the gunman.

"Oscar. Oscar, put the gun down. There's no need for it. Ruby's going to pray, and we'll see what happens. OK?"

Hayes looked aslant as Clark approached and swung the pistol in a slow, circular motion at his side.

"Back off, Clark," Jack growled from the other side.

Ruby opened the door, and her shoulders hunched forward at

the sight of the dead woman. Rain pattered atop the sedan like a maniacal typist. Ruby removed the baseball cap and tossed it to the ground. Then she slid into the seat with Luz's head at her muddy thigh.

"Go ahead, Ruby." Oscar kept swinging the gun. "Wake her up. Next year's our thirtieth. Remind her, OK?"

"Thirty years, huh?" Clark forced a reassuring smile. "That's great. Really great."

Jack scowled and shook his head at Clark's attempt.

Ruby cradled the woman's head in her lap and stroked the thin gray hair. "I'm gonna start, Oscar," she said over her shoulder. "I need you to pray along with me, OK?"

Somewhere in the valley sirens rose. Clark glanced at the house, sure that Ivy called. In response to the sound Clark slipped his phone back in his pocket. In an emergency he estimated the police could be here within three minutes—a lot of time for something to go awry.

Oscar glanced at the men on each side of him and then cocked his head. "Go ahead. You have time. Besides, I'm exhausted, and you don't need me anyway."

She swallowed hard and nodded. Ruby turned back to the corpse and hunched over it. Her head moved side to side, mouth forming inaudible words. But between the hammering rain and her proximity inside the car, Clark could only imagine what was spoken over the rigid gray flesh.

The sirens grew closer, and Clark watched in wonder as Ruby labored over Luz Hayes.

Just five days ago Clark despised the notion of a dead boy rising. Now, for the first time in his life, he found himself pleading for the resurrection of the dead. What must it be like to see a cold, inanimate body regenerate? For a moment the possibility entranced him, and he stood, oblivious to the rain and the loaded gun, watching tired, crippled Ruby plead for a visitation.

After a long drawn-out moment, she grew still. She leaned against the car door and caressed the head of the dead woman.

Oscar heaved a sigh and slumped forward, gun dangling at

his side again. He choked back tears. "If you'da c–come sooner, maybe."

Ruby nestled the woman's head back in the seat, stood, and turned to face them. "Oscar," she said, stepping toward him, "it's not up to me."

"Ruby!" Jack glared at Hayes. "Stay put! The cops'll be here in a minute."

But Oscar's sobbing increased, and he started swinging the gun again.

Clark stepped closer, but Hayes seemed not to notice. "Oscar, you two had a fine life together."

Hayes straightened and lifted the gun to his temple. "Our life's over, Clark."

"No!" Like a trumpet blast, Ruby's voice tore through the liquid curtain.

Hayes jerked at the sound and fumbled the gun. Had Clark not been so stunned by Ruby's shout, he could have used the brief window to wrestle the pistol away from him. Instead Ruby advanced, dragging her bloody leg, eyes fixed on Hayes.

Jack crept closer from the other side. "Ruby, get away. Do not—" He was preparing to pounce, hopefully with more success than his first attack on the warlock.

Across the canyon the lights of the police car whipped off Rivermeer and raced for the bridge.

Hayes watched Ruby approach, shaking his head, jamming the pistol into his fleshy skull. "No, Ruby. No."

She stopped four feet in front of him, sucking air through her teeth. Then she looked into the sky, fighting the torrid rain, blinking with every watery strike.

A crack sounded above them, like the rending of a celestial veil.

She clenched her fists and shouted into the maelstrom, "No! Whatever you are—whoever you are—you don't belong here!" Then she lowered her head and with a tired sigh said, "And you can't have anyone else." With that she lunged at Oscar Hayes, seized his wrist with both hands, and ripped the gun away from his head.

A muffled pop sounded, and Jack barreled at them. He struck Hayes with such force that he drove him off his feet and they hurtled through the air, landed with a splash, and slid across the grass in a muddy heap.

Clark rushed to Ruby, who stood wobbling in the same spot. As he reached for her, she slumped forward and dragged them both to the ground.

"Rube!" Jack called from across the yard, perched over Hayes's limp body. "Ruby!"

Sprawled across Ian Clark's lap, she gulped air in short irregular gasps. She drew her left hand out from under her coat. Her fingertips were stained a vibrant red. She gazed at the blood on her hand, and the tension left her body. Then she settled back in Clark's arms, and with an eerie peace, Ruby Case surrendered to the wound.

Chapter 36

IAN CLARK SHUFFLED THROUGH THE DOOR OF HIS OFFICE tracking mud, dropped his glasses on the desk, and fell into his chair with a sopping thud.

"She had a pulse when they left. Barely. There was a lot of blood."

Vinyette sagged in the doorway, her face pale. "Why? I just can't—I mean, why'd he do it? And why didn't she just leave him alone?"

He slumped forward. "Maybe I went too far, Vin. Maybe we should've left it alone."

Each tick of the wall clock seemed more precious, pregnant with a heretofore-absent urgency. The story had played itself out, and Ruby's ominous precognition had arrived. It was White Creek Chapel all over again. They'd challenged the gods and lost.

The phone in the front office rang, jolting Vinyette. She exhaled and turned to answer it.

Clark held up his hand. "I'll meet you at the hospital. Call as many people as possible. Maybe there's room for one more miracle."

Vinyette drew a deep breath, nodded, and left.

He sat numb, water puddling at his feet, and listened to her muffled voice in the front office. A few minutes later, she leaned through his doorway with her coat and scarf on. "I'll see you there." She stood for a moment, gazing at him slumped in the chair. "You should get out of that stuff." Then she cast a wan smile and left.

On the desk his glasses lay next to the notes for Sunday's message. The promise of a new start now seemed about as empty as the leather chairs across from his desk. Just three days ago Ruby occupied one of them, from which she pleaded for his assistance.

Clark drooped forward.

Because of his complacency and cowardice, Ruby Case lay dying. Maybe she had been correct—the gateway was right there. He unclenched his hands, now smeared pink with her blood.

Could this be the murder he was complicit in?

As he sat staring at his wrinkled, blood-stained palms, a crackling sound singed the air—a stereophonic tingle that made the back of his neck bristle. The foul-smoldering vapor uncoiled about him. He grew rigid. Something thudded to the ground in the far corner, but he remained steady, his jaw clamped. Anger and regret seethed inside him.

Today the haunting would stop!

Clark drew several deep breaths, psyching himself up to confront the demonic entity. Then he bolted out of the chair. Drops of water sprayed the room as he spun toward the corner.

But it was vacant.

He stepped away from the desk and scanned the room for the apparition. The familiar smell of smoke and burning flesh lingered, but he did not see the phantom. Then his gaze came to rest at the foot of the bookshelves, where a large book lay opened. It must have fallen off the shelf with the spirit's passing. Or been placed there.

He crept toward it, half expecting the creature to pounce upon him. With every step his boots produced an annoying rubbery squeak, and he winced at the sound. He stopped and stood puzzling over the book. It was Keen's magnum opus, *The Myth of Religion*. Clark had laid it on the edge of the shelf, and its presence here seemed none too coincidental.

He reached for the massive volume, prepared to return it to the shelf, when he noticed a familiar face.

Clark lugged the book off the carpet, fixated on a photograph in its pages. He carried it to his desk, set it down, and turned the desk lamp on in order to study the photo. The caption below the picture read, "The Ritual Consummation of the Wandering Soul." He leaned over, squinting, and examined the grainy color picture.

Surrounded by tropical flora, Benjamin Keen knelt to the far end of a group of Amazonian natives. Despite their primitive appearance, the khakis and wild gray afro made him look like the oddball in the bunch. Twelve Indian men in crude grass skirts and loincloths, jet-black hair slicked over their angular faces, stood somberly around Mr. Cellophane.

Clark rubbed his eyes. *How could this be?* He spread his hands atop the desk and hunched over the encyclopedia. The young man stood tall with his chest bare and hands folded at his waist. He couldn't have been more than twenty years old. A thin necklace draped his throat, his high cheekbones and large sallow eyes unmistakable.

A shiver passed through Clark. Here was the specter that had tormented him, the phantom in the flesh. What devilry had brought the boy here? And what thread joined the two of them?

Clark glanced around the room again, placed his fingers on the page, and followed the words.

> Like many primitive systems, sacrifice is at the heart of Illuacon society. Intrinsically joined to the Land, this indigenous people group believes the Soul of the Earth is replenished by the blood of the Tribe. Literally, human blood.
>
> For modern Westerners, human sacrifice remains incomprehensible—a barbaric practice relegated to ritual crimes or the most prehistoric of cultures. Nevertheless, the shedding of blood was the religious bedrock for many ancient societies, an honorable act that virtually guaranteed immortality.
>
> Such is the Wandering Soul of Illuacon sacrificology.

Clark rose taut, absorbed over the mystic tome. *The Wandering Soul?* Keen had christened him with the title years ago, when Clark first expressed his doubts about organized religion. That's when the professor gave him the bizarre pendant and pronounced a blessing, launching Clark's nomadic search for truth.

The humidity of the room, combined with his dank clothing,

forced him into a clammy sweat. He stood with his fingertips poised on the book. Despite a growing consternation, Ian Clark continued reading.

> The cyclic drama of death and regeneration inherent in Mesoamerican menology forms the backdrop for the yearly ritual. In the thirteenth month of the Illuacon calendar, during the Festival of Flame, the Chosen One selects his Successor. During the Ritual of Consummation, the Chosen One willingly offers his body—hair, skin, bone, teeth, and, on occasion, lesser appendages such as ears and fingers—to his successor, thus passing the sacrificial torch. At this point the One surrenders himself to the Flame and is incinerated on the altar, initiating the Cycle of Rebirth. The Successor is renamed "the Wandering Soul" and thus begins his yearlong journey. Taking the body parts of his predecessor for remembrance and protection, he is clothed and kept by the sacrifice of the One. Destined to die for the Tribe, his blood will ingratiate the Earth and renew the Cycle at years' end.

Clark swayed backward and gripped the desk to steady himself. The trance of astonishment unraveled. *Sacrifice? Body parts? Kept by the One?* The concepts exploded inside him and tumbled into perfect order, becoming a stark, visceral reality.

He fondled the amulet around his neck.

Suddenly, the look on the warlock's face made sense. No wonder they couldn't touch Clark—*he was clothed and kept by the sacrifice of the One.*

He stood, stroking the crude talisman. If there was a bridge to Keen—a keyhole through a door of darkness—this was it. How'd he become so dim, so unobservant, so negligent? Then he curled his fingers around the choker, grit his teeth, and snapped it off his neck.

The necklace dangled from his fist, and he gazed at it.

With great care he spread it across the desk, hunched over it with his palms flat, and scrutinized the materials. Three unpolished white beads. Fine braided fibers. Diamond-shaped pendant with tiny etched symbols.

Clark pushed himself up and snatched his penholder from the desk. He dumped the contents on the surface and marched to the end of the bookshelves.

On the top shelf sat the assemblage of trinkets and knick-knacks bestowed by Professor Keen over the course of time: the ivory cube, the fluted leather, the lock of coarse black hair, and various charms and beads. He cupped his hand and drew the items into the empty penholder. Then he went back to the desk, poured everything out, and sifted through it.

First he took the tiny leather scroll, untied it, and peeled the soft brown parchment open. *Too soft for animal hide.* Then he took the lock of hair and stroked it. *Not coarse enough for animal hair.* Clark set it down and stepped back. Bone, hair, skin—it was all here.

No wonder the spirit kept materializing in that dank corner. These were the remains of Mr. Cellophane.

The murder he was unwillingly a part of had literally been right under his nose. So this was why Keen kept giving him gifts. The death gods had been summoned by blood, and it was blood that would keep them there. Only this time it would be Clark's. The professor was grooming him to be the next sacrifice.

Ian Clark *was* the Wandering Soul.

He shook himself from thought and scrounged through several desk drawers, searching for something to carry the sacred items in. Then he removed the small cloth pouch from the bottom drawer. He untied and shook it until a gold ring tumbled out to the desktop and rattled about. How long had it been since he'd seen the ring? Cynthia would not mind if he wore it, and he sure didn't. Clark slipped his wedding ring back on, and it fit perfectly.

He took the pouch, filled it with the mummified body parts, and tied it shut. Then he snatched his keys and prepared to settle scores with the great magician.

Chapter 37

BRILLIANT CLUSTERS OF STARS SHONE BETWEEN THE SCUD-
ding black clouds, and the summit of the foothills sheared
the rising moon in half. Clark stood at the gate, surveying the
dark outline of Benjamin Keen's ranch. The passing rainstorm
left the earth alive. Night birds trilled overhead, and the glistening field brimmed with cricket song. In his right hand he
grasped the pouch containing the necklace and the remains of
the martyred boy.

He shoved his keys into the pocket of his slacks, releasing a
damp stink from his waterlogged clothing. Then he opened the
gate and stepped onto the property.

As usual he didn't have a plan of attack. Either way a sense of
necessity—of a looming, inevitable confrontation—gnawed at his
gut. Once again Clark entertained the idea of calling the cops.
But even if the body parts could be traced to someone in the
Peruvian Amazon, nailing Keen for any wrongdoing would be
unlikely. Besides, this battle needed to be fought on another level.

Faint moonlight revealed the path through the front yard,
and starlight speckled the puddles. Clark followed the trail and
passed under the black oak, unconcerned about tree spirits or
fairy folk. Powers much greater than these were on the march.
The Pantheons were raging.

At the far end of the porch the mottled orange window shade
glowed. As he climbed the steps, the timber creaked, but he did
not attempt to conceal his presence. He raised his hand over the
brass knocker but did not strike it.

The winding, tortured road had brought him here. Stacie's
death, his failed marriage, the wreckage of the ministry, and the
professor's malevolent plan were just stepping-stones to this final
confrontation. But the real enemy was not Keen—it never had

been—nor was it the death gods. In the end Clark's own anguish was his greatest adversary. Whatever the outcome, tonight that enemy would be slain.

He inhaled, lifted the knocker, and struck it three times. The metallic sound reverberated in the stillness, and he winced at its sharpness. Footfalls padded inside, the handle turned, and Mr. O stood in a plain linen shirt. "They're expecting you."

This was the first time Clark had heard the man speak, and his delicate, breezy voice seemed to jive perfectly with his graceful demeanor. Mr. O stepped back and motioned him to enter.

Clark knit his brows. How did they know he was coming? And who were *they*?

He gave a curt nod and crossed the threshold. The manservant led him through the room of masks, down the long hallway, and into the study. A rich oily smell mingled with the usual musky spice. Upon seeing him, Jade issued a guttural squall and danced nervously across the perch. Mr. O stopped before the burgundy curtains and motioned for Clark to stay put. Then he swept inside, leaving the thick veil swaying as he passed.

It figured everything would come down here. Clark scanned the library, the ragged colorful spines of books, the curios and trinkets assembled from around the world. He clenched the pouch. How many other dark secrets were contained in this collection?

Mr. O emerged and held the curtains open for him. Clark hustled past the snarling parrot and entered the Temple of All-Father. Mr. O released the thick drapes and remained outside while Clark stood unmoving, allowing his eyes to adjust to the dim torchlight.

In the middle of the room the circular stage rose, and at its apex stood the stone altar. On either side of the rough-hewn table the two bronze lampstands glowed. Inside each basin burned a blue flame, which cast undulating shadows across the ceiling and made the room dance with throbbing, tortured shapes. The altar glistened, sleek and lustrous, dripping oil.

Keen leaned over a display case on the far side of the room

wearing a loose-fitting robe drawn at the waist. "The power of the sacrifice is in the willingness of the participant." He turned and stepped forth, wielding the black obsidian blade. "But neither you nor En'uco chose to go willingly."

"So that was his name."

"A timid soul, I'm afraid." Keen crossed the floor, turning the blade over and back upon his palm. "He served his purpose, however. The good of the tribe, you know."

"I guess you were hoping I'd do it for the good of the tribe as well. To keep the death gods in power."

Keen climbed the steps of the altar and stood beside the shiny, scorched surface. "You were well on your way, Ian. If Jehovah hadn't interrupted. Between your surrender to grief and your misgivings about your own faith, you nearly made it. You would have willingly died, succumbed to despair. Yes, the resurrection threw a monkey wrench into the business. But alas, the Mesos are far too strong. They've held this region for decades—and will continue, in spite of your paltry attempts at rebellion."

Clark held up the pouch. "So you murdered him."

"Ah, you've brought the articles with you. Perfect! They are the bridge to the otherworld. You've discovered that, hmm? But murder is such a"—he stared at the blade—"a puny word. It is so much more. And so much more is at stake. The harmony of the land, resources, health. These are what the gods bestow. It was the Mesos that held the fever at bay. They've brought commerce, prosperity to this valley. And power to some."

"Yeah, but at what cost?"

"Cost? Nothing is without cost. You know that. What makes you think the rules are different on this side of the fence? *The life is in the blood.* Isn't that what Scripture says? The greatest force in the universe is the power of sacrifice."

"And if I don't go willingly?"

From behind Clark, near the entryway, came a second voice. "Then you'll go unwillingly."

Clark started forward and turned to see Coy Barkham stepping from the shadowy perimeter, effectively blocking any sort of retreat. The elder's shaved head shimmered in the torch light, his brow creased in certitude.

The pit of Clark's stomach plunged. His unplanned confrontation had played right into their hands. He had a chance against Keen. But with Barkham added to the mix, those chances decreased significantly.

"So Oscar was good for something after all," Barkham said coldly, unbuttoning his gray twill trench coat and pulling a black scarf from around his neck. "His actions were a pleasant surprise. We figured Ruby would either go mad or just bail. She's a lot tougher than we expected. Who would've guessed Oscar would cave in and take her with him?"

"So she was right. The gateway's in our own church." Clark glanced over his shoulder at Keen, who remained on the platform watching their exchange. "How could you, Coy? How could you pretend to be serving the church and all the while be involved in this?"

Barkham released a snort of laughter. "Look who's talking about pretending to serve the church. You should've had the church in mind a long time ago. But you were too busy wallowing in self-pity, trying to find a way out, a loophole. Really, it was a perfect match. We needed compliance, someone who wouldn't rock the boat. You fit the bill. And your relationship with Keen greased the slide."

Clark stared off, numbed into shameful complicity.

"Besides, how have I hurt the church?" Barkham continued, now with a note of defensiveness. "Canyon Springs has existed peaceably for over fifty years. The blood feud between the Pantheons means nothing to the average member. All they want is a good sermon each week, someone to hear their confession and pat them on the head. You could say we've actually done everyone a favor by not dragging the church into the fray...like White Creek Chapel and Reverend Byrd, that fool of a minister. Reverend Lawrence gave us a scare—he wasn't content sticking to the script. He had to go and force the issue. We're lucky we weren't punished back then."

"So...so is that it, Coy? We don't go snooping around because we might get punished? We don't take a stand because we might stir the opposition? Is that it? I guess if they want your right arm, you offer that up too."

Barkham grinned. "It's hardly a relationship of fear, Reverend. Call it an agreement, an arrangement. We give them what they want, cut them a piece of the pie, and they leave us be. You know, live and let live."

"We're talking about demons! It's a pact with the devil, for God's sake!"

Barkham shrugged. "Call it what you want. Keen's hocus-pocus is intriguing, but our agreement is purely one of practicality. Same for the 'alternative healers' downtown. You know, they're not called witches anymore. But whatever they're called, they pay their rent, bring in revenue. And leave us alone. I couldn't care less about bat wings and magic dust. It's all one of utilitarianism. It has been since it began."

Clark stepped back to get the two men in view. The resolve he'd walked in with quavered before his instinctive need for self-preservation. He needed to buy enough time, consider a coherent plan of attack. So with one ear to heaven, he asked, "So how'd you get involved, Coy?"

Barkham glanced at Keen, who stood at the altar flipping the blade over and back, looking disengaged.

"As I've said before, Reverend," Barkham sighed, "our family goes way back, three generations. My grandfather, Kerwin Barkham, lived in Bridge River. He was one of the founders, owned some mines. He cut the first deal that started it all."

"The deal?"

Barkham removed his coat and tossed it on a nearby chair along with his scarf. He looked even more imposing with it off, which may have been his intent. "After the revival came the fever. That's when it started—this inter-dimensional skirmish—and the first resurrection happened."

"So who was the healer?"

"No one of consequence. A farmer. But the church turned him

into an aberration, an outcast. Between squabbling over miracles and demanding more of them, the poor guy became a freak. Which made the city's decision all the more shrewd."

Clark adjusted his glasses and looked from Barkham to Keen. "And what decision was that?"

The professor stirred from his despondency. "Why, sacrificing him, of course." His charcoal eyes twinkled in the glow of the luminescent bowls. "Strange how healers inevitably become sacrificial lambs."

The sound of Clark's breathing thrummed in his head, and he stood with his jaw slack, letting the awful details align.

"The believers were a faithless lot." Barkham rolled up his shirtsleeves, revealing robust forearms. "The fever raged, but the church was too busy cannibalizing itself to do anything. The Indian immigrants working the mines promised that a sacrifice would lift the fever, invite the blessing of their gods. And guarantee continued production."

"You're not telling me that someone was murdered just so a gold mine would keep producing."

"Hardly. The fever threatened to wipe out half the city. And the Christian God didn't lift a finger. A consensus was easy. The officials turned a blind eye, but they all had a hand in it. He was hung on the hill. My granddad watched. They called it a suicide, but no one really cared. The fever broke, and the church slithered back into the shadows, poisoned by their ineptitude. My family's been recipient of the blessing now for three generations."

Barkham finished rolling up his sleeves and cracked his knuckles. "The church's unbelief and cowardice empowered the curse, gave it life, just as it does today."

"It's a never-ending cycle, Ian." Keen drew an invisible circle with the knife. "The gods are always thirsty. If not for blood, then attention. Obeisance."

Clark stepped back. "If you kill me, the police'll know. They'll search this place, find out about the..." he spat the words, "...the Circle of Knowledge."

Barkham chuckled and exchanged glances with Keen. "The

police will never find out. You've made sure of that. The elder board was never informed about your visits here. Vinyette doesn't have a clue. You've kept this under wraps. Your meetings with Keen have been clandestine, just the way you wanted it. And like the rest of your life, this has been one big secret."

Clark's breath lodged in his windpipe, and he stood unmoving. He had blazed the trail of his own demise.

A slimy, sarcastic grin crept across Barkham's face. "You better close your mouth, Reverend. You might swallow a fly."

"If there's any consolation," Keen said, "it's going to a greater cause."

"Like what?" Clark asked. "Keeping your society secret? Or keeping the city in the dark?"

Keen laughed. "Oh my, much bigger." He set the blade down on the altar, descended, and walked to the far end of the room. He stood before a carved console bookcase of dark mahogany that rose to shoulder height. Reaching into the shadows, he turned on a long fluorescent lamp that flickered to life, illuminating a map posted above the cabinet.

"You really must see this, Ian. Please." Keen stepped back, his boyish enthusiasm showing, and motioned Clark forward.

Barkham wasn't budging from the doorway and probably assumed Clark would try to make a run for it. Clark moved toward Keen, glancing at the altar where the black blade sat unguarded. The irritating squeak in his boots chirped as he approached the map.

It stretched above the length of the bookcase and appeared laminated, marked with notations and symbols along its surface. At first he assumed it was some kind of military chart, with sections of land colorized according to troop deployment, weapons caches, bases, and armories. Clark advanced with one eye on Keen and the other on the map.

"It's been years in the making." Keen stroked his frayed goatee, eyes fixated on the map. "Thus far we've successfully diagrammed our time zone: California, Nevada, the Pacific Northwest. It won't be long before the entire nation is mapped."

Clark stopped seven to eight feet away, glanced at Keen, then the dappled blueprint. Major metropolitan areas—*Los Angeles, San Diego, San Francisco, Reno, Portland, Seattle*—dotted the map in bold block letters. Below each city was a corresponding name. *Abaddon, Moloch, Mammon, Gorgon, Belial, Beelzebub*, and then in suburban areas, clusters of titles speckled the map: *Succubus, Eligoth, Lilith*, and *Leviathan*. Throughout were spherical symbols, slashes, unopened eyes, and watery forks. Clark's mind swooned at the onrushing possibilities.

"The Pantheons. We've identified them, named them," Keen whispered reverently. "And in the naming there is power."

Clark looked from the map to Keen.

The professor's eyes were glazed with ecstatic delight. "They are the Watchers, the Ancient Ones. The Mesos are a drop in the bucket, one unit in a massive invisible army. Stonetree is just the tip of the iceberg, Ian."

Clark stepped back in blank astonishment, his mind fighting for rational footing.

Keen moved to the map and traced his bony fingers atop it. "This is our mission, my boy—*Orbis of Scientia*—to prepare for their coming, the circle of their knowledge. The warlocks and druids, their petty stone rings and incantations are just a shadow. We have discerned a plan much bigger, powers much greater than any man has conceived. Imagine, a society governed by superior intellects. Your God is just one of millions, a pathetic dying entity on the bottom rung of the evolutionary food chain."

Emptiness gnawed the pit of Clark's stomach, and he began to backpedal. In cities all across the land evil entities watched the workings of men, plotting and planning, holding souls in check as they had done him. Corruption, crime, immorality, and malaise were its tentacles, physical manifestations of a vast malignant network. Clark was but a peon, a pawn in the game, a piece to be sacrificed at the whim of the Pantheons.

He took a step back, then another, until his foot struck the circular stairs behind him. He glanced at Barkham, then Keen, then scampered up the steps in reverse. Ducking past the torch, he rushed to the granite slab.

"The blade!" Barkham lunged toward the foot of the altar. "Quick! The other side!" He motioned to Keen, who shook himself from his euphoric stupor.

Clark bounded up the steps with the pouch in hand and seized the obsidian blade.

"You can't stop it." Keen prowled around the opposite side of the platform with a maniacal grin on his face. "It's too big for you, Ian. You've no choice but to surrender. Join your sister—*join Ruby*—in the Great Cycle."

Barkham stood on the other end, at the foot of the steps, watching Clark's every move. "Let's not make this difficult, Reverend."

The blade's jagged edges sparkled seductively in Clark's hand. Maybe he *should* die for the tribe—penance for his selfish disregard and neglect. Or maybe he could impale himself upon the altar in exchange for Ruby. Neither option seemed admissible. Despair scuttled across the bedrock of his brain. How had this happened?

Keen climbed the first step, his frizzy mane accentuating his crazed stare. "For the tribe, son. For the tribe."

Heat from the torches forced perspiration from Clark's flesh. He swept the dagger in front of him in wide, reckless arcs. Then he drew the back of his opposite hand—the hand with the pouch—across his forehead. "You'll never get away with it. This—this'll all be found out."

Barkham stood at the bottom step of the altar. "I used to think that. But I learned. You underestimate them, these Pantheons. Their influence is great; no one's immune. Scientists, senators—they're all puppets." His wide eyes and reverent tone belied the influence of darker forces. "The police'll find your body burned beyond recognition in your car at the base of the highway. Like the rest of them. All trace of DNA incinerated. And life will go on like it has. Until another sacrifice is required."

Clark blinked back sweat, trying to maintain focus upon his

attackers. His inner ears had become a punching bag for his heartbeat. It might be possible to immobilize one of the men with the blade. But the other would do him in. If there weren't so much distance to cover, he could dash for the exit. However, the chances of eluding Barkham, ex-QB, ex-jock, were slim. Fear suffused through Clark's body, a tangible stiffness that constricted his joints.

Follow your dreams.

Clark inhaled the words as if they were fresh air in a poisoned mineshaft. He'd already surrendered far too much, something Stacie would never have approved. The least he could do was put up a fight, make one final stand. For her. For Ruby. For himself.

He glanced at the torch on his left, then his right. Oil drooled off the edges of the stone table. The legs of the altar were nothing more than four, squat columns. And between them was a gap with just enough space for a man to squeeze through. Especially a desperate man. He gripped the slick handle, and his wedding ring glinted in the torch light.

Clark flashed a look at the soot-covered chimney overhead. How many sacrifices had already been conducted here? How many souls had been poured out on this altar?

Barkham ascended the first step, and Clark swiped the blade through the air. The elder leaned back and chuckled, clearly unfazed by Clark's spastic motions.

Follow your dreams.

Clark rose tall and nodded to himself. Yes. His dreams. Amidst the wreckage, the disappointment, and loss, a seed of hope still existed inside him. It always had. Maybe Stacie's death *was* a type of sacrifice. She died pursuing her dreams, and she wanted that for him. He'd survived this long, protected by forces he did not completely understand, preserved for one final confrontation. His chances now seemed meager, but this time he would not surrender.

"There's been enough sacrifices, Professor Keen." Clark spoke with tremulous resolve. Then he held the pouch up, and Keen's eyes widened. "And it's time we gave this one a proper burial."

With a smooth underhand motion, he tossed the pouch into the burning basin to his right. It thudded into the flame, sending a small shower of sparks cascading.

Both men froze, apparently stunned by the move.

"The amulet!" Keen gasped.

Barkham took two stair steps in one stride, landing on top of the platform in a crouch, no more than six feet away. Keen scampered up, his eyes darting from the seething torch to Clark. The men crept forward, forcing him back against the stone altar.

"It's your destiny," Keen hissed. "You're the One, Ian. The Wandering Soul."

Clark slashed the blade in front of him. "That's a possibility, Professor. But my wandering's not over yet."

The pouch blazed in the basin, crackling and showering the ground with a hail of glowing embers. Barkham remained focused on Clark, his face mottled by the pulsating torch light. Keen's attention, however, was deflected between his prey and the combusting amulet. Sparks careened through the air and landed sizzling atop the altar.

Clark switched the dagger to his right hand and swiped it before him in wide arcs, all the while squinting and dodging the fireworks.

Barkham sneered and crept sideways, preparing to pounce.

As Clark tensed and readied for their attack, a familiar odor struck him.

The air tingled, charged by a wave of static energy, and the scorched, reeking stench of burning flesh uncoiled at the altar. Clark's eyes stung and filled with moisture. And behind his attackers the ghostly figure rose like a surreal, transparent curtain.

In that split second, as Keen and Barkham became aware of the fantastic presence, Clark tossed the knife over the altar and dropped on all fours. He jammed himself under the stone table and thrust his body between its legs.

The opening was much smaller than he anticipated.

His torso lodged between the legs of the altar, his rear end exposed behind him. The obsidian blade lay balanced on the edge of the steps, waiting for him. But Clark wriggled, trapped between the four squat columns.

Sparks showered off the altar above, tumbling down the steps before him. He managed to squirm one arm through, making room for the rest of him, when someone cried out and a great ball of flame erupted overhead. Its blazing underbelly engulfed the platform and momentarily sucked the oxygen out of the air.

Clark bellowed and heaved himself through the legs of the altar. He slithered out the other side, rolled, snatched the blade, and raced down the steps.

The entire room pulsated, the altar having become a swirling inferno. Horrid gurgling sounds, combined with the devouring wildfire, sputtered inside the maelstrom. He stumbled back from the steps with one arm shielding his face, fixated on the gruesome consummation.

Mr. Cellophane unfurled above the platform, twice the size of his normal stature, a canopy of throbbing, translucent organs hovering atop the room. The atmosphere sizzled, and the temple radiated with the spectral splendor, sending shards of light and shadow orbiting wildly across the ceiling. Its eyes, once sad and empty, glared with vengeance upon the two men who lay writhing upon the stone table.

Clark stood limp, the blade dangling from his fingers, too terrified to look away, too awestruck to flee.

The apparition, swollen and sustained by the flaming pyre, stared down on the sacrifice. Its elastic arms stretched serpent-like, coiled around Barkham and Keen, pinning them to the charred granite table. The men lay squirming in a pitiful, scalded mound. Curdled hands clawed the air and then shriveled into decomposing matter. Clark grit his teeth as their shrill cries became nothing more than garbled, nonhuman yowls.

The curtain of flame finally deadened by degrees until it turned into an elegant blue veil, shimmering like a gaseous celestial cloud. Atop the altar Keen's and Barkham's bodies were bubbling masses of liquefying flesh.

Clark tore his gaze away, his stomach churning with revulsion. The very altar built to perpetuate the unholy sacrifice had received its final offering. The professor's vaunted theories about the afterlife could now be tested—firsthand. Sorrow and regret stabbed at Clark's heart.

The corpses curled upon the slab, now nothing more than heaps of frothing lard. The ghostly bonfire swirled, becoming a funnel, and sparks danced amidst the rising pylon, flitting to the ceiling. At its peak Mr. Cellophane's head rested, buoyed by the inferno. It stared down upon Reverend Clark, the once-sad eyes now placid and peaceful. The mass churned, spinning itself into a formless vapor. Then the spirit's body faded and evaporated in the ascending smoke.

Clark massaged his eyes and blinked as the room returned to shadows. Except for the crackling charcoal forms, the temple remained silent. This was the battle Ruby made way for, the last, great stronghold to be neutralized.

He tossed the blade on the steps, and it landed with a dull thud. Then he walked around the perimeter of the room and stopped before the map. *Abaddon, Moloch, Mammon, Gorgon, Belial, Beelzebub.* Itzcoliuhqui was a pinprick on the landscape. Could Stonetree really be just the tip of the iceberg, just a squad in a massive network of mythic powers, influencing and interacting with the world of men? How many more unnamed entities lurked, waiting for acknowledgment?

Clark rubbed the joint of his hip and limped toward the burgundy veil. As he made his way there, the curtains parted and a figure stepped into the doorway and stood motionless.

Mr. O studied the room. His tiny eyes glinted in the torchlight as he grew still and gazed at the smoking forms on the stone table. Then he looked at Clark.

Unable to comprehend another battle, Clark's shoulders slumped forward. He glanced at the blade on the steps and then shook his head and approached the servant. For a brief moment they stood, squared off, examining one another.

Then Mr. O bowed before Ian Clark—a slow, reverent gesture. He remained there for a moment, rose, and stepped aside.

Reverend Clark exhaled and hurried out of the Temple of All-Father, hoping that he could make it to the hospital before Ruby Case went to heaven.

Chapter 38

THE JEEP BARRELED DOWN THE RAIN-SLICKED ROAD. Clark cradled the cell phone between his ear and shoulder as he spoke to the dispatch operator. "I don't have time to explain. Just, please, get someone up here."

He clicked off and glanced at the digital in the dash. Ten thirty-seven. He swerved, the tires squealed, and he eased his foot off the gas. Adrenaline pumped through his body, and his hands trembled atop the steering wheel. The last thing they needed was another death. In an attempt to calm himself he drew a deep, concentrated breath, held it, and expelled the air.

Before he put the phone down, Clark replayed Vinyette's message. "Where are you? I called everyone I could, like you said. She's in surgery." A long silence followed her words. "The bullet hit an artery. They won't say much more. Hurry."

No wonder there'd been so much blood. But the doctor's silence was not encouraging. Clark set the phone on the passenger seat and fixed his attention on the road. He could be to the hospital in forty-five minutes. Forty if he got daring.

The net of storm clouds had grown sheer, revealing icy moonlit skies behind them. As he plunged into the valley, a stiff onshore breeze beat against the vehicle and sent the clouds racing.

How had it come to this and spiraled out of control so quickly? Or *was* it out of control? Could this be part of a divine plan, something far beyond his ability to grasp? Perhaps the Pantheons were simply rearranging the chessboard, preparing for another game with the unsuspecting pawns. But how his actions fit in this plan, Clark could not fathom. If he made it through this, there'd be plenty of time for philosophical noodling. At the moment, however, he could think only about Ruby. It was her simple resolve, her childlike faith, that had forced this confrontation.

And in the end her faith was more instrumental than all the powers combined.

Stonetree Valley Hospital lay nestled in the southeastern foothills, just outside the downtown area. Bordered on both sides by a wall of oleander, the structure rose into canyons with granite outcroppings and arid streambeds. A multi-winged, single-story facility, it contained a large underground complex with operating rooms and a morgue. Local witticism tagged it the city's one-stop drop.

He cut across the outskirts of the parking lot and followed the eastern oleanders toward the delivery docks. A van sat parked with its rear doors open, and two men stood talking at the ramp, stamping in the cold. He recognized one of the men as Abel, a hospital warehouse worker who attended Canyon Springs sporadically. Clark pulled up and rolled down his window. Abel motioned to his companion and jogged to the Jeep, leaving a trail of steam behind him as he spoke.

"What's up, Rev? You here for the gunshot?"

"You heard anything?"

"Nothin' coming out." After a brief, uncomfortable moment of silence, he shrugged. "Well, c'mon." He pointed to the spot along the ramp where they allowed clergy to park. As much time as a minister spent at the hospital, learning the shortcuts became a necessity. This was one of them.

Clark pulled over and hustled out. The asphalt glistened after the rain, and his hurried boot steps echoed across the parking lot. He passed in front of the cargo van, whose driver sat inside filling out paperwork, and joined Abel at the ramp.

The man's furry eyebrows arched in surprise as Clark approached. "You been mud wrestling, Rev?"

Clark glanced down at his clothing. "Uh, I guess you could say that."

Abel grinned and turned up the ramp. "Lot goin' on tonight," he said over his shoulder. "Kinda weird."

"What do you mean?"

The man stopped and pointed west, toward the downtown

area, where an inky curtain of smoke brooded over the city, its underbelly brandished a pulsating red.

"What is it?" Clark asked. "What's going on?"

"Heard it from the EMTs. About an hour ago a big fire broke out. Some of the shops downtown, I guess. No one's hurt, so's far as I know, but sounds like there's a lotta damage. A lot."

He shrugged and continued up the ramp. But Clark stood for a moment watching the throbbing cloud. The hellish bonfire at Keen's ranch had blistered his mind. A bizarre symmetry was occurring; dimensions far beyond his understanding had over-lapped. Were these two blazes parallel universes of some ominous, encroaching reality? After a moment contemplating the distant fiery shroud, he shook his head and hustled up the ramp.

The pneumatic doors hissed open as Abel marched through. This shortcut led straight to the OR waiting area. Clark had been here three times since his arrival. However, he feared this might be the worst visit yet.

They entered a cold warehouse with tall metal shelves, neatly labeled, and a small office with a floor heater glowing. Near another set of pneumatics a security guard stood managing a steaming cup of liquid. He tipped his head as Clark passed.

The doors opened into the hospital, and Clark squinted at the flood of obnoxious fluorescents.

"Good luck, huh." Abel patted him on the back.

"Thanks."

The hallway formed a T, corridors running to opposite sides off the central passageway. Clark went toward the nearby stair-well, ducking first into the restroom. It smelled soapy, and paper towels overflowed the trash receptacle. He removed his glasses, splashed water on his face, and gazed in the mirror. It looked like he'd been swimming in motor oil and blow-dried by an industrial hurricane fan. Matted hair complemented his bloodshot eyes. He drew his jacket collar to his face. It reeked of smoke and oil. Then he gripped the sink and hung his head.

Barkham. Keen. Stacie. Cynthia. Ruby. How much wreckage lay scattered in his wake? Perhaps it was his destiny to ruin friends and lovers, the backwash of his own cowardice. But just as he was about to flagellate himself with a new round of self-condemnation, angry voices rose in the hallway.

He exhaled, wiped his eyes, and pressed his wrinkled clothing down to no avail. Clark slipped his glasses on and raked his fingers through his hair. Then he left the bathroom and passed into the bright, sterile hall.

At the warehouse doors, the security guard and Abel stood in animated conversation with a familiar figure.

It was the reporter from *Rippington*'s. Mace Wilflee turned toward Clark with his plastic Hollywood smile. His wraparound sunglasses perched on his spiky bleached hair, blue eyes radiating a borderline madness.

"Hey, Rev," Abel called, stepping in front of Wilflee with obvious disdain. "We caught this guy snooping around, following you or something. Some news hack, I take it."

Wilflee shook off the security guard's grip and stepped around Abel. "I knew this city was ripe the moment I stepped foot in it. Lotta skeletons. And lotsa closets. You folks shoulda just spoke up when you had a chance, saved me the headache and your-selves the embarrassment. But I got my story. Just like I said." He stared into the lights with a glazed, ecstatic sneer. "Healer Slain by Satanist." Then he looked at Clark with crazed gratification. "So how does it feel to have been harboring a devil worshiper, Reverend?"

"Hayes?" Clark pondered aloud. "You think Oscar Hayes is a—?"

Wilflee leaned toward Clark with a wolfish gleam. "Question is, how many more o' those you got in that church." Then he leaned back and exclaimed, "This is huge. Huge!"

"C'mon," the security guard growled. "Get outta here."

With Abel's assistance, they turned the reporter around, one on each elbow, and escorted him back out through the warehouse.

"Stonetree!" Wilflee proclaimed over his shoulder. "Gateway to hell! Yup, I got my story!" The doors closed on the reporter's maniacal cackling.

Clark stood with his mouth open. Did these tabloid guys ever get it right?

As he started to turn, someone called to him from the adjoining hall. Two policemen strode toward him, footsteps echoing through the bleak corridor. Ivan and Bean worked the night shift. They approached and Clark stiffened, his mind racing in anticipation of the confrontation. Surely he'd be cuffed and taken away. At least interrogated by Gramer, or someone worse. But he couldn't leave the hospital without word on Ruby. Clark grit his teeth in preparation for the showdown.

"We barely had a chance to get coffee," said Ivan, scanning Clark with a look of puzzlement. "Whadya do, get run over by a diesel?"

Clark brushed off the front of his jacket. "Something like that."

"I dunno what you've been up to, Reverend. But it's caused quite a flap." Ivan strapped his thumbs through his holster. "And this whole time I thought you was some mild-mannered milquetoast and all."

"I've been told that recently."

"We just heard from county." Bean shot a glance at Ivan. "It sounds like they've got half the force up there. I'm sure they'll be needing to question you."

"But for right now, looks like you're off the hook." Ivan peered at Clark with dark, skeptical eyes. "Say, what was going on up there anyway?"

Clark scratched his head and winced. This would not be easy. He'd told the dispatch officer as little as possible, that a fire had erupted at Keen's ranch and left two men dead. No doubt, once the sheriff caught sight of the bizarre sanctuary and altar, they'd have more than a few questions. But how could he even mention gods, curses, and human sacrifices without sounding like a complete lunatic?

Clark cleared his throat, preparing to stall, when Bean stepped closer and lowered his voice. "This'll probably break the case wide open."

"What do you mean?"

"The butler squealed," Ivan interjected. "Told the sheriffs everything. Spilled the beans about the murders. Guess he led them to the missing college girls, all three of 'em. Or at least what was left of them. The nutty professor kept their bones and hair for some kinda weird ritual. Regular *Silence of the Lambs* stuff. This guy was a real screwball, Reverend."

"So it was Keen?"

Ivan nodded. "Sounds like it. Guess he had a cult following at the university. His classes tickled the fancy of some of these local loons. Stupid kids. But they got more than they bargained for." Then Ivan squinted at Clark and asked, "You weren't involved with this guy, were you, Reverend?"

"Almost too involved." Clark shook himself. "Listen, I'll tell you everything you need to know. But I've gotta get downstairs, find out about Ruby, the woman from my church."

"The miracle worker?" Ivan asked facetiously.

Bean scowled at his partner. "You mean Mrs. Case?"

"Yeah. You heard anything?"

"Nothing. Mr. Hayes is at the precinct. Probably'll get sent off to the shrink. It's a shame, though. He's a nice guy. And she seemed like a nice lady. With her trying to save him and all, it makes it pretty hard, huh?"

The doors hissed open, and the security guard emerged from the warehouse, wiping his hands together. "Hey, Will. Kevin. How ya guys doin'? I've got some hot coffee in the back if ya care for some."

"Now you're talkin'." Ivan turned to Clark. "Good luck, Reverend. And keep your schedule open. I'm sure they'll be needing to ask you some questions about Dr. Frankenstein." He joined the security guard, they shook hands, and the doors closed behind them.

As Clark excused himself and turned down the hall, Officer Bean interrupted. "Reverend Clark?"

"Yeah?"

The plump, youthful man stared at the ground with his brow furrowed. "This city, you know...I mean everything going on...the murders, the Watcher's Woods, that thing at Goldman's..." Then he leveled his gaze at Clark. "This is outside our jurisdiction, isn't it?"

Clark thought for a moment, then nodded. "Yeah, Kevin. I guess you could say that." He patted the officer's shoulder and then hurried down the hall.

Instead of waiting for the elevator, he took the stairway, which was his custom. He stepped out of the stairwell and followed the signs to the OR waiting room. As he turned the final corner, Clark stopped in his tracks.

Hunched in a chair with his baseball cap pulled down over his eyes sat Jack Case. At the sound of Clark's footfalls, he lifted his head to reveal red-rimmed eyes. Immediately Jack rose.

They studied each other for a taut moment. Jack's stolid gaze was unnerving. A cool detachment stayed his features, the kind of detachment that often comes with the acceptance of some grim reality. Or perhaps he was just sizing up the bedraggled minister, preparing to drive Clark's nose into the back of his skull. Still, no single punch could hurt more than the emotional pain of losing Ruby.

"D'you fall down a sewer?" Jack finally muttered.

Clark glanced at his clothing and sighed, partly in relief that he hadn't been socked. "Something like that."

Jack issued a curt snort of laughter and started to turn away. But Clark placed his hand on his shoulder. "Listen, Jack. I am so sorry."

Jack stood nodding, looking spacey.

Just then the waiting room door opened. Vinyette gaped at Clark before clomping over and embracing him with such fervor he stumbled backward and fought to steady himself. And until that moment, Ian Clark realized he had never felt another's tears on his neck. Vinyette's sobbing lasted only a moment. She quickly separated, as if the expression of emotions might be misconstrued, and stood wiping her eyes.

"Where were you? I called and texted."

"I'm sorry, Vin. It's a long story."

Then she looked him up and down and wrinkled her nose. "And what were you doing? You're filthy."

Clark glanced down at his sooty, oil-stained clothing. "I'll live. So what've you heard? What's going on?"

Jack and Vinyette looked at each other.

Then Jack sighed, "She got lucky."

"It wasn't luck, mister." Vinyette's words were less banter than reprimand. "She's alive, and it was a miracle. Just like this whole thing's been."

After his skirmish with the occultists and knowledge of the city's dark religious underbelly, Clark was not about to object to Vinyette's assessment. Ruby had survived—whether by providence or medical know-how. He heaved a great sigh, and a week's worth of exhaustion exploded inside him, turning his knees into rubber.

"You all right?" Vinyette reached across to steady him. "Here. Sit down."

"No, just—what happened?"

"Well, where do I start? When I got here, she was in surgery, and there was no word for the longest. Marcella and Mondo came, Pat Raynee. We prayed. But they kept us waiting and waiting. Finally the surgeon came out, said the bullet had grazed an artery and she lost a lotta blood. And, I guess, at one point—" she glanced at Jack, "they lost her."

"You mean—?" Clark peered forward.

"Yeah, she flatlined." Vinyette's swollen eyes sparkled with a fresh wave of emotion. "Clinically dead for two or three minutes."

Silence hovered between them.

"They was about to give up when she came to." Vinyette wiped her eyes and recomposed herself. "Now, it's going to be awhile before she's up and about. And she'll probably have some side effects, nothin' major, they said. But, bottom line, we got her back."

They stood quietly in that sacred moment, pondering the implications of all that had unfolded, before Jack spoke up.

"God can't be explained, but like Ruby says, He can still be trusted." He shrugged. "So there it is."

Clark laughed and shook Jack's hand, while Vinyette did a little two-step under the fluorescents. Eventually they sat together in the waiting room and revisited the events of that last week, drifting occasionally into tired, giddy ramblings. Clark said nothing about Mr. Cellophane, the ghastly sacrificial system, and the Pantheons wrestling unseen for their allegiances. Some time after one in the morning the doctor allowed Jack to visit Ruby. To Clark's surprise, he requested that the minister accompany him, which Clark was eager to do.

Ruby drifted in a medicated dream world. Whether inside her body or out, she could not tell. The smell of rubbing alcohol and newly washed sheets awakened distant memories, but the dull pain and drugs overpowered her and she yielded. A pastiche of faces, both friend and foe, wandered through a rich, subliminal gallery. She ambled there without worry.

But something greater, larger, lurked nearby. A coliseum of nameless faces surrounded her, eyes rapt upon her every move.

Through warm spacious corridors she meandered, until Ruby stood before the great oak once again. Yet its ominous aura was gone. The hideous gray gave way to soft living tissue, and the red sky melted into a bright, glistening dawn. From high above the dazzling ray descended again, as in her previous dream. And she surrendered to its embrace. Inside the luminous fold, amidst the healing quietude and the cloud of witnesses, Ruby rested. So great was her joy that she wished never to leave.

But two figures caught her attention, and she approached, captivated by their motions. Underneath the majestic tree Aida Elston danced—without a cigarette—her withered body now vibrant and whole. She twirled and leaped in graceful refrain, a rambunctious sprite, her white hair sweeping behind her like a gossamer mane. Her eyes sparkled, struck by the radiant beam. And across from Aida, a stout man with overalls had her hands and swung her wide. It was Aaron, the beloved farmer, the healer of yesteryear. As Ruby watched, heavenly laughter rose and wakened the world, reviving leaf and limb. And the old oak roused from its slumber.

Then the tree faded; Aida and Aaron were no more. A pang of sorrow filled Ruby's heart at their passing. Figures emerged in the foreground, voices nearby, and she struggled to focus. Two people hovered on each side of her. Had Aida and Aaron come for her? She tried to speak but couldn't. So she steadied her gaze until the forms melted into clarity.

Jack stood on one side of her hospital bed with tears tumbling down his face, and on the other, Reverend Clark with a great smile. Ruby tried to raise her hand, to comfort her husband and bless her minister. But she could not speak, and her strength failed her.

Soon the images faded and drifted into raw color, green and vibrant, and blended with the distant outline of the tree. And as Ruby watched, the Sailor's Oak grew bright and clear, and the two men standing on each side shone with it, as if part of some great universal chemistry that wrapped the world in its workings. Then her heart swelled, for she knew that her struggle was not in vain, that something far greater was bleeding itself into the earth, drawing souls heavenward, and that she was part of its circuit.

And for the first time that entire week, Ruby lay her head back in great peace and fell into a deep, restful sleep.

Chapter 39

RUBY STARED OUT THE PASSENGER SIDE WINDOW OF HER SUV, aghast at the carnage. The odor of burnt wood and chemicals clung to the air like the aftermath of a great war.

"What happened?" Sean wriggled in his car seat with his nose pressed to the glass.

But Ruby sat gaping.

"What does it look like?" Jack glanced back at his sons, then at Ruby. "There was a fire."

"Well, I guess." Ruby peered at the charred rubble lining the downtown marketplace. Yellow caution tape cordoned the street, and a temporary chain-link fence stretched along Bapho's, Mars, and the Green Man Pub. Large sections of storefront stood blackened by soot. Collapsed rooftops with charcoal planks were visible behind shattered glass. Along the sidewalks mounds of ash and debris sat, and hand-drawn "Do Not Loot!" signs hung on several doors. Ruby's eyes watered from the lingering burnt stench.

"They said it was a welding accident." Jack stared out the window. "The fire just took off, I guess."

"Weird," Ruby said to herself.

Jack shifted into gear. "Let's git, or you'll be late for your meeting."

They circled through the downtown marketplace, turned on Rivermeer, and headed toward Canyon Springs. The sun had yet to crest the hills, and Ruby found herself gazing at the ridgeline, following it with her eyes until she spotted the Sailor's Oak perched against the powder blue morning sky. Would the cursed oak really grow again? It seemed so far-fetched. But after the last week, was anything impossible? Fear and wonder mingled inside her. Yet the thought of inspecting the tree and traversing the ancient cemetery again sent chills up her neck.

Jack glanced at her. "You all right?"

"Yeah, just..." she ran her hand up and down her forearm. "Yeah."

Between the camphor trees the church's Spanish tile roof shone deep red, like a beacon in an ocean of green.

"Guess the Springs is in for some changes, huh?"

"What do you mean?" Ruby asked.

"What I mean is that the chairman of the board is dead, another's in a nuthouse somewhere, and Millquint resigned, which he shoulda done a long time ago."

"Jack," she scolded.

"Hey, I told you those guys were up to no good, didn't I? Maybe you'll listen to me now. And with Clark resigning..."

"I know. I don't understand it."

"Hey, it's probably the most manly thing he's ever done."

They turned off Rivermeer and pulled into the church driveway. As they passed the wooden sign, Ruby did a double take. Someone had finally fixed its broken leg, and the sign stood straight and tall. She smiled and shook her head. They wound through the avocado and olive grove to the back of the church. After three days in the hospital, the sight of the church nearly made her bawl. This was where it all started, but everything seemed so different.

Jack pulled to the back and parked outside the office, where Vinyette and Marje stood waiting. Vinyette had her hands on her hips and tapped the toe of her boot on the asphalt, nodding and smiling.

Leaving the car idling, Jack circled around to the back, popped open the hatch, and removed Ruby's wheelchair. He unfolded it and wheeled it to her side. She opened her door. A scent of spring blossoms graced the air, and her nostrils perked at the fragrance. She carefully swung her legs out.

The girls applauded.

"I thought she was gonna wheel herself here," Vinyette said to Jack.

"Can you believe it, Vin? I'm telling you. She's convinced she could make it here without help."

"Well, I *could*," Ruby protested. "It's not *that* far."

But her stubborn self-reliance wasn't what it used to be, and she gave up without a fight. Some things *were* just too big for her. *Ain't that the truth.*

Ruby slipped out of the car, pivoted on her good leg, and plopped into the wheelchair. Jack wheeled her toward the group, and they surrounded her with embraces. As they did, Reverend Clark walked out of the church office carrying a box, which he put in his Jeep along with the rest of his belongings. He glanced at the group, retrieved something from his front seat, and joined them.

"Ruby, you'll be happy to know you made the front cover." Reverend Clark displayed a copy of *Rippington Weekly*. A grainy close-up of Ruby graced one side of the cover, and across the page, a separate picture of Breyven, eyeliner and all, with his arms folded, leaning against the black Hummer. Over the top, in bold italicized letters, it read *Supernatural Standoff.*

"Oh, brother." Jack snatched the tabloid and read from the caption. "*Small coastal town is epicenter of psychic showdown.* Can you believe this?" He rolled his eyes and handed the paper to Ruby. "I shoulda beaned that guy when I had a chance."

"Who?" asked Clark. "The warlock or Wilflee?"

"Both!"

Ruby scanned the tabloid, unable to stifle a grin. "Well, I guess he got his story."

Clark laughed. "He doesn't know the half of it. Does he?"

Ruby gazed at the minister, fixated for a moment. For in his eyes was something she had never seen, something she could only describe as joy. Aida was right—lots of other people had a stake in this. Maybe more than she'd ever know.

Ruby handed Clark the paper. "So you're leaving."

"I am."

"Thanks for coming for me. On the mountain, ya know."

"It was the least I could do."

They looked at each other without speaking for a moment.

"You fixed the sign out front." Ruby motioned toward the street.

"Yeah, well. I figured I'd leave the church with at least one good thing to remember me by."

"So where to?"

"At the moment? I've got a one way ticket to Darfur. Gonna finish what my sister started. After that?" He shrugged. "I'll just wander, I guess. Maybe that's my calling, huh?"

"Well, you can't wander forever."

"Yeah," Clark conceded. "You're right." He smiled, bent, and they embraced. "Thank you for everything, Ruby."

Then Reverend Clark swept back into the office as Ruby brushed back tears.

"I'll be back at noon." Jack circled around the SUV. "Vin, you'll keep an eye out, right? Make sure she doesn't join a marathon or somethin'."

"You ain't stayin'?" Vineyette folded her arms and glared playfully at him.

Jack paused with his hand on the door. "I'm, uh..." He looked at Ruby. "I'm workin' on it."

Sean chattered something from the back seat. Jack saluted the girls, got in the car, and they drove away.

"And after all that!" Vinyette steered Ruby's wheelchair over the curb. "He's next on our list, ya know that, Rube."

"In due time, Vin." Ruby gazed into the sky. "In due time."

Afterword

What Is Mr. Cellophane?

OVER THE COURSE OF WRITING *THE RESURRECTION*, questions and speculation regarding the nature of Mr. Cellophane have repeatedly been proffered. Some have gone so far as to suggest that Christian publishers, because of the ambiguity of the character, might hedge on the book. Once again, I am indebted to Strang Communications for allowing me to tell this story, characters intact. Nevertheless, this does not eliminate potential confusion or concern on the part of readers.

While the Christian church is largely resolved as to the nature of the afterlife (heaven and hell) and its denizens (angels, demons, and human souls), there is no consensus as to an "in between" state and possible "overlaps" therein. Are the dead aware of us? Can they interact with us? If so, what forms do those interactions take? Or is all such "contact" categorically evil?

The more questions that are asked, the further we get into territory beyond our explaining. This, however, has not stopped us from trying to explain spiritual phenomena. Ghosts are no exception.

Evangelicals, for the most part, have come to define ghosts as demons. There are several reasons—good reasons—to do so. One is the Bible's position on death: "...man is destined to die once, and after that to face judgment" (Heb. 9:27).* Souls don't get second chances. And hauntings seem to lack the finality that Scripture suggests. Another reason is the fixed nature of our eternal state. It's either heaven or hell. Forever. (Even those who

---

* All scripture quotations in the Afterword are from the Holy Bible, New International Version. Copyright © 1973, 1978, 1984, International Bible Society. Used by permission.

believe in purgatory see it as a holding tank for one or the other.) As such, the Bible provides glimpses of souls in eternal torment or eternal bliss. Frankly, we don't see many souls traipsing about unsure of where they're headed. A final factor in the "ghosts are demons" position is the biblical warnings about "deceiving spirits" (1 Tim. 4:1; 1 John 4:1). We are in a "struggle" against "spiritual forces of evil in the heavenly realms" (Eph. 6:12). Not only are there spirits out there, but also many of them want to do us in and perpetrate "another gospel" (Gal. 1:8). The medium who claims to speak to the dead but communicates a message contrary to the gospel is probably speaking to someone other than Uncle Bob's ghost.

But while there is good reason to see ghosts as demons—at the least, something malevolent—the Bible seems to offer some "contrary" evidence as to their nature and existence. The most famous and perhaps the most puzzling "ghost incident" in Scripture is Saul and the witch of Endor (1 Sam. 28). When Saul compels a seer to summon the prophet Samuel, they witness "a spirit coming up out of the ground" (v. 13). The spirit is recognized as the dead prophet, who validates himself by prophesying against Saul (vv. 16–19). So, was Samuel a ghost? And where was he before his invocation? Whatever your answer, the manifestation of Samuel's "ghost" is possible evidence of another category of existence, neither demon nor angel but disembodied man, still able to interact with our earthly plane.

Another monkey wrench in the "ghosts are demons" case is the Mount of Transfiguration (Mark 9:2–8), where two dead prophets—Moses and Elijah—manifest alongside Jesus. Complicating matters is the fact the prophets "were talking with Jesus" (v. 4), engaging in a sort of inter-dimensional conversation. Were they ghosts? Had they been physically resurrected? Were they still in paradise? Scripture is unclear.

Still another account is Jesus's appearance to His disciples after His crucifixion. Luke records this:

> While [the disciples] were still talking…Jesus himself
> stood among them and said to them, "Peace be with you."
> They were startled and frightened, thinking they saw a
> ghost. He said to them, "Why are you troubled, and why
> do doubts rise in your minds? Look at my hands and my
> feet. It is I myself! Touch me and see; *a ghost does not have*
> *flesh and bones, as you see I have."*
> —LUKE 24:36–39, EMPHASIS ADDED

Notice, the disciples immediately assumed they'd seen a ghost, suggesting that ghosts were an admissible category within their culture. Even more interesting, Jesus does not rebuke them for this belief. In fact, He seems to substantiate it: "a ghost does not have flesh and bones, as you see I have." This is important because Christians have historically maintained that Christ resurrected in His same body. Even though the risen Jesus had the ability to vanish (Luke 24:31) and suddenly appear in locked rooms (John 20:19, 26), He was not a ghost. Among other things, this tells us that ghosts are not resurrected souls (and vice versa), which means they are…something else.

Do these stories validate the existence of ghosts? Maybe. Maybe not. More importantly, what they do is to expand the boundaries of possibility and our understanding of paranormal phenomena. It is simply too easy to resign all paranormal phenomena into the category of the demonic. Samuel's "appearance" was not viewed as demonic, nor was the transfiguration of Moses and Elijah. Furthermore, we have no need to "test the spirits and see whether they are from God," as 1 John 4:1 instructs us, if all spirits (or spiritual phenomena) are categorically evil. So while the Bible cautions us about deceiving spirits, it does not go so far as to say that all "encounters" are necessarily of the "deceptive" order.

I understand that this might trouble some folks. The larger issue, as I see it, is coming to grips with the world we live in. Scripture paints a universe of vast mystery, teeming with intellects (visible and invisible) both good and evil, and phenomena beyond our wildest imaginings. This is why the Bible contains wondrous stories—stories we often take for granted—about miracles, visions, reviving corpses, warrior angels, talking mules, fiery chariots, demonized swine, tongues, and prophecies. We simply live in a supernatural world. The downside—paranormal phenomena do not always fit tightly into our theological framework.

While the Bible is not definitive as to the nature of ghosts, nor how the dead interact, if at all, with our world, Scripture is clear in its denunciation of necromancy, sorcery, and witchcraft (Deut. 18:9–12). We are forbidden, in explicit terms, from summoning, consulting, or communicating with the dead. So whatever conclusion a believer reaches about ghosts, inviting them, consulting them, or letting them hang around is the wrong thing to do. Seeing our world as a supernatural place is one thing; validating every supernatural phenomenon is another. In this, we do well to exercise great caution.

So what is Mr. Cellophane? He could be a vengeful disembodied spirit. He could be...something else. But to say with any certainty would be to eliminate all the fun. In the simplest sense, Cellophane is a fictional construct, part of a vast, complicated universe infused with mystery and wonder. What I am advocating is a worldview that tolerates (at least, in a "fictional" sense) a being that defies neat categorization. Ghost, demon, or something other? The answer is as much about theology as it is the reader's imagination.

Coming soon from Mike Duran—

The Telling

Chapter 1

HE USED TO BELIEVE EVERYONE WAS BORN WITH THE MAGIC, an innate hotline to heaven. Some called it intuition, a sixth sense; others called it the voice of God. Zeph Walker called it *the Telling*. It was not something you could teach or, even worse, sell—people just had it. Of course, by the time their parents, teachers, and society got through with them, whatever connection they had with the Infinite pretty much vanished. So it was, when Zeph reached his twenty-sixth birthday, the Telling was just an echo.

And that's when destiny came knocking for him.

It arrived in the form of two wind-burnt detectives packing heat and a mystery for the ages. They flashed their badges, said he was needed for questioning. Before he could object or ask for details, they loaded him into the back seat of a mud-splattered Crown Victoria and drove across town to the county morgue. The ride was barely ten minutes, just long enough for Zeph Walker to conclude that, maybe, the magic was alive and well.

"You live alone?" The driver glanced at him in the rearview mirror.

Zeph adjusted his sunglasses. "Yes, sir."

"I don't blame you." The detective looked sideways at his partner, who smirked in response.

Zeph returned his gaze to the passing landscape.

Late summers in Endurance were as beautiful as a watercolor and as hot as the devil's kitchen. The aspens on the ridge were showing gold, and the dogwoods along the creeks had already begun to thin. Yet the arid breeze rising up from Death Valley served as an omnipresent reminder that beauty always lives in close proximity to hell.

They came to a hard stop in front of a white plaster building.

The detectives exited the car, and Zeph followed their cue. A ceramic iguana positioned under a sprawling blue sage grinned mockingly at him. Such was the landscape décor of the county coroner's building. The structure doubled as a morgue. It occupied a tiny plot of red earth, surrounded by a manicured cactus garden complete with indigenous flora, bison skulls, and birdbaths. Without previous knowledge, one could easily mistake the building for a cultural center or art gallery. Yet Zeph knew that something other than pottery and Picassos awaited him inside.

The bigger of the two detectives, a vaquero with a nifty turquoise belt buckle and matching bolo tie, pulled the door open and motioned for Zeph to enter. The man had all the charm of a cage fighter.

Zeph wiped perspiration off his forehead and stepped into a small vestibule.

"This way." The cowboy clomped past, leaving the smell of sweat and cheap cologne.

They led him past an unoccupied desk into a corridor. Bland Southwestern prints adorned sterile white walls. The stench of formaldehyde and decay lingered here, and Zeph's stomach flip-flopped in response. The hallway intersected another, where two lab technicians stood in whispered conversation. They straightened as the detectives approached. After a brief nod from one of the white-jacketed men, Zeph's escorts proceeded to an unmarked room.

"We got someone fer you to look at." The cowboy placed his hand on the door and studied him. "You don't get sick easy, do ya?"

Zeph swallowed. "Depends."

"Well, if you're gonna puke, don't do it on these." He pointed to a set of well-polished eel skin boots. "Comprende?"

"No, sir. I mean—yes! Yes, sir."

The detective scowled, then pushed the door open, and stood waiting.

By now Zeph's heart was doing double time. Whose body was he about to look at? And what condition was it in? His mind raced with the possibilities. Maybe a friend had suffered a car accident. Although he didn't have any friends to die in one. Perhaps the Drifter, that mythical apparition who stalked the highway in his childhood, had finally claimed another victim. More likely Zeph's old man had finally keeled over. However, he was convinced that his father had stopped living a long time ago.

Zeph drew a deep breath, took two steps into the room, perched his sunglasses on his head...and froze. In the center, framed under a single oval swath of light, lay a body on a gurney— *a body that looked strangely familiar.*

"Take a good look, Mr. Walker." The detective's boots clicked with precision on the yellowed linoleum. He circled the rolling metal cart, remaining just outside the reach of the fluorescent light. "And maybe you can help us figger this out."

Yet Zeph remained near the door, hesitant to take another step into the room.

"Go ahead." The second detective sauntered around the opposite side, gesturing to the body. "He ain't gonna bite."

The detectives positioned themselves on either end of the gurney, where they stood watching him.

A black marble countertop, its surface dulled by a thin blanket of dust, ran the length of one wall. In front of it sat a single wooden stool. The low-hanging lamp bleached the body monochrome and forced the outskirts of the room into shadow. Zeph had seen enough procedurals and CSI knock-offs to know this was not an autopsy room. Perhaps it was used for viewings, maybe occasional poker games. But as the detectives studied him, he was starting to wonder if this was an interrogation room. Scalpels, pincers, saws. Oh, what exotic torture devices one might assemble from a morgue! Nevertheless, this particular room appeared to have not been used in a long time. And by the fevered sparkle in their eyes, these men seemed inspired about the possibility of doing so.

Zeph glanced from one man to the other, and then he edged toward the corpse.

Its flesh appeared dull, and the closer he got, the less it actually looked like skin. Perhaps the body had been drained of blood or bleached by the desert sun. He inched closer. Sunken pockets appeared along the torso, and he found himself wondering what could have possibly happened to this person.

The head lay tilted back, its bony jaw upturned, cords of muscle taut across a gangly neck. He crept forward, trying to distinguish the person's face. First he glimpsed nostrils, then teeth, and then...something else.

And that *something else* brought Zeph to a standstill.

How could it be? *Build. Facial features. Hair color.* This person looked exactly like him. There was even a Star of David tattooed on the right shoulder—the same as Zeph's.

What were the chances, the mathematical probabilities, that one human being could look so identical to another? Especially in a town the size of Endurance.

"Is this...?" Zeph's tone was detached, his eyes fixated upon the body. "Is this some kinda joke?"

The detectives hunkered back into the shadows, without responding to him.

Goose bumps skittered across Zeph's forearms as the overhead vent rattled to life, sluicing cool air into the room. He took another step closer to the cadaver until his thigh nudged the gurney, jolting the stiff, and bringing Zeph to a sudden stop. He stood peering at the bizarre figure.

A white sheet draped the body at the chest, and just above it a single bloodless hole about the size of a nickel notched the sternum. Yet their similarities were unmistakable. The lanky torso and appendages. The tousled sandy hair. Thick brows over deepset eyes. *This guy looked exactly like him!*

However, it was one feature—the most defining feature of Zeph Walker's existence—that left him teetering in disbelief: *the four-inch scar that sheared the corpse's mouth.*

Zeph stumbled back, lungs frozen, hand clasped over the ugly scar on his own face.

"Darnedest thing, ain't it?" The cowboy sounded humored by Zeph's astonishment. "Guy's a spittin' image of you, Mr. Walker."

Zeph slowly lowered his hand and glanced sideways at the man. "Yeah. Except I don't have a bullet hole in my chest."

The detective's grin soured, and he squinted warily at Zeph.

"Indeed you don't." The second man stepped into the light. "But the real question, young man, is why someone would want to put one there."